LOVE SONG

As a vulnerable seventeen-year-old, Beth Paterson gave a fellow student private tutoring. She didn't expect to fall in love with him and have her life changed forever in a couple of months. And she didn't expect him to vanish without saying goodbye. Now an accomplished businesswoman and doctor, Beth's life is thrown into turmoil when Charlie Campbell comes back to town to help his family. He's now a big star on the alternative rock scene — but he remembers Beth and seems as mad at her as she is at him. Embroiled in the community's struggle, Beth can't help but cross paths with Charlie any more than she can fight the resurgence of wild attraction between them. But Beth Paterson is no dummy — there's no way Charlie Campbell is ever getting back inside her heart . . .

Books by Sasha Wasley
Published by Ulverscroft:

TRUE BLUE

SPECIAL MESSAGE TO

THE U
(registe
was estab ... to provide funds for
research, diagnosis and treatment of eye diseases.
Examples of major projects funded by
the Ulverscroft Foundation are:-

- The Children's Eye Unit at Moorfields Eye Hospital, London
- The Ulverscroft Children's Eye Unit at Great Ormond Street Hospital for Sick Children
- Funding research into eye diseases and treatment at the Department of Ophthalmology, University of Leicester
- The Ulverscroft Vision Research Group, Institute of Child Health
- Twin operating theatres at the Western Ophthalmic Hospital, London
- The Chair of Ophthalmology at the Royal Australian College of Ophthalmologists

You can help further the work of the Foundation
by making a donation or leaving a legacy.
Every contribution is gratefully received. If you
would like to help support the Foundation or
require further information, please contact:

THE ULVERSCROFT FOUNDATION
The Green, Bradgate Road, Anstey
Leicester LE7 7FU, England
Tel: (0116) 236 4325

website: www.foundation.ulverscroft.com

SASHA WASLEY

◆

LOVE SONG

Complete and Unabridged

AURORA
Leicester

First published in Australia in 2019 by
Penguin Random House Australia

First Aurora Edition
published 2019
by arrangement with
Penguin Random House Australia

The moral right of the author has been asserted

A catalogue record for this book is available
from the British Library.

ISBN 978–1–78782–203–0

Published by
F. A. Thorpe (Publishing)
Anstey, Leicestershire

Set by Words & Graphics Ltd.
Anstey, Leicestershire
Printed and bound in Great Britain by
T. J. International Ltd., Padstow, Cornwall

This book is printed on acid-free paper

Dedicated to the people of the Kimberley, who inspired the stories in the Paterson sisters books.

1

Beth leaned against a fence post and looked across the red dirt paddock, puffing.

The run to the Paterson Downs gate and back was only 3 kilometres, but it was the best running trail at the station. The straightest, flattest, least dusty trail. No cow pats. And even a short run was better than no run at all.

She turned to observe the house. *Hopelessly outdated.* How many times had she subtly suggested renovation to her father or Willow? Barry barely seemed to listen, while Willow always gave her the look that meant 'Are you insane?' Willow adored the old homestead and seemed blind to how unfashionable it was. But all it would take was a little bit of rendering on the mission-brown brickwork — perhaps a dark grey — and a classy stone portico right over the top of that ridiculous arch . . .

What was the point in envisioning renovations to the Paterson Downs homestead? Even if Beth managed to talk her father around, Willow would just veto the idea. Beth caught sight of her mother's dragon-embellished doorbell swinging gently in the morning breeze and her heart softened. There were some things even she wouldn't change about the old place.

Willow came out through the front door and checked the boots that lived on the doorstep for snakes or toads. She caught sight of Beth.

'Good run?'

Beth approached, nodding. 'A bit short but it's too hot to run now anyway. I slept in.'

'It's only eight,' said Willow. 'And it's a Sunday. I think you're permitted a sleep-in after dealing with Mount Clair's diseased all week. By some people's standards, this is revoltingly early.'

'But by yours, it's late in the day,' Beth said with a smile. 'What are you up to this morning?'

'Tom and I are heading over to Quintilla. The goats have arrived!' Willow's dark eyes sparkled.

'Oh, that's exciting! Are any of them coming to Patersons?'

'Not yet. These guys were raised organic so they're certified already. We'll keep them at Quintilla until Patersons is fully certified, so they don't lose their organic standing.'

Tom stepped outside behind Willow, his blond hair flattened where his hat had been sitting. 'You been jogging, Beth? Crazy woman.'

Beth wiped her forehead with her arm. 'I don't have hard manual labour to keep me fit like you two do. I have to do something.'

Willow laughed. 'That's not why you jog.'

Beth looked at her in surprise. 'Why else would I do it?'

Willow hesitated. 'I don't know. I figured it was a stress release for you.' Beth raised her eyebrows. 'I mean, no-one needs to run for over an hour every morning *and* night to stay fit, do they?'

It did sound fanatical, put like that. Beth's cheeks warmed. 'Yeah, I guess it's a good way to wind down.'

Tom nudged Willow. 'Goats wait for no man — or woman.'

'Coming!' Willow approached Beth for a hug. 'In case you're gone when I get back.'

'I'm all sweaty,' Beth protested.

'Yeah, that's gross — don't get your sweat all over my sweat.' Willow grinned and took off after Tom.

Beth watched as they climbed into a farm vehicle, discussing their new livestock in animated tones. Just over two months pregnant, Willow had no baby bump to speak of so far, but soon enough she would have to tell the world. Willow would be so embarrassed by all the attention she would get — and Tom would glory in it. Beth smiled as warmth stole over her heart. Tom Forrest was the only man she considered good enough for her precious sister — the only man she really trusted to value Willow properly. And never to hurt her.

As for Free's boyfriend, Finn — well, the jury was still out for Beth. He seemed to adore Free like she should be adored, and he'd certainly had an anchoring effect on the youngest Paterson sister. For the first time in her adult life, Free seemed happy to stay in one place for more than a few months at a time. Finn had been around for almost a year now, but Beth would reserve judgement until he'd lasted a couple more. Beth pictured Free's sunny, open face and soft golden hair and was hit with a stab of love so fierce it almost took her breath away. If he hurt Free, Constable Finn Kelly wouldn't want to face Beth's wrath.

She waved Tom and Willow off and went inside for a drink. Barry was in front of the television, sound down, frowning over his planting diary.

'Morning, sweetheart. You been jogging out there? Bloody hot. You'll get heat stroke if you don't watch out.'

'I'm fine, Dad. I'm used to it.'

'Hmm.' He focused back on his diary as she went for the water jug in the fridge. 'You want a cuppa, Bethie?'

'Not yet. I'll have a shower first. Have you eaten? Do you fancy a cooked breakfast?'

Barry's face lit up. 'Bacon and eggs?'

'Dad.' She didn't even have to finish. He raised his hand in defeat. 'Poached eggs on toast,' she said.

'Sounds beautiful, sweetheart. Don't tell your sister this, but you'll always be the best bloody cook in Mount Clair.'

Beth was unable to help a smile. 'Taught by Mum — the master. But you only think I'm better than Willow because I cook with meat.'

He chuckled. 'Nah, you've got magic in your fingers. Go and have your shower and I'll get the kettle on.'

Beth enjoyed the slow morning at the station. She nattered and joked with her father, and found some clean washing to fold in the laundry, knowing how hard Willow and Tom worked. Coming back to her childhood home never failed to remind her to live life at a gentler pace — or at least to try.

On the drive back to town in the afternoon,

Beth thought about the next couple of days. They already looked crazy. She had appointments at the clinic until six on Monday and she still had to ask Paul or Carolyn if they could take any of her late appointments on Tuesday afternoon, since the Madjinbarra stakeholders had called a special meeting at five. Then she had a networking function at seven. She hoped there would be food there, because at that rate, she'd be lucky to squeeze in dinner. She had to get her own tests booked, too: a mammogram and a cervical screening. She'd never had an abnormal result but it was better to be vigilant, with her family history.

Her mind wandered back to the stakeholder meeting. She wasn't sure why the meeting had been called — it wasn't on the usual schedule. Her first thought was funding. Most extraordinary meetings were about funding problems, in Beth's experience. Things were always changing in the government department that funded her role as Madjinbarra's fly-in doctor, and she'd seen whole programs scrapped in the blink of an eye. Beth hoped this wouldn't be the fate of the Madjinbarra program. They needed the medical visits, and she treasured her regular treks out there to see the members of the remote community. The work got her out of town for a few days every month and she'd connected with many of the people there, making a difference to their health. Her mind settled on Pearl, the big-eyed toddler with cerebral palsy, and her older sister, Jill. Beth was particularly fond of those two. Her warm thoughts clouded over for a moment as she contemplated Pearl. *If only she lived in Mount Clair.* The child needed more care than she could get out in the tiny town.

She would discuss the matter with Mary Wirra next time she saw her. As the girls' guardian and a community elder, Mary was sure to want to explore options for Pearl's wellbeing.

★   ★   ★

Beth was already exhausted when she headed to the Madjinbarra meeting at the Department of Communities office on Tuesday. She'd been called out to the hospital the night before when an unexpected rush in Emergency left them short on doctors. She hadn't gone to bed until two in the morning and was up at six to get ready for work.

Maybe I'll pass on the networking function later . . . But she hated missing any opportunity to build her business and connect with the movers and shakers of Mount Clair. Beth sighed as she pulled the Beast into the diagonal street parking outside the department office. Something would have to give, and the chamber of commerce function was the most dispensable activity in her day. She hadn't been for a run, either, she recalled with a pang.

The big office with its worn carpet was full of people, and Beth got a shock when she recognised Mary Wirra, as well as Harvey Early. They were the most senior members of the Madjinbarra community, but it wasn't often that they would come all this way just for a meeting.

It must be serious. Mary caught sight of her and waved, so Beth joined them, kissing Mary's cheek in greeting.

'Hi, Mary, Harvey. What's going on?'

Mary grimaced. 'It's bullshit, Doc. Gargantua wants to put in a mine camp.'

Beth understood in an instant. Mining conglomerate Gargantua held a lease close to the tiny town. The Madjinbarra community had been living under the threat of Gargantua calling in its rights for decades.

'Oh, no,' she said.

'We already said no to them putting the workers' camp into Madji,' Harvey told her. 'They've been going on and on, saying they'll bring money and work to the community.'

'And other things,' Mary muttered.

'We told them no way,' Harvey went on. 'Now they reckon they'll build the workers' camp at the mine, instead. Billy and me drove out there the other day to check how far it was. Didn't even take us an hour to get there from Madji.'

Beth shook her head. 'That's too close.'

'We built the camp at Madjinbarra forty years ago to get away from town life.' Mary's voice shook with emotion. 'We don't want our young folk getting into grog and trouble.'

Beth squeezed Mary's hand, wishing there were something she could say to reassure the woman. She wondered why *she* had been called in to this meeting — after all, it wasn't as though Beth would have any say in what happened. She glanced around and spotted Lloyd Rendall, a local solicitor, as well as some suits who must be from Gargantua. There were people she knew from the department, too, and a few other unfamiliar faces — thirty or more people in all.

'Have you got legal representation?' she asked.

'Not yet,' said Mary.

'This is just the start,' said Harvey. 'You watch. They've called us in to make us see how small we are compared to all their executives and lawyers.'

Beth's heart sank further. He was probably right.

'We've got some good people though.' Mary tried to rally Harvey. 'Doc, we can rely on you to support us.'

'Of course.'

Mary beamed at her. 'And my nephew. He's famous. He's coming this arvo, too. He'll stick up for us.'

Lloyd called everyone to attention and invited them to take a seat in the large meeting room, where chairs had been set up for the purpose. He took his place at the front of the room, clad in a well-cut suit. He was dressed to impress today. Normally Lloyd wore chinos and short-sleeved button-down shirts that strained over his slight beer gut. Gargantua would have to be one of his most valuable clients ever, Beth thought. He'd probably been seconded by the Gargantua legal team as a local face.

Lloyd nodded his greying head once or twice and thanked everyone for coming. 'I'm a neutral party for the purposes of this evening's meeting,' he said. 'I'll simply be acting as a think-tank facilitator.'

More like a shark tank. Beth was vaguely aware of more people arriving, taking seats behind her while Lloyd introduced the team from Gargantua and the Madjinbarra elders. Clearly, this matter was polarising the community.

'As you'd all know, we're here to talk about the mining operation that's proposed to open near the Madjinbarra remote community. When the mine is approved by the Mining Department, Gargantua employees will need a workers' camp, but representatives of the Madjinbarra community have a few concerns about the matter. Gargantua's position is that they can bring much-needed improvements to Madjinbarra — employment, business, amenities, and so on. I'm sure you'd all know that what's in place out at Madjinbarra is pretty substandard. The couple of hundred people who live there have electricity, of course, and water. But it's water drawn from a bore, and there's very little phone or internet signal out there — sketchy satellite coverage at best. There's a small co-operative where they sell mostly packaged staples; a run-down, under-resourced school; and a health clinic staffed once a month by a FIFO doctor.' Lloyd paused and looked around. 'Not what you'd call a thriving metropolis.'

Beth glowered. This was so unfair. Yes, the place was a little rough — when Beth visited it was like being in a different country — but she understood precisely why they valued it. It had been an oasis of calm for its inhabitants for generations. The children there were schooled by a devoted team of teachers — including locals who had been specially trained. Some of the kids had never even been to a big town. The community took in and rehabilitated the occasional outsider — people of Aboriginal heritage who were struggling with issues stemming from ongoing cultural trauma. Beth always came away from her monthly visit buzzing and re-energised, her faith in humanity restored.

'The point of contention, as I understand it,' Lloyd went on, 'is the wet mess — the pub. A workers' camp needs a pub, or you're going to struggle to attract workers. But Madjinbarra's elders claim that it's been a dry community — alcohol free — for around . . . ' He checked his notes. 'Fifteen years. And they're a little concerned that a wet mess close by might cause problems in the town. Now, I think it would be advantageous at this point to hear from a few of the people involved.'

Lloyd called up a Gargantua executive first. The guy talked about the rich resources that had been identified through exploratory work and the potential fiscal benefits to the Madjinbarra community. He took care to remind everyone that Gargantua would not be infringing on Aboriginal land — the location of the proposed mine was just outside the native title on which Madjinbarra sat. He used all the right words: 'community partnership', 'engagement', 'financial empowerment'. Beth sighed inwardly. This was going to be an uphill battle.

Harvey got up to speak next and he didn't pull any punches. He said quite bluntly that the community wasn't interested in Gargantua's fiscal benefits and wanted to stay as it was. Beth cheered him privately, but her objective side knew he wasn't as convincing as the Gargantua bloke — not to the decision-makers.

'There have been some concerns raised about the problem of health care out at the community,' Lloyd said when he reclaimed the speaker's position. 'Dr Paterson, you undertake regular visits to the community through the Remote Health program. I believe you have concerns that some residents at Madjinbarra cannot obtain the care they require while they're so far from medical facilities, is that right?'

Beth went cold. Suddenly she knew why she had been invited. At the last chamber of commerce networking event, she'd been chatting to Lloyd. He had asked her about her role providing care out in the community. Unaware that Gargantua was sniffing around, she'd said it was rewarding, but confessed she was worried about a child who needed more care than she could get out at the community.

Beth saw Harvey look at her in shock and she stood, composing her features. 'That's incorrect. The Remote Health program is working extremely well for the Madjinbarra community.'

Lloyd frowned. 'I understood there were members of the population out there who require more specialist care than a GP can provide through monthly visits. A child with a congenital condition, wasn't it?'

'Not quite, Mr Rendall. There is a child with cerebral palsy. From time to time, she will need

11

specialist care. However, her family are giving her excellent care and she has all the equipment she needs, for her developmental stage.'

'And the others? I'm aware there are a couple of older adults with diabetes, heart conditions; a recovering cancer patient. None of *them* require more than a monthly fly-in GP visit, even with such serious health conditions?' Lloyd held her gaze, his face impassive.

Jerk. He'd done his homework. *Neutral facilitator, my arse.* He was here solely for Gargantua.

'It's not up to me to make that call,' she said, watching him steadily. 'The Remote Health working group has investigated thoroughly and deems a monthly GP visit to the community appropriate, in addition to the Madjinbarra clinicians, of course — a very competent nurse and an Aboriginal health officer.'

There was a noise behind her — someone else standing up. 'Excuse me, Lloyd,' came Mary's voice. Beth sat, grateful to be out of the firing line. 'My nephew's come to Mount Clair to put his voice behind our community. He's well-known all round Australia, and the TV and radios are pretty interested in what he's got to say. He's here tonight and has a few things to tell you fellas from Gargantua.'

Lloyd's eyes flickered across the room and settled somewhere behind her — presumably on this nephew of Mary's. Beth had a little moment of satisfaction, watching discomfort creep over Lloyd's face. He even cast a hasty look at the Gargantua blokes. *This has got to be good.* Beth turned to check out the nephew herself, wondering who could be important enough to unsettle poker-faced Lloyd Rendall.

Oh, hell.

★   ★   ★

Charlie Campbell. It had been seventeen years.

Of course, he'd been back to Mount Clair since that time — on many occasions. He'd played at Mounties Hotel and, when his singing career really took off, at the Muster Festival. He was considered a homegrown talent and Mount Clair was proud of him, even though it had only really been his home for that one year of high school.

High school.

Beth tried and failed to shut her mind to the thought. She knew that Charlie had lived in a remote community before he came to board in Mount Clair, but she'd had no idea where. She certainly hadn't suspected it was the very same one where she now worked for three days each month. No-one at the community shared the Campbell name.

'The Madjinbarra elders invited me here to have a say,' Charlie said, getting to his feet and crossing his arms over his chest.

Beth took in his serious, tanned face with those startling green eyes, his slightly wry mouth, and the thick hair, quite long, and regularly raked upwards from his forehead with an impatient hand. Even after such a long break, he was still deeply, unnervingly familiar.

Charlie was watching Lloyd with an even gaze, full of loathing. A glance back at the lawyer showed Beth that Lloyd had made his face carefully blank. *Odd.* Did they know each other?

'I grew up in Madjinbarra and I'll defend it with my dying breath,' Charlie said. 'I think even you blokes from the city know about the problems Aboriginal people face — substance abuse, health, education and jobs. If this mine gets approved — *if* — then you can take your wet mess somewhere else, because the Madjinbarra community has got it right and we're thriving. That's too important to ignore.'

A shiver of excitement went through the room, although Beth wasn't sure if it was because of his words, or because Charlie Campbell was here speaking up for his home town. Lloyd gathered his wits and went on with proceedings. He thanked Charlie for his contribution and invited a shire councillor to take the floor and talk about the benefits of bringing more jobs to the region.

Beth barely heard a word for the rest of the meeting, so flustered was she to be in the same room as Charlie after all this time. He was taller than she remembered, and stronger-looking. He'd always had something — people sat up and took notice when Charlie Campbell entered the room — but now his presence was undeniable. Years of performing, growing ever more famous in the alternative rock music arena as he travelled around the country, had given Charlie an air of confidence. Even the puffed-up Gargantua executives shrank a little before him.

Charlie didn't speak again — nor was Beth

called upon for her opinion. Lloyd closed the meeting at six-thirty, although the issue was nowhere near resolved. He added that reports would be compiled and meetings convened before a decision was made on the workers' camp. Beth couldn't help but think Lloyd's words were a tad premature, given the Mining Department hadn't even formally approved the mine yet.

She stood and headed straight towards the door, desperate to escape, but Mary caught her arm. Charlie arrived at the same moment and stood next to his aunt, Harvey on his other side. Beth didn't know where to look.

'Hang on, Doc. Me and Harvey are in town for a couple of nights, and Charlie's staying local while we sort this bullshit out, too,' Mary told her. 'Come for a feed with us down the pub.'

'I'd love to, but I've got this thing I'm supposed to be going to,' Beth stammered. 'And, um, I'm quite tired. Late one at the hospital last night.' She took a breath and tried to pull herself together.

Mary nodded, her expression sympathetic. 'You're a bloody hard worker. But we want to get together this week, talk about our battle plan. You reckon you could come along?'

After the way Lloyd had tried to drop her in it, using her innocent comment about little Pearl needing extra care, Beth was eager to show her commitment to the community. She nodded. 'Please send me the details. I'd love to come.'

Mary gave her a warm smile and let her go.

Charlie Campbell never even looked her way.

15

2

She should have gone straight home. Seeing Charlie had left Beth seriously rattled. But she went to the chamber function at the premises of Snowman Air Con, the business that was hosting this month. Beth couldn't stand it when anyone wormed their way out of going to something they'd committed to, and she refused to be that person.

Pam Twomey, a woman in her late fifties with henna-red hair, greeted her like an old friend. Although she wasn't president, Pam was the one who held the Mount Clair Chamber of Commerce together. She took care of all communications, even the weekly newsletter, and organised its regular functions.

'How are you, love? Goodness, you look so pretty in that white top! How do you get away with wearing white? I'm a magnet for sauce or coffee whenever I try to wear a light colour.' Pam peeled a name label off her sheet and patted it onto Beth's left breast without batting an eyelid. 'You hungry? I got Marcel's Deli to do the catering for us, half-price!' Her face glowed. 'Sushi and pastries they were going to chuck out, so they could hardly argue with giving us a good discount.'

'Nice one.' Beth concealed her disappointment. She wasn't about to eat anything that carried a risk of food poisoning. Looked like

16

she'd be subsisting on carrot sticks and supermarket hummus for the evening.

Gary from the Water Tank Warehouse brought her a glass of wine and Beth mingled with a small group of people she knew from previous chamber functions — Gary, Hermione from Cristo Geo Surveying, and Gino from Safe-Tee-Quip. Across the room, she could see the new, very young radiographer who worked part-time at the pathology clinic and in the hospital's imaging lab. She'd been intending to make his acquaintance but wasn't up to socialising with new people tonight. She was still too shaken up by the stakeholder meeting. Annoyingly, Lloyd Rendall turned up and made a beeline for her group.

He smiled at Beth as he joined them. 'We must stop meeting like this.' Hermione gave him an inquiring look, so he explained. 'I literally just saw the lovely Dr Paterson at a different meeting.'

'Is that so?' Gary lifted his eyebrows. 'A meeting for two?'

Lloyd chuckled but Beth had to swallow her revulsion.

'A stakeholder meeting regarding Madjin-barra,' she informed Gary. 'Gargantua wants to put in a miners' camp right next to the community.'

Formality crept into Lloyd's manner. 'We're not really supposed to discuss it at this stage.'

'Oh, really?' Beth feigned innocence. 'It's early days — all up for discussion at this stage, isn't it, Lloyd?'

'I suppose so,' he said. 'I just wouldn't want misinformation floating around.'

'True.' She caught his eye. 'You wouldn't want to make some generalised comment that might later be used against you, even in the safety of a social night like this.' She looked away just before he could be certain she was having a dig at him. 'I saw your new ad on television the other night, Gino. Was that your baby granddaughter I spied in the background?'

Gino launched into an enthusiastic telling of the story of his latest ad production, which had starred, as usual, most of his extended family. He thanked her profusely for dropping a casserole around to his daughter in the days after the birth. Beth deflected his gratitude by asking after the baby, whose delivery she had attended. Lloyd recovered and joined in the conversation, but Beth couldn't stand to look at his smoothly shaved face for much longer and excused herself to join Pam's group.

Thankfully, the other business owners were just as keen as she was to keep things moving so they could all go home to bed. Beth listened patiently throughout the introductory speech from Snowman Air Con. She smiled mechanically throughout the door prize draw. She crunched carrot sticks with dip, counting the minutes until she could leave. Finally, someone else departed, giving Beth the green light to make her own move.

'Thanks, Pam,' she said as she passed the welcome desk, where Pam was packing raffle ticket books, markers and labels into a tin. 'You did a great job, as usual. I'll be watching my inbox for next week's newsletter.'

'Thanks, Beth — and don't forget, it's your turn to host at the clinic next month,' Pam said.

'Looking forward to it. I'll have to open up the courtyard, I think, or we might not all fit!'

At last, she could go home and reflect on the hell of a day she'd just been through. Although knackered, Beth rolled the bin out to the verge and checked the moisture levels in her pot-plant collection on the porch before letting herself inside. Going for a run was out of the question. It was dark, after nine p.m., and she didn't feel safe running at night.

For all her love of cooking, Beth didn't have the energy tonight — and uneasiness was still swirling around her insides. She dug out a portion of pumpkin soup she had frozen for this sort of occasion and fervently thanked her own preparedness as she dropped it into a pot. Beth dialled Rikke's number, stirring the frozen lump over the gas burner.

'Hello, you.' The soft accent and smile in her best friend's voice were an enormous comfort.

'Hey, Rikke. I know it's late to call. Are you in bed?'

Rikke snorted. 'Are you for real? *Downton Abbey* starts at nine-thirty.'

Beth laughed. 'Hallelujah for *Downton*. How's work?'

'Good. It's been a quiet week. I'm waiting for the autumn viruses to kick in, then I'll be busy again. And football season injuries. You?'

'Busy, here. Staff shortages at the hospital, and

gastro's going through the schools like wildfire, so that's kept me on my toes — among other things.'

Rikke listened to the ensuing silence for a moment and, when she spoke, her tone was suspicious. 'You're stressed out. What's going on?'

'Ugh, you always know when I call to whine.'

'Shush. Just whine.'

'Well, you know the Madjinbarra community I work with every month?' Beth poured out the story of Gargantua and the mine, and the stakeholder meeting, including Lloyd Rendall's dick move. 'And then Mary called up her nephew to speak . . . ' She hesitated. Was this too humiliating to talk about, even with Rikke?

'Her nephew? Who's that?'

'Charlie Campbell.'

There was a pause and then a gasp. '*No! The* Charlie Campbell? The singer? The guy who . . . '

Rikke was the only person in the world who knew this story. Beth didn't need to confirm it, either. Her friend was already letting loose with a string of curse words, in both English and Danish.

'How dare he show his face in Mount Clair after what he did to you?'

'He's been to Mount Clair a heap of times,' Beth said. 'I've just avoided seeing him until now. Easy to do when his face is on posters all over windows, telling me exactly when and where he's performing. But I didn't expect to see him at a community stake-holder meeting.'

'Did you speak to him?'

'God, no.'

'But he recognised you?'

Beth thought of the way Charlie hadn't looked directly at her face. 'I think so.'

'And do you think you'll see him again?' Rikke pressed.

Beth sighed. 'It's quite likely.' Her pulse gave a strange flutter at the thought, a blend of dread and hope. She was annoyed at herself. 'His aunt seems to think he's here to see the community's fight through. Who knows, though?'

'Oh, no, that's so uncomfortable,' Rikke moaned. 'Hang on, I've got my laptop right here. I just want to google him.' There was some rustling and clicking. 'I've seen stuff about him online, of course, and I took notice because of your history, but I've never had a really good stalk. Here we go. Photos from last year's tour.' There was a pause that lasted several moments. 'Well, he's certainly got the face of a heartbreaker. And — *wow* — the body of a rock god.'

Beth gave a weak laugh. 'Uh-huh. He was always a good-looking guy. The girls at school were falling over themselves to get to him. He was pretty quiet back then, though.' She pictured Charlie standing up to speak at the stakeholder meeting. 'He doesn't seem so quiet any more.'

'I wouldn't have thought he'd be shy these days.' Rikke was still clicking on her laptop. 'Hmm, he's really quite famous, isn't he? He hasn't released anything new for a while, though. There are lots of articles speculating about his next album. Hang on, here's an interview from

21

two weeks ago.' She paused, reading. 'He says he's got some family responsibilities to deal with before he goes back into the recording studio. Guess we know what that means now, don't we?'

Beth heard a song start up through the phone. Rikke must have clicked on a video of Charlie singing. She didn't know the song — she'd actively avoided listening to Charlie's music — but his voice was instantly recognisable and it turned a knife somewhere deep in her heart. She scowled at herself.

'You were at the same boarding house, weren't you?' Rikke asked.

'No, I was in Durack House, the girls' accommodation, and he was in Grey, next door. He came from a small community — Madjinbarra, I now realise — and the school there didn't offer tertiary pathways. He boarded in town so that he could go to Mount Clair High.'

'Ah,' said Rikke. 'He wanted to go to university?'

'Yeah. He had some catching up to do, so he was doing Year Eleven while I was in Year Twelve.'

'Wasn't that around the time your mum passed away?' Rikke's voice softened a little. 'A vulnerable period.'

'Yes, Dr Rikke,' Beth said. 'Oops, your psych specialisation is showing.'

Rikke gave her usual throaty chuckle. 'Sorry. So how did you get to know him, if you were in separate boarding houses?'

'I tutored him after school. Biology, maths and English.'

'And you fell for him?'

'Yeah. I thought it was mutual but . . . ' Her throat tightened but she forced a laugh. 'Typical man — got what he wanted and cleared out.'

'You had sex?'

'Yes.'

'First time?'

Beth cringed. 'Yes. He was my first.'

Rikke puffed out a long breath. 'Look, it stinks. But Beth, you shouldn't say 'typical man'. Not all men are like that. Not all of them want only one thing.'

'Don't they? Funny, from where I stand it sure looks that way.'

'You've just been unlucky,' Rikke insisted. 'The guy was, what, seventeen, eighteen? He was immature.'

'And Sebastian? He was thirty-eight. Was he immature too?'

'No, he was just a sneaky, unfaithful bastard. But what happened with Sebastian, that could have happened to anyone. He fooled us all, and I have no doubt he's out charming some other poor woman at this very moment while his wife is at home with his kids. You shouldn't give up on men because of two jerks. Most women go through half a dozen jerks before they find one decent guy.'

'You're not exactly convincing me that there are loads of wonderful men out there,' Beth said with a laugh.

Rikke joined in with her own chuckle. 'Well, I'm not exactly living proof of a successful relationship! But maybe one or the other of us

23

will find a nice boy yet.' She gave a sudden gasp. 'Oh, shit, I have to go! *Downton* is starting!'

Beth said goodbye and sat down to eat her soup. She steered her thoughts away from the men who'd screwed her over and gazed at the living room from her seat at the kitchen table. She hadn't yet got the decor right in there. There was something a little sterile about it. Perhaps she could try a wallpapered feature wall? Definitely new light fittings. She'd seen some startling and rather lovely new trends last time she was in Perth. It would be good to do something really unusual — a chandelier of flattened silver forks had caught her eye in a city café in November. But her neat little house wasn't quite right for that sort of rustic quirkiness. Modern and understated would work better here.

Her mind wandered back to the afternoon's meeting. Charlie looked different these days. Of course he did — he'd been eighteen years old the last time she saw him in the flesh. Now he was thirty-five. Beth had avoided looking too closely at pictures of him over the years because they still triggered that old sting. As a result, seeing him in person in the department office tonight had been her first proper glimpse of Charlie in a very long time. He looked older, obviously, but not unpleasantly so. She'd thought of him — of them both — as grown-up when they were eighteen, but now, with his solid strength and the stubble on his jaw, Charlie was a man.

He'd been smooth-faced when they had studied together in the school library. They'd revised together after school, building up from two sessions per week to every day. The increase in frequency happened quite naturally. Charlie simply said, 'Can we do this again tomorrow?' at the end of their session, and Beth jumped at the chance to spend more time with him. She looked forward to their library session all through the school day and lingered over thoughts of him when she lay in bed every night. During the tutoring sessions, she carefully kept their revision on track, although at times Charlie made her laugh. But as they walked back to their boarding houses from the library, they talked. They crammed as much as possible into the ten-minute stroll, walking slower and slower each day, loitering on the bridge over the Herne River, until the ten-minute walk stretched to an hour. It was as though they could talk about anything and it would be interesting, from family, to school, to university, to music, to food, travel, dreams, politics — anything.

They'd only known each other a month on the day of their first kiss. Beth had been reading aloud from a list of animal classes, pausing in between for Charlie to answer with the correct phylum. Then he startled her by pressing his lips momentarily on her cheek. Beth whipped her head up and stared into those sea-green eyes, heart jumping into a gallop.

'What are you doing?' she whispered, checking that the library teacher wasn't watching.

'Sorry,' he said, but he didn't look sorry. He was looking at her mouth and Beth hesitated, unsure what to do. Move away from him and get on with their studies? Or stay where she was, pulse racing, waiting to meet his full lips with hers . . .

Beth blinked into her pumpkin soup. *Jesus*, she thought, mentally slapping herself. Where the hell had *that* memory come from? She remembered the afternoon in astonishing detail, from the hush of the empty library to the scratched table where they sat, side by side. She'd tried so hard to bury it all since then, pulling her thoughts back sharply each time they threatened to slip towards the foolish little teenage love affair. She wasn't about to let those memories back in *now*. Beth stood, collecting her bowl, and headed for the living room. She would curl up on her big sofa and join Rikke in a bit of escapist television.

Anything to stop thinking for a while.

3

Beth snapped her head up. 'What are you doing?'

'Sorry.'

Charlie's eyes were locked on Beth's mouth and warmth thrilled through her. She sat up straight so she was out of his reach.

'You can't just go around kissing girls,' she whispered.

'I only kissed you.'

'Why?'

'Because you're so pretty.'

'Well, there are plenty of pretty girls in town, Charlie, so why don't you go kiss one of them? I'm supposed to be revising biology with you.'

His eyes sparkled. 'I don't want to kiss them. I want to kiss you.'

Beth's pulse fluttered but she returned her gaze to the biology book. 'Gastropod.'

He sighed. 'Mollusca.'

'Oligochaeta.'

'Annelida.'

'Very good. Arachnid.' She sneaked a glance at his face and his sea-green eyes were still on hers.

'Arthropoda.' He moved closer and reached out a hand, brushing her straight hair back over her shoulder. 'Your hair's exactly the same colour as a hazelnut.'

Beth tried to find the next word to test him,

but the letters seemed to wriggle around on the page.

'And you've got a freckle on your cheek,' he went on. 'I wanted to kiss that spot from the day I met you. That's why I did it.'

'Charlie,' she whispered furiously. 'Miss Chomsky will hear you.'

He glanced across the room at the library teacher. 'She's got her back to us.' He inched closer again and Beth wondered if her heart could possibly beat any faster. She tried to slow her breathing. 'Know the other place I want to kiss?'

Heat rushed into her cheeks. He'd better not say anything disgusting right now . . .

'Here.' He placed a finger very gently on her neck, just below her earlobe. 'It looks so soft there.'

Beth opened her mouth to tell him they had to get back to revising but his eyes were on hers and so serious, and she'd secretly been imagining this moment for weeks now, and his lips looked like they would feel amazing on her skin . . .

She placed her book on the desk and checked Miss Chomsky was still facing the other direction. Then Beth tucked her hair behind her ear, breathing fast, and tilted her chin ever so slightly up and to the side so Charlie could kiss that spot under her ear.

⋆ ⋆ ⋆

Her phone alarm broke into its usual trilling chime and Beth squinted her eyes open, reaching

28

out to swipe it off. She pulled her hand back and touched the spot under her earlobe. The dream had been so real — and it was so precise a replay of that day in the library. Good God, she still felt warm and turned on from it.

Incredibly annoyed with her subconscious for taking her back in time like that, Beth shoved her doona away and pulled on her running gear. She swept her hair up into a ponytail and stepped briskly out of her front door. Only pausing to do some stretches, she set off at a jog. She would run the stupid dream off.

She was 2 kilometres into the run before she really settled into her pace. As her breathing regulated, legs moving rhythmically beneath her, Beth's logic kicked back in. Of course Charlie's reappearance in her world had rattled her. She fell hard for him all those years ago and threw herself into the relationship with complete abandon. His sudden departure without even a word of explanation had hurt so much she'd cried every night, trying to muffle any noise in her pillow so she wouldn't alert the other girls at Durack student accommodation. Or worse still, Hen. Julie 'Hen' Henderson, the unyielding but comforting house supervisor, would have taken her into the kitchen for a warm Milo like she did with the homesick Year Eight girls whenever she caught them crying at night.

For three weeks, Beth had silently wept, longing for Charlie to return, willing to forgive him if he would just come back. Then she gathered the courage to ask the principal about him. Mr Ogilvie told her they'd contacted

Charlie but he'd said he didn't want to go to university or finish high school, after all. He'd gone home and would pursue his music — and if that didn't work out, learn a trade.

'I really appreciate the work you did with Charlie this year, Beth,' Mr Ogilvie had said. 'I hope you're not too disappointed that he decided not to see it through. Perhaps he'll rethink his decision someday, but there's no point pushing him if his heart's not in it.'

At that moment, Beth had decided to get on with things. She shoved back the sadness every time it hit her and worked harder than she'd ever worked in her life. She topped her year and gave the valedictory speech at graduation, and easily soared into the medicine course. She even had her name listed in the newspaper as a high achiever. Every single day, she told herself that Charlie Campbell was in the past, and everyone had a love-gone-sour story, and she should be thankful that hers had happened while she was just eighteen and had her whole life ahead of her.

At university, she met the round, blonde Rikke, an international student, and they became best friends as they studied medicine together. After graduation, Rikke found a job in Perth while Beth flew home to start her GP career. All in all, things had gone pretty smoothly for Beth after the Charlie incident.

Well — except for Sebastian.

Beth checked her pace and the time on her wrist monitor. Not bad. Pulse was up slightly, but that was probably just the weather. At six twenty-five, it was already cloyingly humid.

Sebastian. He was the complete opposite of Charlie — that was what had made her think he'd be a good choice. Sebastian had short fair hair and warm brown eyes, had been to private school in the city, and had connections. He didn't play guitar or sing. He played tennis. Beth had met him during a student internship at the children's hospital, where he worked as a paediatrician. It was his sweet manner with a frightened burn patient during a dressing change that had first softened Beth towards Sebastian.

He'd seemed like the ideal man. Over ten years older than her, Sebastian was clever, thoughtful and confident. He took Beth, who still had a little of her wide-eyed country girl wonder, to expensive restaurants, to concerts, on holidays at stunning resorts. Secretly awestruck by how distinguished Sebastian was, Beth had decided that when he asked, she would agree to marry him. He was perfect.

Until the day she received a text message from a woman named Shannon, asking Beth to end the relationship. *Perhaps you don't even know he's married. Please finish it so I have a chance of saving my marriage. Seb won't. But I will fight for this marriage, for my children's sake.*

The words were burned into her memory forever, and after dumping Sebastian in horror, Beth hadn't done anything more than casually date or flirt at parties since.

And Rikke wondered why Beth didn't trust men.

Wow — she was nearly home. Beth barely remembered running the 10-kilometre circuit through town. She was on autopilot, she realised, lost in her thoughts. But that was precisely what she tried to avoid through running. She was supposed to be present, in the moment, focused on her breathing, her legs, the morning air in her lungs.

She slowed to a walk as she reached home and did some warm-down stretches on her porch, watching the sun rise beyond the roofs and boab trees. Today was a regular Wednesday, so long as the hospital didn't call on her. Paul and Carolyn were both in the clinic on Wednesdays, so they shared the load when there was a walk-in or an emergency. Paul usually cranked through appointments at a superhuman pace — his patients were the ones who preferred short and sweet — so he generally saw most of the walk-ins, anyway. She could have a normal day at work and come home on time. She would take another run — remembering to practise a little mindfulness this time — and cook herself a stir-fry filled with fresh vegetables, garlic and ginger.

She would not think about Charlie, or anything else that might stir up old pain.

★   ★   ★

Mount Clair's gastro bout appeared to have eased. Only one vomiting child visited Beth that day. She cleaned everything down with antiseptic wipes and sprayed the room after the patient left. The last thing she needed was a stomach bug.

During the day, Mary sent her a message. *Me*

and Harvey heading home tomorrow. Can you meet us tonight? Mounties 6pm.

Beth paused over her reply. This might mean seeing *him* again. But she'd promised she would help — and she genuinely cared about the Madjinbarra community. She didn't want to see them get screwed over by Gargantua and bloody Lloyd Rendall. She replied in the affirmative and then, before she left the clinic, spent a few minutes tidying her hair and applying lip gloss. She loathed herself for it, but she did it anyway. *Confidence*, she told herself. *I'm making sure I look presentable so I feel confident when I face him again.* She couldn't let Charlie think he'd left her broken and lonely. She said goodbye to her colleagues and drove to the pub.

Inside Mounties, Beth bought a sparkling water at the bar and went to hunt for Mary and Harvey. She found them sitting across the far side of the beer garden. Harvey was frowning over his phone and said something to Mary, which prompted her to remove her glasses and hand them over. He put them on and focused on his phone again. Mary sat back and folded her hands over her tummy.

No Charlie.

Mary saw Beth and waved. 'Evening, Doc.' She pointed Beth into a chair as Harvey thumbed keys on his older-model phone.

'I got a message from Charlie,' Harvey said, looking up. 'He says he can't come down right now. He's got business to attend to.'

Mary sighed. 'What a nuisance. I'll go rustle him if he doesn't get his arse down here shortly.'

33

Beth, who knew precisely why Charlie didn't want to join the meeting, was determined to push on without him. 'Have we got a plan of attack?'

'We've invited the Minister for Mining out to the community,' said Mary.

Beth blinked. 'Wow. Really?'

'Best way to show him how good things are out there,' Harvey said.

'The Minister for Aboriginal Affairs is already on our side,' Mary put in. 'We figure we might need the personal touch with the mining bloke.'

'When did you do this?' Beth asked.

'Today. Charlie did it for us. It's a *strategic* move, he reckons.'

Beth had no doubt that it was a strategic move, but she wasn't sure it would come off. Still, if the minister did come, it could be an extraordinary coup for them. Seeing the Madjinbarra community in action was sure to — at the very least — make him think twice about letting Gargantua cause problems for them.

'I was thinking about the media,' Beth said. 'Maybe we could speak to the newspaper and regional radio about the issue. Start to raise awareness of how strong Madjinbarra is — put a bit of public pressure on Gargantua.'

Mary was nodding vigorously. 'That's what Charlie reckons, too. He's got contacts in the media.'

Beth sat back, fidgeting with her straw. 'It sounds like Charlie has a good solid plan. I'm not sure you even need me. Perhaps I could assist when I'm needed but take more of a back seat.' Mary's disappointment was plain on her face and Beth scrambled to clarify. 'I don't mean I don't want to help. I just think Charlie's got things under control and you might not need my help.'

'We need you,' Mary told her firmly. 'I want you to bring the minister, if he says yes. *Escort* him. He might want to fly out there, but it would be better if he goes by land. The road's pretty good at the moment, and it tells a bit of a story, the drive out there. You don't get that same feeling if you go in a plane.'

'It does give you a more accurate sense of distance,' Beth agreed.

Mary looked at Harvey with an air of triumph. 'Told you. She knows how to say things right.'

'I never argued with you,' he said mildly.

'There's Charlie.' Mary stood and cooeed across the beer garden.

Charlie had been walking towards the exit but saw Mary and waved, changing direction. Then he saw Beth at their table. He stopped.

Beth fought to keep her composure. *What's wrong, Charlie Campbell? Scared you might get an earful from the girl you ditched?* She picked up her water, sipping in as unconcerned a fashion as she could muster. Charlie continued, but at a slower pace. Some of the younger patrons of the pub stared and whispered, clearly recognising him, but most of the older people didn't take any notice. At last, he was standing at their table. Beth lifted her eyes to his face.

Charlie looked stern and oddly blank, like he

was covering something. Was he experiencing his own discomfort? *And well you should be*, Beth thought, but she refused to look away.

'Hello, Charlie.'

He nodded, a shadow crossing his face. 'Beth.'

'Do you know each other?' Mary asked in surprise.

'A little,' said Beth.

'From school,' Charlie supplied, shoving one hand in his jeans pocket.

'Oh, yeah.' Mary laughed, resuming her seat. 'That didn't last long. You were at the high school, what, six months before you got so homesick we had to come get you.'

He didn't sit, Beth noted. He clearly couldn't even face the thought of sitting at the same table with her. He knew exactly how bad it was, the way he'd abandoned her after all those lies. Charlie's eyes flicked to her face and for an instant she saw Charlie Campbell, the boy who'd sat next to her in the library and wanted to kiss the soft skin under her ear. Her hands lost their steadiness and she shoved them into her lap, locking her eyes on the table.

'Doc's agreed to drive the minister out to the community,' Mary told Charlie, and she sounded so pleased that Beth didn't have the heart to remind her she'd done no such thing.

'I can drive him if it coincides with my treatment visit,' she put in. 'I can't just abandon my clinic whenever I feel like it, unfortunately.'

Mary was nonchalant. 'I reckon we can work something out. Should we get a feed? Charlie, you shouting?'

'I'm shouting,' he confirmed.

'Order us a steak sandwich, would you? Harvey?'

Harvey added his order and they looked at Beth expectantly. 'I'll sort out dinner at home,' she hurried to assure them.

'Rubbish. Charlie's loaded.'

'No, truly, I'm fine.'

Charlie shrugged and headed to the counter, where Beth could see him ordering and paying for the meals. She had to keep her head up and show him she wasn't disconcerted by this meeting. *She* wasn't to blame for what he did, after all. She wondered suddenly if he'd ever told anyone about them. Oh, Christ, what if he'd poked fun at her with people in Madjinbarra? What if he'd talked about doing the 'wild thing' with Dr Beth Paterson? Beth felt sick and wished there were some way she could escape.

Her phone pinged with an email and Beth scrounged in her bag for it, glad of an excuse to look busy. Ugh, it was from Lloyd Rendall. She opened it.

Hi Beth, can we catch up? I was hoping to talk about the Madjinbarra matter — just an informal chat. Would appreciate an hour of your time. Lloyd

She switched off her screen. She could deal with him later — and he'd reminded her of something she wanted to clear up. Beth leaned forward to get her companions' attention.

'I have to say this, Mary, Harvey. What the lawyer, Lloyd Rendall, said last night about me saying the health care at Madji isn't good enough — that was a twisted version of the truth.' Charlie returned and took his seat, and Beth continued as if she weren't unsettled by his presence. 'What I actually said was that I wished one of the children there had access to more care. Pearl, obviously. The way Lloyd said it sounded like I'd been criticising the community.'

Charlie spoke to her directly, his voice sharp. 'What's this about Pearl?'

Mary shushed him. 'Don't get your jocks in a knot, Charlie. Beth's been a bloody good doctor for us, and she's got a way with Pearl and Jill. She even gave Tish a nice recommendation to help her land a job at the restaurant here in town last year.' She explained Charlie's reaction for Beth's benefit. 'Charlie is uncle to Pearl and Jill — his sister's kids. He pays for all Pearl's equipment. The wheelchair and the special potty and all that stuff.'

'I see,' said Beth, surprised all over again. She glanced at Charlie. 'Pearl's equipment is excellent. And Jill takes wonderful care of her little sister, especially considering she's only fifteen. But Pearl would benefit from regular physiotherapy and perhaps some qualified educational support when she reaches school age, particularly for learning to write and doing physical activity. An occupational therapist could assess her equipment needs, too, and regular speech therapy would be great for her. I do what I can, and I know Mary has brought her to Mount Clair a few times, but her needs are greater — '

'I can take her to Darwin or Perth for

treatment, if need be,' Charlie interrupted. 'But she should be able to call Madjinbarra home. That's where her sister and family live.'

'Intermittent treatment is not quite what I'm getting at,' Beth said. 'I'm saying it would be better if she lived in a town — in an environment where she has continuous access to specialists and therapies.'

Mary chimed in sadly. 'I've been telling him, Doc.'

Beth looked back at Charlie. 'You don't want Pearl to live away from the community, even though she needs extra care?'

He hitched a hand in one pocket and stared at the table. 'I want her to get the right care. But she won't be happy away from her home and her people. I know that from personal experience.'

He didn't lift his eyes and Beth was silenced.

It was Harvey who cleared his throat and spoke. 'Pearl not getting the care she needs out at Madji — it might not look good to the government, Charlie. And if anyone asks the doc here, well, she can't be expected to lie and say Pearl's fine. We want to look as good as we can to the government fellas while we're fighting against Gargantua, and if we've got a baby needing special stuff we can't give her, they'll start looking at us sidewards.'

'Pearl stays at Madjinbarra,' Charlie said, his jaw tight. 'I can fly the specialists out there when she needs them.'

Beth sighed inwardly. Pearl needed more consistent therapy. Surely there were foster carers in Mount Clair who would take her on

— the child was a delight. And she coped so well with her disability. Beth understood that Jill was Pearl's world — the teenager had almost taken a parenting role with her little sister since their mother took off — but Pearl could still thrive with a caring Mount Clair family, even if they weren't related by blood. And Harvey was absolutely right about the government's views on this kind of matter.

'And what if you run out of money, Charlie?' Mary was demanding. 'You're doing well now, but music's a fickle business. What's Pearl going to do if suddenly Uncle Charlie can't afford to get the physio out once a month?'

Beth wanted to say that once a *week* was more what she'd had in mind, but dared not. Charlie's eyebrows were drawn down in a frown. They were railroading him, she realised.

'Pearl's happy, healthy, and well cared for,' Beth put in, attempting to defuse the moment. 'But regular access to therapy is certainly worth thinking about. Perhaps you could at least consider relocating her before she hits kindy age.'

Charlie forced a nod, still not looking her way. Mary made a wry face at Beth.

'You're all heading back to Madjinbarra tomorrow, are you?' Beth asked her.

'Yep, but Charlie's staying in Mount Clair,' said Mary. 'He's going to talk to some of the bigwigs. He might need a bit of help, actually, Doc. You know lots of big cheeses in town, don't you? The business owners and shire councillors and all that?'

'I do. I'd be happy to help.' *Oh, God.* Why had she said that?

But Charlie stood up. 'I won't need any help, thanks. I need to make a phone call,' he added to his aunt, and strode away.

'What's up his nose today?' Harvey was bemused.

'Buggered if I know.' Mary shot Beth an apologetic look. 'Sorry. The stress must be getting to him. He hates the thought of Madjinbarra going down the crapper. He's not normally rude like that.' She muttered something about Charlie not being too old for a 'clip round the ear'ole'.

'It's fine,' Beth said. 'The point I was trying to make is, I'll help in any way I can. You know that, don't you?'

They both nodded. 'I wouldn't put stock in anything that Rendall snake says,' Mary assured her.

'Good.'

'Charlie hates the bloke's guts, that's all,' Harvey added. 'And no wonder.'

Beth waited but Harvey had finished. 'What do you mean?' she asked.

'It was Rendall who tried to get Jill taken away from us, years ago,' Mary explained. 'When he worked at Child Services.'

'What? I didn't know that.'

Mary nodded. 'A teacher at our school, she told the government Jill wasn't being looked after proper. Charlie's sister, Justine, she wasn't going too good.'

Harvey made a noise of warning and Mary hesitated.

41

'She was sick.'

'Sick' could mean a lot of things in Mary's parlance, but it often meant 'abusing substances'.

'Justine was struggling to look after Jill?' Beth ventured.

Mary shot a look at Harvey but nodded confirmation. 'Child Services came out and said Jill needed to go into foster care,' she said. 'There was a white couple working at the church — they took Jill in. Charlie was off making music while all this was going on, missed most of it until it was all settled. When he got back he was bloody pissed off, and went straight to Child Services. He said him and me could look after Jill and she shouldn't be with people who aren't even her family. But the couple what had Jill, they wanted to keep her. The case worker — that was Rendall — he went in to bat for them. Played hardball. Pulled up every bit of dirt he could on Charlie, which wasn't much, but made up all sorts of shit about the celebrity life and how bad it would be for Jill. Said stuff about Charlie, like he would be taking drugs and drinking grog, and mixing with rough crowds and loose women, and went on about how Jill was happy and well looked after where she was. Child Services decided Jill belonged with her family, thank Christ, so we got her back. Charlie and me are her legal guardians now. Then bloody Justine turned up three years ago with Pearl and said she couldn't keep her neither.'

Harvey harrumphed again and Mary scowled, swearing at him.

'This is the doc,' she said. 'We can trust her.'

Harvey raised his thick eyebrows but sipped his lemon squash in silent consent, and Mary continued. 'So Pearl's now legally Charlie's little girl too, but he's been worried about the girls being taken away ever since. And he hates the air that Rendall dickhead breathes.'

The story had given Beth a whole new reason to dislike Lloyd. She was vaguely aware he'd been a Child Services case worker at least a decade ago — well before he did his law degree — but she hadn't known he'd been embroiled in a battle over Charlie's nieces. She was also experiencing a confusing tug of pity towards Charlie — and indignation at the thought of Lloyd accusing Charlie of leading a wanton lifestyle. It was completely unfounded indignation, since Beth knew nothing about how Charlie lived these days. Still, she struggled to imagine the Charlie she remembered as a deadbeat parent.

Beth shook herself mentally. Charlie was still nowhere in sight, and she had an opportunity to escape before he got back and spilled his unpleasantness on her again. She got to her feet, shouldering her bag.

'Keep me up to date with how things are going, if you can, Mary. I'll keep my ear to the ground around here. Hopefully the minister will agree to tag along on my next trip out to Madji in — what is it — two weeks?'

'We'll get Charlie to talk to him.' Harvey was confident.

Beth farewelled them both and headed for the

car park. To her dismay, Charlie was outside, talking on the phone as he paced back and forth on the footpath, a hand jammed into his pocket. He caught sight of her and lost his words for a moment before turning deliberately away. Beth held her head high and made for the Beast, sliding gratefully into the driver's seat. When she glanced back his way as she pulled out of the hotel car park, Charlie had gone.

4

Beth walked beside the principal, crossing the red-dirt-stained paving of the quadrangle towards his office.

'Thank you, Bethany, for agreeing to help Charlie out. It's not that he hasn't had an education in the community where he was raised, but out there, they're focused on basic literacy and numeracy. The staff there are already working beyond capacity, trying to deliver the curriculum for almost seventy kids, from five right up to sixteen years of age. Charlie's a very intelligent young man, and he's doing an excellent job of picking up the Year Eleven content, but obviously extra support will be valuable.' Ogilvie gave her a sidelong glance. 'I don't want it to interfere with your own studies, though.'

'I think it'll be fine,' Beth answered. 'I'm treating it as revision time. I tutored Lyall McGovern last year, so I kind of know what's involved.'

'And the good news is, because of Charlie's circumstances, and because you're putting your tutoring payment towards boarding instead of taking the cash, you can cite it as community service on your university entrance portfolio.'

That was a bonus. She hadn't realised this tutoring gig would help her out in that way.

Mr Ogilvie pushed open the door to his office

and, inside, a boy was waiting in one of two chairs at the principal's desk. His brown skin was smooth and he had longish dark hair, brushed back from his forehead. His gaze was on his shoes, and Beth saw long lashes in profile above strong, handsome features. When she stopped beside him, Charlie looked up and Beth blinked into a pair of clever eyes, the same light green as the waters of a calm beach. She'd seen him around school in the distance, she remembered, but never up close. She certainly would have noticed. 'Hi,' she said with a quick smile.

He smiled back. Whoa. This guy was not just good-looking — he had a smile that lit up the room. Any lingering hesitations about taking the tutoring role vanished in an instant. Beth took the seat beside him.

'Charlie, this is Bethany Paterson, who's agreed to give you some extra tutoring,' said Mr Ogilvie. 'You can use the library. Miss Chomsky's there until four-thirty every after-noon, so you can hold your sessions straight after school, on any days that work for you both. We want you to do a minimum of two sessions per week.'

They nodded and Mr Ogilvie turned to Beth. 'Here are the English, biology and maths course outlines for Charlie's classes this semester. It's broken down week by week. All you need to do is work through any homework with Charlie and do some revision and quizzing on the topics. You learned it all last year, so it should be pretty straightforward.'

'No problem,' she said.

'If it gets too much, don't hesitate to let me know. We can arrange a break or for another student to take over.'

'Thanks,' she said.

'When do you want to get started?' the principal asked.

Beth looked at Charlie, but he was watching her, waiting for her to make the decision. 'Tomorrow?' she said, raising her eyebrows at him.

He smiled and nodded. Mr Ogilvie stood.

'Good stuff. Charlie's a fast learner,' he told her, and then looked at Charlie. 'And Bethany's an outstanding student. I'm sure this will be a very successful arrangement.' He paused, a thoughtful look crossing his face. 'Perhaps you can walk back to the boarding houses together after your tutoring sessions. As you know, there's no wandering around town permitted on weekdays after school.'

Beth got the feeling Mr Ogilvie wanted her to escort Charlie back to Grey after tutoring — like he thought Charlie might go on an unauthorised trip to the arcade if she didn't see him home. I'm not a babysitter, she thought. If Charlie Campbell wanted to wander around Mount Clair, that was his choice.

But she didn't mind walking home with him if he was okay with it.

They departed, hesitating outside the administration office. Charlie glanced at Beth. 'Are you walking straight to Durack?' he asked, and it was the first time she had heard his voice. It was deep, but had a warm, natural timbre to it. Her pulse picked up in pace.

'Yes . . . '

'Want to walk with me?'

Beth nodded with a kind of shrug so she wouldn't seem too eager. She shouldered her backpack and Charlie did the same.

They walked in silence for a few minutes but Beth couldn't let that go on. She felt silly, like a shy nine-year-old walking with a new friend, unable to think of anything to say. That wasn't her — not normally. She was in the debating club, for God's sake.

'What do you think of Mount Clair High?' she asked, and then wished she hadn't. Dumb question.

But Charlie gave her his big, warm smile again. 'It's okay. Pretty serious, compared to my old school.'

'What do you mean?'

'Well, I went to a mixed-age school, so we had to cater to all levels. There was always lots of sport and singing. I liked the sport, but every damn week at Friday morning assembly, we had to sing 'Do Your Ears Hang Low?' The little kids loved it.'

Beth laughed. 'Yeah, that would wear a bit thin.'

'Ogilvie said you're, like, the top student.' Charlie studied her and Beth's cheeks grew warm. 'You're going to uni?'

'Yes. I want to be a doctor.'

He gave a low whistle. 'That's about the hardest thing to get into, isn't it?'

48

'Almost. I think I can do it.'

'You going to travel? Go and be a doctor in Europe, or America, or whatever? Or in the city?'

Beth checked the road before stepping out to cross. 'No, I'd like to work here in Mount Clair, actually. The population's increasing here, and we always have to wait so long to see a doctor. It's only going to get worse as more people settle in town. If someone opens another surgery, I might be able to get a job there, and if they don't, I might do it myself. I'd love to own my own clinic.'

'That's cool. We don't have a doctor out where I live. We have a nurse, but if we need a doctor we have to drive for hours.'

'What about in an emergency?' Beth asked, astonished.

'Flying doctors.'

'Oh, right.' She contemplated that. It must be difficult for them. Why didn't they have a doctor? It would be scary for elderly people, or parents of newborns, to have the nearest medical help so far away.

Charlie broke into her thoughts. 'Why d'you want to stay in Mount Clair?'

'My family has a cattle station here.'

'Which one?'

'Paterson Downs.'

'Oh, yeah. I know it.' A teasing glint came into his eye. 'You're a pastoral princess, then?'

'A what?'

'One of the rich kids from the big stations.'

She laughed again. 'We're not rich!'

'Rich is relative.'

She hitched her bag higher on her shoulder. 'Okay, fair enough. But we're not that rich. And I'm not a princess.'

'Princess Beth from Paterson Downs,' he mused. 'I reckon there's a song in that.'

'Stop it,' she said, but she couldn't help giggling.

Unexpectedly, Charlie broke into a melody. 'She came from the valley with a golden crown, Princess Beth of Paterson Downs.'

Startled, still smiling, Beth gazed at him. 'You've got a really good voice.'

Charlie grinned. 'Thanks. My dad was a country music singer.'

'Was? But not any more?'

Charlie gave a lopsided shrug. 'He died when I was a kid.'

'I'm so sorry.' Beth paused, then spilled out her own story. 'My mum died recently.'

'How recently?'

'April.'

'Shit.' Charlie stopped walking and watched her, his vivid eyes filling with sympathy. 'My mum died, too. Two years back. Lung cancer. She was a smoker.'

Beth stopped as well. 'My mum got breast cancer. Not a smoker. Just bad luck.'

They watched each other in silence, but a moment of understanding passed between them. For the first time in a while, Beth felt tears threaten. She resumed walking, eyes glued to the footpath.

'My mum grew up in the community, like

me,' he said, keeping pace. 'She met my dad in Roeburke, working in the pub. He was touring and did a show out there. They didn't have much of a relationship, but he visited us from time to time after I was born. I remember him, just a little bit.'

Beth was grateful he wasn't asking about her mother. 'Did he teach you to sing?'

'Nah, I've always sung. Been singing for years.'

'"Do Your Ears Hang Low"?'

Charlie cracked up. 'Smart-arse.'

She glanced at his hands. 'Do you play an instrument?'

He looked at her in surprise. 'Yeah. Guitar. How'd you know?'

'I can see you playing guitar.'

Charlie smiled at her again and her heart skipped. Beth attempted to focus on walking but all of a sudden his hand shot out and grabbed her arm, pulling her back off the road just as a car whooshed past. Beth regained her balance and stammered a thanks.

'All those years on a cattle station must have made you lazy about looking out for traffic,' he said, looking down at her with a frown.

She wanted to argue that she was, in fact, extremely diligent and careful, both with traffic and more generally, but her brain emptied of all sensible thought as she looked at those sea-green eyes, acutely conscious of his hand on her arm. Something completely new happened to Beth on that street corner in the dry July air. Looking up at Charlie Campbell's handsome, challenging

51

face, she saw a man, not a schoolboy, and abruptly Beth knew that she wanted him. She wanted him with every nerve ending in her body. She couldn't speak. She couldn't even hear him speak.

She just wanted him.

Charlie urged her on across the road and she walked, unseeingly, to Durack House.

'I'll see you tomorrow.' Charlie gave a light wave as he walked on to the boys' accommodation.

And all Beth could do was croak an awkward goodbye.

★ ★ ★

For Chrissake.

It had happened again. She'd dreamed about bloody Charlie Campbell.

These were not like her usual dreams, where she processed the day's events and wandered through confusing, nonsensical situations. These were clear, accurate flashbacks — vivid replays of her lame little eighteen-year-old heartbreak. And Beth did not welcome them.

She pulled herself out of bed and washed her face at the bathroom basin. What a rubbish night's sleep. It had started with a few hours of insomnia and ended with that unwanted subconscious rehashing of the first time she'd met Charlie.

A run, that was what she needed.

She dressed in her running gear and tied up her hair. Charlie was staying at Mounties, so she would avoid that part of town. She would skirt the new housing estate instead. It was unlikely she would bump into Charlie at six in the morning, but . . .

What the hell am I doing? Planning a trajectory around town to avoid Charlie Campbell — the guy who had been utterly brutal with her heart when she was still innocent and clueless? He didn't deserve that kind of consideration. If anything, he deserved to get a good hard dose of Beth's face whenever he least felt like seeing it, just to remind him that it wasn't cool to treat women like that. She would run her usual course, dammit. Right past Mounties.

Beth didn't see him, not even to hold her nose in the air and show Charlie she didn't care in the least whether she saw him or not.

★ ★ ★

Lloyd Rendall messaged Beth again during the day so, after work, she reluctantly called him.

'Hey, Beth. How's things?'

'Good, thanks. What can I do for you, Lloyd?'

'Well, I feel like we got off to a bad start on the Madjinbarra issue, and I wanted to have a chat about it.'

She repressed a sigh. 'I'm the wrong person to talk to, Lloyd. I don't have any influence over an outcome. All I know is, the community won't go down without a fight.'

'Yes — but, sadly, there's very little chance they'll win. I don't want them to suffer, though.

You're on good terms with them, aren't you? Mary Wirra and Charlie Campbell? And old Harvey what's-his-name?'

'Harvey Early. I'm on moderately good terms with Mary and Harvey but I don't know Charlie well at all.'

'Well, I'm not sure if you know this, but Gargantua offered the Madjinbarra elders the chance to build the mine workers' camp right in town, to bring new facilities into their community.' Lloyd paused to add gravity. 'They said no.'

'Yes, I knew that.'

'Oh, really?' He sounded surprised. 'Well, it means that Gargantua needs to start from scratch, putting in all the infrastructure for a workers' camp. But even that's not good enough for the Madjinbarra elders. They seem to think that simply having a workers' camp nearby will be a problem for them.'

'Lloyd, they don't just *think* it — they know it. Everyone knows it. The mine site's too close to Madjinbarra.'

He still didn't seem to get it. 'Gargantua can't budge on the site,' he said. 'That tract of land contains the richest deposits, so they'll need a workers' camp.'

'Exactly, and the workers' camp will have a wet mess — a pub — only an hour's drive away from the community.'

'And they honestly think that will be a problem?'

She explained in simple words so this moron would understand. 'Lloyd, the Madjinbarra locals will seek work on the mine. If they work at

54

the mine, they'll have access to the workers' pub. And even if they don't, booze will be available close to home. The Madjinbarra community is dry — no alcohol. If some of them get into drinking, they'll start bringing the problem home.'

'It's not a foregone conclusion that they'll get into drinking,' he said.

'Is there any reason why Gargantua can't have a dry miners' camp?' Beth countered. 'Out of respect for Madjinbarra?'

He paused, then chuckled. 'That's a little naive for a smart lady like you, Beth.'

Her temper flared. 'The Gwini nation could have a native title claim over that land, you know. If they submit a claim now, there will be lengthy delays while it goes through the tribunal.'

Lloyd was unflustered. 'Well, they tried once before to get native title on the area in question and the court ruled against them. There was no evidence that it was ever anything significant to the Aboriginals. So I doubt a claim would even get heard.'

Beth's spirits sank. If Lloyd was telling the truth, it didn't look promising for the community.

'Here's the thing,' he went on. 'I was hoping to present an idea to the elders but if *I* do it, they won't like it. They don't like dealing with lawyers. I was thinking: if it comes from you, they might be willing to consider it.'

'What idea?'

'We've got a solution in mind,' he continued. 'I'd like to tell you about it but it's a bit involved.

Can we meet? I was thinking I could take you for a meal at the Sawmill so we can have a proper chat.'

'Can't you give me a rough idea now?'

'No, it really needs a full explanation, Beth. Let me shout you dinner.'

She heaved a silent sigh. 'I'm a bit busy this week.'

'You don't have any nights free at all?'

Beth felt put on the spot, but she owed it to Mary and Harvey to find out what this *solution* was. 'How about I come to your office . . . '

'Let a bloke take you out for dinner,' he said in a jovial tone. 'I promise I won't bore you with legalese.'

That wasn't what she was worried about. Having suffered through Lloyd's unwanted attention for years, she didn't want him thinking this was some kind of date.

'I'll meet you on Sunday night, if that suits,' she said. 'A business dinner. I'll pay.'

'I wouldn't hear of it.' Was he trying to be gallant now? Beth rolled her eyes. 'My shout, and no strings,' Lloyd went on. 'Seven p.m. Sunday at the Sawmill, for a nice meal and a cosy chat.'

Cosy chat, my arse.

There was a bang on her front door and Beth was saved from the retort she'd been going to make.

'Okay. See you then, Lloyd. I need to go — I have a visitor.'

She hung up and dashed for the door, opening it to Free. Her sister had her arms full of foliage and her sweet face broke into a smile as Beth

56

unlocked the screen door.

'Look what I've got for you, Bethie! Old Mr Craddick across the road did all these cuttings for me, you know, so I can make a pretty garden like he's got. But I don't know what to do with them and I didn't have the heart to tell him, so you can have half if you teach me how to make them grow.'

Beth waved Free inside. 'How did you get yourself into this situation?'

'Reg is always out in the garden, and whenever I'm out the front I get stuck in a conversation with him. He has a really nice front yard and I've mentioned it a few times, so I guess he thought I wanted a nice front yard too. He gave me all these and I'm scared I'll kill them and he'll be disappointed in me.' Free dumped her load of plants on Beth's sideboard.

'You could have said *no thanks*,' Beth reminded her.

Free's eyes opened wide with the scandalised look that always made Beth want to laugh. 'I couldn't do that! He'd be hurt.'

Beth knew Reg Craddick — he was a patient — and she knew he wouldn't be hurt by something like that. But she also knew she would never convince Free of that fact, so she turned her attention to the plants.

'Oh, these are easy. You just stick them in some soil, and water them for a few weeks. They grow a new root system and then they're pretty much fine by themselves.'

'Do I need to fertilise them, or graft them or anything?'

'Graft them!' Beth watched Free in amusement. 'Do you know how to graft plants, Freya Paterson? Because if you do, I'll hire you to come and tend my garden.'

Free giggled, a little sheepish. 'They seriously only need to be planted and watered?'

'I promise.'

'Okay.' Free surveyed her greenery. 'I'll give it a go. If they start to die, Finn can take over. He's good at everything responsible.'

'*You're* good at lots of things, too.'

It still bugged Beth whenever she remembered the disagreement they'd had the year before. How could her sister have assumed Beth thought so little of her capacity to do — well, anything much at all? Beth blamed herself. She should have been nicer to Free over the years — not so bossy or controlling. She watched Free, her smooth forehead wrinkling as she inspected the plants, oblivious to the trace of blue paint on her arm and the singlet strap hanging off one shoulder. Free was like a whirlwind of talent and passion, and every time she paused to think about her, Beth almost wept with love. It remained a punch in the guts to know she'd inadvertently hurt one of her sisters.

'Stay for dinner,' Beth said.

Free thought about it. 'Okay. Thanks. Finn's working tonight and I was going to do pasta for myself but I'm so sick of pasta. What are you having?'

'What do you feel like?'

Free brightened. 'Curry?'

'I can do a tikka masala for us.'

58

Free practically wriggled with delight. '*Yum!* I'll help.'

This meant her evening run was out the window, but Beth preferred her sister's company. They cooked and ate together, then chatted on the sofa, and when Free got a message from Finn at nine p.m. to say he was heading home, Beth was sorry to see her sister jump up to leave.

'I want to beat him home,' Free said, gathering her things hastily. 'I've painted this creek bed and it looks *exactly* like Finn's eyes! I'm so excited. Can't wait to show him.'

She departed in a rush, forgetting about the mass of cuttings she'd left on the sideboard. Beth watched Free drive off and gathered up the plants, placing them in a bucket of water. She could drop a few off at Free's place tomorrow after work. Beth tidied her kitchen and sank back onto the sofa to check her phone for messages. *Nothing.* Quite abruptly, she felt lonely.

To her vexation, Beth found her thoughts drifting back towards Charlie. It was the same loneliness she'd felt at Durack all those years ago, mourning her mother and missing her father and sisters; wishing for home but too determined to succeed to admit it. Maybe that was why she fell so hard for Charlie way back then — because he was lonely too, having lost his parents and left his home. He understood what it felt like for Beth. With the benefit of age, basic psychology training, and distance from the situation, it all made sense. She'd been longing to connect with someone who understood.

Charlie had come along, and he got it — or seemed to.

Or maybe it was because when he sang about me it reached into my soul, when he touched me it lit my body on fire —

Oh, for Chrissake. This was ridiculous. She needed someone to talk some sense into her. Beth snatched her phone off the coffee table and dialled Rikke.

'Hello, you.'

Beth's heart flooded with relief when she heard that soft Danish accent. 'Hi, Rikke. I'm sorry. I've called you late again.'

'What's wrong? You sound upset.'

'I'm not upset. Just a bit rattled by all this . . . ' *Ugh, I sound ridiculous.*

'All this what? Oh, wait, do you mean Charlie Campbell?'

Beth gave up trying to fake some dignity. 'Rikke, I'm having these weird flashback dreams and I need your psychologising to help me.'

'What weird dreams?'

'These super vivid dreams where I relive moments with Charlie, right down to the most accurate detail. And I want them to stop.'

'When you say accurate, do you mean — '

'I mean, totally accurate! No embellishing, no psychedelic swirls or random raccoon appearances. These dreams are like watching my life back on video.'

Rikke gave a whistle. 'Episodic dreaming. Very rare.'

'What the *hell?* Episodic dreaming — what does it mean?'

'No idea. There are theories, but who knows for sure?' Rikke paused. 'If you pushed me, I'd say it means there are some events in Bethany Paterson's life that have been squashed down and repressed. And they're coming out now.'

Beth bristled. 'I never repressed anything. I remember what happened with Charlie perfectly well.'

'But did you find peace with it?'

Beth was silent.

'Beth? You there?'

'Yes. I never really thought of it like that. I suppose I moved on in the sense that I stopped mourning him and had boyfriends and was happy. But I never had it out with him. Never told him what a bastard he was to do what he did.'

'Maybe now's your opportunity,' Rikke suggested.

'No way. Do you realise how unhinged it would look to suddenly start berating Charlie over dumping me seventeen years ago?'

Rikke gave her low chuckle. 'You don't need to berate him. But if you find yourself in the appropriate circumstances, you could touch on the topic. Ask him what was going on for him.'

Beth recalled Charlie's hard face as he'd turned away from her in the Mounties car park the night before. 'I'm not convinced I'd get any answers, even if I found the courage to ask.'

'I wonder if there's more to it than you think,' Rikke said.

For a second, Beth wondered if Charlie might have some sort of explanation, after all. Then she

61

sighed. 'He probably just thought of me as a fling. A conquest.'

'Probably.'

Rikke's bluntness hurt but it was a good reality check. 'How can I get rid of the dreams?' Beth asked.

Rikke guffawed. 'Did you hear yourself just now? These are episodic dreams, not a nasty case of herpes! They'll stop when your subconscious mind agrees that you've moved on, I'm guessing.'

'Rikke.' Beth felt helpless. 'This is so humiliating.'

'The dreams?'

'All of it. Him coming here and messing with my mind. My stupid memories, dreams and emotions. Ugh! Get me out of here.'

'Why don't you take a little break, babe? Come to Perth and stay with me for a while. How far ahead are you booked up at the clinic? If it's just a week or so, why not give yourself a little getaway?'

'Maybe.' Beth was doubtful. She was almost always booked a month ahead because some of her regulars liked to sort their appointments out well in advance. Plus she had the Madjinbarra visit in two weeks' time. 'Enough about me, anyway. What's going on with you?'

'Nothing whatsoever. I'm living my romantic life vicariously through you at the moment. The biggest thrill of my social life is going to see the latest Dwayne Johnson movie next cheapskate Tuesday.'

Beth relaxed into laughter. 'You and The

Rock! I will never understand that obsession.'

'You're just jealous that I have sweet dreams of Dwayne every night and you get some jerk who screwed you over twenty years ago.'

'I am not jealous of *Dwayne Johnson*, for Chrissake, Rikke. If anything, I'm relieved he's too busy visiting your dreams to take a wrong turn into mine.'

'He'd better not turn up in your dreams.' Rikke was giggling now, too. 'You wouldn't be able to handle him.'

The phone call ended a few minutes later with Beth's promise to check her bookings and think about an escape to visit Rikke. Beth contemplated her living-room wall for a few minutes, thinking about wallpaper patterns, and then took herself off for a shower.

She needed to get to bed if she was going to achieve the extra-long run she had planned for the morning.

5

One-thirteen a.m.

Beth's phone was ringing. She fumbled for it, swiping to accept the call, eyes too bleary to read the caller's name.

'Hello?' she practically whispered.

'Hi, Dr Paterson.' It was Yolanda Clement, the hospital registrar. 'Sorry to wake you. Could you come in?'

'No problem,' Beth managed. 'Anything specific?'

'There's been a car accident and we've had three trauma patients come in. We've got Mrs Leaman, who had hip replacement surgery yesterday, and a labouring mum in maternity, as well as the usual contingent of late-night emergency cases and time-wasters.'

'Okay. I'll be there as soon as possible.'

'Thanks, Beth.' Yolanda's usual hard-as-nails voice softened slightly. 'I hope you know we appreciate it.'

Just those few words of gratitude rallied Beth's spirits. Yes, she was tired, and yes, she'd be even more tired when she started work in the morning, but at least the team at the hospital knew they could rely on her. It was good to feel needed — trusted.

She was there until four. Beth fell into bed at four-thirty and dismissed her jogging alarm at five-thirty, going back to sleep until eight. Then she had to scramble to get dressed and make her first appointment. She fell behind during the morning thanks to Reg Craddick insisting he had Ross River virus because he'd been bitten by a mosquito and now he had a dreadful sore throat. He wouldn't leave until he'd convinced Beth to request blood tests. She worked through lunch to bring her appointments back into some semblance of order, and finished at quarter to six, starving and stressed.

Going out to Madjinbarra would feel like a vacation, at this rate.

Beth said goodbye to Paul, who was just inviting his last patient into his room, and her young receptionist, Dani, who thankfully loved the overtime pay. Weariness hit before Beth had even stepped outside — replaced by a jolt of alarm when she saw Charlie standing in the clinic car park. He wore sunglasses and stood with his hand jammed in one pocket, as was his habit. When he saw Beth, he crossed to stand near her car — not too close, but close enough to indicate he had something to say.

'Hello, Charlie,' she said, when it became apparent he wouldn't speak.

'Aunty Mary wanted me to give you a message.'

'Yes?'

'We heard back from Nigel Winston, the Minister for Mining. He's willing to visit the community. He can be here in town in two weeks, at the same time you're due to head out there. My vehicle's a bit rough, and Aunty Mary reckons you'll be a good advocate for

Madjinbarra. Would you drive Winston and one of his staff?'

'Of course.' Beth was slightly shocked. 'That's — that's great he's going to take a look at the community. How did you manage to convince him?'

Charlie seemed lost for words. He shrugged a shoulder. 'Just asked.'

'I guess it's hard for him to ignore someone of your public standing.'

Right on cue, a car passed them, and the driver must have recognised Charlie because he went into a frenzy of honking and waving. Charlie glanced up and waved back, which clearly made the guy's day. He farewelled them with a huge grin and a long blast on his horn.

Beth watched wordlessly. When Charlie turned back, his face was serious once more and she was struck anew by his coolness. She couldn't help feeling a little outraged. He was acting like she was the one who'd wronged *him*.

'Is that all?' she asked.

His expression changed. His eyebrows tugged down and his mouth tightened. 'Aunty wanted me to ask if I can ride with you and the minister. I want to take advantage of having the guy as a captive audience for five hours or so.' Charlie paused for a moment to let her digest this idea. 'Any problem with that?' he added stiffly.

Of all the cheeky . . .

'No problem.' She made her voice ice-cold. 'Four will fit comfortably in my vehicle.'

Charlie nodded. 'Where should I get Winston to wait for you, and what time?'

'I'll be leaving at five a.m. and I'll collect you and the minister on the way, if that suits everyone. You'll still be at Mounties?'

'Yeah.'

'And the minister at the resort?'

'Probably.' The breeze blew Charlie's hair across his forehead and he pushed it back. 'I'll confirm when I can.'

Beth realised they probably needed to exchange numbers. Charlie had fished his phone from his pocket and the uncomfortable look on his face told her he'd thought of the same thing. She dug in her handbag for her own phone, her cheeks warming with each moment that passed as she searched for it. At last, she gave up.

'My phone's hiding right down the bottom,' she said. 'I'll give you my number and you can text my phone so I've got yours.' She rattled off her number and Charlie entered it into his phone. He thumbed a message and hit send, and Beth heard her phone beep from inside her bag. 'If you could confirm where I need to collect the minister from, when you know, that would help.'

'Yeah, I'll keep you posted.' Charlie lifted his gaze to her face for a second. 'Is there anything Pearl needs? While I'm in town, I could get it for her.'

Beth thought about it. 'I was pleased to see the gait trainer appear. I assumed it came through government funding but Mary said you've organised all Pearl's equipment. How did you even know Pearl needed one?'

'Aunty Mary said you'd recommended it.' Charlie jammed that hand in his pocket again and Beth recognised it as a sign of discomfort. 'Not everything at Madjinbarra relies on government funding.'

Beth straightened. 'I suggested Mary request funding for the equipment, which is why I assumed it had come through a grant of some kind. I had no idea *you* were Pearl's uncle until Monday.'

He didn't speak and Beth's resentment swelled. How dare he act like she'd injured him — his community — in some way? She'd never done anything but try to help the residents of Madjinbarra.

'Pearl's interested in drawing lately,' she said, keeping her voice cool. 'You might like to get her some drawing and colouring books, preferably stapled in the middle so the pages stay flat, since she might have difficulty pinning a glued book open. She'll also need some large, easy-to-grip markers or crayons. Nothing that snaps too readily or requires fine motor skills.'

He gave a nod. 'Thanks.'

Charlie loped away towards his 4WD, parked on the road. Beth climbed into the Beast, letting out a slow breath. How long had he been waiting in the car park for her to appear? Why didn't the idiot just come inside the clinic and leave her a message? It was ludicrous, the lengths he was going to just to show her how little he enjoyed interacting with her.

She'd really got him wrong all those years ago. He'd seemed hopeful, warm, gifted in his music as well as his mind. Sure, he'd proven to the world he had musical talent, but his warmth must have been all performance. Nowadays, his personality was cold and hard. Or maybe he reserved that for her. Mary and Harvey had seemed surprised by his behaviour at Mounties. Maybe Charlie felt as embarrassed as Beth did about their history, and his coolness was a way to cover it up.

Or maybe he just saw her as a forgettable past conquest.

She groaned aloud as she pulled the Beast out into the lazy evening traffic on Mount Clair's main street. Having Charlie Campbell in town was seriously damaging her equilibrium. She needed another weekend at Patersons to regain a little sanity.

She arrived home within minutes and checked her pot plants, then got ready for a run. As she fitted her phone to her arm strap, Beth saw the terse text message from earlier. *Charlie Campbell's number*, he'd written. She saved it in her phone, uneasiness washing over her.

It felt weird having his number.

★   ★   ★

'You got an A!' Beth lifted her gaze to Charlie's face. 'Holy crap! I'm glad you're not doing Year Twelve, or I'd be feeling competitive right now.'

Charlie grinned, but he followed it with a quick shrug. 'Miss said my grammar and punctuation have improved 'phenomenally'. I'm guessing I might not have done so well without your editing.'

Beth waved a dismissive hand, reading the

69

English teacher's written comment. 'That stuff — spelling and punctuation — it's just for decoration. It's only noticed when you get it wrong. But listen to this. 'Charlie, your grasp of the metaphors in Wilfred Owen's poetry is extremely high-level, and your way of expressing yourself has demonstrated your skill with language. Your essay is as much poetry as it is about poetry'.' Beth met his eyes. 'She's right, you know. You write like a poet.'

'Not a poet,' he said with a slight groan. 'Bloody hell. Songwriter.'

She thought of his silly ditty about her from the first time they'd met four weeks earlier. She had it memorised and thought about it way too often, vividly remembering the strength of his voice and that cheeky, sexy expression in his eyes when he'd sung to her.

'You could be big someday, you know, Charlie. With your writing talent and your voice.' She ducked her head and pretended to be perusing his English assignment again.

'You reckon?' She heard the smile in his voice. 'I hope so. I want to do something big. I kind of want to be a lawyer, but another part of me thinks that would be pretty much the most boring job on the planet. I'd want to skip the part where you study big fat wads of legislation and jump straight to the bit where I defend the little guy in court and annihilate the crack legal team on the other side.'

Beth shook her head. 'You don't talk like someone raised in a tiny remote community.'

'You don't talk like a pastoral princess,' he

shot back. 'You still haven't mentioned the rainfall figures or the size of your father's property.'

She laughed a little too loudly and Miss Chomsky looked up from her magazine at the library desk. Beth smiled apologetically at the teacher and she smiled back, her face warm.

Charlie waited for Miss Chomsky to return to her magazine and then gave Beth a cynical look. 'You know how to keep the teachers wrapped around your finger, don't you?'

Beth shrugged. 'They trust me because I don't mess with them. I don't see the point. It means I get pegged as the goody-two-shoes, though.'

'Do you get hassled over that?' he wanted to know.

'Not really. I did before.'

'Before?'

'Before everyone got older and more mature.' She paused. 'And before my mother died.'

His mouth twisted. 'Everyone's a bit nicer to you now, huh?'

Beth didn't answer. She didn't need to.

Charlie stared down at his long legs stretched out beneath the table they were sharing. 'At my old school, one of the teachers was a complete bitch. Hated me. No reason, just hated me. She was nice to the girls but seemed to have it in for most of the boys.' He glanced at Beth. 'The day I came back to school after my mum died, she did a full about-face. Suddenly she couldn't do enough for me. Pats on the shoulder, better grades, smiles, house points.'

Beth felt angry for him, but she got it, too.

71

People could be arseholes sometimes, and it took something awful to soften them towards you. Her classmate Cyndi Hanrahan had been nasty to her for years. She couldn't forget the name-calling. Suck-arse. Brown-nose. Tight snobby bitch. Then, the week after Beth's mother died, Cyndi had come up at school out of the blue and hugged her. Beth had wondered if Cyndi was trying to stick gum in her hair, it had been such a shock.

'Maybe your teacher felt guilty about how she'd acted,' she said to Charlie.

He tipped his head. 'Maybe. I still hated her for it.'

Some of Beth's carefully repressed resentment towards Cyndi suddenly gushed out like hot water spraying from a faulty pipe joint.

'Yeah. Fair enough,' she said.

Charlie eyed her in surprise and gave a soft chuckle. 'I thought you were going to tell me it was better to forgive, empathise, let the anger flow away like the new rain washes the debris out of the riverbed every year.'

Even though he was messing around, it was like every word he said made Beth's emotion surge. Somehow Charlie could speak her feelings. 'Where did you learn to talk like that?'

'Like what?'

'Like a poet.'

He grabbed her arm and looked her in the eye — jokingly, but it made Beth forget to breathe. 'Don't you call me a poet,' he threatened, a hint of a smile on his lips. 'Songwriter, I told you, woman.'

72

'Okay — where'd you learn to talk like a songwriter?' she asked, her voice steadier than she felt.

'My dad left me something.' Charlie released her arm and sat back. 'And my mum made sure I got it. A record player. It would have been top of the line when it was made. It still works. And I've got the biggest collection of vinyl of any kid in the Kimberley, you can bet your arse. Hundreds. I know every record, every track, every line.'

Beth frowned. 'What's that got to do with anything?'

'Songwriters,' he said. 'I was raised by them.'

★   ★   ★

When she woke up on Thursday morning, dragging herself out of yet another Charlie Campbell replay, Beth cemented her decision to go to Paterson Downs for the weekend. She was floundering — her mind was all over the place — and she needed somewhere to recalibrate. She talked Free into coming with her, since Finn was rostered on to work both Saturday and Sunday. Free's only condition was that she be home by two in the afternoon on Sunday so she wouldn't miss her art circle.

Beth got through the next two work days and collected Free from her unit on Marlu Street on Friday afternoon. On the drive to Patersons, Free fretted about how much she would miss Finn, as though Beth were taking her on a long vacation.

73

'Have you got any travel plans in the pipeline?' Beth interrupted when she could take no more.

Free gasped with recollection. 'Yes! We're going to Kuala Lumpur with Devi and Si at the end of muster season. It's going to be *amazing*. We're bussing it out of the city to stay in Devi's village. Si's never even been out of Australia, can you believe that?'

Beth considered it. 'Si's only young, isn't he? Lots of people don't travel overseas until they're older and start to earn their own money.'

'Si's twenty, though. I've been helping him get his passport organised. He's so excited.'

'How long are you staying?' Beth asked. 'Or is it open-ended?'

'No way. Finn's got work, but also — my customers and students! I can't just abandon them. We're going for two weeks, though — a decent stay.'

Beth couldn't help a laugh. 'Is this Free Paterson I'm talking to? I remember when you wouldn't have got out of bed in the morning for anything less than a month's trip.'

Free giggled. 'I know, right? But that was before I met Finn, and before I, you know, had a proper job, or whatever.'

'You've put down roots.'

'Yeah. I still love travelling, though. I'm organising an artists' retreat in Italy next year. A nice long trip. I thought I might rent a villa in Pisa for four or five weeks, and people can join me throughout the month. I've already got six people interested, and my friend Flavia has found me the perfect place with four bedrooms. I can have three other people staying with me at any one time, or more if they're willing to share. My student Tia — she's in Year Twelve — she's already saving up to come during her uni break.'

Beth thought longingly of a summer stay in Italy. Hell, she needed a holiday. 'And Finn?'

'His parents are coming here to visit in December, so next year will be perfect for us to visit them. He'll come meet me at the end of the retreat and we'll go to Ireland for a few weeks.'

'Won't you miss him while you're in Italy?' Beth teased.

Free didn't pick up on the sarcasm. 'Yes! But I'll survive. I should be so busy doing art museum tours and plein-air day trips that I'll get through it okay. And he has to stay here to look after Maxie-Boy, anyway.' Free cast an adoring glance into the back seat where the tabby cat lay sleeping in his carrier basket. 'Jay said she can take him for a couple of weeks while we're both away, but not the whole time I'm running the retreat, so Max will need his daddy.'

Max was the most spoilt cat in the state, Beth thought. Even Barry, who loathed cats as a general rule, was soft on Max.

Willow and Tom were at Quintilla for the night but they'd promised to come for a Paterson family dinner on Saturday. Barry, Beth and Free had the option of eating in the station dining hall but Beth offered to cook steaks and steamed vegetables for them so they could have a quiet night in private. She didn't feel like socialising.

'When's your next stint out at the Madjaballi community?' Free asked over dinner.

75

'Madjinbarra,' Beth corrected with a smile. 'Ten days from now. I'm chauffeuring the Minister for Mining, believe it or not.'

Barry's eyebrows shot up. 'What's that, sweetheart?'

Beth gave them an outline of the Gargantua problem, and her father shook his head, impressed. 'I'm bloody surprised you could talk him into driving out there. Hell of a trip. Half of it's unsealed roads, isn't that right?'

'Yes, but the Beast can handle it. It wasn't me who talked the minister into it, though. People from the community did the hard negotiating.'

'Someone who lives there?' Free asked.

'Used to.' Beth realised too late that she'd sparked their interest. 'More gravy, Dad?'

'No, thanks, sweetheart. Beautiful dinner.'

'Who was it?' Free wanted to know.

Beth sighed inwardly. 'Charlie Campbell.'

'Oh my God!' Free's fork clattered to her plate. 'You're working with *Charlie Campbell* on this? I'd heard he was in town. I've been hanging around Mounties with Phoebe whenever Finn's on evening shift, trying to catch a glimpse of him. I *love* Charlie Campbell! Beth, you are so sneaky. Why didn't you tell me? You know I'm crazy about his music. I go see his shows every time he comes to Mount Clair and I've been waiting over two years for his next album!'

'I didn't know that,' Beth lied. 'Anyway, I'm not working *with* him. He happens to be involved in the campaign to protect the community. I saw him at a stakeholders' meeting, and I'm giving him and the minister a

76

lift out there, that's all.'

'I'm passionate about your work at Madja-birri,' said Free. 'I could join in the fight.'

'Madjinbarra.' Tension made her voice sharp and Free flinched slightly. Beth felt terrible. 'Sorry. I'm worried about this stuff with Gargantua. I don't want them to win.'

Free studied her in that painfully honest way she had. Her eyes were filling with tears. 'Is there anything I can do to help?'

'Oh, God, Free.' Out of nowhere, tears had sprung to Beth's eyes as well. 'Don't set *me* off! It's okay. We're working on a plan. Charlie's involvement will make a big difference — he's high-profile, and the media's interested in what he says and does. It will put pressure on the government and Gargantua.'

Her father was rubbing his chin, deep in thought. 'Is this Campbell bloke any relation to that kid you used to help out at school, sweetheart? I remember old Ogilvie telling me about an Aboriginal kid called Campbell, back when he asked my permission for you to do that tutoring job.'

Seriously? Her father remembered that? Beth wanted to slink from the room but she bravely kept her face up.

'Yes, I tutored Charlie for a short while in Year Twelve. But he didn't see out his studies.'

Free goggled. 'You tutored *Charlie Campbell* in high school? Why the hell am I only finding out about this now?'

'It was very short-lived.'

'Why?'

Free's eyes were on hers and it brought Charlie's eyes to mind. Beth transferred her gaze to her father, and his eyes — also green — were watching her expectantly. *Bloody hell . . .* They were a different shade, but still. Green was one of the most statistically unlikely eye colours to occur, and yet she was surrounded by it.

Beth clenched her fists under the table. 'He decided to pursue a music career,' she said, keeping her voice perfectly steady.

'Thank the universe for that!' Free laughed and tucked back in to her meal. 'It's a good thing you weren't a better tutor, Beth, or we might not have Charlie's beautiful music today.'

Beth's appetite vanished. She forced down some pieces of broccoli and pushed her steak around on her plate so it would seem like she was eating. *So unfair.* She'd been a bloody good tutor, as a matter of fact.

Well, I was a good tutor before I completely lost my mind over my student and started sneaking out of the library with him to . . .

Beth grasped her wineglass and took a large sip. 'How did the *Born and Bred* wall survive its first wet season?' she asked Free. 'It still looks good to me when I go past it, but I'm no expert.'

This was enough to take the heat off her. Free happily launched into a description of how amazingly perfect her tile wall still looked, and then went on to talk about the primary school mural she had worked on in Broome over the previous couple of months. Beth kept pushing food around her plate and nibbling bits of vegetable. And her stomach continued to churn every time her mind drifted towards Charlie Campbell.

★ ★ ★

'Why won't you look at me, Princess Beth of Paterson Downs?'

She couldn't keep the smile from her lips no matter how hard she tried. 'I have a duty to revise biology, English and maths with you.'

Charlie tipped his head to one side. 'That makes me your customer, yeah?'

She met his eyes and lifted her eyebrows. 'Customer?'

'Yeah. Your job is to revise. To tutor me. You're the worker, I'm the customer. And the customer's always right.'

'Whatever.'

She turned back to the biology textbook but Charlie caught her hand and leaned in close. 'The customer doesn't want to revise biology.'

Beth's mind went blank, although her eyes kept running blindly over the biology book. 'Is that so?'

He leaned even closer. 'That's so. You let me kiss you yesterday.' Charlie was whispering, and his warm breath on her cheek sent a shiver through her. He reached up a hand and touched her neck, just beneath her earlobe. 'Right here.'

'So?'

'So, today I want to kiss you somewhere else.' Beth stared hard at the open book but the text and pictures all swam together. Charlie ran his finger from her ear, across her cheek, and stopped at the corner of her mouth. 'Here.'

She didn't answer because every single part of her yearned for exactly what he was promising. She pressed her lips together, barely breathing.

'Beth?'

'Miss Chomsky's right there,' she managed.

Charlie looked up. The library teacher was seated facing them, immersed in an administrative task — or maybe reading her magazine again. Who knew? The point was, she could see them if she looked up.

Beth shifted slightly. 'We're studying arthropods today,' she said. 'Maybe we could do some . . . some field work.'

Charlie frowned. 'Huh?'

'Arthropods, Charlie Campbell. What are they?'

'Organisms with an exoskeleton.'

'Like?'

He sighed and rolled his eyes. 'We did this on Monday.'

'Examples?'

'Spiders, insects, scorpions, crabs.'

She took a breath. 'So I want to know if you can identify one in the wild.'

Charlie's eyes lit up as he realised what she was suggesting. 'I'm up for the challenge.'

Beth rose, shoved her books into her bag and headed for the exit, Charlie trailing behind her. Miss Chomsky looked up as they passed.

'Finished already?' she said.

Beth gave the teacher her best good-girl smile.

'We're going spider-spotting. I want to see how well Charlie knows his arthropods.'

The woman laughed. 'Well, you're braver than me!'

They headed for the lake and found a spot to sit on the grassed bank.

'Look, an arthropod,' Charlie remarked, pointing at the grass next to Beth's schoolbag.

Sure enough, an ant was crawling among the blades of grass.

'Correct,' she said.

'What's my reward?' he asked, his sparkling eyes catching hers.

Beth checked that no-one was watching and leaned swiftly forward, her heart pounding. She kissed his lips — just for an instant. 'Every time you get a question right, that's your reward.'

His eyes seemed darker all of a sudden. 'I'm motivated.'

'What are the main characteristics of an arthropod?' she asked.

Charlie's gaze was locked on hers, making her weak with longing. 'Um, an exoskeleton?'

She leaned forward to place another quick kiss on his mouth. 'Correct.'

'Ask me more.'

'What else characterises the phylum?'

Charlie had moved closer by now and she would have forgiven him for abandoning the quiz, but he paused to consider her question, exploring her face.

'Segmented bodies.'

She was overjoyed he'd got it right because

she desperately wanted another kiss. She leaned in and their lips met. They held the kiss a little longer this time.

'Correct,' she said at close range, her breathing uneven.

He seemed to be thinking hard, his shoulders heaving with the effort to control his own breathing. 'Legs,' he said. 'Six legs.'

'Wrong,' she sighed.

'Not six,' he corrected himself hastily. 'Sometimes more. But jointed. Arthropods have jointed legs.'

She smiled and moved in for another kiss, but this time Charlie slipped an arm around her waist, the other hand on her upper back, fingers tangling in her long hair. This was the first time Beth had ever kissed a boy — really kissed anyone. She felt clumsy, certain she was doing it wrong, but at the same time she didn't care. Charlie's lips were soft against hers and all she wanted was more.

Their revision was finished for the afternoon. They had precisely thirty-three minutes to kiss as deeply and hungrily as possible before they reluctantly started the walk back to their boarding houses.

'Which university are you going to?' Charlie asked.

'The University of WA,' she said. 'It's the only one that offers medicine.'

'Then that's where I'm going,' he said.

'You want to study medicine?' she asked in surprise.

'No. I want to be where you are.'

★   ★   ★

In her old bedroom at Paterson Downs, Beth gazed at herself in the mirror. She had dark hollows under her eyes. She looked her age today, she realised, sighing.

Damn you, Charlie Campbell, for coming back to town, back into my life, and messing with my peace of mind.

She went out into the yards to find Willow. Her sister was in the treatment shed, pregnancy-testing cattle with Vern and a cohort of stockmen.

'It's a glamorous life,' she called, catching Willow arm-deep in heifer.

'Yeah, but you do this with humans, you sicko,' Willow called back, grinning.

'Let's run away and become ballerinas.'

Willow checked the remaining half a dozen heifers, calling her verdict to Vern, who entered it into a spreadsheet on a tablet. Then she discarded the plastic gloves, cleaned herself up and joined Beth away from the action.

'Still keeping your news under wraps?' Beth asked in a low voice.

'Yeah. Tom's dying to tell the world, but I made him promise to wait till the three-month mark.'

'No morning sickness at all?'

Willow shook her head. 'Makes me wonder, and worry, sometimes.'

Beth laughed. 'Do *not* wish for morning sickness, Willow. One of my patients was sick every day of her pregnancy. She was vomiting

83

while she was in labour. You don't want that.'

'I've had a couple of food aversions,' Willow said, brightening. 'Bananas. And coffee.'

'Coffee! You?'

'Yep. Probably better for me to avoid coffee, anyway.' She checked for eavesdroppers but they were standing well away from everyone else. 'I've stopped horseriding but Tom wants me to stop doing cattle treatment, too. Like the preg-testing this morning. We had a big argument about it last night.'

'Who won?'

Willow shot her a look. 'Didn't you heckle me for preg-testing cows just five minutes ago?'

Beth grinned. 'Poor Tom. I can understand his concern. You were well clear of the kick zone, from what I could see, but it's always a risk. I hate to say it, but he's right.'

The look on Willow's face told Beth exactly what she thought of that.

'As you get bigger, it will be harder to do those things anyway,' she reminded Willow. 'You might as well get used to letting the boys do the heavy work for a while.'

Willow heaved a sigh, stubbornness and common sense at war in her expression. 'What about Amy Weston? She went on muster *and* competed in a rodeo when she was five months pregnant. Her baby's fine.'

'Yeah, but she didn't realise she was pregnant. She got lucky. No mustering or rodeos for you, please.'

'I couldn't go on a muster even if I wanted to,' Willow said with a grimace. 'The crew would get tired of me having to stop for a pee every half an hour.' Beth chuckled and Willow inspected her face, frowning a little. 'What's going on? You don't seem yourself.'

Beth hesitated. For most of Beth's adult life, Rikke had been her go-to girl for spilling problems, but Willow had carved her own place as a confidante in recent years. Beth cherished her new closeness with her sister.

'If I tell you, do you promise not to tell Dad and Free?'

'Of course.'

They walked around the perimeter of the yards and outbuildings, and Beth spilled the story of Charlie Campbell's connection to Madjinbarra. Then, with deep embarrassment, she confessed the short-lived high school love affair, or at least the bare basics of it. She needed Willow to understand why the current situation was so uncomfortable. Maybe this confession would help exorcise the turmoil from her heart.

'Why did you never tell me this before?' Willow asked.

Beth shrugged. 'I don't know. We never used to tell each other stuff, not after Mum got sick. We stopped talking about *all* feelings, remember? And when we finally started talking again, it didn't seem relevant.'

'You told me about Sebastian, though.'

Willow was too smart, Beth thought to herself. They stopped to lean on a fence railing in the shade of a tree.

'Was it because the bust-up with Charlie

meant more to you than the one with Sebastian?' Willow asked.

Beth forced a smile. 'The softer you are, the harder you bruise.'

'The first cut is the deepest?' Willow grinned. 'Are we quoting songs at each other now?'

Beth nodded, smiling. 'Just don't quote any of Charlie's song lyrics at me.'

Willow transferred her gaze to the cattle yard. 'Any idea why he just up and left? Had something happened out at the community? Occasionally, if there's a death in the family or something, our Aboriginal staff here just need to leave, sometimes for weeks on end.'

'I don't think it was anything like that. If it was, why wouldn't he have told me? He just left, no explanation, no goodbye. I'd never felt so utterly . . . unimportant.'

Sadness flashed across Willow's face. 'Shit. I've been on the dishing-out side of that sort of thing before. I'm just lucky Tom was willing to forgive me. Maybe it's a similar situation — maybe there's more to what happened with Charlie than you know.'

This was what Rikke had suggested too, and part of Beth wanted to believe it. She forced herself to remain cynical. 'Or maybe he just decided he wanted a life of fame and stardom. Money and women.'

'I guess it's possible.'

'And now I have the pleasure of his company for a five-hour drive to look forward to,' Beth added with a grimace.

'Isn't there someone else who could do it?'

Willow asked. 'I mean, why can't Charlie drive the minister himself?'

'Mary and Harvey wanted me to be involved, and Charlie says his car's not suitable. I'm not sure what that means. It would handle the roads, but it's a bit worse for wear — older than the Beast; battered and dirty. Maybe they want the minister to have a more comfortable journey.'

'Could you try to forget about what happened at school?' Willow asked. 'I mean, maybe he feels bad about it too. If you both just focus on saving the community from Gargantua, you might be able to develop a reasonable working relationship.'

'Sounds good in theory, but I go tense every time I'm in his presence. I'm terrified that if I'm friendly he'll think I'm flirting.'

'Or he'll think he got away with what he did?'

Beth was startled. How did Willow do that — say something so devastatingly insightful in that mild, sensible voice she had?

'Hmm' was all she could say in reply.

'You could back out of the trip . . . ' Willow suggested gently, and Beth stiffened. 'Ha, stupid idea. Beth Paterson never backs out of a commitment.'

'I'll just get it over with,' Beth said, slapping a hand on top of the fence rail. 'I've promised Mary and Harvey I'll help them push back against Gargantua, and I will. Hopefully this drive will be the most contact I'll need to have with Charlie Campbell. Perhaps he'll lose interest in the fight and go back on tour.'

'I hope not,' said Willow as they resumed

walking. 'He's probably the best chance of success they've got.'

6

After the drive back to Mount Clair on Sunday, having dinner with Lloyd Rendall was the last thing Beth wanted to do. She even caught herself checking her phone for a call from the hospital. No such luck. Beth dropped Free home, tidied her quiet little house, went for a run and then showered. Arriving at the Sawmill restaurant as promised at seven p.m., she found Lloyd already seated with a bottle of wine in a cooler bucket on the table.

He stood up when he saw her and leaned forward to kiss her cheek. Beth had to stop herself from recoiling.

'You look lovely, as usual,' he said, looking her over. She'd deliberately dressed plainly but Lloyd still seemed to like what he saw. 'You like sauvignon blanc, I believe?' he asked as he helped her into her seat.

'I wasn't going to drink — ' she began.

'Just one, then,' he said, pouring her a glass. 'I think we'd better order our meals soon,' he added, lowering his voice. 'It's quiet here tonight, and we're pushing our luck with a seven o'clock booking.' He winked. 'Small-town restaurants, eh?'

Beth took the hint and selected a grilled barramundi from the menu. Lloyd went for the steak and, once the waiter had left them, launched into a long story about the golf game he'd played with the Chamber of Commerce president that day. Beth gave polite smiles in the right spots.

'So, what's this idea you wanted to talk about?' she asked when Lloyd had got his story off his chest.

Lloyd looked amused. 'All business, aren't you? Not a problem. So, put bluntly, the Madjinbarra folk haven't got a hope in hell of winning this one.' Beth raised her eyebrows. 'They don't,' he said, his tone slightly apologetic. 'There's no native title, Gargantua owns the mining lease, and the government wants the jobs and wealth a mine would bring. Frankly, there's no reason why Gargantua can't come in and build a mine tomorrow — and a camp with a wet mess.'

Beth shook her head, annoyed. 'What's the big deal with the wet mess? Can't the workers do without it? I mean, imagine the health benefits — Gargantua could use the concept to show what a responsible employer it is.'

Lloyd gave a half shrug. 'You won't get workers to sign up without a drinking hole on site.'

She fixed him with a stare. 'Madjinbarra's been dry for fifteen years. It's a strong community with extremely low levels of antisocial behaviour and domestic violence. Doesn't that mean anything? What gives Gargantua the right to bring a licensed venue into the middle of that?'

'The mine's going to mean more workers and visitors will be living in the area — and they've got the right to enjoy a quiet beer at the end of a hard day's work.' Lloyd paused to sip his wine. 'The Madjinbarra residents don't *have* to visit the wet mess. No-one's got a gun to their heads.'

Beth kept her temper with an effort. 'The remote location of Madjinbarra has been part of their success in maintaining a dry community, Lloyd. They're at least five hours from anywhere. The sheer distance and inconvenience of driving to a town with a pub means residents can't do short runs to party or smuggle alcohol back in. And they're not governed by any local legislation so they can choose to remain dry, a decision upheld by the elders. It's strategic, their remoteness from pubs and liquor stores. Bringing a wet mess within an hour's drive could cause all kinds of problems.'

'Okay, I hear you.' Lloyd sat back, stroking his smooth chin. 'And this brings me to the idea I mentioned. How about this, Beth? Is there any reason why they can't set up their dry community in a different location that will meet all their needs? Maybe even more of their needs — somewhere closer to infrastructure. Closer to health care and education.'

She kept her voice even. 'Why should they have to move?'

'Because they're running out of options,' he said. 'But the good news is, we've got a plan B for them. Like I said, Gargantua doesn't want to see them unhappy. They've identified a piece of land that sits under the same native title claim as Madjinbarra. It's a similar size, plus it's got water and sealed roads. Subject to planning approvals, Gargantua's willing to relocate the buildings and even construct some new ones for the residents. Madjinbarra Mark Two.'

This was unexpected. Beth reached for her wine. 'Where is this location?'

Lloyd opened a folder on the table and shuffled through papers until he found some printouts of maps. He pointed to the area in question. Beth examined the page.

'It's substantially further from Mount Clair than the current location,' she said.

Lloyd nodded. 'About 350 kilometres further — but two hours closer to Roeburke.'

'They'd need permission from the native title corporation to settle there.'

'Of course,' he said, 'but I doubt there would be any objections.'

'What's the catch?' she asked.

Lloyd's face relaxed into a smile. 'So suspicious, Dr Paterson? No catch. Quite frankly, everyone wins. It costs Gargantua a bit of money, but a drop in the ocean compared to the profits they can potentially make from their mine.'

'But you haven't presented this idea to Mary and Harvey yet?'

Lloyd shook his head. 'They've nominated Charlie Campbell as their liaison person for the matter. The guy's a roadblock. He's fixated on keeping that community exactly as it is, and, quite frankly, we don't even want to talk to him about this yet. He'll veto it, and that means they won't give it due consideration as an option.' Lloyd leaned his elbows on the table and gazed into Beth's face, his eyes earnest. 'I was hoping you'd talk to Mary and Harvey about it and see what they think — before we involve Charlie.'

'It's really not my place. I'm just their doctor, Lloyd. I don't belong to the community and I can't make their decisions.'

'God, no.' Lloyd gazed at her, seemingly aghast. 'All I'm asking is that you be the one to present the idea to Mary and Harvey. Charlie is prejudiced against everything Gargantua does, so he won't give the idea a fair hearing.' Beth listened sceptically. *More like Charlie hates everything you do, Lloyd, after you tried to get his niece taken from him.* 'You've got more objectivity,' Lloyd was saying. 'Balance. If you explain it to the community elders, we can trust that the option won't be dismissed out of hand.'

The waiter brought their food and Beth half-listened to Lloyd chat about their mutual acquaintances while they ate, turning the idea over in her head. The relocation sounded, well, not ideal, but reasonable, which made her suspicious. She wouldn't be surprised if Gargantua had an ulterior motive. Perhaps government funding — or a kickback for developing an Aboriginal community space. Tax savings, maybe? Charitable donations were non-taxable . . . Or maybe this project would let them meet their Indigenous engagement goals in one hit?

When they had finished their meals, Beth declined coffee and explained that she was tired and needed an early night. 'I'll pay my share on the way out,' she said, rising and collecting her handbag from where it was slung over the back of her chair.

'Don't you dare,' Lloyd said, wagging a joking finger at her. 'I've been looking for an excuse to take the most beautiful woman in town out for dinner for years now.'

I'll be lucky to keep my dinner down if you continue on like that. 'Well, thank you for dinner, Lloyd. Could you do me a favour and email me an outline of the proposal you told me about this evening?'

'An outline?' Lloyd got to his feet, frowning. 'Er . . . '

'Gargantua must have something in writing we can see.'

'It's just kicking around as a concept at this stage,' he said.

'Oh. Well, when they've scoped it out, get them to send it over to me and I'll work out whether I'm able to present it to the Madjinbarra decision-makers.' She gave him a pleasant smile.

'Perhaps you could make a few inroads with the idea of relocation, Beth. You're fairly close with Charlie Campbell, aren't you?'

Beth froze. *What the actual . . . ?* She studied Lloyd's face, looking for a deeper meaning. *Inconclusive.*

'Not really. I barely know the guy. Like I said, send me something and I'll consider it.' She stuck out her hand to make it clear there would be no more cheek-kissing, but Lloyd had the audacity to use her hand to pull her in close and brush the side of her face with his dry lips. Beth repressed a shudder.

'See you around, Lloyd.'

Beth hurried for the exit before he could think of escorting her to her car. Letitia from Madjinbarra — the young woman she'd supported to find a job in Mount Clair — was at the payment counter as she went past.

'Hi, Dr Paterson!' the girl called as Beth reached the door.

'Hi, Tish!' Beth glanced back to see if she was in any danger of pursuit but, back at their table, Lloyd was already looking down at his phone screen. She approached the desk. 'How's it going?'

'Good.' The girl gave her a huge smile. 'I've started my silver service training.'

'Ooh, that sounds fancy!' Beth said. She dropped her voice. 'The Sawmill's not silver service — are you moving up in the world?'

Letitia checked around for co-workers but the coast was clear. 'I like this job but I want to get a job at Black Pearl in Broome.'

'Oh, wow. I've heard so much about that restaurant.'

Letitia nodded. 'My boyfriend works in Broome, so I want to move there. But I don't want to end up working in a fish and chip shop. So I'm doing this silver service course. It's weird shit we're learning, Doc.'

'I bet,' said Beth. She checked on Lloyd, who was still on his phone. 'Well, I'd better be getting home.'

'Do you want your bill?'

'No, Lloyd said he'd get it.'

'Yeah, I saw you were sitting with Mr Rendall.' Letitia eyed Beth curiously for a moment.

'It's not a date,' Beth told her firmly. 'A business meeting.'

Letitia smiled. 'Well, you drive safely, okay?'

'I will. Good to see you, Tish.'

⋆   ⋆   ⋆

Propped up on one elbow, Charlie ran his fingers down Beth's bare back. 'Damn, you're beautiful.'

She glowed inside. She'd been told that plenty of times by friends, family, even other boys, but it was different coming from Charlie. It mattered. She wanted to be beautiful to him. She was lying on her stomach, cheek pressed against the layer of Durack-labelled blankets they'd put down in the furniture storeroom. It was dim and cool in there and, surrounded by unwanted tables, chairs and bed frames, it was a little like hiding out in a darkened forest.

Charlie lay down beside her so his cheek was on the blankets too, and gazed at her at close range. Beth examined his mussed hair, the faint sheen of perspiration on his skin from the energy they'd just expended. And those amazing eyes. The love inside her threatened to bust her heart open, it was so huge — so powerful.

'Why don't we just stay here forever?' he said. 'Live here? I'll go out on food-finding missions at midnight, but other than that, we've got everything we need.'

'Showers? Toilets?' she reminded him. 'Clothes?'

'You won't need clothes,' he assured her.

She laughed softly. 'Pretty sure I won't get into the medicine course if I hide in here having sex with you all day, every day, Charlie.'

'Pfft, who needs medicine or university, or crap like that? You've got me, I've got you, babe.' He broke into an old song Beth knew from her father's favourite radio station, which was mostly talkback and news, with a few classic tunes thrown in.

She loved his voice but put her hand over his mouth when he got louder. 'Charlie, shh.'

He frowned, removing her hand. 'I thought you said no-one else was here.'

'None of the girls are here, and Hen's out shopping, but I don't know what time she'll get back.'

'You worry too much.'

'It would be a disaster if we got caught.'

He nodded seriously. 'Yeah, we'd have to find another hiding spot.'

She laughed again, then went quiet, her heart swelling as she locked her eyes on his. She almost wanted to cry, love ached through her so hard.

'I've never met anyone like you,' she told him.

Charlie grinned. 'I'm one in a million.'

'You are.' She wasn't laughing.

Charlie lifted a hand and stroked the back of his fingers down her cheek. 'Beautiful Beth, the Paterson Downs princess who's going to be a doctor and cure the Kimberley.' Beth's lips curved into a smile. 'I used to hate Saturdays, with the other kids heading home to their stations,' he added. 'I'd be stuck at Grey with Dave and Badger. Now weekends are my favourite part of the week, even if Badger does the worst farts ever and Dave's a racist. Because beautiful Beth stays at Durack and sneaks me into the storeroom when Hen's out shopping.'

'I gave up my weekends at home for this,' she said.

'I know. Has your dad made noise about you not coming back to the station for the weekends?'

'So far he's been pretty understanding. I told him I can concentrate better here. I'll probably have to go home soon, though. At least once this month.'

He nodded. 'Wish I had that option.' He stretched, sweeping a gaze over her. 'Hey, do you want to go get something to eat later? You've got rec time till four, right?'

'Yeah.' Beth chewed her lip. 'I don't think that's a good idea, though. We'll get seen.'

'By who?'

'Anyone.'

Charlie's eyebrows knitted. 'So?'

'If people see us doing boyfriend-girlfriend stuff together, they'll suspect something.'

'I thought we were boyfriend and girlfriend.'

She melted and shuffled closer to kiss him. 'Yes, but we can't let anyone know at the moment, Charlie. The school thinks we have a tutoring arrangement, nothing more.'

He cocked his head. 'You don't reckon they suspect something more's going on, what with us

98

turning two days of tutoring into five days a week?'

'I hope not!' she exclaimed. 'If they knew, they wouldn't let me stay at Durack on the weekends — they probably wouldn't even let me tutor you any more. I don't think they know. Mr Ogilvie probably just thinks I'm trying to get my points up.'

'Huh?'

'You know. My community service points. I get some for tutoring you. It'll look good on my uni application.'

'Community service?' Charlie's expression darkened slightly. 'What — because I'm Aboriginal?'

She shrugged. 'I suppose.'

He sat up abruptly. 'Is that why you agreed to tutor me?'

'No, of course not.' Beth sat up beside him and tried to see his eyes, which were locked on the blanket. 'I agreed to do it because it's a good refresher. It helps me with my Year Twelve work. The points thing was just a bonus.'

He was silent for so long that she started to think she should have stayed quiet about the service points.

'I'm not sure I like being your community service project,' he said at last.

'Jesus, Charlie.' She got up on her knees and grabbed his shoulders, shaking him so he would look at her face. 'I don't care about the points. I wanted to tutor you. And anyway, Mr Ogilvie never asked me to do anything except tutor you. This, you and me — it's got nothing to do with tutoring, or points, or anything.'

His eyes softened, then sparkled with wicked pleasure. 'You mean our extracurricular activities don't count towards your little points tally?'

She couldn't hide her amusement. 'If they did, I'd be raking in the points. I could probably get a bloody scholarship to Harvard.'

Charlie laughed and reached for her. Beth sank into his kiss, making a small noise of approval as he ran his hands over her skin. They were still sitting up, face to face, and his bare chest against hers made her tingle and shake.

'What should we do now?' he murmured in her ear, slipping a hand down over her buttock and ducking to kiss her neck.

She shivered with the pleasure of it. 'I don't know. What do you want to do?'

He whispered a description and Beth wondered if it was possible for her blood to run any hotter.

'Beth,' he added. Unexpectedly, he'd stopped moving his hands.

She pulled back, trying to focus. 'What?'

Charlie's startling green eyes seemed to bore a channel directly through flesh and bone, right into her heart. 'I love you. I love the hell out of you.'

Beth opened her mouth to reciprocate and only managed a sob.

7

'We must stop meeting this way,' Carolyn quipped as she directed the light between Beth's thighs.

'Your turn next month,' Beth reminded her.

'Funny how quickly they invented a non-invasive prostate test for men while we still have the joy of the speculum.' She paused. 'Ready?'

'As I'll ever be.' Beth closed her eyes and tried to think happy thoughts.

'All done,' Carolyn said just a minute later.

Beth sat up and rearranged her clothing. 'Thank you, Dr Shen. I'll book yours in for you.' She grinned wickedly.

Carolyn rolled her eyes. 'Maybe I'll just be like my patients and conveniently forget about pap smears or cervical screenings for ten years.'

'Not on my watch,' said Beth.

Carolyn tipped her head to one side, observing her.

'What?'

'Is everything all right?'

Beth shrugged. 'Why do you ask?'

Carolyn was still watching her with a ruminant expression. 'Your good cheer seems a little forced.'

'Hey, you just stuck a medical instrument up my hoo-ha,' Beth protested. 'Am I supposed to be hopping around the room with glee?'

'Not just now. I mean for a few days. At least since the weekend. Is everything okay with your dad?'

'Yes, he's fighting fit.'

'You're off to Madjinbarra on Sunday, aren't you? Is that what's bothering you? Is it getting a bit much?'

Beth attempted to appear nonchalant. 'No, I enjoy it. I'm just tired and in sore need of some time off.'

'Always tired.' Carolyn shook her head. 'If I were your doctor, I'd recommend dropping one or two things from the Beth Paterson diary and having more time to yourself. Know what I did last week? I said no to a patient's baby's christening and played tennis. Nothing and nobody will make me miss my two social tennis sessions per week. They're my indulgence.' She quirked an eyebrow at Beth. 'You need an indulgence.'

'Like what?'

'Like a weekly massage. A book club. Something fun.'

Beth groaned. 'Don't get all *work-life balance* on me, Caro. I've got a clinic to run.'

'No, seriously.' Carolyn nodded at her patient's chair to indicate that Beth should sit. 'What do you do for fun?'

Beth sighed and sank into the chair. 'Lots of things.'

'Like?'

'Spend time with my family. Socialise with friends — '

'Hang on,' Carolyn put in. 'When do you

socialise with friends?'

'I haven't for a little while,' Beth said with dignity. 'But I went to an engagement party last month.'

'That was a patient.'

'It was still a social outing.' Beth kept her gaze on Carolyn's. 'Seriously, I'm fine. I have my running, my family, I do a bit of gardening at home, and there's the chamber of commerce meetings — '

'Stop right there.' Carolyn glared. 'Do *not* try to tell me networking with the chamber is about fun. That's *work*.'

Beth gave her a lopsided grin. 'Yeah, all right — you got me.'

'I think you need to inject a little more fun into your life, Beth. There really isn't much balance.' Carolyn looked genuinely concerned. 'Even the running is mechanical for you — just a way to keep your body fit so you can keep up with all the demands of your life.'

'It used to be social,' Beth reminded her. 'But I lost my running partner to tennis.'

'Have you looked for another running buddy?'

'No-one could replace you.'

'Beth, I'm being serious. I don't want you overworked and lonely. What about dating? It would be nice if you had some lovely guy to look after you — to take you out and give you some fun. Or at least a good shag.' Carolyn shot her a mischievous smile.

Beth rose. 'And on that note, Dr Shen, I am returning to my appointments.'

'I hear there's a cute new radiographer

working at the imaging clinic,' Carolyn called after her.

'I'll think of some more tests to add to your appointment next month if you don't stop,' Beth stage-whispered back through the door, and Carolyn lifted her hands in defeat.

Beth went back to her consulting room to prepare for her next patient. *Bloody Carolyn.* She was right, Beth knew. Everyone was right.

She worked too hard and didn't have any balance in her life, but there was nothing she could do to fix that right now. She had to run the clinic. She had to see her patients. She had to keep her business competitive and well-attended, and she had to meet her own expectations, writing comprehensive patient notes, not to mention ensuring compliance with Medical Association standards.

And not one of those things could be shifted aside to make room for 'fun' at this point in her life, no matter how much anyone said she was overworked.

★   ★   ★

Beth's alarm woke her at four-thirty a.m. on Sunday. She had half an hour before she would collect Charlie from Mounties and the Minister for Mining and his assistant from the Mount Clair Resort. Then they would be driving until at least midday; longer if there was water on the roads.

She was ready in twenty minutes, her bag and medical kit packed into the back of the Beast.

She'd refilled her fresh water bottles the night before and checked the spare tyre, the extra fuel container, her first-aid kit and toolbox. She grabbed her fully charged radio and set off.

The dawn sky had just started to break through the darkness when she pulled in to Mounties' empty car park and parked beneath a pool of orange from a streetlight. Charlie stepped out of the shadows near the hotel doorway, and Beth's throat tightened. He held a backpack and his guitar case, and a shopping bag hung from his arm. Charlie strode to her vehicle and opened the back to load in his gear without saying a word. Then he came around to the passenger side and climbed in with a gruff 'Morning'.

'Good morning, Charlie.' She could be polite, even if he couldn't.

He shut the door and buckled up. Beth pulled out of the car park and headed towards the resort. She forced herself to take some silent, slow breaths, locking her eyes on the violet and amber horizon. *I've done nothing wrong*, she reminded herself. *He wronged me all those years ago. If anyone should feel uncomfortable . . .*

'Got the colouring stuff.'

She actually jumped, his words were so unexpected. 'Pardon?'

'The colouring-in stuff for Pearl. I couldn't find thick crayons, so I had to get textas.'

'Oh. Yes, those crayons are quite specialised these days. I've only seen them at educational stationery stores. There are some websites where you can order them, though.'

He didn't answer, and she blushed that she'd been so eager to respond to him. God, this was nothing like her normal self. How did Charlie still have the power to turn her into a simpering schoolgirl?

'I've checked the roads,' he said. 'We should get a decent run out there. Most of the water's dried up.'

'That's good.'

They drove the rest of the trip to the resort in silence. Beth pulled in to the drop-off zone and an inattentive-looking porter stared at them from a chair near the lobby door. Charlie unbuckled.

'I'll see if I can track Winston down.'

It was ten minutes before Charlie finally returned with the minister. Nigel Winston was a small man with unnaturally black hair, dressed in shorts and a buttoned shirt. His assistant, Melody, could not have been older than twenty. She had sharp eyes behind classic nerd glasses and carried an iPad, on which she either snapped photos or tapped notes, seemingly without pause. Charlie seated Nigel in the front beside Beth, and the minister greeted her, talking fast. Melody asked her to stop at the *Welcome to Mount Clair* sign as they left town so that she could take a photo of the minister with Charlie. As an afterthought, Melody took a couple of shots that included Beth positioned on the other side of Nigel.

Yay. Captured for posterity in a photo with Charlie Campbell.

At first, she thought Nigel was nervous, but after half an hour on the road, Beth realised that talking fast and jumping from topic to topic were simply his way. Melody asked a lot of questions about the Madjinbarra community and tapped away as Charlie answered. The minister interjected with his own questions from time to time but he seemed distracted by dealing with emails on his phone.

A tightness crept up Beth's spine as they drove. It was clear that Gargantua's lobbyists had spoken to the minister's office. Nigel only seemed interested in hearing about the problems of the community. Charlie was doing a good job of turning things around and framing his replies positively, but she could hear him losing his patience. If he snapped at the minister, it would be completely understandable but disastrous for his cause.

'The education completion rates are pretty low out there, isn't that right, Mel?' Nigel checked with his assistant.

She tapped, swiped, tapped. 'Fifty-seven per cent high school completion.'

Nigel looked at Charlie, whose composure was admirable. 'Yep, but they're staying at school longer than Aboriginal kids in other places. The national rate's fifty per cent. And the population's small at Madjinbarra — probably too small to be representative, anyway. There's only about eighty kids in the whole school. Even if they don't always get their high school certificate, they're staying in school longer and turning up more often than the Aboriginal kids in the bigger towns and cities.'

There was a silence as Melody took notes and

Nigel scrolled through emails.

Beth cleared her throat. 'The kids who come from Madjinbarra really have their heads screwed on straight,' she said. 'One of the girls, Letitia, she's eighteen. Fantastic kid. She got herself a job at the Sawmill restaurant in town and she's enrolled in a course at the local TAFE, learning silver service. She's hoping to get a job at a top restaurant. She knows what she wants in life and is steering well clear of trouble.'

'Hmm,' said Nigel. 'Tell us a bit about what you do out at the community, Dr Paterson.'

'Beth,' she said. 'Well, there's a great little clinic that's open weekdays, run by Maud, an Aboriginal health officer, and Christine, a community nurse. They take care of the day-to-day health issues and minor emergencies. If it's fractures or surgeries, anything critical like that, the patient is generally airlifted by the RFDS to Mount Clair or Darwin Hospital, depending on the severity. I spend a few days at Madji every month. My role is to assess and treat ongoing health problems, check the records at the clinic and follow up on anything that I feel needs it, prescribe and dispense medication, consult with new patients or cases that come in — whatever's needed. But Maud and Christine handle the rest. They are absolutely amazing. There's not much I could teach them about health care.'

'What about specialist therapies?' Melody asked. 'Physio, podiatry, optometry. How do you manage that?'

'If I think a specialist therapy is required, I

first check how it could be managed at Madji. Maud and Christine can provide an impressive array of therapies between them. But if that's not feasible, then I'll talk to the patient to find out how and when they'll be able to get to a bigger town, and I help them make a plan. Then we'll set something up with the therapist and make sure there's a reminder system so that hopefully the therapy takes place. It doesn't always pan out, but usually they'll get to town for treatment at some stage.'

Melody paused. 'So it can be a bit hit-and-miss?' she prodded.

Beth kept her face expressionless. 'Like anywhere, some patients won't prioritise specialist therapies. It can depend on how much discomfort they're in, or their day-to-day commitments. My Mount Clair patients are just the same — some follow up, others don't.'

'What about a course of treatment?' Melody pressed. 'I mean, it's one thing to go and get a glasses prescription updated when you're visiting town, but if someone needed weekly treatment — physio or speech therapy, for instance — what would happen then?'

Beth caught Charlie's eye briefly in the rear-vision mirror. Did they know about Pearl?

'Generally, I'd look at who might have the aptitude to deliver ongoing treatment. For example, if it was speech therapy for a child, I'd make a recommendation that one of the teaching staff at the school get some specific training in how to work with the pupil. If it was physio, then the nurses, or even the parents or carers, could probably get some training in how to provide the treatment.'

She wasn't completely convinced by her own words. In Beth's experience, some cases were beyond the capacity of the community to manage — like Pearl's. But this wasn't the time or place to show doubt in Madjinbarra's ability to self-support.

'It sounds like the community would benefit from some infrastructure,' Nigel remarked. 'Why are they so set against the mine going ahead and bringing new facilities closer to home?'

Beth glanced at the man. Did he really have so little understanding of the issues? Or did he want to hear it directly from a Madjinbarra resident? Beth remained silent, waiting for Charlie to answer.

'It's *our* community,' Charlie said, repressed passion in his voice. 'Our place. We believe in it as a place to raise kids who are strong, healthy and happy. We're protecting them until they're old enough to make their own choices. If Gargantua moves in next door with a whole bunch of FIFO workers and builds a camp where anyone can stay, it will change things. It won't just be ours any more. Outsiders will bring in grog and drugs; there'll be demand for sex workers, skimpies, fast food. It'll totally change the way we live, and not in a good way.'

Melody was silent and Beth could see in the rear-vision mirror that the girl was impressed. Nigel tipped his head in a manner that suggested he acknowledged Charlie's words but was not particularly persuaded by them. It made Beth's anger fire but she didn't say anything. No point in riling the guy.

Melody swiped and tapped on her iPad. 'Oh. No internet. When's the next point I'll have a signal?'

Beth hid a smile. 'There's no more signal now. Well, there's satellite, but it's sketchy.'

'I don't think I'm set up for satellite. Does your phone use it?' the girl asked. 'Could I hook into yours?'

'Sure. It might be a bit slow.'

Nigel sighed and pocketed his phone. 'Can we take a pit stop? How far's the next roadhouse?'

Roadhouse! The minister's briefing process must have broken down somewhere along the line. Beth checked the mirror and saw Charlie grinning in the back seat.

'No dunnies until Madji now, I'm afraid,' he said. 'Bush pit stops only.'

Nigel was aghast. 'You're joking!'

'I need to go too,' Melody said in a small voice.

Beth sought out a spot with a decent number of rocky outcrops and boabs, and pulled the Beast over. She passed a packet of tissues to Melody.

'I'll go left, you go right, Nigel,' Melody said, putting on a brave face.

Nigel scowled.

'Watch out for ticks,' Charlie called after him, and Beth couldn't help a snort of laughter.

She looked in the mirror at Charlie's face. For a moment, they were smiling at each other. Then Charlie's smile dropped away and he broke eye

111

contact. Heat crept up her cheeks.

When they got back on the road, Charlie had more of the minister's attention, since the guy's phone signal was gone and he couldn't read his emails any more. Melody continued with her note-taking, and Charlie pointed out sights of significance to the Madjinbarra community.

'Just here,' he was saying, 'this is our cemetery — see through the scrub?'

'It seems a long way from the town,' Melody said. 'Aren't we still over an hour away?'

'Yeah, you're right, but this was where the mission originally stood. See the ruin through there?' He pointed. 'That was the church. We moved the community away from here once we gained independence from the mission, but the cemetery stayed.'

'Why did you move away from here?' Nigel asked.

'It's a better piece of land where Madji sits now,' Charlie told him. 'More water, flatter, more space. Plus a few bad things happened here at the mission that people wanted to get away from.'

Nigel nodded knowingly. Charlie pointed out the remains of a well and some stone footings that had once been an infirmary. As they drove, he dropped in an occasional story from his childhood. Beth sensed that Charlie was trying to give Nigel a personal connection to the place so that he would think twice about approving Gargantua's mine application.

'This big boab up ahead, the one with the split, it's been there as long as anyone can remember. It tells you we're just an hour away from Madji. There's a track out west of there to a waterhole. Around this time of year, the river dries up but the waterhole's still got water and the fish are trapped in there. Fantastic fishing. Uncle Harvey Early used to take some of us kids out.' Charlie shifted a little. 'He's one of the elders, and a recovered alcoholic. He had cancer, too, but he's in remission. Coming out to live at Madjinbarra saved his life, he reckons. He works with other people stuck on the grog now, using his own alcohol abuse recovery program.'

'Like Alcoholics Anonymous?' Melody asked.

'A bit like that, but adapted for local culture.'

'How often do you get out here, Charlie?' the minister asked, adjusting the air-conditioning vent. 'You must be busy with touring and recording much of the year.'

'I loved your last album.' Melody went pink in the cheeks as she said this.

He smiled at her. 'Thanks. Yeah, I don't get out here as often as I'd like. Three or four times a year is usual.'

'You still have family living at Madjinbarra?' Melody wanted to know.

'Many of us are related in some way or another. My closest relatives here are my aunt, Mary Wirra, and Jill and Pearl, my sister's daughters.'

'Oh, so your sister's out here?' Nigel asked.

Charlie's face was impassive. 'She's living on the east coast at present. Her two daughters are still out here, though, living with my aunt.'

'How old are they?' Melody said. 'Kids or grown up?'

'Jill's fifteen. Pearl's only three.'

Melody nodded. 'And their dad?'

'Not in the picture,' Charlie said a little stiffly. 'But they're well looked after.'

'They must love having a celebrity singer uncle,' she remarked, cheeks going pink again.

'Your father was a wonderful musician' was Nigel's comment. 'My parents loved his music. It must have been a great help to have a foot in the door of the music industry through him.'

Beth blinked. That was rude — it almost sounded like Nigel didn't think much of Charlie's music. Charlie's face in the rear-view mirror was still neutral, although he exchanged a fleeting glance with Beth and she knew he was thinking the same thing.

Strange how they could still read each other, even after all this time.

Beth smothered the thought and focused on driving. The last hour into Madjinbarra was on rough, unsealed road, rutted and furrowed from the recent wet season. They hadn't seen another car for a couple of hundred kilometres now. Thin grey trunks of saplings and bright yellow tufts of grass lined the red track on either side. Beth slowed down, spying scraggly looking cattle on the road up ahead.

'Someone's cows are out!' Melody said with surprise.

'Everyone's cows are out round here,' Charlie told her. 'Those ones could be feral, though.'

Once the cattle meandered off the road, Beth

114

sped up again. Charlie pointed out some chunks of dull, faded metal dotting the sides of the road.

'Old World War II relics,' he said. 'There was an air force base and a radar station in the region around that time.'

Melody was astonished and Beth slowed the Beast so the girl could take pictures with her iPad.

'Lots of history out here,' Nigel remarked.

'At least sixty thousand years' worth,' Charlie said, and Beth had to press her lips together to stop herself smiling.

Nigel looked uncomfortable and murmured acquiescence, and Charlie actually raised an eyebrow at Beth in the rear-vision mirror before he remembered himself and turned back to Melody to point out another wrecked fuselage.

8

At last they reached the colourful *Entering Madjinbarra* sign and Melody exhaled with relief. 'Thank God. I thought my bladder was going to burst. How the heck did you last that whole trip, Beth?'

'I've been in training for a couple of years,' Beth answered with a laugh. 'But sometimes I have to make a pit stop.'

When they hit the town site, people peered at them to see who it was and, recognising Beth and Charlie, waved. Kids ran along-side the Beast and three of them jumped up on the rear bumper for a free ride. Melody exclaimed in a panic, then giggled when she realised the kids were okay. They parked at the health clinic, which was just a couple of buildings down from Mary Wirra's house. Beth was touched to see that someone had marked out a reserved spot in chalk on the paved clinic driveway. It read *The Doc* and had a drawing of her — a stick figure with big, sultry lips and long, straight hair.

'Looks like Jill's artwork,' Charlie said, his voice a little strange.

Jill was already trotting down the street to meet them, with three-year-old Pearl on her hip.

'Hi, Doc!' she called, smiling. 'Hi, Uncle Charlie!'

Pearl was waving her arms around, just as excited to see Beth and her uncle as Jill was.

Charlie took the little girl from her sister's arms and hugged them both. Jill clung to her uncle with genuine adoration, but she didn't take her eyes off Beth. Beth's heart went warm. Jill was endlessly fascinated by Beth's medical work, full of questions and offers to help. She suspected the girl would have a future in health care.

'I love the portrait,' she called.

Jill was laughing. 'I gave you Hollywood lips.'

Beth shot her a grin and opened the back of her vehicle to unload her gear. Jill left Pearl with her uncle and came to help.

'Is that the government bloke in your car, Doc?' Jill asked, dropping her voice. 'Aunty said you were bringing him.'

'Yep, the Minister for Mining, Nigel Winston. Your uncle's showing him around Madji.'

'Is he a good fella?'

Beth shrugged. 'I don't know him very well. Hope so. Could you get the esky, Jill? Those medicines have to go straight into the fridge.'

After she and Jill had unpacked the gear, Beth approached Charlie. He was still standing by her car holding Pearl, with Nigel and Melody hovering nearby. Pearl put her arms out to Beth for a cuddle and, after a moment's hesitation, Charlie passed her across. It was an awkward exchange, both of them trying not to make physical contact — which was pretty well impossible while handing over a wriggly toddler. Beth tried not to notice when his warm hand brushed her arm, her thoughts flying against her will to her dream about the Durack furniture storeroom . . .

'Are you taking the minister to his accommodation now?' she blurted. 'Want to use my vehicle?'

'Um, yeah. Cheers.'

He looked so tense that she wondered for a moment if she'd done something wrong by making the suggestion. She held out her keys and he took them, not meeting her eyes.

'What's next on the agenda?' Nigel asked with somewhat forced jolliness. 'Shall we come in and take a look at the clinic?'

Beth glanced at Charlie but it seemed unlikely he would speak so she answered. 'Why don't you go with Charlie for now? He can show you where you'll be staying and let you freshen up. The first step will probably be to introduce you to the community elders. Is that right?' Charlie nodded. 'But you're welcome to drop in to the clinic after that, or any time over the next few days.'

'Next few days — ' Nigel began, but he was interrupted by the clinic's health officer, who'd poked her head outside and spotted Beth.

'Good to see you, Doc,' Maud called. 'We got Billy Early in here with bloody horrible sores on his feet. The silly bugger won't keep 'em clean.' There was a muffled shout from inside — Billy protesting Maud's claim, no doubt. 'Well, it's true,' she retorted over her shoulder. 'I reckon he needs an antibiotic.'

Beth hurried to the clinic, torn between wanting Nigel to comprehend the real world of Madjinbarra and wishing they could present a façade of perfection to these outsiders.

118

As always, there was no opportunity to unpack properly or even take a breather after the long drive. Beth was launched straight into consulting. The health clinic was supposed to be closed on week-ends, but Maud and Christine opened it if someone needed them. This qualified. Billy Early's foot ulcers were nasty, and it took Beth some time to clean and dress them properly. Pearl scooted around the clinic floor with her funny little bum-shuffling gait while Beth worked. The child had almost mastered walking, despite her spasming muscles, but she tended to bum-shuffle because it was easier. Jill watched avidly as Beth treated Billy's feet, wincing in sympathy whenever Billy flinched.

'Doesn't the pus bother you, Jill?' Billy asked her.

'Nah,' she said with a grin. 'Pus is cool. I love watching the doc clean it all out.'

Definitely destined for a career in health care, Beth thought, smiling. She applied antiseptic and then a clean dressing.

'These sores are pretty bad, Billy,' she told him. 'How long have you had them?'

'Few days,' he said with a shrug.

'Are you in a lot of pain?' He shrugged again, and Beth fixed him with a serious look. 'You need to be careful with your feet, as a diabetic. Even a little scratch can turn serious and you could end up in a bit of strife. Are you taking your medicine every day?'

He avoided her gaze. 'Yeah.'

Beth was dubious. 'You heading into Mount Clair soon, Billy? Need a ride? I'm heading back on Thursday — I'll drive you.'

'I'll probably get there in the next couple of weeks,' he said, standing up. 'I'll drop in to see ya then, yeah?'

She gave him a high-strength antibiotic, and when he'd left Beth sat down and went over the clinic's treatment records with Maud and Christine.

Jill unloaded the shopping bag Charlie had handed her. 'Look what Uncle Charlie got for you, Pearl!'

Jill set up the colouring book and fat textas on a table and heaved Pearl up onto a chair. Pearl's enormous brown eyes lit up, and in a moment, her fair curls were bent over the colouring book, her face a picture of concentration.

'Uncle Charlie's the best,' Jill said, seeing Beth's gaze on them. 'He always gets good stuff for Pearl.'

'Charlie's a godsend,' Christine agreed. 'If anyone needs anything in Madji, he sorts it out.'

'He's our bloody fairy godmother!' Maud wheezed a laugh.

'I don't understand how I didn't know Charlie was from Madjinbarra,' Beth said, shaking her head.

'Didn't you?' said Jill. 'Maybe it's 'cause he's never been here at the same time as you. I've talked about him to you heaps, I reckon.'

Beth suddenly recalled mentions of 'Uncle Charlie' in the past. She'd always assumed he was an elder. The way they all talked about him held such love and respect, she'd never imagined the revered Charlie was a younger man.

'Charlie was the one who set up the drive-in,' Christine said.

'He paid for the big screen and projector and the outdoor speaker system. He wanted us to have a cinema in the dry season and sorted out a licence so we can watch new movies — sorta new, anyway. Anything Charlie reckons will be good for our community, he works it out for us.'

'Uncle Charlie rocks.' Jill's face was alight with pride and love.

'Unca Jarlie,' Pearl mumbled in agreement as she scrawled with her texta, curls bobbing.

Beth concealed the pain this praise caused her. She honoured Charlie's generosity — it sounded like he was indeed a wonderful patron for Madjinbarra. It didn't give him the right to treat her like crap seventeen years ago or today, but at least he was fundamentally a good man. She took a breath and decided she could be bigger than her teenage heartbreak. She would take Charlie at face value and try to be positive towards him, for Jill and Pearl's sakes, if nothing else.

'Hopefully these colouring-in things will stop Pearl from zoning out,' Jill said quietly. 'I reckon she gets bored a lot.'

'She's a smart little thing,' Beth remarked. 'Like her sister.' She gave Jill a wink. 'It's a pity she can't start three-year-old kindy.'

'Do they have that in Mount Clair?' Jill asked.

'Yes. Just a couple of mornings a week.'

'She'd love that.' Jill watched her sister, then switched her attention to Beth. 'Is it a good school, in Mount Clair?'

'The primary school?'

'The high school.' Jill fidgeted with one of Pearl's textas. 'Do lots of the kids there get their certificate? And go to uni, or whatever?'

Beth tipped her head. 'Some do, some don't. I went to Mount Clair High School. It was good. Supportive teachers. Both of my sisters and I got into uni.'

Jill nodded, and after a moment's hesitation spoke again. 'How smart do you have to be to go to uni?'

'Depends on the university and the course. And it's not necessarily about being the smartest, but whether you know how to get the results. Common sense and organisation.'

'No-one in my family's been,' Jill admitted.

'Your uncle could have, if he'd wanted to.'

Jill raised her eyebrows. 'Really? Uncle Charlie? How do you know?'

Crap. She shouldn't have said that. 'I was at school around the same time. He had the ability.'

'Uncle Charlie went to your school?' Jill seemed amazed. 'What happened? Didn't he get the score he needed for uni?'

'He didn't stay to see the year out. I don't know why not.'

Jill's brow furrowed. She looked oddly disillusioned. 'Huh.'

'Camp fire tomorrow night, Doc,' Maud broke in. 'You coming along, yeah?'

Beth was cautious. She was usually knackered at the end of the day here in Madjinbarra. 'Hope so.'

'I say we close up now — what do you reckon,

122

Chris?' Maud asked.

Christine was in agreement and they shut the clinic, walking with Beth to Mary's house, nattering about recent happenings in the community. Jill insisted on carrying Beth's bag, and Beth held Pearl's hand, encouraging her to walk.

Mary was sitting on her front porch and she lifted a hand in greeting when she caught sight of Beth. Jill went inside, and Beth knew she would find her gear in Jill's little single-bed room later. Jill always gave up her own bedroom and slept with Pearl when Beth stayed, despite Beth's protests.

Served a meal of boiled frozen vegetables and grilled fishcakes, and refreshed with a quick shower, Beth sat on the darkened porch with Mary, a cool glass of water in her hand, to catch up on the latest. Jill got Pearl off to bed and then plonked herself between them. They were talking about Pearl's progress with walking and had moved on to Mary's back pain when Jill broke in, her voice anxious.

'Why do ya reckon Uncle Charlie left school, Doc?' She paused. 'Too hard, maybe?'

'What's this?' Mary asked in surprise.

Beth hastened to explain. 'I mentioned to Jill earlier that Charlie and I were at school together.'

Mary just laughed. 'Your uncle wasn't cut out for school. He got homesick.'

Jill still sounded worried. 'Will I get homesick, if I go to Mount Clair?'

Beth was startled. 'Are you thinking of going

123

to town to finish school, Jill?'

The girl shifted in her chair. 'I wanna be a nurse or a doctor — to look after Pearl properly. Miss Gloria, our principal, she reckons I should go to Mount Clair. Go board there, so I can do my uni entrance.' She stopped and regarded Beth awkwardly, as though she expected naysaying, but Beth gasped, delighted.

'Jill, that's brilliant! Every time I come here, I think how good you'd be in a healthcare job.'

In the dim light of the porch, the smile that broke on Jill's face was beautiful. 'Miss Gloria applied for a spot for me. But what if I can't keep up with everyone else?'

'I think you'll be fine. If you need support, I'll be around.' Beth had no spare hours in her day, but if it helped Jill, she'd make some.

Jill's face lit up again. 'Thanks, Doc. Is it hard? Like, really hard?'

'It will be a challenge compared to what you're used to, but you're up to it. Boarding at Durack House, there's lots of rules and regulations. You have to be on time, do your jobs, get your homework done. Strict bedtime. It takes a bit of getting used to, but I quite liked it in the end. It helped me gain self-discipline in my study and sleep habits.'

'That might be good,' Jill said. 'Our school's a bit slack, and half the kids are late every day. No-one does any homework. Sometimes I wish it was stricter.'

Mary cackled. 'Our school runs on Gwini time.'

Beth knew the expression. It meant family and

community needs were prioritised over punctuality for appointments or schedules. She'd heard business owners in Mount Clair using the phrase in exasperation, as if it were just a way to excuse laziness. She watched Jill fiddling with the hem of her shorts, staring out across the front yard. Jill would probably thrive on the routines of boarding at Durack. She was certainly committed.

The unmistakable sound of the Beast rose from the road. It came to rest in Mary's driveway and Charlie climbed out, his movements weary. Jill bounded up to help him unload his gear from the back of the vehicle. She took his guitar case and slung it carefully over her shoulder.

'Hi, Aunty,' Charlie called, approaching the dim porch. 'I brought the doctor's car back. Where's she staying?'

Mary burst out laughing. 'Here, ya nong.'

Beth shifted and Charlie must have caught sight of her in the darkness because he stopped for a moment before resuming his approach. He came to a halt on the porch and directed a question Beth's way. 'You're staying with Aunty Mary?' he asked.

She attempted to explain, feeling like an upstart. 'I used to stay in the temp workers' lodge, but Mary was kind enough to offer me a room a few months back.'

'Better to have you close to the clinic since you're always working late,' Mary said. 'And the girls bloody love you.'

Jill rested Charlie's guitar case on the porch

125

railing, staring at him like she could hardly wait another moment to interrogate him. 'Hey, the doc says you were at school together in Mount Clair but you didn't finish. Why not, Uncle Charlie?'

Beth wanted to slink under a chair. Charlie didn't even look at her. 'You still going on about school in Mount Clair? You can finish school here, Jill. Just as good.'

She mumbled something that sounded like 'No, it's not'.

'She won't be able to get her uni entrance here, Charlie,' Mary objected.

'She can get that later,' he said, dropping into a chair. 'No need to rush off now. Best to finish school here, among family and friends, and worry about uni later.'

Beth was surprised. Madjinbarra couldn't take a teenager to tertiary entrance. The school didn't offer the required classes. If Jill wanted to sit her university entrance exams, she would need to board in Mount Clair — and as soon as possible. Beth fought her desire to say so; too much history hung in the air around them.

A scowl crept over Jill's face. 'I don't wanna be years older than everyone else. You said I'm smart enough. Why can't I go now?'

Charlie was silent for a few moments, his gaze on an invisible point in the dark street. 'We'll talk about this another time.'

Jill slouched back against the porch post, dissatisfied.

'Did you get the minister some tucker?' Mary asked, smoothing over the moment.

'Harvey gave them a meal,' Charlie answered. 'I asked the two of them to come back here for a cuppa but they said they wanted to get a bit of work done and get off to bed.' He paused. 'Winston seems a bit underwhelmed.'

'What does that mean?' Mary demanded.

'I'm starting to think it'll take a bit for him to really appreciate what we've got out here.'

This was clearly difficult for Charlie to admit. In spite of herself, Beth felt her heart go out to him. She also felt like Nigel had been surprisingly unsympathetic — even uninterested — in the things that were good about Madjinbarra. It worried her. But Charlie was right — a couple of days, and the minister might start to connect with people in the community and get a deeper understanding of the issues they faced with the looming Gargantua mine. Perhaps Charlie could introduce Nigel to Harvey's work with recovering alcoholics. Preventing substance abuse was a big part of the argument for keeping Gargantua out of the region, after all.

'Were you homesick, Uncle Charlie?' Jill couldn't let the topic go. 'Mary says so.'

Charlie heaved a sigh. 'Not too homesick. I just decided I wanted to concentrate on my music.'

'But you could have done both. You could've finished school and come back to do music later.'

'Town life isn't all it's cracked up to be,' he said.

'Why not?'

'There's a lot of false people out there. Lot of two-faced people who don't give a shit about anyone but themselves.'

Charlie's voice had gone hard and Beth felt a pang of pain — and shock. A new sense of realisation sprouted. Had something happened to Charlie all that time ago? Something that made him leave town without saying goodbye? Maybe he wasn't the gigantic bastard she'd assumed. After all, in Madjinbarra he was loved without exception — his whole community seemed to consider him a hero. But Charlie's words hinted at a painful deception, or even a betrayal, in Mount Clair at some stage.

Who'd burned him?

Maybe Rikke and Willow were right and there was more to his abandonment than Beth knew. Maybe she should talk to him about it . . .

Jesus, no. Too much time had passed since then, and talking to him would only reveal how painful the abandonment had been to her. No way would she let him see that he'd broken her heart.

'You mean someone stabbed you in the back?' Mary had become curious now. 'Back when you were at school in town?'

Charlie stood up. 'I reckon I'd better go get some sleep. I'm stuffed after playing tour guide all day.'

'Where're you sleeping, Charlie?' Mary asked.

'Doc's got my room but you could have the couch,' Jill suggested.

Even in the darkness, Beth saw his discomfort.

'Nah, I'll borrow a bunk at Harvey's.'

Beth spoke. 'Take the Beast. My car,' she corrected herself. 'I won't need it in the morning. I'll be in the clinic all day.'

He hesitated, and she tossed the keys at him. He caught them and nodded at her. 'Cheers.' Charlie swung down the porch and got into the Beast.

'Does he normally stay here?' Beth asked Mary above the noise of the engine.

'Yeah, Jill gives him her bed.'

'Oh, no.' *Ugh, how awkward.* 'You should have said. I could have stayed at the lodge this time.'

'Bullshit' was Mary's stout reply. 'Charlie doesn't care where he sleeps.'

'I'd rather *you* stayed here,' Jill chimed in, 'so we can talk about school in Mount Clair. Uncle Charlie's being a pain in the arse about it.'

Beth chuckled. 'Let's talk about it tomorrow. I'm pretty tired myself, and I wouldn't mind going to bed.'

In the same bed where Charlie regularly sleeps. She cringed inwardly.

'Maybe you could put a word in with Charlie,' Mary told Beth. 'About Jill going to Mount Clair for her uni entrance. You boarded, didn't you? You could tell him how well they looked after you. How you stayed out of trouble.'

Beth pretended to be distracted by knocking dust off her boots, thankful for the darkness that hid her intense blush. She gave an offhanded 'Yeah, let's talk about it some more tomorrow', and made a hasty escape.

'You shouldn't walk with me,' Beth said.

'Why not?'

'Because people will suspect.'

'Suspect what? That I just had my hand up your school shirt behind the bike shed?'

'Charlie!' she hissed, looking around. There were a bunch of younger girls hovering around the admin block verandah, but they were too far away to hear.

He laughed and caught her hand. She shook him free, shooting him a glare.

'I'm serious, Charlie. I don't want anyone knowing.'

'I want the whole world to know — ' He sang until she smacked his arm. 'Hey! Violence is never the answer, Pastoral Princess.'

'Please, Charlie. If anyone knows, they'll stop us from seeing each other.'

He tugged her to a stop and faced her, stroking her hair back from her forehead with a tender hand. Beth glanced anxiously at the group of girls but they were deep in conversation, facing the other way.

'Nothing and no-one could stop me from seeing you,' he said, completely serious.

Beth fell speechless, her love welling inside her, building into that familiar ache. She couldn't get enough of him. If they spent every moment of every day together, it still wouldn't be enough. She checked on the girls again and leaned in to press her lips briefly to his.

'Go. I've got to get to this meeting. Mr Ogilvie

went to lots of trouble to arrange it.'

'I know.' Charlie grinned. 'I'm next in the queue.'

'What?'

'I'm seeing this university sheila too. Told you. I'm going where you're going. I've got the next appointment after yours. I might as well sit in the waiting room till you're done.'

She couldn't hide her smile as they entered the office together. Year Eleven student Leanne Clegg was already seated in one of the waiting room chairs, and Charlie greeted her. Beth knew her from the boarding house, and Charlie obviously knew her too — maybe she was in one of his classes. He chatted with Leanne as the three of them waited together.

Beth contemplated next year. If only he were in the same school year as her. Perhaps she could defer uni and take a gap year, live in town and get a job? Be close to Charlie, keep tutoring him in private and make sure he got into university as well so they could go together. They wouldn't have to hide their relationship if she wasn't a boarder any more — there would be no risk of them being kept apart. And they would be adults, well and truly. If she rented a cheap place, Charlie might even be able to stay with her on weekends . . .

'Bethany.'

Mr Ogilvie's big voice shook her out of her reverie and he beckoned her into his office. Charlie flicked her backside sneakily as she stood, and she prayed Ogilvie hadn't noticed.

'This is our prize student, Miss Bethany

131

Paterson,' Mr Ogilvie told the woman seated in his office. 'Beth, this is Karen Kristovic from the University of WA. She's in charge of a regional student program that's aiming to get more students from remote areas into courses.'

Beth smiled and shook the woman's hand, doing her best to make a good impression. There were scholarships available, she knew, which would help with university boarding fees. Mr Ogilvie was rattling off a list of Beth's academic achievements, and Karen was nodding, looking more and more delighted.

'Mr Ogilvie tells me you're hoping to get into medicine,' Karen said as soon as the principal paused for breath, and Beth nodded. 'That's wonderful. It sounds like you're on track to achieve the score required for entry into med. As a regional student with such good results, you'd certainly be considered for our funded residential program. Do you have family in Perth, or were you thinking of boarding in one of the residential colleges?'

'I don't have any family in Perth, so I'd definitely need to board,' she answered.

'I'll make sure Mr Ogilvie passes on the application forms, then.' Karen gave her another warm smile. 'It's a buzzing social scene on campus. Do you get involved in any team sports or clubs, when you're not studying?'

'I like netball,' said Beth. 'I used to play but then my mum got sick and — um, I stopped.'

Mr Ogilvie shook his head. 'Unfortunately, Bethany lost her mother to cancer a few months ago.'

Karen's eyes clouded with sympathy. 'I'm so sorry. Aren't you amazing, soldiering on with your studies during such a sad time?'

'Studying's a good distraction,' Beth said with a shrug.

She second-guessed herself as soon as she said it. Hopefully the woman wouldn't think she was using study as a crutch. Which I kind of am, she thought with a pang of guilt.

'I know Mum would have wanted me to keep at it,' she stumbled on. 'She knew how important it was to me that I get into the course I wanted. I've been thinking of taking up netball again, now things have settled down, and I'm boarding in town for the rest of the year.'

'Bethany's very balanced in her approach,' Mr Ogilvie jumped in to rescue her. 'Yes, she was obliged to give up netball, but that didn't stop her from continuing with the debating club. And she's committed to her community service portfolio, too. She's tutoring an Aboriginal student who's struggled to keep up with coursework. Bethany's taken him under her wing, recognising his academic barriers, and really brought him along. The poor lad was getting an abysmal education out at the remote school he was at, and he's got a lot of potential. If he achieves university entrance, it will all be down to Bethany's hard work.'

Karen looked impressed. 'Is that so?'

Beth didn't like the way Mr Ogilvie had described the situation, but she couldn't deny she was tutoring Charlie.

'Yes, I started working with him about three months ago.'

'She worked with another Indigenous student last year,' Mr Ogilvie went on. 'Lyall McGovern. He'd looked like failing, but Bethany worked very closely with him, rescued his grades.'

Lyall McGovern was Aboriginal? Beth guessed he could have been. Best not to say anything in front of Karen. Lyall had left school now anyway, so it was beside the point.

'Look, I'd love to see you achieve your dreams,' Karen was telling her, her face earnest. 'Your intelligence and initiative are just the qualities we're seeking in candidates for our residential scholarships. Please do put in an application.'

'I will, for sure,' Beth said, smiling her thanks.

'We'd better crack on, or we won't get through all our appointments,' Mr Ogilvie said. He checked his list. 'Speak of the devil, I've got the boy we were just discussing coming in next.' He grasped the door handle. 'I'll check if he's here yet. He might be running on Gwini time.'

Beth wondered what 'Gwini time' meant, but Ogilvie was laughing at his own remark and Karen had a little smile on her face so Beth smiled too as she left the office. Charlie got to his feet and stepped forward in response to Mr Ogilvie's gesture, so when Beth passed him they didn't even have time to exchange a look. She paused for a minute after the principal closed the door. She could hear his booming voice giving his next advertorial-style introduction to Karen, singing Charlie's praises. Beth grinned to herself.

Charlie would go along with it, but he'd probably have something to say about Mr Ogilvie's performance later. Hopefully there were enough scholarships floating around.

One way or another, they'd work it out. They'd be together.

9

Not a great night's sleep. Apart from yet another wretched 'episodic' dream about Charlie, Beth's muscles were tight from the long drive and the lack of a daily run. She'd woken several times in the night and thought about being in the same bed that Charlie sometimes slept in. Each time she had the thought, she experienced an unsettling wrench, somewhere between discomfort and — *ugh* — arousal. It was the dreams, she told herself. All that horny teenage action replaying in her brain was stirring her up. Everything was stirring her up: the memories and dreams, spending time with Charlie, Jill's stalemate with her uncle over high school, not to mention the Gargantua problem. No wonder she felt so out of whack. As soon as life got back to normal — that was, *no Charlie* — things would settle down. Then she'd be back to daily appointments, late-night hospital call-outs, monthly networking functions and planning the redecoration of her living room.

The thought left her flat. When had life become so stupidly, relentlessly busy — and so dull? Once, every day had been an adventure. She had thrived on building her business, networking with other driven people, and creating a beautiful home. Now, the thought of going back to her well-planned life in Mount Clair left her uninspired.

Hell, she *really* needed a holiday.

Beth got up at sunrise, determined to go for a run and ease some of the tension in her body and mind. She crept out of the house and jogged quietly along the grid of dusty roads through the residential part of the community. It was peaceful out here, and it reminded Beth of mornings at Paterson Downs — mellow, still and burnt orange in the dawn light. She ran past the co-op where a food truck trundled in and dropped off a load of groceries once a week during the dry season, the school with its native animal mural, the community meeting centre and the new drive-in. She paused to stretch and check her heart rate at the drive-in, eyeing the big weatherproof screen and outdoor speaker system, and the tin shed that must be used as a kiosk. Charlie's gift to the town.

Honestly — how could she not have known he was from Madjinbarra? There were dozens of remote communities dotted throughout the region, and several of them were home to a largely Gwini population. But how could she have spent every spare moment with a man, be desperately in love with him, sneak around having the best sex of her life with him, for God's sake — and not even know where he came from?

Because you didn't care where he came from, she reminded herself. *You only cared that you didn't lose him.*

Maybe it was age and disillusionment that made people care about where someone came from. She was innocent back then, unaware of bigger issues affecting society. All she'd cared about was that Charlie was hers and that no-one would take their love away from them.

She'd never imagined *he* would be the one to take it away.

Beth sighed to herself. She was so used to hating him for what he'd done, but seeing Charlie in his own space, surrounded by people who loved him, working so hard to give back to the community, had changed things. The comforting resentment was wavering. Yes, he'd hurt her, but they'd been little more than kids. There were bigger things going on than she'd understood. The scene from this morning's dream came back, hitting her with a wave of clarity. Had Ogilvie truly made some condescending joke about Charlie running on 'Gwini time' to that woman from the university? Charlie, who'd worked his arse off to do everything right in a new school environment away from his family, because he wanted to be a lawyer and fight for the little guy? Had Ogilvie honestly credited Beth with Charlie's progress at school, as though it were all down to her and not Charlie himself? Anger shook through Beth, and then self-reproach. Why hadn't she stood up for him?

At the time, she hadn't even realised how bad it was that her principal had put Charlie down like that. She'd just figured he was buttering up the university woman to make Beth look good. It hadn't occurred to her how detrimental it was to Charlie for Ogilvie to, in one breath, claim Charlie's success was all down to Beth, and in the next, invite Charlie in and pretend he thought the world of his 'disadvantaged' student. What a dick their principal had been! And what a self-absorbed ignoramus she'd been to let him get away with it.

She'd loved Charlie so much she would have done practically anything for him. But she'd refused to go public with their relationship — all because she was terrified of missing out on time alone with him every day after school. *Nothing could stop me from seeing you,* Charlie had promised. And yet she'd never even let him hold her hand in the schoolyard. She'd been consumed by her narrow world view, by her selfish need to protect their little secret bubble of a relationship. Charlie had probably thought she was ashamed of being seen with him.

Beth resumed running, then stopped. These thoughts had churned up her stomach to the point where, quite suddenly, she thought she might be sick if she kept running. She took a few breaths and set off at a hard walk instead. The sun arrived over the horizon, making long shadows from buildings and trees shoot across the red-dirt-stained bitumen.

Oh, God.

Had her insistence on secrecy — the way she'd failed to stand up for him — been why Charlie had left? Maybe he'd overheard that conversation in Ogilvie's office: overheard her agree that she'd been the source of his academic success, that Charlie was merely a 'disadvantaged' student who ran on 'Gwini time'. And Charlie had so much pride. He would have — quite rightly — *hated* to hear that.

How long after that day had he left? She made desperate calculations and felt like her heart slammed against the bottom of her gut she when realised it had been less than a week after their appointments with Ogilvie and the university representative. It was just days later, when she went into the office to ask Mr Ogilvie for the scholarship forms, that she'd discovered Charlie was gone.

'Charlie Campbell's been marked as absent from English this morning,' one of the office women said to another as Beth waited for Mr Ogilvie.

Her colleague didn't pause in clacking at a keyboard. 'Oh, yes — I meant to let you know. He's left the school. His uncle picked him up this morning.'

'What, for good?'

'Yep. They were driving straight back to their community.'

The woman chuckled sadly. 'Another one bites the dust. Pity, he was a lovely kid.'

Beth slowed her pace and sat on a bench outside the closed co-op. If only she could remember exactly what had happened that week. Had Charlie talked about any of this stuff with her? Shown any sign that he was hurt or angry? All she knew was that she'd been utterly oblivious to anything being wrong, and the news that he'd left had hit her like a punch in the chest. The very thought of that moment still brought back the nights of sobbing silently into her blankets, the utter, helpless confusion, like it was yesterday.

She dropped her face into her hands and tried to clear her mind of the memory and its breathtaking pain. *Dammit.* She had to somehow get a hold of herself. She had to process this stuff later. *I will remain composed whenever I am around Charlie for the next three days.*

And then share a long drive back to Mount Clair with him.

She stood up, fought her nausea, and forced herself back into a jog.

★   ★   ★

Mary generally joined Beth at the clinic during consulting days. She sent Jill off to school, brought Pearl with her, and held court in the outer room, where she had a good view of anyone coming in through the glass doors. Beth understood. It was an opportunity for Mary, as an elder of the community, to reconnect with people she hadn't seen for a while. The residents of Madjinbarra tended to save up their nagging ailments for Beth's monthly visit, only using the clinic nurses for urgent injuries or sickness, and Mary liked to know what was happening in their lives. Pearl was quite happy, playing with the clinic's collection of toys and board books and any other children who came in.

Beth heard the Beast pull up midmorning and her shoulders tensed. She attempted to focus on assessing old Helen's blood pressure, wishing the inner room's door was shut so she wouldn't be distracted by Charlie's presence — but no-one ever closed the door unless they needed to discuss something deeply private.

'G'day, Charlie' came Mary's voice as the clinic door slid open. 'What's wrong?'

'Nothing.'

'Bullshit nothing. You look mad as a cut snake.'

The door shut and Charlie's voice replied. 'It's that dickhead Winston. You won't believe this, Aunty.'

'What's he done?'

'He's left.'

Beth almost dropped the blood pressure pump.

'Could you give me a moment, Helen?' she asked.

'Not a worry, love.'

Beth stepped into the outer room. 'Did you say Winston's *left?*' she asked Charlie. 'How?'

He pulled a hand through his hair, clearly agitated. 'I just dropped him at the airstrip and saw him onto a charter flight. His assistant kept apologising. Said he had 'urgent parliamentary business'.'

Beth stared at him, mind whirring. The look on Charlie's face was deeply cynical.

'Did he look at *anything* before he left?' she asked.

'Not much. Harvey and I drove him around to the school and the meeting centre, he met a couple of the blokes on Uncle's program, and then he got a call. I heard him saying, 'Thanks, mate, thanks so much. It's pretty dire.' I reckon he put out a distress call when he saw his accommodation last night and they sent a plane for him this morning.' Charlie looked at Mary. 'The prick couldn't hack it here, so he called for a rescue crew. I bet he'll be back at the Mount Clair Resort in no time, taking a dip in the pool before he catches his flight home.'

'Wanker.' Mary sounded more sad than angry, and Charlie's expression matched.

Beth tried to buoy them up. 'His assistant, Melody — she was pretty switched on. We should try to make contact with her.'

Charlie sank into a chair. 'What's the point? She's just one of Winston's staff. She's probably writing his report on why Gargantua coming in to build a mining camp nearby is exactly what Madjinbarra needs.'

Mary looked so stricken when he said this that Beth hastened to reassure the woman. 'Okay, this is a setback, but it's taught us Winston is no good to us. That's a positive. We need to know our enemies as well as our friends.'

'Thank heavens for you, Beth,' Mary said, her eyes glistening. 'At least *you're* our friend.'

Charlie shot Beth a look that could have frozen her blood in her veins, it was so filled with disgust and anger. He seemed to be barely holding back, ready to say what he really thought. Bewildered, Beth waited, her gaze locked on his green eyes. But he glanced at Mary and reined in his ire.

'I'm getting a cuppa. Want one, Aunty?'

'Yeah,' she said, wiping her eyes.

'Maud?' he called. 'Aunty Helen? Cuppa?'

They all called their thanks, and he headed for the kettle in the tiny kitchen.

'Don't forget the doc,' Mary called after him.

'I'm fine,' Beth said quickly, fighting the heat that burned her cheeks. 'I'm busy with Helen at the moment, anyway.'

She pulled the door shut on her way into the consulting room. Screw the open-door custom. She didn't need Charlie Campbell messing with her equilibrium while she was trying to care for a patient. Helen looked startled by the bang of the door.

'What's going on out there?' she asked. 'Charlie sounded like he wanted someone's guts for garters.'

Beth forced a smile. 'He's fine. Now, let's get this blood pressure checked, so you can go and join Mary for a cuppa.'

★ ★ ★

Beth worked without a pause all day, determined to shut out the memory of Charlie's public snub. Her regret over the past and those fledgling thoughts of trying to move on had stalled in the face of his unpleasantness. She finished close to five o'clock, when Maud and Christine declared it time to pack up and started turning people away.

'Come back tomorrow,' Maud called out to some latecomers. 'Doc needs a feed and a rest, yeah?'

Beth hated seeing people knocked back but couldn't help feeling grateful. There was no way

144

she would see so many people in one day back at her clinic. Her clinic days were a blend of fifteen- and thirty-minute appointments, and she normally got a little breathing space here and there because some preferred to be in and out within five minutes. Here, she was lucky to get a couple of minutes with one patient before the next one was shown in. Maud and Christine managed a steady flow in and out of her consulting room to stop her getting stuck with any one patient, which ensured she worked through her long queue.

She thanked them both and held Pearl's hand for the walk home to Mary's house.

'You should have yourself a quick rest, I reckon,' Mary said. 'Camp-fire meal tonight.'

'Shoshage' was Pearl's contribution.

Mary nodded. 'Too right. Sausages, spuds. And the blokes caught a few fish at the waterhole today. Should be a good feed. We'll wake you up before we head over.'

Beth crashed on Jill's bed and slept hard, barely aware of Pearl's squawks, Mary's carrying voice, or Jill's movements when she fetched something from her bedroom. The next thing she knew was Jill's warm hand on her arm, shaking her gently.

'Doc. Hey, Doc, you wanna come get some tucker?'

'Mm,' Beth managed. 'Have I got time for a super-quick shower?'

'Yeah, no worries. I'll wait for you. Aunty's already gone with Pearl.'

Beth dived in for a lukewarm shower, rinsing

sweat and red dust out of her hair, and washing away some of the day's tension. She scrambled into shorts and a T-shirt, but there was no time to make herself anything more than relatively tidy, not with Jill hopping from foot to foot, eager to set off. Beth rubbed the towel through her hair and brushed it at lightning speed, and threw on a pair of boots, dashing outside to join the girl.

Jill had her uncle's guitar case hitched over her shoulder, and Beth remembered with a sinking heart that Charlie would, of course, be at the camp fire.

'Did you talk to Uncle Charlie about me going to Mount Clair High School?' Jill asked as they walked.

'No, not yet,' Beth said. 'I think he's been a bit distracted with the Gargantua stuff and showing the minister around. But I haven't forgotten.' *Jesus, why did I say that?* She was the last person who could convince Charlie to send his niece to Mount Clair. Or do anything, for that matter.

'Okay,' said Jill, her voice full of trust.

Beth cast her gaze over the street, which was darkening as the sun disappeared. Who knew where the Beast was? This happened sometimes — someone borrowed it, then she barely saw it for the few days she stayed in Madjinbarra.

'Uncle's really upset about this Gargantua stuff, I reckon,' said Jill, scuffing the dust as she walked. 'He's bloody grumpy. He's never grumpy, not normally.'

Beth remained silent.

'I've been thinking,' Jill continued. 'What you

146

said last time about Pearl needing massages and stuff . . . '

'Physiotherapy?'

'Yeah. And the talking stuff. Do you reckon I could learn it, so I could help her properly?'

'Absolutely.' Beth glanced at Jill. 'There are courses. You could do physiotherapy, speech therapy, occupational therapy. Disability studies. You've got loads of experience, too. You'd be fantastic at any of those.'

Jill nodded, but her eyes stayed on the ground as they walked. 'I'm just worried about who'd look after her if I'm off studying.'

Jill had a point. Mary was a wonderful mother figure, but she was ageing, and didn't have the energy or physical strength to look after Pearl like Jill could. This was another reason why Pearl would do better in town.

'Maybe we could find somewhere for Pearl to live in Mount Clair while you study,' she said. 'Do you have any family there?'

Jill pursed her lips, thinking. 'There's some relations of ours living in town. Not sure what they're like. Uncle Charlie'd know.'

'He doesn't seem keen for Pearl to leave Madji,' Beth said, recalling Charlie's reaction when she'd mentioned it a few weeks ago.

Jill's expression changed. 'Yeah.' She sighed. 'Guess I'm stuck here, then.'

'That's not very fair on you,' Beth said. 'You're only fifteen. You shouldn't be stuck raising a toddler — being a carer.'

'I've got to look after Pearl. She's my baby sister. Aunty Mary can't do it all.' Jill gazed at

147

her thong-clad feet, crunching over the hot bitumen. 'I reckon Pearl needs to live in town. I get worried about her. She keeps zoning out. It's like she's tired, or sad. I dunno. She needs more than what she's got here.' She looked at Beth for a split second. 'What about . . . '

'What about?' Beth prompted.

Jill took a breath. 'What about if Pearl and I went into foster care in town together? I mean, a doctor could recommend it . . . '

Beth was speechless. This was a huge thing for Jill to suggest. Was this driven by Jill's desire to finish her schooling in Mount Clair? Or her concerns about Pearl? Both, Beth realised. Two birds, one stone.

'Are you asking me to help you out, Jill?'

The girl's eyes remained on the road. 'I don't know what else to do.'

They'd almost reached the crackling camp fire, surrounded by dozens of locals. Beth touched Jill's shoulder.

'Let me have a think, okay? One way or another, you'll be able to do what you need to do. You hear me, Jill?'

Jill nodded and took off at a run to join some friends. She off-loaded her uncle's guitar case on the ground beside him as she trotted past. Beth spotted Mary nattering with some other women and Pearl wasn't far away, bum-shuffling around in the dust after some young kids playing chasey. Makeshift grills held scores of sausages, the smell making Beth's mouth water, and a couple of men were pulling foil-baked fish and potatoes out from the ashes.

148

'I think I got here just in time,' Beth said when Mary shuffled over on her log seat to make room for her.

The feast commenced. Pearl was right in there, Beth saw with delight, clamouring among the other kids for a sausage. She wasn't treated differently to any of them, either. Beth's heart squeezed. She *got* that Pearl belonged here at Madjinbarra, as Charlie said, but she couldn't help but worry about that doe-eyed child with her big smile. She winced as Pearl dropped her sausage and scrabbled it out of the dirt, cramming it straight back into her mouth. *Oh, well.* A bit of dirt was good for the immune system.

Beth got a blisteringly hot potato in foil and a big hunk of baked fish to go with it. *God, this is so good.* Carbs and protein — exactly what she needed after her busy day. She devoured it, not even thinking about table manners until she glanced up and saw Charlie's eyes on her across the fire. Her simple joy in a good feed after a hard day's work fell away. Did he have to judge every damn thing she did or said?

There were stories, jokes and arguments around the giant camp fire. Beth was grateful for the fall of darkness so she could barely see Charlie any more where he sat with Harvey, Billy and a few other blokes. She could almost have pretended he wasn't there except for Pearl's occasional shouts at her 'Unca Jarlie'.

But then the singing started.

Normally, Beth loved the singing. There was a mix of outback country music, Gwini songs,

149

kids' songs, and old rock 'n' roll tunes. Occasionally, someone brought an instrument along. The conversations usually continued throughout the singing, people joining in or talking over the singing as they wished. It was chaotic but somehow wonderfully soothing.

Tonight, with Charlie present, the pressure was on him to lead the singing. They teased and shouted at him until he pulled his guitar out of its leather case and tuned it, the dissonant plinking and adjustments mellowing into a gentle strumming that brought a sense of quiet, sociable happiness to the party. Beth tried to ignore it, straining to listen to the jolly, meaningless conversation going on around her.

But the bastard played so beautifully.

She couldn't control her thoughts as they drifted towards Charlie's guitar. She pictured his fingers moving over the strings, and it made her think things about his fingers that she hadn't thought in a very long time. She hated herself.

'Sing, Uncle Charlie.' Jill's command cut through the darkness, and Charlie began to sing.

Apart from a few stray conversations, the camp-fire circle fell mostly silent to listen to Charlie sing. *God, that voice.* Beth dropped her head, pretending to rest it wearily on her forearms, but really she was hiding her face, because Charlie's voice cut deep into her. It wasn't even knife-like. It was a pickaxe, hacking into the hard surface she'd cultivated around her heart.

Those around the camp fire joined in the singing, but one or two of his songs were too solemn for anyone to sing along. Instead, people just made noises of agreement or appreciation. They were songs of betrayal and regret, memorials to those they'd lost. However, Charlie never let the mood get too morose. He always brought them back to happiness with an old ballad about the land or one of his father's country songs. He understood his audience.

No. He understood his community.

Beth had never permitted herself to listen to Charlie's music before, and tonight she learned why he'd been so successful. He had that magical combination of melody, voice and words. She wanted to leave. She longed to get up and walk away, to go and hide at Mary's house. But his music held her there. She loathed the situation and yet she could not leave. Every time he took a break his voice echoed in her mind, that stupid two-line song about *Princess Beth of Paterson Downs*. And when he sang again his voice called to her, capturing her like the very first time she'd heard it, until she couldn't resist the temptation any longer and sneaked a look across the fire at his face. Her eyes met his and, for a moment, Charlie sang to Beth.

Then he faltered, pulled his eyes away and laughed at himself, pretending he'd forgotten the line.

And Beth knew she had to talk to him.

10

'We'll finish you up at three today,' Christine told Beth in the morning. 'You gotta go out and see Gurrungah.'

Gurrungah was an old woman who lived in a rough bush shanty, forty-five minutes out of the community. She refused to come into the centre of Madjinbarra. People from the community dropped in to visit the woman from time to time and reported back to the clinic any time she was in need of health care. It was an accepted fact that Beth would simply need to pay a house call when Gurrungah required medical attention. She normally went out with Mary or Maud.

'Anything specific?'

'She's huffing and puffing. Reckon it's her heart again.'

'I'll need to track down my vehicle,' Beth said. 'If you hear where it is, could you let me know?'

'We'll get it back here for you, Doc.' Maud was confident.

Mary and Pearl turned up once again, and the day went on as busily as the one before. Midafternoon, Charlie arrived in the Beast. Beth heard him handing the keys to Mary in the outer room.

'You can head out with the doc to see Gurrungah this arvo,' she told him. 'Take some supplies, and deliver those blankets and tarps you brought.'

'No, I can't. I'm busy.'

I bet, Beth thought bitterly.

'You bloody can and you will,' Mary informed him. 'You can drive Beth out there, in fact. She's working her fingers to the bone in here while you're out gallivanting in her car. You can do her the favour of driving her.'

'Aunty, I can't — '

'You'll go and pay your respects to Gurrungah,' Mary commanded. 'And stop being such a rude prick to the doc, while you're at it. What's she ever done to you?'

There was a silence followed by the sound of the sliding door as Charlie left the clinic. No argument. Beth's heart rate bumped up. Maybe this would be an opportunity to speak to Charlie — if he obeyed Mary, that was.

Maud and Christine closed up shop around three, as promised. Beth tidied her consulting room and loaded up a backpack with items she might need for her visit to Gurrungah. In the outer room, Pearl was asleep in Mary's lap.

'Want me to carry her home?' Beth asked, shouldering her backpack.

Mary nodded. 'Ta. Charlie's got some stuff to give to Gurrungah, so he's going to drive you out.'

Beth would believe that when she saw it. She took the sleeping Pearl from Mary and smiled down at the little girl's long lashes and open mouth. They walked back to Mary's place, where the Beast waited in the driveway. Charlie was sitting on the porch, messing with his guitar.

So he's here, waiting? For me? Maybe he did

intend to go with Beth to visit Gurrungah. She wasn't going to let him drive her, though. That would put him in control, and she would rather have the upper hand during their forced time alone together. She murmured a greeting and he nodded, focusing quickly back on his guitar. Beth took Pearl inside and laid her on the couch, pushing a cushion up against its base in case the child rolled off. After freshening up, she took the keys and went outside to the Beast. She climbed in and adjusted her seat, which was positioned for a taller driver than her. The moment she turned the key and checked the fuel levels, Charlie appeared at the passenger side with a shopping bag of food and a bundle of tarps and blankets. He dropped them onto the back seat and climbed in beside her wordlessly.

Beth hid a smile. Mary's word was law, even for the big celebrity grumpy bastard, Charlie Campbell.

She waved to Mary and drove them out of town, turning the vehicle onto the track that would take them south towards Gurrungah's hut. When they'd been on the road for ten minutes and neither had spoken, Beth began to panic that the opportunity would pass before she found the fortitude to speak.

After three false starts, she pushed out the words. 'Charlie, could we talk?'

There was a long silence. 'About what?' he said at last, his tone hard.

Rather than being intimidated, Beth felt her temper flicker. 'About why you're so pissed off at me.'

154

'I'd rather not.'

'I'm sorry to hear that. But I think we need to. We've got a battle ahead of us with this Gargantua stuff, and I'd rather we put our past to rest so we can work together.'

He didn't reply. Beth twisted the wheel to avoid a deep furrow in the track.

She forged on. 'I've been doing a bit of thinking. I'd always assumed you took off — left Mount Clair all those years ago — because you got tired of it all. But you seem resentful towards me. I'm starting to wonder if you left in anger.'

She felt his eyes on her, and when she checked his face, saw utter disbelief. 'Seriously, Beth?'

Baffled, Beth squeezed on the brakes so she could navigate a difficult piece of track.

'Yes, seriously,' she said when she could concentrate again. 'I don't get it. I was upset with you for leaving. You never even said goodbye. But you're acting like it was all my fault.'

His voice was low and cold. 'Do you take me for a moron?'

She frowned. 'What are you talking about?'

He gave a short laugh. 'Of course you do. You do take me for a moron. I know what was going on back then, and I don't want to discuss it. You and I are nothing to each other. As for the Gargantua stuff, we don't want or need your *help*. The sooner you go back to Mount Clair and leave us to it, the better.'

Beth was shocked into silence. She fought against the pain his words had sparked and tried to focus on things around her to calm herself

155

down. *Trees, birds, blue sky, potholes in the track*. To cry in front of Charlie would be her worst nightmare. She couldn't even manage anger — she was too hurt. She fixed her eyes on the road and pressed her lips together to stop them trembling. Charlie turned his back and stared out the window, and they drove the remainder of the trip without speaking.

Gurrungah's camp consisted of ropes strung between spindly trees, a rough corrugated-iron shack, a decaying vinyl couch, and an array of metal barrels and tools scattered over the dusty ground. Scrawny dogs wandered to and fro, and rabbit skins lay drying on an improvised wire rack, high enough to prevent the dogs from thieving them.

Gurrungah hobbled into view when they pulled to a stop. She was a white-haired woman with deep brown skin darkened further by years in the outback sun. She accepted Charlie's gifts with a quiet nod and invited them to join her at a little fire for billy tea in cracked, dusty cups. The odd thing about Gurrungah's tea, Beth always thought when she came out here, was that it was the best she'd ever tasted. Dirty cup and all.

Beth performed some tests and found Gurrungah's heart and blood pressure were certainly worse for wear. There was no chance of talking her into a hospital visit. The woman spoke mostly in her people's language but had enough English to understand Beth's questions and give her answers, albeit with plenty of gestures and some translation from Charlie.

Beth dispensed two types of medication but wasn't sure if Gurrungah could read the directions. Charlie took on the responsibility of explaining how to take the pills. He asked Beth for paper and a marker, and drew a picture of a sunrise, high noon, and the moon, with the number of tablets to take at each time and an apple to show her she needed to take the medicine with food. He stuck it to the inside of Gurrungah's hut wall. Beth was impressed in spite of herself. Such a simple way to remind an old, possibly forgetful woman how to take her medication.

They left her munching on a fresh banana, the sun getting low in the sky. Beth wasn't sure she would have been able to communicate successfully with Gurrungah on her own and was glad Charlie had been there to help.

Even if he *was* being a complete arse.

When they were bumping along the track again, Beth permitted her thoughts to wander back to Charlie's glacial attitude. It was odd how loved and admired he was around Madjinbarra, even with a personality like a spoilt six-year-old. Mary had accused him of being a 'rude prick' to Beth and seemed genuinely surprised to see him behaving this way. Jill had also said he was being uncharacteristically grumpy. Did he reserve this unpleasantness specially for Beth? She looked at him and found him watching the track ahead, his face pensive.

'How long has Gurrungah lived out there?' she asked.

'As long as I can remember,' he said. 'At least thirty years.'

'Does anyone know how old she is?'

He shrugged.

There was silence for several minutes, and then Charlie shifted, turning slightly towards Beth.

'Gurrungah was born to a Gwini woman and a white stockman. The government took her away and put her in a home. They christened her Gertie. She was raised in that home with about a hundred other 'half-castes', and she was raped by this mongrel superintendent who was supposed to be looking after them. She got pregnant at thirteen and then they took her baby away, too. She never found her mum and never saw her son again, either. She's so sad that she doesn't want to be around people at all. She's chosen to live out here on her own so she won't infect other people with her sadness.'

Heart heavy, Beth nodded without speaking. Gurrungah's story wasn't unique but it cut her heart to know personally someone it had happened to. She pictured Gurrungah's weathered face, the long, slow erosion of her hope.

'That's why you are *not* taking Pearl away from Madjinbarra,' he added.

Oh, for Chrissake. 'Why the hell would I want to see Pearl anywhere in the world except safe and happy?' Beth snapped. 'Stop making out like I'm the bad guy here.'

He clamped his mouth shut and stared at the track ahead, a deep frown on his forehead. Beth hit the brakes and the Beast slid to a halt in the gravel. She switched off the engine and climbed out of the car.

'Get out,' she ordered.

Charlie unbuckled slowly, storm clouds gathering in his expression. 'What are you doing?'

'We're going to talk about this. Right here, right now.'

He slammed the car door, and she came around to stand before him.

'This is childish,' he said. 'Give me the keys.'

'No. Tell me what I did wrong.'

Charlie's angry eyes bored into her face. 'Give me the god-damned keys.'

She shook her head. 'Tell me.'

He made a swipe for the keys, and she swung them out of his reach. He tried to stretch around the other side of her to grab them, so she twisted away and pulled her tank top open at the neckline, dropping the keys down the front. Charlie froze.

'What the . . . ?' Disbelief crept over his features, then the tiniest hint of amusement.

She couldn't quite believe she'd done it either. Clearly, Charlie still had the capacity to make her do things that were completely out of character. She took advantage of his slight improvement in mood and stepped forward.

'Please.' Her voice softened. 'It was really confusing when you just took off all those years ago. I've wondered for years why you did it. I assumed you were just using me, but it's obvious you're mad at me for something. I honestly don't know what I'm supposed to have done.'

He practically choked. 'You assumed I was using *you*?'

'Yes.' She took a breath, trembling a little. 'I figured you got what you wanted — to screw the pastoral princess — then got bored with me.'

A look she didn't quite understand crossed his face — something between caution and regret. He slumped against the car, pushing a hand into his pocket.

'I wouldn't do that, for Christsake.'

She swallowed the sudden urge to cry. 'Well? What was it, then?' He still seemed unwilling to talk, so she blurted out her suspicion. 'Was it because you thought I was taking credit for your grades?'

Charlie's eyes met hers again, reflecting the sun dropping behind her. 'Is that what you reckon?'

'I've been thinking about that time Ogilvie called us in to meet with the university rep. That was about a week before you vanished. Ogilvie was being his smarmy self, talking me up and going on about the *community service* I was doing by tutoring you. To be honest, I didn't think much of it at the time. I didn't really get it. But recently, when I remembered what he said, it occurred to me that it must have been really insulting to you — if you happened to overhear it.' She waited, heart hammering.

Charlie shrugged. 'I remember that. I did overhear it. It wasn't exactly a pleasant thing to hear but I figured Ogilvie was making you look good to the university rep, so I let it slide. It wasn't your fault he talked that way.'

'No, but I could have stood up for you,' she admitted. 'It was cowardly of me to just stand there and let him say that crap.'

Charlie's mouth was hard. 'I was used to being talked about like a charity for well-meaning people to donate to.'

'So . . . ' Beth chewed her lip. 'That wasn't why you left?'

He shot her a scathing look. 'No. Let's just say that paled in comparison to finding out you'd been screwing around on me.'

Beth sucked in a breath and stepped back in shock, but her foot hit a rut in the track and she stumbled, falling heavily onto her backside. She made a stupid *oof!* noise as she hit the ground, and pain shot up from her tailbone into her back.

'Shit.' Charlie took a step towards her, reaching out. 'Are you all right?'

'I'm fine,' she said, getting to her feet.

Owwww. Her heart was racing, but whether from her fall or his words, she wasn't sure. She searched his eyes for something that might explain why he'd said that. 'What are you talking about, *screwing around?*' she demanded.

He gave a slight roll of his eyes to show her he didn't buy it. 'You want to know how I found out? When you went in for your meeting with Ogilvie that day, I was chatting with a friend I knew through my classes. Leanne.'

'Leanne Clegg, in the waiting room? She was living at Durack with me.'

'Yeah. She saw me . . . ' He looked awkward. 'She saw me touch you when you went into Ogilvie's office, and she asked me if you and I were a thing.' Charlie stuck his hand back in his pocket, dropping his gaze. 'I knew you didn't like anyone knowing, but I said yes, we were.'

Beth waited, rubbing her lower back. It stung horribly from her fall.

'She said, 'You're not the only bloke in town Beth Paterson's been getting around with, you know.''

Beth's mouth fell open. She closed it, swallowing with difficulty. 'Right. What else did she say?'

'She said you used to give Lyall McGovern private tutoring too, and everyone knew what you'd been getting up to with him. That you had a habit of offering extra *support* along with your tutoring services. She said — ' Charlie stopped, a dark look coming over his face. 'You know what? Who cares? We were just kids. Shit happens. Let's get back.'

She didn't move. 'No. I want to know exactly what Leanne said about me.'

'Beth, if we don't get back in the car soon, we'll be negotiating this shitty track in the dark.'

She clutched the keys under her shirt, in front of her stomach. 'We're not going anywhere until I have the full story.'

He sighed. 'Fine. Leanne told me about a crack you'd made about me to the girls at Durack.'

Could this get any worse? Beth tried shifting her feet to relieve some tailbone pain. 'What *crack?*'

'Your comment about me. 'Charlie Campbell will never get into university. He's just as dumb as Lyall McGovern, but not as good in the sack.''

Charlie kept his green eyes on hers, challenging her to deny it — but, try as he might, he couldn't hide the pain of reliving Leanne's words.

Beth didn't even flinch. 'And you believed her?'

He raised his eyebrows. 'Actually, no, I didn't. I thought you were the best thing since sliced bread, so I figured it must be bullshit. I had no idea why Leanne would say a thing like that about you.'

'Maybe because she had a thing for you herself,' Beth suggested, her voice sardonic.

He tipped his head. 'Don't know. Whatever the case, I doubted her. I didn't mention it to you, either, because I thought it might upset you. It wasn't until you went home to your station the next weekend and I bumped into Lyall that I realised it was closer to the truth than I'd thought.'

'Oh, really?' Beth was increasingly disgusted.

He echoed her cool tone. '*Really*. I didn't know him very well, but his folks were friendly with my father when he was alive. Lyall said he'd heard you were tutoring me, and you were a bit of a snob but a 'good root'.' He watched her, eyes narrowed. 'I realised, with that much smoke, there had to be fire.'

She struggled to control her voice. 'So, based on a snide remark about me from a girl who had a crush on you, and the lewd, completely unfounded claims of a guy you barely knew, you assumed I was screwing around and lying to you?'

'Are you going to try to tell me you weren't?'

'Yes, Charlie, I am.' She took a steadying breath. 'I was not screwing *anyone* else. You were . . . ' *God*, this was humiliating. 'You were my first, and my only, in high school. I never thought you were anything resembling *not smart enough* to go to university, and I certainly never said anything like that. The only negative thought I ever had about you was that you made me feel cheap and stupid when you left.'

If Beth stayed there right now, talking to him, she might scream at him or — worse — cry. She yanked at her tank top, pulling it out so she could retrieve the car keys, and marched around to the driver's side. She climbed in and started the engine. Hell, her tailbone hurt. Could she have fractured it? Wouldn't that be just her luck, to break her tailbone out here when she had to do this bumpy ride back on the southern track. And then a long drive back to Mount Clair on Thursday.

These thoughts were a useful way to push his dreadful accusation from her head.

Charlie climbed into the passenger seat. Beth took off, wincing with pain every time they went down a dip or up a mound. She refused to look at Charlie. They must be arriving at the smoother part of the track soon. A particularly rough bump made her suck in a gasp of pain.

'Beth, stop,' Charlie said.

She permitted herself a glance at him. 'Why?'

'Just stop the damn car.'

She complied, bringing the Beast to a halt and pulling on the handbrake. Beth looked at him expectantly, ready to defend herself against more accusations.

'You've hurt yourself, haven't you?' For once, Charlie's eyes weren't full of repressed anger. 'Your back? Or your . . . '

'My tailbone,' she interrupted with as much dignity as she could muster. 'It's either badly bruised or fractured. It's quite painful.'

'I can see that from the way you practically rip off the steering wheel every time we hit a bump. How about you let me drive? You can lie down in the back, maybe.'

'I'm fine.'

'Beth.'

She huffed a sigh. 'Okay. I'm not going to lie down, though. I'm not driving without a seatbelt on — but not having to use the pedals might help.'

They climbed out, Beth gritting her teeth through the pain caused by the step down from the car seat, and changed places.

Charlie resumed the drive. She could tell he was trying to take it as easy as possible, but it was still agony every time they hit an undulation in the track. At last they reached the bend that marked a better-graded section of the track and increased their speed. By now, the sun had sunk below the horizon, and Charlie had to slow for kangaroos more than once.

It was after six when they finally saw the lights of Madjinbarra up ahead. Beth could have wept with relief. She need painkillers — strong ones. She sent up thanks for her bag full of pharmaceuticals.

'Don't know how you're going to go on the drive home.' Charlie put voice to her concern.

'Maybe it will feel a bit better in a day or so.' She bloody well hoped so.

'You might need to sit on a cushion.' A hint of humour had crept into his voice. 'Princess-style.'

She grimaced. 'Bum injuries hold no dignity.'

Charlie made a sound of amusement. Her thoughts threatened to wander back towards what he had revealed — that he'd believed a couple of random losers who'd lied about her. That he'd taken off on the basis of what they'd said, without even speaking to her. This betrayal was almost as hurtful as believing he'd simply used her for sex and vamoosed. He'd told her he loved her — and yet all it took was a couple of meaningless slurs for him to think she'd played him.

She dragged her mind back to the present. She could process that stuff later. Right now, she just needed to get back to Mary's place, get hold of an icepack and take some painkillers.

Charlie pulled into the driveway. Beth was clambering out of the Beast before he could even switch off the engine, inhaling a silent breath as the pain hit again. It was okay when she walked — it seemed only a bump or trying to climb caused a problem. From Mary's place, Beth heard the clatter of plates and Pearl's piping voice. The smell of chops cooking wafted through the screen door. She reached the porch, pausing to eye the couple of steps apprehensively.

'Hey, wait a minute,' Charlie said.

She waited. He slammed the car door and hit the button to lock it, then approached, holding out her keys.

'Here.'

She took them and turned back to the house but Charlie reached out, grasping her arm in his big warm hand for an instant. Beth froze and he let her go, pulling his hand back, clearly aghast at himself.

'We didn't finish our conversation,' he said by way of an excuse.

'No, probably not,' she said. 'But now's not a great time.'

He hovered for a few more moments, then nodded. 'Yeah. Okay.'

Charlie's confusion was plain on his face. He looked almost disorientated, as though his disillusionment with Beth had been holding him in position for all these years, and now he didn't know what to lean up against any more. At last, he dropped his eyes to the ground between them. He took a step back and shoved a hand in his pocket.

'Hope you feel better.'

He turned and headed down the road towards Harvey's place.

11

'It's all purple, Doc.'

Jill was examining Beth's bruise for her, since the house's only mirror was thirty centimetres wide and hung at face height.

'Looks sore. How'd you do it?' Jill wanted to know.

Beth pulled her shorts back up, wincing, and sat gingerly on the edge of the couch. She eased the icepack she'd fashioned from a tea towel and a packet of frozen peas down onto her tailbone.

'I stacked it on the gravel, of course,' she said.

Jill tried to hide a smile but Mary guffawed. 'And you weren't even wearing your high heels, Doc.'

'Ha-ha, Mary.'

Mary disappeared back into the kitchen, chortling.

'Did you talk to Uncle Charlie about school yet?' Jill asked.

'Oh, bugger. I'm sorry, Jill. It slipped my mind.' The girl's eyes dimmed in disappointment. 'I'm really not sure he'll listen to me,' Beth admitted. 'But I'll try, I promise.'

Jill went to help Mary, and Beth stared at the Disney movie Pearl was watching, replaying Charlie's words in her mind. She was so wound up inside. Beth would have paid every cent she owned for the opportunity to go for a run, just to ease the tension coursing through her body. But the ache in her lower back put the kibosh on that. She could barely walk from one side of the house to the other, let alone jog. Charlie's eyes were on pause in her memory, full of hurt as he repeated the foul words that had been said to him all those years ago.

Exactly the same hurt that had sliced through her own heart every time she'd thought of him since.

Had they really lost each other over such a stupid misunderstanding? For an instant, Beth sank into deep, crushing despair. It was so pointless. So unfair.

Why the hell had those jerks said those things to him? She knew the answer before she even asked the question. In the Durack common room, Leanne Clegg had been quite clear about what she thought of Charlie. She'd made lascivious remarks about him, openly speculating about the size of what Charlie kept in his jeans. Beth had despised Leanne for it, but had also secretly gloated, thinking of Charlie's lean, muscular body, the intensity in his eyes as he kissed every inch of her on their Saturday mornings in the furniture storage room. The way he questioned and teased her, brought her outside of herself — outside of the clever, self-controlled Bethany Paterson. The way he'd made her crash headlong into love just by singing to her.

And Lyall, the guy she'd tried to help through English and science when she was in Year Eleven. He did okay in semester one, but he was never especially focused and, after the novelty of working with Beth had worn off — and she'd knocked back his invitation to the senior ball — he appeared to lose motivation. She could barely get him to listen for their weekly one-hour study session. Finally, he'd announced with glee that he had scored an apprenticeship at the local air-conditioning repairer. Beth had congratulated him, a little surprised, and had never seen him again.

It was breathtakingly stupid. A girl lusting after Charlie. A guy annoyed by Beth's rejection. With almost stunning synchronicity, they'd both driven shards of doubt into Charlie's heart, and it had broken something unutterably precious.

Get a grip, she scolded herself. They were kids. Every love felt special at eighteen. She had to be one of millions of eighteen-year-old girls who'd thought she'd met the love of her life.

Her angry teenage ghost rose up from nowhere and screamed at Charlie, *You imbecile, how could you think that of me? You had every single part of me. I surrendered every piece of my love, my soul — I gave myself to you more completely than ever before or ever again — and you believed the insipid lies of those nobodies!*

The immature heart that hid under Beth's very adult self was raging, thrashing around in its cage, wanting to slap Charlie's beautiful goddamned face. Wanting to hate him.

And completely unable to.

Beth adjusted the packet of frozen peas, eyes watering with the pain — or something. She focused on Pearl, sitting back in a bean-bag. The light from the television made the little girl's fair curls a soft white-blue. Beth's weariness took over, and she pulled herself into a sideways position as carefully as possible, allowing her body to relax into the gritty couch. Pearl's soft profile glowed, the long lashes drooping, fluttering, drooping again.

⋆ ⋆ ⋆

'Have you ever tutored anyone else?' Charlie asked, his eyes trained on hers.

Out of habit, Beth checked the position of the library teacher. 'Why do you ask?'

'You seem pretty experienced.'

She half-smiled. 'In tutoring, I assume you mean?'

He didn't appear to find that as funny as she'd expected. 'Have you?' he pressed her.

'Yes. I tutored another kid last year. He wasn't really interested, though. He dropped out.' She gave Charlie a self-conscious glance. 'I felt like a bit of a failure. I mean, he was never going to run the country, but I was hoping he'd at least finish high school.'

Charlie's gaze rested on the copy of Othello lying open before them.

'Key themes,' she said.

'Huh?'

She pushed his arm. 'What are the key themes in Othello?'

'I don't want to study today.'

She tipped her head. 'You think this is bad. Next year, it's Macbeth, you know. And Pride and Prejudice.'

He ignored her warnings, his eyes running over her face. 'Why are you interested in me?'

Beth pulled back, surprised. 'What?' Charlie waited. 'Because you know all the characteristics of arthropods.'

He kept waiting and she realised he was being serious.

'Because you're smart, gorgeous and talented,' she said, wondering why he needed to hear this right now.

He dropped his gaze, and a muscle moved in his jaw. Beth checked that Miss Chomsky was facing away and leaned close to Charlie, throwing her inhibitions to the wind.

'I love you because you make my heart feel like it's bigger than a planet.' Beth waited until he lifted his eyes, which were strange and anxious, and then her words crowded out, suddenly unstoppable. 'I swear to God, I love you more than anyone ever loved anybody else. I promise you, I'll be yours until the day I die.'

Charlie breathed heavily, relief washing over his expression like the crashing of waves, and he seized her in a hug so tight it was almost painful. She pulled back just enough to smash her mouth fiercely against his, for once not caring if Miss Chomsky or anybody else saw.

★ ★ ★

Beth woke with tears on her cheeks. It was dark, and she was still on Mary's couch. She'd been wrenched from sleep several times in the night, startled awake by the pain in her coccyx. She attempted to wriggle into a more comfortable position, peeling her damp top away from her chest.

Something was nagging at her — something outside the bloody mess that was Charlie and her; something outside the pain in her lower back. Something she should have noticed. She racked her brain to locate it, replaying the evening. A hastily nibbled chop and overcooked frozen vegetables, Pearl watching Disney, Jill's gentle ministrations to Beth's injury. But Charlie's face dominated her thoughts — his green eyes watching her closely as he listed her sins; his pain as he described the things he'd believed about her. She fought the vision, as much from her aversion to Charlie's suffering as from the need to think clearly.

Dammit. Whatever it was she needed to remember, it was eluding her.

Sleep was ruined. Beth rose to a sitting position, discovering an unpleasant sodden patch where the frozen peas had thawed on the couch cushion. She rose stiffly to her feet, sucking in a breath as she used the muscles around her thighs and hips. Had to be a fracture or a dislocation. With a stab of fear, she recalled a patient who'd presented with a 'bruised' tailbone but in fact had a tumour on the sacrum, a secondary cancer. The woman had been in remission, but the cancer had metastasised.

Beth's own mother had died of aggressive cancer.

Beth was sensible, with her regular cervical screening tests. She even got mammograms every couple of years, because of her mother's history. But she'd avoided the genetic testing you could get for breast cancer, and she had never quite worked out why. Getting a positive or a negative result seemed so . . . final. *Yes*, a death sentence, or *no*, you're clear. It was like having all control of your own destiny ripped out of your hands, and something about the idea of knowing for sure made Beth feel like she might come unanchored inside.

She attempted to roll her eyes at herself. Knowing you had the gene mutation wasn't a death sentence. And a sore tailbone was highly unlikely to be cancer. But Beth had seen cancer too often to completely dismiss the thought. She located her phone where she'd left it on Mary's kitchen bench and checked the time. Five-twelve a.m. Too early to be up; too late to go back to sleep. She might as well watch the sunrise. As quietly as possible, Beth made herself a coffee and went outside to sit on the porch. She lowered herself into a chair —

Scratch that. *Stand* on the porch.

She leaned against the porch post and surveyed the street, grey in the slowly rising dawn. She lifted her eyes to the dark sky, where the number and brightness of the stars were almost overwhelming. Beth scanned the sky above her, locked motionless for a few minutes by the vision of those stars, forgetting even to sip her coffee. When she came back to the present, Beth was bewildered at herself anew. Since when was she a day dreamer?

Who the hell is this woman?

'You're up early.'

She started violently at the sound of his voice. For a moment, Beth thought she might have conjured Charlie again — that this was another dream. But there he was in the middle of the road, a shadow on the bitumen. Looking at her.

She found her voice. 'So are you.'

'How's the bum?'

Beth's face heated up in the darkness. 'Fine.' When he didn't answer, she caved. 'By which I mean, so painful I'm contemplating putting a shot of morphine in my coffee.'

Charlie stepped forward, and she could see the curve of his smiling lips. The sight fed a hunger in her that she'd thought long dead. The cool morning air was no longer quite cool enough.

'You got one of those haemorrhoid rings in your doctor's bag of tricks?' he asked.

'If only.'

Charlie climbed the porch and leaned against another post. He looked up at the sky.

'Are early-morning walks your thing?' she asked.

He shook his head. 'Absolutely not. This is a one-off.'

'As you get older, your body clock changes,' Beth remarked.

'You start to rise earlier.'

'I'm not old enough for that yet. I just happen to be a bit restless.'

'Must be the rock star in you.' Beth sipped her coffee, hoping her trembling was invisible in this low light. 'It's too dark and quiet out here after experiencing that big, bright life of yours all over the country.'

'It will never be too dark or quiet out here for me.'

His scent had drifted up the steps with him, and it was so familiar it made Beth's breath catch in her throat. She remembered going back to her room after hours in the Durack storeroom with Charlie, and how all her senses were filled up with him, shivering as she relived the touch of his fingers on her skin, inhaling his scent with every breath as if he were lying right beside her. She lifted her coffee cup and breathed in the vapours of her hot drink, trying to break his unintentional invasion of her body.

'Last day on the job for you,' he commented, as though he wanted to keep the conversation going but wasn't sure how.

'Yes, for another month. I wonder if today will be as crazy.'

'What's the biggest health problem out here?' he asked.

She considered. 'Overcrowding, probably. Infections spread like wildfire because everyone's piled in together, ten to fifteen people crowded into two-bedroom homes.'

He sighed almost inaudibly and she knew why. This problem was nigh on impossible to fix.

'Also, diabetes and related conditions,' she said.

He lifted his head. 'What would help with that?'

'For most of my patients, the damage was done years ago. If it were up to me to try to address the problem, I'd be focusing on the kids. Preventative stuff.'

'Like?'

Beth faced him more fully. The line of his jaw was visible in the slowly brightening air, and his eyes were on hers, more open and uncertain than she'd seen them since Charlie came back into her life.

'A canteen overhaul. It's great that they provide breakfast at the school, but Coco Pops and Froot Loops should *not* be on the menu. The lunches aren't the best, either. They need more salads, proteins, wholegrains, fruit, pulses — that sort of thing. Less white bread, tinned spaghetti and pies.'

Charlie nodded thoughtfully. 'Right.'

He kept his gaze on her face as the sun broke over the horizon. She sipped her coffee, watching him in return. It was a relief to be able to look at him without pretending she wasn't. She explored the changes in his face, her eyes pausing over the stubble on his jaw, the laugh lines starting around his currently serious mouth.

'How do I know you were telling me the truth yesterday?' he asked suddenly, almost blurting the words.

Beth's stomach tightened. She turned back towards the road and stared at the sky, hoping it would take some of the sting out of what he'd said. After a few breaths, she was able to reply. 'You don't. I suppose you just need to make your own decision.'

He was silent. Anger rattled through her, making the hand holding her coffee shake.

'What does it matter, anyway?' Her bitterness spilled out. 'I hoped that knowing the truth would give you some peace of mind — but obviously not.'

She made to step away from the post so she could go back inside the house, but Charlie shot out a hand and caught her wrist.

'Hang on.' She had stilled as soon as he touched her but he didn't let go, although his big hand loosened slightly. 'I'm sorry. It's . . . it's been a bloody strange night. I haven't even slept.'

'Been awake trying to find the holes in my story?' she asked coolly.

'Come on, Beth.'

He was still holding her. She looked at his hand on her arm, then up at his face. He had that same vulnerable anxiety in his eyes that she'd dreamed about in the early hours of the morning. As much as she wanted to shake him off and walk away, Beth couldn't.

Charlie relinquished her arm at last and took a step back. 'We need to talk. Don't walk away from me,' he said, a plea in his voice.

'*You* did,' she answered.

He sagged against the post and pulled a hand through his hair. Beth ached to do something — anything — to get them past this moment of limbo. Slap him. Kiss him. She couldn't do either, of course. All she could do was stand there holding her cooling coffee, watching the dawn light colour Charlie and the rest of the world tangerine.

'Did you ever consider contacting me?' she

asked. 'Even just to shout at me?'

He nodded. 'I did. A lot.'

'So why didn't you?'

He shrugged. 'I was already completely humiliated. I couldn't handle the thought of you laughing at me.'

She stared. 'You didn't even know me, did you?'

His eyebrows tugged down. 'Bullshit. I knew you.'

'Then how could you have thought that? How could you have thought I would do what Leanne and Lyall said I did, and then laugh in your face about it? You didn't know me at all, Charlie.'

Her words seemed to cut him. 'It wasn't that I didn't know you, it was just that I was scared of looking like even more of a fool.'

'Seems like a lot to throw away for your pride.' Beth wished she hadn't said that as soon as the words were out. In one short statement, she'd admitted how important their love had been to her. She had her pride too.

But it seemed he already knew, because Charlie didn't bat an eyelid. 'I realise that now,' he said. 'I was naive. I didn't think anyone would lie about stuff like that. I doubted it when it was just coming from one person, but when someone else backed it up, I figured it was case closed. Maybe it wasn't the most sensible conclusion to reach, but I was a bit of a hothead, I suppose.'

'Just a bit.'

'You thought I'd taken off,' he countered. 'You thought I'd taken off and I didn't give a damn about you. Shows how well you knew *me*.'

Beth raised her eyebrows. 'You *did* take off. I had no way of contacting you. What was I supposed to think?'

Charlie slumped back against the post and was silent for a long moment. 'All right. Yeah, you're right. I was the one who screwed up.'

Clearly, he enjoyed admitting this as much as she was enjoying the thought of a long drive with a tailbone injury. But she was relieved that he *had* admitted it. They watched the sun gleam through the scrubby trees across the street, the orange of dawn transforming into brighter, bluer daylight.

'I'm going fishing with some of the other blokes today,' he said. 'Hoping to bring back a feed for a mob over at Harvey's.' There was a long pause before he added, 'You should come over for dinner.'

'Are you coming back to Mount Clair with me tomorrow?' she asked.

'Yeah. I've got no other transport.'

Beth flicked the dregs of her coffee onto the dirt. 'I wasn't sure if you were thinking of staying longer and catching a lift back with someone else.'

'No, I'll go with you — if that's okay?'

Beth nodded. The prospect of the drive back alone with him didn't seem so bad any more. 'If I'm still sore, I might get you to drive, if you don't mind.'

'No problem.' He glanced her way. 'It'd be a *bummer* if you knocked your injury. But I promise not to make you the *butt* of any jokes.'

Beth groaned, but couldn't suppress a smile.

'You're such a *crack-up*,' she told him. Charlie laughed.

Noise arose in the house, and Beth guessed Pearl was up, thumping her way to the bathroom where her special potty sat on the floor. Charlie dropped down the step off the porch and rammed a hand in his pocket, nodding at Beth.

'Catch you later.'

She went inside to check on Pearl.

12

Beth's hopes for a quieter day went unmet. Knowing this was her last day in town, the ones who'd been putting off their visits made the effort to come in. It was so packed in the clinic that Maud and Christine started to filter the queue, checking out the complaints and conditions, assessing whether they were urgent, could be dealt with by one of the nurses, or could wait until Beth's next visit. Mary was there for a couple of hours but it got too crazy even for her, and she took Pearl home late in the morning.

'You better see Billy again before you go,' Maud said with a sigh, rubbing her forehead. 'His ulcers are acting up. You been out fishing again, you silly prick,' she barked at him. 'Standing in the murky bloody water.'

'Come through, Billy,' Beth told him before he could snap back at Maud. 'Why don't you and Christine finish up now?' she said to Maud, who was obviously past the point of no return. 'I'll lock up the clinic and drop the key off to you later.'

Neither argued. They packed up and left with an air of relief.

Beth examined Billy's sores and his foot more generally. He winced with pain. 'Be honest, Billy. How long has it been like this?' she asked.

'Couple weeks.' He shrugged.

'One week? Two? Or longer — like five or six weeks?'

He shrugged again, discomfort in his face. 'Maybe a couple months, I s'pose.'

Beth cleaned and dressed Billy's foot ulcers, gave him painkillers and yet another dose of antibiotics, then told him he needed to come into town for a stay in hospital.

'I can give you a lift,' she said. 'Tomorrow.'

'Nah.' He seemed alarmed. 'It's not that bad.'

'Billy, these ulcers are necrotic. That means the flesh is dying, and it's spreading. If we don't sort it out urgently, you might lose a foot.'

'Bullshit.' He looked deeply uncomfortable. 'It's just midge bites. Doesn't even hurt.'

Billy couldn't be more than mid-forties, but he looked much older. Beth sat opposite him, keeping her eyes on his face. 'Your diabetes means your blood doesn't move around your body like it should, and that makes your nerves die off so you don't feel much pain when you hurt yourself. Any sores and scratches you get don't heal as well, either, because the blood's not flowing past, keeping everything healthy. You need to come to the hospital and put your feet up for a few days so we can heal those sores. Then you need to start wearing boots or water shoes when you go fishing, Billy, or it will happen again.' She looked him in the eye. 'Now, will you come to town with me, or do I need to send an ambulance for you?'

His lips twisted with vexation. 'I gotta coach the footy kids.'

'You won't be able to run around on the field

183

with them if you only have one foot.'

Billy swore. 'All right, all right. I'll get a lift in with Kanga on the weekend. He's going in to stay with rellies.'

'Perfect. I'll tell the hospital you're coming, and they'll call me when you arrive.'

Beth checked the outer room, but it was empty, and night had fallen. She wondered if dinner was definitely happening at Harvey's place.

'Can I give you a lift somewhere, Billy?'

'Yeah, me dad's place. We caught a good feed of fish down the waterhole today.'

Beth raised her eyebrows. 'So Maud was right. You *were* fishing in the muddy waterhole.'

He had the decency to look slightly ashamed. She stuck an adhesive waterproof cover over his dressing, and Billy waited in his thongs and clean dressings that wouldn't be clean for long. Beth packed up her gear and pulled out the gifts for Maud and Christine that she'd been concealing in her bag all week. Fancy stationery holders in new-season colours — rose gold and pastel aqua, full of matching pens, staplers, tape dispensers, markers and other office essentials. She knew Maud in particular would go crazy over them. She loved 'tarting up' the clinic, as Christine called it. Beth added organic, sugar-free lollies and a load of bright stickers to give the kids getting their shots, and locked up.

She and Billy loaded her gear into the Beast before Beth got behind the wheel, surreptitiously bundling an old towel onto the seat so she was elevated off her tailbone. She drove down to

Mary's house first to see what was happening with the evening meal.

'Thought you'd never bloody finish,' Mary called through the screen door. 'We're going over to Harvey's for tea.'

'Hop in,' Beth called back.

Mary, Jill and Pearl filled up her back seat.

'You got her booster?' Beth asked Jill, and the girl groaned. 'We're not moving until she's in it.'

Jill jumped out again and dashed back to the house for Pearl's booster seat. It was mouldering on the rear verandah, covered in dust and cobwebs. Jill gave it a bang on the porch post as she ran back and shoved it under Pearl.

Mary wheezed a laugh. 'It's the only time we use the bloody thing, when you're in town, Doc.'

Beth hoped that was simply because they didn't own a car. She dropped in at Christine's house to give her the key to the clinic and a grateful hug, then they drove to Harvey's place, which was lit up and heaving with people. Harvey had an older-style fibro house instead of one of the new cyclone-rated, insulated transportables. It was built back from the road, so parties at Harvey's were held out the front — and that meant lots of gatecrashers. Kids were running around on the road, kicking a footy or playing spotlight with torches. A fire burned in the centre of the broad, sandy yard.

'Hope you and Uncle Charlie caught a lotta fish,' Jill said to Billy from the back seat.

Pearl jabbered away while Jill unbuckled her and heaved her out, and Beth discerned the word 'footy'. Pearl loved playing with the kids in the dusty road. They regularly chucked the ball her way and cheered for her when she touched it.

Beth caught sight of Charlie. He was standing under a spotlight that was hitched up to the gutter, manning a gleaming stainless-steel barbecue. It looked out of place beside a couple of older, blackened, rickety ones. She was willing to bet it had been his gift to Harvey. No-one could accuse Charlie of being selfish with the money he'd made from his music. Watching him listen to the chatter around him as he checked the status of the fish made Beth wish she'd tidied herself up a little.

Charlie lifted his head and spotted her vehicle. Even at this distance, Beth saw how his face changed, brightening with . . . with interest, she supposed. He straightened, as well. Beth fidgeted with her top and smoothed her hair, then made an effort to climb out of the Beast without looking like she had an injured backside. Her heart was thumping, she noted with disgust. She tried not to look at Charlie's face as she trailed into Harvey's front yard behind Mary and Jill, but it was a fruitless task. He kept checking on her, and she was doing the same thing to him. Was he still trying to work out whether he believed her story?

People called out to her as she wove through the crowd to the front door after Mary, and Beth returned their greetings, making a concerted attempt to keep her eyes off the pale blue T-shirt stretching across Charlie's chest in a way that would make any red-blooded woman stare.

Especially since he was still following her with his amazing eyes, now barely even pretending to listen to the chatter around him. She was almost relieved when she made it through the door and was met inside by a couple of young women.

'Hi, Doc. Hi, Aunty Mary.'

One of the women, Debra, had a baby perched on her hip. She was chopping celery with her spare hand. 'Charlie went and got a whole heap of stuff from the co-op, so we can have salad with the fish.'

'He didn't get spuds, but,' the other woman commented. Cynthia, Beth thought her name was. 'Does he want us to wrap up these sweet potatoes in foil for the fire, d'you reckon?'

Beth examined the ingredients on the table. He'd bought lettuces, capsicums, lemons, bean sprouts, avocados, tomatoes, English spinach . . . *Did he buy out the entire vegetable shelf at the co-op?* He'd picked up a heap of dressings, too. She spied a dusty bottle of balsamic vinegar. It may have been sitting on the co-op shelf for years.

'I've got a great salad recipe,' she offered. 'If you guys do a green salad, I'll do my spinach and sweet potato one.'

'Sounds like something Tish'd make at work,' Cynthia said with a grin, and Beth remembered that she was the older sister of Letitia who worked at the Sawmill.

She smiled at the young woman. 'Not quite that fancy.'

In the absence of a working oven, Beth parboiled and sauteed cubes of sweet potato. She washed the sand off the spinach but it was only one bunch, so she finely sliced a lettuce to add bulk. Then she folded chunks of tinned beetroot and sweet potato through with olive oil and the balsamic vinegar, squeezed some lemon and sprinkled salt and pepper over the lot. Beth pushed the bowl back on the bench when it was done, and Mary bent over to stick a fork into it. She munched thoughtfully.

'Bloody good, Doc. And I don't like salad, as a rule.'

'Who does?' Beth laughed. 'Make them taste good, and then people will like them.'

Billy came inside, thongs slapping on the raw concrete floor.

'What ya making?' he asked Debra.

'Salads,' she said.

Billy's lip curled in disgust. 'Bloody rabbit's tucker.'

Debra ignored him. 'What can you do with this one, Doc?' she asked, one-handedly chucking chopped carrots into the enormous garden salad.

Beth cast her eye over it and looked back at the other items scattered across the table.

'Oh, I know,' she said, reaching for the avocados.

She scooped the flesh into a battered metal bowl and poured in a healthy serve of coleslaw dressing, lemon juice and a bit of salt. While she was checking the fridge for something to give it a bit of flavour, she spotted a jar of anchovy spread. It looked okay — not too old or crusty — so she scooped a teaspoon into the bowl, took

188

a fork and whisked like her life depended on it, wincing from the pain the movement caused to her lower back.

'Here, let me,' said Cynthia.

She'd found a rotary whisk in Harvey's drawer and took over from Beth, who checked the pantry for dried herbs. Nothing — but she spied a container of dried parmesan cheese. *Perfect.* She sprinkled it in around Cynthia's quick hands and dipped a spoon in for a taste. Not bad. A pretty close approximation of a pimped Caesar dressing.

'Taste,' she said to Cynthia, and the woman obeyed.

Her eyes opened wide. 'That's bloody good.'

Beth smiled and drizzled it over the garden salad. 'Hopefully our salads have a chance of being eaten, yeah?'

'Hey, you 'member the last doc, Aunty?' Debra nudged Mary.

'The time he came down to Harvey's for a feed?'

Mary burst out laughing. 'Bloody hell, I almost forgot about that.'

She looked at Beth and her broad face trembled with mirth. Debra and Cynthia waited for the story, grinning. They didn't dare tell it. Mary was the boss.

'We had this bloke coming out four times a year back then, before the government made it a monthly thing. White as that piece of bloody butcher's paper there, and a fish out of water. He kept to himself, got through the people he needed to see, then hightailed it outta here as quick as he could every time. But one time, there was bad weather, too bad to fly, and he had to stay over. We asked him round for a feed. Felt sorry for the poor bastard, and anyway, he'd helped Edwina with her sick bub, so we were feeling pretty friendly towards him that day. Harvey and the blokes had been out fishing and caught themselves a couple of turtles, and we were baking 'em up on the fire, and this doctor, he caught one look at them and almost keeled over. Said he was sorry but he couldn't eat them. Reckoned he was allergic.' Mary laughed so hard she couldn't speak.

'Allergic to turtles!' Debra plonked herself into a chair and popped out a nipple for her baby, who had started grizzling. 'Like he'd even bloody know!'

'Remember what he said?' Cynthia was giggling. 'Said he was allergic to shellfish! Even I know turtles aren't bloody shellfish.'

Beth couldn't help a laugh. She was lucky — she'd been raised in Mount Clair and knew a little about bush tucker. She'd never been offered turtle, but she had tasted crocodile. And camel.

'Salads are all done,' Mary decreed, and led the way back outside.

Charlie looked around as Beth came through the door, and that ridiculous thrill of nervous tension shot through her again. *Gawd, who invited the high school girl?* Then the food was ready and everyone lined up for a paper plate of fish or a sausage. Beth normally felt relaxed and included during her time in the line to eat, people teasing and chatting around her, but knowing Charlie was serving screwed her up tight inside. She kept a smile glued to her face, pretending to listen to the chatter around her, until at last she was there at the barbecue. Any moment now, her cheeks might ignite in flames. The universe had mistimed things, however, and Harvey was the one who served her. Charlie was loading up someone else's plate and practically dropped the bit of fish he had in his tongs because he was too busy looking at Beth. Her cheeks survived the moment and she found herself a seat on the edge of the verandah with a plate of food, Charlie no longer in sight.

Mary demanded everyone take a bit of salad, and there was praise for the flavours. Even the kids were sighted eating greens. Beth was declared the salad master, although the grilled sooties were the real heroes of the day. After they'd eaten, everyone settled down in chairs, on paving slabs or even in the dirt around the half-barrel fire. The conversation trickled on. As the night grew late, many departed, until only a dozen or so diehards were left, including Mary, who was never averse to a social occasion.

There were so many moments when Beth had looked over at Charlie to find his gaze on her that she felt jittery. She would have no clue what to say to him if he approached her right now. She sat and listened to the talk around her, as gentle and ephemeral as a babbling creek. Across the fire, just beside the point where she'd been allowing her gaze to fall, Charlie stood and made as though he was coming around to join her.

191

Jill stopped him with his guitar and a camp stool. 'Everyone wants you to play, Uncle Charlie.'

It was the second-best thing to having him come around and join her, and a lot less panic-inducing. Charlie sat on the camp stool and tuned his guitar, focusing on the strings — which gave Beth the opportunity to really study him. She let her eyes roam all over him, from his roughly swept-back hair to his eyebrows frowning over the guitar-tuning; from his lean jaw to his full mouth, the bottom lip caught absently between his teeth while he concentrated. His muscular shoulders to his narrow waist; his sinewy forearms to his nimble fingers — and all the way down his jeans to those worn leather boots.

Holy hell — almost two decades later, he was even sexier than he'd been at eighteen. How was that even legal?

Then Charlie played, and Beth was again swept up in the aching beauty of his music. He sang once or twice, tunes the group knew, and they sang along. But mostly he just played a gentle, rambling melody, the soundtrack to their conversation. She didn't dare look at him this time, because if he saw her face, he would know exactly how his playing made her feel. Beth kept her chin on her arms and her eyes on the fire, fighting the temptation to glance up and meet his eyes. It was bad enough to be feeling these things, without revealing them as well.

A wail cut the air. That was Pearl. Jill jumped up, dashing for the road where two or three kids were still kicking the footy around. Beth stood, watching as Jill scooped up her little sister and inspected her, then crossed back to Beth.

'She stacked it,' said Jill. 'She's bleeding.'

Beth checked the grazed knee but it wasn't anything serious. A clean-up and a bandaid would fix it. Pearl had gone quiet and Beth started to tell her she'd be fine, but the little girl's expression stopped her words. Pearl was limp in her sister's arms, her eyelids drooping.

'Pearl,' Jill said, giving her a little shake. 'Pearl!' She caught Beth's eye. 'See? She zones out sometimes.'

In a flash, Beth knew what she'd been trying to remember early that morning: the vision of Pearl's eyelids flickering and drooping as she watched her Disney movie the night before. This was exactly the same thing. She took Pearl from Jill and carried her into the house, watching her little face with concern. Pearl blinked and focused on Beth for a moment, before drifting off again, her eyelids fluttering. In the living room, under the light of a fluoro tube, it was abundantly clear what was going on. Beth lowered the child gently onto the sofa and waited.

The screen door banged and more people joined them, but Beth was only interested in Pearl at that moment. The big dark eyes were on hers again within seconds, and Pearl's face screwed up into tears.

'Shhh,' Beth whispered, dropping her face down to kiss Pearl's forehead. 'You're okay. Just a bump on your knee. You were very brave.'

Gradually, Pearl calmed down and permitted Beth to clean her graze and place a SpongeBob bandaid over the injury. Beth looked up and found Mary and Charlie hovering nearby, waiting. They'd seen her reaction; they knew something was wrong.

'Jill, could you give Pearl a cuddle for a few minutes, and maybe sing her a song?' Beth asked.

Jill nodded but she looked worried too; she'd also realised something was up. Beth gave the girl a reassuring smile and left her to sing to Pearl, who sniffled in her sister's arms. She headed for the kitchen, followed by Charlie and Mary.

'That was a seizure,' Beth said when she was sure they were out of Jill's earshot. There was no point hedging around the truth.

Mary looked astounded. 'What?'

'An absence seizure. Jill's mentioned Pearl zoning out. Does it happen a lot?'

'What's an absence seizure?' Charlie interrupted.

'Most people understand seizures as shaking or spasming. This is a specific type, where Pearl simply blanks out for short periods. She goes quiet, can't see or hear anything. She might even look like she's daydreaming.'

'That's a seizure?' Mary looked aghast. 'She does that a lot. At least a few times a day.'

Beth's heart dropped. She looked at Charlie.

'What does it mean?' he asked.

'I'm not sure. We'll need to do scans. She could have epilepsy.' She looked at him warily.

194

'She needs to come to town for tests, I'm afraid.'

He cast a frantic look at the living room, where one of his nieces was singing to the other.

'Epilepsy . . . ' Charlie turned his attention back to Beth. 'What does she need?'

'She needs to be in hospital while we work out exactly what's going on. There are medications that work really well to control seizures, but we need to be sure of what's causing them and get a proper diagnosis.' She watched his tight mouth. 'She might need to stay in the ward for a few days. If it's more complicated than Mount Clair can handle, they'll send her to Darwin.'

'Is it bad for her? The absence thing?' Mary asked.

'Seizures aren't normal. She's basically losing consciousness several times a day. If she starts school without controlling the seizures, she'll struggle — and it can be dangerous because she could collapse without warning.' Beth transferred her gaze to Charlie's face, knowing he was the one she had to convince right now. 'Also, her seizures may worsen. They might look harmless right now, but she could end up having more violent seizures, which would be very scary for her.'

He pulled his hand through his hair and dropped his eyes to the floor again — the move that showed Beth just how distressed Charlie was. She reached out to put a hand on his shoulder, which was what Dr Paterson always did when someone was upset, but recalled halfway there that this was Charlie Campbell, and they had a shitload of history. She pulled her hand back sharply and placed it on the back of her neck. Charlie looked up.

'Can we take her back to Mount Clair with us tomorrow? Or is it more urgent than that?'

'No, she'll be fine overnight.' Beth looked around Mary to check on Jill and Pearl, snuggled up together on the sofa. 'Jill will probably want to come to town too.'

Charlie shook his head. 'Jill can stay here. I don't want her missing school. I'll look after Pearl while she's in Mount Clair.'

Beth suspected he'd have a fight on his hands but said nothing.

'I'd better get them home to bed,' Mary said.

Beth agreed. 'Disrupted sleep patterns can have an impact on how often the seizures occur.'

'Shit,' Mary muttered, and Beth realised she'd inadvertently made the woman feel guilty but couldn't think of a way to unsay it.

'She's still our little Pearl,' she tried, pulling her keys out of her pocket. 'She's going to be all right. She just needs the right medicine. She'll be back home in no time, tearing up the footy field.'

Mary called to Jill, and they said a hasty goodbye to the remaining partygoers.

'I'll pop round tomorrow,' Beth heard Mary say to Harvey — code for *I'll fill you in on the important news when we have some privacy.*

Charlie walked them to the Beast and helped Jill buckle Pearl into her seat.

'The doc and I are taking Pearl to town for a visit tomorrow,' he told his teenage niece.

Beth practically heard Jill's sense of injustice snap to attention. 'To town! Let me come.'

'No.' His voice was firm. 'You've got school.'

'Bullshit! This is bullshit!' Jill sounded close to tears and Pearl squawked in protest.

'Watch your mouth,' he said, but Beth heard veiled sympathy. 'You've got school, and Aunty Mary needs you here.'

The girl was silent, but clearly desperate to argue. Best to get her away from here before this turned into a shouting match. Beth started the engine and Charlie shut the back door, tapping the side of the car as a farewell. He watched them drive away. Beth knew this because she was watching him in the rear-view mirror.

'It's not fair,' Jill burst out as soon as she thought it was safe. 'I look after Pearl. If she's sick, I should be there.'

'Button up, Jill,' Mary said comfortably.

'But — '

'Hey,' Beth interjected, her voice rising over Jill's. 'How about we talk about this in a little while? We don't want *anyone* getting unnecessarily concerned, do we?'

Jill caught her meaning and glanced down at Pearl beside her. She clamped her mouth shut, conceding Beth's point but no less pissed off. They arrived at Mary's house within a couple of minutes and Mary said she would sort Pearl out for bedtime. Jill watched Mary carry Pearl off to her little room and turned to Beth.

'What's wrong with her?' she asked, her young face suddenly frightened.

Beth explained the seizures and, because Jill looked so shocked, took her out onto the porch for some fresh air. It was there that the girl started to cry. Beth hugged her tight.

'It's going to be okay,' she said, stroking Jill's hair. 'Pearl's going to be fine.'

'I don't understand why Uncle Charlie won't let me go with her,' she wept. 'I'm the closest one to her.'

'I know, but it makes more sense for you to stay here. I don't know how long we'll need to keep Pearl in town. It might take a while to get the test results and get her medication sorted out. Charlie doesn't want you missing so much school.'

'If he'd let me go to school in town, it wouldn't be a problem,' Jill said, sniffing.

'If I get the right moment, I'll bring that up,' said Beth. 'I haven't forgotten. It's just, things have been . . . '

'Tense?' Jill hazarded, and Beth shot her a quick look.

'Busy.'

Jill rubbed her face with her arm but kept her gaze on Beth.

'Why doesn't he trust me?'

'I don't think it's *you* he doesn't trust, Jill. It's other people.'

'I'm not stupid. I wouldn't get into trouble. And I would *stay*,' Jill added stoutly. 'I wouldn't throw away the opportunity like Uncle Charlie did.'

Beth's heart ripped a little to think of Charlie giving up on school because of his stupid mistake about her. But the same thought gave rise to her anger. *How could he think that of me?*

'How did it happen, Doc?' Jill asked, and for a

moment Beth feared the girl knew what was going through her mind. 'Why's she got seizures?'

Beth breathed again. 'I'm not sure yet. Epilepsy can be quite common in people with cerebral palsy. You remember I told you about how Pearl got CP?'

'From not getting enough oxygen when Mum was having her?'

'Yes. That can cause epilepsy, too.'

Jill stared gloomily at the dark street. 'I just want her to get better.'

Beth put an arm around her. 'I believe we can make this better. She just needs a little stay in hospital. You hold the fort here, help Aunty Mary out, and your uncle will have Pearl back in no time.'

Jill didn't answer, and just looked more dissatisfied than ever.

13

Pearl was excited for the first part of the trip, babbling and asking questions. Then she grew restless, complaining that she was hungry, thirsty, needed to go to the toilet. Finally, after they'd stopped for a toilet break, stuffed her full of sandwiches and entertained her with I-spy for what felt like hours, she fell asleep, her water bottle clutched to her chest.

'Thank Christ for that,' Charlie breathed, sinking back against his car seat.

Beth glanced at the rear-view mirror. 'At last.'

'How are you holding up?' he asked. 'I'll drive, if you want.'

He was referring to her sore tailbone, she realised. 'I'm okay for now, but I'll probably take you up on that before much longer.'

They were being so civilised. It was a long way from the awkward drive out with the Minister for Mining and his assistant. They were even discussing her rather embarrassing injury in a mature manner. Beth pushed away thoughts of the vast unspoken issue between them. They had other priorities right now.

'I'll come into the hospital with you to get Pearl admitted,' she said.

'I don't know how she'll go in hospital,' he said. 'She's never really been away from Jill. Will they let me stay, if she's freaking out?'

'Yes, definitely. They won't want her distressed.

If it's quiet and they have spare beds, they'll let you bunk in with Pearl. If there're no beds, you can still stay but you'll be stuck in a chair.'

'That's fine.'

The track had evened out, Beth noted with relief. They'd be back on sealed roads any minute now.

'I'm sorry you got hurt,' he said out of the blue.

'Uh — thanks.'

'No, I mean, *I'm sorry*. I caused it. What I said . . . shocked you. I don't think you would have fallen over if I hadn't said that. You're not exactly the clumsy type.'

'I have my fair share of klutz moments. That was a pretty stellar effort, though. I just hope it's not dislocated.'

'Better than a fracture, right?'

She gave a short laugh. 'Not if you know how they relocate it.'

He thought about that for a minute — just long enough for her to regret saying it. When she risked a glance his way, he was grinning. She rolled her eyes.

'Laugh it up.'

'Hopefully it's just bruised,' he said, but the grin remained.

'Anyway,' she went on in a tone that said *let's move on*, 'it definitely wasn't your fault.'

The smile disappeared. 'Not this time, maybe,' he muttered, and Beth's pulse seemed to bump along as erratically as the rough track.

They drove in silence for some time. At last they hit the turn-off to the highway and she brought the Beast to a halt, pulling on the handbrake.

'Hello, bitumen,' Beth said with a sigh of relief. 'Would you drive for a bit now?' she asked Charlie.

In answer, he got out and came around the front of the vehicle. Beth adjusted the seat so he could climb in more easily, and when she turned around he had opened her door and reached out to help her. There was nothing else for it but to take his hand and allow him to take some of her weight for her descent. Was it her — uncharacteristically fertile — imagination, or did he hold her hand an instant longer than he needed to? When he released her, she stretched gingerly, trying to work out how she felt about his sweetness, and his guilt about her fall. His beautiful eyes and strong, warm hands. *Ugh*. She didn't need to work out how she felt. She knew exactly how she felt, because her heart was racing and her cheeks were warm, and she was getting those old *Charlie* emotions — the ones where she glowed with the joy of feeling special and adored.

This was utterly insane.

They hadn't even worked through the stuff that had happened between them — not properly. She didn't know him any more. Seventeen years of gaping absence and Beth had no idea what Charlie had done during that time, what he'd been like. Who else he'd hurt. He knew nothing about her, either. He didn't know her habits, her tastes, her friends — what she cared about. As she climbed into the passenger seat, Charlie turned around to check on Pearl, still in an angelic repose in her booster seat.

Well, that was one thing she knew they both cared about.

In a strange, inexplicable way, it felt as though she did still know Charlie. She could read his feelings no matter how he tried to hide them, and she was pretty sure he saw straight through her as well.

Still, it was insane. She shouldn't be so hasty to forgive. Or heal. Or *feel*. She'd always jumped in too quickly with Charlie — in every way — and there was no way she would be so stupid again.

★   ★   ★

Getting Pearl admitted to hospital was the easy part. Beth hadn't counted on how unsettled or tearful Pearl would be. The toddler wailed unstoppably, repeating one word over and over until Beth's head was competing with her tailbone for the title of most painful body part. She could see Charlie was tense about the whole situation. Maybe Pearl was picking up on that.

'What's she saying?' she asked him over Pearl's screaming, snotty face.

He shook his head in frustration. 'I can't make it out. No, Pearl,' he said when she tried to clamber off the hospital bed for the umpteenth time.

'It sounds like *dummy*,' Beth said, frowning. 'She doesn't suck a dummy, does she?'

'No.' He caught his niece as she clambered

towards the end of the bed once again.

Beth watched Pearl's tearful face for a few moments as the child fought her uncle, waving her arms. She followed Pearl's line of sight and saw the girl's bag sitting on a chair. Beth crossed to the grubby Barbie backpack and unzipped it, digging through Pearl's clothes in case there was a pacifier in there after all. If Pearl still sucked a dummy, now wasn't the time to put her on restricted access. Her hand landed on a tatty toy elephant and she pulled it out. Maybe Pearl would appreciate something to cuddle, too.

'Gummy!' Pearl shouted, then dissolved into more wailing, reaching frantically for the elephant.

'This is Gummy?' Beth brought it to Pearl, who snatched it out of her hand. She immediately hooked it under one arm, shoved her thumb into her mouth, and brought her other hand up to twiddle her ear. Classic self-soothing. She hiccuped a small sob, and Charlie let out a long breath.

'Gummy. Her elephant. I bought her the damn thing. I completely forgot that she asks for it when she's upset. God, what an idiot.' He gave Beth a rueful look. 'Uncle fail.'

She laughed, more from relief than amusement. 'Thank Christ Jill packed it.'

Charlie kicked off his boots and climbed up on the bed beside Pearl, pulling her into a cuddle. Her eyes began to droop, and for a moment Beth thought a seizure might be starting, but it seemed she was just tired. The child sighed and wiped her damp face against her uncle's T-shirt.

'Thanks for staying through all of that,' Charlie said to Beth, ignoring the fact that his shirt was now smeared with toddler mucus. 'Might be a good opportunity to get your war wound checked out,' he added. 'Being here at the hospital, I mean.'

'That's not a bad idea.' She looked him over, then remembered she shouldn't do that and pretended to check that Pearl's patient chart was in place. 'Hope you get some sleep.'

He smiled. 'Not likely. But thanks.'

Beth said goodbye and left the room. She made her way down to the radiography department and begged for an X-ray. Eunice Obwalden was the formidable nurse on shift and she caught the young radiographer before he left for the day. Beth recognised him from her most recent networking event.

'Harry, Beth's gone and bashed up her tailbone,' Eunice said in a voice the whole ward could hear. 'Can you take a quick squiz?'

Harry looked about twenty, although Beth knew he must be older. 'Have you seen anyone about it yet?' he asked, by which she understood he was asking if she'd had a rectal exam.

'No. I thought I'd cut out the middleman,' she said with a weak smile.

He chuckled. 'Fair call. Come on through and we'll throw some electrons at you.' He scanned her clothing. 'You got metal buttons on those shorts?'

She checked. 'Yes.'

'Better pop you in a gown, then,' he said.

He asked the standard questions and, once

she'd answered to his satisfaction, invited her to hop onto the table. Beth lay on her side in her underwear and a hospital gown while Harry took the images. She'd worn a hospital gown before for mammograms and had never been bothered by them, although she'd heard plenty of complaints. They were clean and roomy, she thought — what was the big deal? But as she got off the table, the gown got caught underneath one leg and gaped, so she unintentionally gave Harry an eyeful of her stomach, knickers and thighs. She scrambled to pull it shut again and reminded herself that he was a professional. He probably saw that happen twenty times a day. Harry left her to get dressed, then she sought him out in the consulting room.

'Good news,' he said. 'Tailbone's intact, not dislocated. You've avoided the rubber glove by the skin of your nose.'

'If that's my nose, you must be looking at the X-ray upside down,' she said, and he guffawed. 'It's just bruised, then?' Beth peered at the image on the light box, searching for any sign of anomalies — masses, tumours, lesions. She was no radiographer but everything looked pretty normal. When she pulled back, Harry was watching her.

'Did you suspect something more sinister?' he asked.

She shot him a self-conscious smile. 'I was just checking for paranoia. There it is — a great big lump of it beside the hypochondrial gland.'

Harry grinned at her. 'You finished for the day? Want to go grab something to eat?'

'I drove five and a half hours today, and I have an appointment with my bed,' she said. 'But thank you. Next time.'

'I'll hold you to that,' he said, and she realised from his expression that he meant it. *What's he doing, chatting up doctors at least ten years his senior?* Maybe it was difficult to meet women in Mount Clair.

Beth thanked him again and he walked her to the reception area. She hesitated before she stepped out into the car park, thinking about Charlie. What would he do for a meal? Last she'd seen, Pearl had her uncle in a death grip and was half-asleep. She changed her mind about leaving and bade Harry goodbye, zipping over to a snack vending machine. She bought a prepacked BLT and an orange juice and dashed back to the children's ward. Charlie had dimmed the light and had the television on with the volume low. Pearl was curled up, sound asleep in his arms. A wave of tenderness crashed through Beth, so powerful she almost changed her mind and scurried away. *Grow up,* she scowled at herself and entered the room, placing her offerings on the table beside the bed. Charlie looked up, startled.

'Something for your dinner,' she whispered.

Charlie's eyes held hers for a moment that stretched on too long before she wrenched her own gaze away and departed.

At home, she checked her phone while she waited for a frozen curry portion to heat up. A message arrived from Charlie.

Thank you. For everything.

Beth hastened to turn on the television and watch something silly and lighthearted so she would stop picturing his face and feeling his lips on that spot under her ear.

★　★　★

Beth woke at seven. She hadn't bothered with an early alarm, since she couldn't run properly while her lower back was still so sore. Her thoughts flew to Pearl and Charlie. She had work today and it would probably be a long day, but she could message him to ask about the test results. Then she would visit them in the evening. In fact, if Pearl was still being clingy, she could offer him a break. She would stay with Pearl so that Charlie could go back to Mounties for a shower and some dinner.

Decision made, she got ready and dived into her workday. Free left her a message during the morning to ask Beth to join her and Finn for Friday-night drinks at their place. Normally, Beth would have enjoyed that. Pubs weren't really her scene any more — too noisy. She preferred quiet get-togethers. But today she sent her excuses.

Willow messaged as well. *It feels like someone released a flying insect in my belly. Is that normal?*

Beth replied, grinning. *You just felt your baby move.*

This is the weirdest thing I've ever been through.

Lloyd Rendall phoned during the course of

the afternoon but Beth missed the call. He didn't leave a message so she didn't bother to call back, but it stirred the memory of his community relocation idea. Beth checked whether he'd sent more information yet. Still nothing. She fired off an email to him.

Hi Lloyd,

Don't forget to send through the details of Gargantua's relocation idea. I can't discuss it with the Madjinbarra elders if there's nothing for me to show them.

She added a smiley face to pretend she was being amicable and signed off. Then she took a steadying breath and messaged Charlie.

Any word on Pearl's tests yet?

He replied a short time later. *Not yet. Doctor's coming by in the late afternoon to discuss. Pearl's much happier today. She's made a friend.*

That made her smile. She sent a reply to let him know she'd drop by the hospital after work and he responded with a thumbs up.

Between appointments, Carolyn popped her head around the door. 'Got a second?'

'Yep, what's up?'

Carolyn came in and shut the door. 'Not that it means anything, necessarily — as you know — but your cervical test came back with a follow-up recommendation.'

Beth went cold. 'What is it?'

Carolyn gave her a long look. 'The usual — atypical cells. But we'll get a gynae to do a colposcopy to be safe, yes?'

Beth nodded, heart thumping. She saw

Carolyn staring at Beth's hands and looked down to find they were clenched together and shaking.

'It'll just be inflammation,' Carolyn said.

'I have a family history.'

'I know, but that was breast cancer, and you know there are no credible links between breast and cervical cancer, don't you? You're *not* at heightened risk, Beth. And anyway, how often have you sent a patient for a colposcopy and had it come back clear?'

'I know, I know.' Beth attempted to control her shaking.

Carolyn watched her with worried eyes. 'You don't have any other family history, do you?'

Beth hesitated over the words. She'd never admitted this to anyone before — maybe not even herself. 'My grandmother — Mum's mother — she died of cancer too.'

Carolyn's brow creased ever so slightly. 'What sort?'

'I'm not sure. Mum never told me about it. I only found out from Dad a few years ago. He didn't know what sort of cancer but thought maybe bowel.'

Carolyn's frown deepened. 'How old was your mum when she was diagnosed?'

Beth cleared her throat. 'Forty-two.'

'Do you know if your mum's cancer was linked to a BRCA-1 or -2 mutation?'

'No, not sure.'

'And you're, what, thirty-four?' Carolyn paused. 'Now might be a good time, if you're thinking of getting the genetic testing done.'

'I've tried not to be ruled by my fears,' Beth said. 'That's why I haven't gone for genetic testing before.'

'I understand, but it might put your mind at ease. While you don't know, every pain or funny test result is going to freak you out.'

This was true — just look at her paranoia over the bruised tail-bone. Beth imagined getting a bad result; learning she had between a thirty and eighty per cent chance of developing breast cancer. *Hell.* What would she do? She would need to get a preventative mastectomy. She'd have to get Willow and Free to do tests, too. Oh, God, what if one of *them* tested positive —

'Beth?'

Beth blinked and focused back on Carolyn. 'Yes, you're right. Can you write me a request for the genetic test? I'll make an appointment with Bainbridge for the colposcopy.'

Unexpectedly, Carolyn leaned in and hugged her. 'I know this is like telling you not to breathe, but could you do me a favour and try not to stress out over this? Almost every woman gets a dodgy test result once or twice in her life and it usually means nothing. You're healthy and have everything going your way. And once you've had the genetic test, you'll feel so much better — free of the burden of worry.'

Unless it comes back positive.

'Yes, I know.' Beth forced a smile. 'And if it's positive, I can take control. It's the wisest thing to do.'

Carolyn squeezed her shoulder and departed. Fingers still trembling, Beth tapped out an email to the hospital's head gynaecologist to ask for an appointment. Once the cells had been biopsied, they could — hopefully — rule out cancer. Or pre-cancer. She wouldn't put off the genetic testing any longer, either. Time to take control of this cancer fear that had hung above her for all these years.

Beth shoved the thoughts to the back of her mind and got on with her schedule. When her day's appointments were complete, she cleared out as quickly as she could. She didn't want any delays to stop her from seeing Pearl before the child went to sleep for the night.

The Beast was waiting for her in the clinic car park, its sides coated with a thick layer of red dust. Normally, she took it through the car wash the day after she got home, but Beth was too busy to worry about that right now.

Charlie was right about Pearl having found a friend. She and a little boy with a bandaged head were seated together on one bed, an array of plastic animals between them. They were alternately creating zoos and simulating attacks. Pearl used a zebra to savage her friend's tiger as he watched, quite solemn. Then his tiger attacked her hippopotamus while Pearl squealed with excitement.

Beth caught the boy's mother's eye and the woman shrugged. 'It keeps them entertained.'

Pearl noticed Beth and gestured at her with the zebra. Beth went over and kissed the top of her curly head, pausing to listen to Pearl's enthusiastic gabbling as she showed her each animal.

'That's a lovely bunch of animals, Pearl,' she told her. 'Where's Uncle Charlie?'

'Dunno.' Pearl launched another zebra ambush on her playmate's elephant.

Beth went to find Charlie. He was in the waiting area, standing in discussion with the paediatrician. He saw her and waved. Dr Bernard Grahame looked around.

'Oh, hello, Dr Paterson,' he said, smiling under his grey moustache. 'Pearl's your patient, I believe.'

'Yes. What are we looking at?'

'Mr Campbell tells me you suspected epilepsy characterised by absence seizures. Spot-on. We witnessed two of the seizures today. Mr Campbell caught one of them on his phone camera — very quick thinking. And the other was observed by a nurse. The scans show some scarring on the brain, probably a result of the damage sustained when she was born. I think that scarring is the focus of the epilepsy but obviously we'll need to do a bit more testing to rule out any other problems — an EEG. In the meantime, we'll try her on a low dose of Ethosuximide to reduce the frequency of the seizures. Then we can increase the dose until we get it right.'

'Is it safe?' Charlie asked. 'The Ethothing?'

'Ethosuximide?' said Bernard. 'Provided she's on the right dose and you don't give her any other medicines without checking with us first, it should be very safe. It's usually our first option in this sort of situation. You might see some side effects — nausea, sleepiness. That's why we'll start low, and in syrup form, since Pearl's not really capable of taking tablets at this stage.' He looked at Beth. 'Who's going to be giving her the medication?'

'Me,' said Charlie. 'And Pearl's older sister.'

'She's fifteen — and very switched-on,' Beth told the doctor when he looked dubious.

Bernard nodded.

'How long do you reckon she'll need to stay in hospital?' Charlie wanted to know.

'She's had her first dose already. We just need you to keep a very close eye on her and record the number and duration of seizures, if there are any. If there are no adverse effects and the EEG is clear, she can be discharged tomorrow.'

'Tomorrow?' Charlie looked surprised. 'That's great. What happens next?'

'Bring her back in to see me next week and we can adjust the medication, if necessary,' said Bernard.

Charlie's brow creased.

'Pearl lives out on a remote community,' Beth explained for Bernard's benefit. 'It's over five hours from here.'

'Ah.' He considered the problem. 'Can she stay in town for a couple of weeks while we get the medication right?'

Charlie nodded. 'But not in the hospital?'

Bernard shook his head with a benevolent smile. 'No, no, she doesn't need to be here the whole time.'

Beth expected to see relief on Charlie's face, but his frown deepened. 'Okay,' he said. 'Thanks.'

The doctor departed and Beth turned to Charlie. 'It's good that she doesn't need to be in hospital very long. Right?'

He nodded. 'I just didn't count on having to find somewhere for us to stay.'

She saw his dilemma. Pearl could hardly stay at Mounties with him. It was loud there and could get rough — not an environment for a child. And definitely not a place for a child suffering from seizures.

'Don't you have any family or friends in town?'

'One or two, but they're mostly in Darwin and Madji.' He stared absently at the ground, as though flipping through a mental Rolodex, hunting for a suitable place to crash for two weeks with a toddler. A newly medicated toddler, with cerebral palsy and epilepsy.

'How about she stays with me?' Beth heard herself asking before her brain had time to intervene.

Charlie met her eyes and gave her a quick smile. 'No, it's fine.'

'If there's nowhere else suitable, then it makes sense. It's good to have a doctor on hand while they're getting her medication right, too.' *Gawd.* She was practically begging him and Pearl to stay with her. Pathetic.

Charlie studied her. 'No, I can't do that to you. You've got work — your business to run. You can't be looking after a kid.'

Ah. He thought she was offering to look after Pearl. 'Yes, I have to work. I meant both of you could stay. At mine. If you want.'

215

'Both of us . . . '

Beth gave a vague shrug, attempting to make it look like she didn't care either way. Then she wanted to undo the action. Charlie was so damn proud. There was no way he would accept her offer unless he thought she actively wanted him to stay —

'Wow. Thank you.' His beautiful eyes had lit up with relief. Warmth. 'I can't think of anywhere else I'd feel okay about staying with her. I mean, the other option is I could book us in to the resort, but she'd be at me all day about the swimming pool, and I don't think she should be in the water right now.'

Beth nodded. She hunted for something to say. 'Are *you* due anywhere soon? Gigs, or touring or whatever?'

'Not for a couple of months. My manager knows I'm trying to fight Gargantua, so I'll be tied up for a while.'

'Well, it's the weekend now, so I'll be at home. Why don't you let me know when Pearl gets discharged, and I'll expect you shortly after that?'

He nodded. 'I'll pick up some DVDs for her to watch. I got her a few toys already today.'

Beth smiled. 'I saw her ferocious zebra. We need to teach her about food chains.' Ugh, that sounded all co-parent-y. 'And don't worry about food,' she added quickly. 'I get a delivery from the supermarket every Saturday, so there will be plenty there.'

'Right, then.' Charlie didn't say anything else. His green eyes wandered over her face until she suspected he could see the blush in her cheeks. Beth turned to leave. 'I'll see you tomorrow.'

★　★　★

Halfway home, Beth decided on a detour. If she went home now, she would turn into a nervy psycho, cleaning her perfectly tidy house in preparation for her guests. She'd already caught herself contemplating baking biscuits. And if it wasn't that, she'd get online and scour medical journals until she terrified herself with too much information about cancer and genetic mutations. She stopped at the bottle-o and picked up a bottle of white — she and Free shared the same favourite — then drove past the busy pub and takeaway shops to Marlu Street. Three cars were on the verge at number 17B. *Hmm.* If it was too noisy for Beth's taste, she could just stay for one drink and then make her excuses.

Free's eyes, a bluer green than Charlie's, opened wide when she saw Beth on the doorstep. 'You came!'

Beth stepped into Free's hug. 'I've missed you.' She handed her the wine. 'Are you guys having a party?'

'Briggsy just picked up pizzas, and Hendo's pretty drunk already,' Free confided. 'I hope they all clear out by nine, because *I Gotta Sing* is on tonight.'

Beth chuckled. She didn't share Free's obsession with reality talent shows, but she sure knew about it.

She was greeted loudly by the crowd and went

around exchanging hugs and kisses. Beth had a soft spot for Briggsy, who was one of the most forward-looking and open-minded police officers she'd ever met. She wasn't quite as keen on his girlfriend, Kate. Beth was only a year older than Kate, so she knew her from school, and remembered how the girl's behaviour had raised eye-brows in the senior common room. As a teen, Kate had been an attention-seeker, and Beth had seen her busting up other people's relationships. As far as Beth could tell, Kate was still a bit that way inclined. Nathan 'Hendo' Henderson was there too, with his bubbly girlfriend, Karlia.

'Oh, my God, Karlz, I forgot to tell you!' Free exclaimed. 'Beth just spent the week with Charlie-freaking-Campbell!'

Karlia turned her attention to Beth, her eyes round with awe. '*What?*'

'No.' Beth tried to laugh it off. 'Not quite. I drove Charlie out to Madjinbarra, where he grew up. And gave him a lift back to town yesterday.'

'What's he like?' Karlia asked. 'I follow all his social profiles. He seems really fun and chatty. His photos are gorgeous.'

Beth struggled to picture Charlie being chatty on social media.

'He's very dedicated to his community,' she said, hoping that would suffice.

'Beth was at high school with him,' Free added, barely waiting for Beth to finish. 'Can you believe it? I nearly died when she told me. And get this — she used to *tutor* him!'

'There were rumours about you two, you

218

know, Beth,' Kate put in, her dark eyes sparkling with mischief — malicious mischief, Beth thought. 'That something was going on.'

Free was in danger of popping out an eyeball or two. '*Was* there something going on?' she breathed.

Beth mustered a casual smile. 'Yes, there was. I was tutoring Charlie in English, maths and biology.'

'There was a girl in my year who absolutely *insisted* you and him were, you know, having a thing,' Kate went on. 'What was her name again?'

Leanne Clegg, Beth thought sourly. 'Good old high school gossip,' she said aloud.

'Charlie was so shy. He hardly talked to anyone.' Kate sighed. 'But so hot.'

'Hey,' Briggsy protested. 'I'm right here, you know.'

Beth was thinking about Charlie being *shy*. He wasn't shy about making a move on her in the school library when the urge took him. He'd never struck her as shy at all. She suspected he was just extremely picky about who he mixed with. He didn't trust people easily.

And people lost his trust easily, too. She was living proof of that. Her anger flashed again. *How could he think that of me?* And yet, just half an hour earlier, she'd invited him to stay at her place indefinitely. What a sucker.

No, I'm just trying to care for a patient —

'Beth?'

'Huh?'

Free bounced in her chair impatiently. 'Is

219

Charlie doing a show in Mount Clair while he's here? The manager at Mounties said he asked him, but Charlie wasn't sure if he could make it happen.'

'As far as I know, he's just here to help Mary and Harvey push back against Gargantua putting in a mine workers' camp right next door to Madjinbarra.'

Finn extricated himself from a discussion about football with Hendo. 'I heard on the radio today that the government's going to make a decision on the mine next week.'

Beth's heart dropped. *So soon?* It wasn't likely to be the result they wanted, not if it was already practically done and dusted. She had better go over Lloyd's relocation offer with Charlie if things were moving this fast.

'I reckon it'll be good for 'em' was Hendo's opinion. 'There's bugger-all work out there at Madjim-whas'name. Gargantua does Indigenous employment. They'll give some of them jobs on the mine and around the camp.'

Briggsy dived into the argument, making all of Charlie's points about the problem of putting a wet mess next to a dry community, but Hendo was drunk and adamant that the mine was a good thing. Beth vaguely recalled that he worked in construction. Perhaps he hoped to get a FIFO job there himself.

She sighed and took a slice of pizza. So much for getting away from thoughts of Charlie.

14

Beth's house had three bedrooms. She spent Saturday morning preparing for her guests — making up the guestroom for Charlie and creating a space for Pearl to stay in the spare room. She kept a few boxes of stuff in there: old Paterson family cookbooks she couldn't bring herself to throw away, shawls crocheted by her grandmother, a collection of photos from her university days and the odd trip she'd taken overseas, a letter her mother had written to her before she died. Beth stacked the boxes in the closet and placed a foam mattress on the floor, making it up with the one and only single sheet set in her linen collection.

She wondered how to make the room welcoming for a three-year-old. Beth had absolutely nothing for children in her house. She made a mad dash to Mount Clair's only department store and bought some picture books and a miniature fold-out lounge with the Barbie logo on it. Pearl appeared to be a fan of Barbie, and she could take it with her when she eventually went home. On impulse, Beth grabbed some lilac bunting and a mobile of felt farm animals from the baby department. She could give them to Willow for the baby once Pearl was gone.

She questioned herself all the way home. God, she was going to look like a complete nutter,

221

decking out her spare room for Pearl's short stay. If she put all this stuff up, it would be fancier than Pearl's own room at home. What if Charlie thought she was trying to ingratiate herself with him, or play Mummy to his niece? She shoved back against her fears. *I bought these things for Pearl because I want her to feel happy and relaxed, goddamnit.* She wasn't trying to manipulate anyone or pretend to be something she wasn't. Why did she always second-guess herself when it came to anything to do with Charlie?

This was a hopeless situation. She should never have invited him to stay. What a god-awful mess.

But Pearl . . .

She was still sticking up bunting when her phone buzzed with a message.

We're done here. What's your address?

Beth texted her address to Charlie and tidied up the blu-tack, scissors and empty packets, surveying her handiwork for a moment. It actually looked really cute in there, with the lilac bunting draped on the wall above Pearl's foam bed, made up in those sage-green sheets, felt animals bobbing from the ceiling fan. The soft pink Barbie mini-sofa sat in the corner with a neat stack of board books within easy reach. Beth pictured Pearl asleep in the bed, thumb in mouth, Gummy the elephant clutched to her chest, and was overcome with warmth and longing.

Hurry up with that baby, Willow. She really needed a niece or nephew in her life.

When Charlie knocked on the door, she'd composed herself somewhat, but it was still a speechless moment for both of them, looking at each other across Beth's doorstep. Pearl broke the tension by reaching for Beth to give her a cuddle.

'Hello, little one. What's going on? Did you have your lunch yet?' Beth carried her inside.

Charlie nodded but Pearl disagreed.

'No. I hungry.'

Charlie's face showed amusement mixed with indignation. He gave a resigned shrug.

Beth chuckled. 'I'd better get you something to eat, then.'

She quickly assembled a platter of finger food for Pearl — cherry tomatoes, cheese sticks, snow peas, and slices of a cold boiled egg she had in the fridge. Beth set her up at the kitchen table, and Pearl proceeded to devour whatever she didn't drop on the floor. Beth tried not to think about the mess Pearl was making. She'd need to brush up those bits of crumbly egg yolk before they found their way onto Pearl's knees or bottom, and ended up ground into the carpet —

'I really appreciate you putting Pearl up like this.' Charlie's voice snapped her out of her fretful neat-freak moment. 'Us,' he added, discomfort in his tone. 'Putting us up.'

'Happy to help. Would you like a tea or coffee?'

'No, thanks.'

Pearl ate, oblivious to the adults' awkwardness, and they stood in the kitchen watching her.

Finally, Beth thought of something they could do.

'You can bring your gear down to the bedrooms, if you like,' she told Charlie.

He picked up Pearl's backpack and followed her down the hall. To Beth's relief, he barely glanced at the pretty bedroom.

'Where's your bag?' she asked him.

'I left it in the car.'

'Oh, well, this is your room.' She indicated the guestroom and he flicked a gaze across its neutral decor.

'Thanks. Nice place you've got.'

'It's not huge but I like it. It's only me here, anyway.' *Way to make him think you're declaring yourself on the market, Beth.* 'Bathroom's in there, and there's a games room but I use it as an office, so it's not very kid-friendly.' The tour concluded in the living room.

Charlie couldn't help an amused glance. 'And the rest of your house *is* kid-friendly?'

Beth glanced around. Glass coffee table, expensive floor-standing vases filled with faux reeds, a white rug. A *white* rug, for goodness sake. She gave him a crooked grin.

'I guess not. This place might be about to get the Pearl treatment.'

'If there's anything you really care about, you might want to shut it in your office,' he answered, a ghost of a smile on his lips.

They went back to the kitchen, Beth thinking about her decor. Was there anything she particularly cared about? Not really. It was just *stuff.*

'I'll move the vases,' she said. 'They might fall on her. Other than that, I'm not worried.'

As if to test the theory, Pearl clambered down and bum-shuffled some egg yolk across the kitchen floor. Charlie scooped her up and brushed off her backside.

'Come and see your room,' he said, carrying her down the hall. 'You're gonna go ape over this.'

Beth hastened to brush Pearl's food scraps into the bin, happiness lighting her up inside when she heard Pearl's appreciative squawk and giggles from down the hall.

Charlie was a good uncle, Beth discovered as the afternoon wore on — and not just because he paid for things. He spent time with Pearl, helping her with her toys so she could play, and reading books to her. Pearl had a new collection of blocks and spent quite a long time building enclosures for her plastic animals while Charlie sat close by, watching her or exchanging messages with people on his phone.

A girlfriend, maybe? Beth wondered, surprised by how flat the thought made her feel. She cast the speculation away and fussed around reorganising drawers in the kitchen, not really achieving anything useful. Normally if she had guests, she would spend time with them. When her father stayed with her, Beth spent hours making tea, nattering about family and friends, baking scones and doing crosswords with him. But the history with Charlie hung between them like a dense fog and she couldn't think of anything to say. Her solution was simply to stay out of their way.

It wasn't possible at all times, of course. When she'd cooked dinner, a ginger beef stir-fry, she was obliged to sit at the table with the two of them. Pearl ignored the vegetables and tucked into the meat and rice, but declared she 'no like' the beef and ended up just eating rice for her dinner. *Hmm, that dish was not a hit.* Beth should have realised the strong flavour of ginger was more of an acquired taste, and stir-fried vegetables would not be terribly palatable to young tastebuds either. Charlie ate all of his, at least, and thanked her afterwards.

Charlie bathed Pearl after dinner and then got her into bed while Beth tidied the kitchen. She flicked the television on while he was gone. It would fill the ghastly silence between them if they both sat in the living room. When Pearl was asleep, he did indeed return to the living room to sit down. He fiddled with his phone and Beth went past the doorway several times, willing herself to join him in there. It didn't happen. Instead, she grabbed her phone and scurried down the hall to shut herself in her office, where she sank into her chair and texted Rikke.

You won't believe what I've done.

Rikke phoned twenty seconds later. 'Well?'

Beth kept her voice as low as possible. 'His niece has epilepsy and they needed somewhere to stay while she's getting treated in town.'

Rikke paused for some time, obviously trying to make sense of Beth's words. Then she gasped. 'Are you talking about Charlie Campbell?' she cried. Beth's silence was all the answer she

226

needed. Rikke swore. 'Beth, what are you doing?' she wailed. 'After what he did to you!'

'I know,' Beth moaned. 'But there was nowhere else and I really care about this child.'

'Are you sleeping with him?'

'No! He's got the guestroom.'

'This makes no sense. You never let yourself get played, Beth. I don't know anyone who trusts men less than you. But you've let this guy into your home, after he broke your heart. What were you thinking? Have you even discussed what he did back then?'

'Yes, sort of. It turns out he was under the impression I was sleeping around.'

'Uh-huh.' Rikke's voice was deeply sceptical. 'So it wasn't his fault, right? It was all just a misunderstanding.' She sighed. 'Classic victim blaming.'

'No, he doesn't blame me — '

'But he doesn't hold himself responsible for skipping out on you either, right?'

'It's not quite like that.' Beth heard herself and cringed. Was Rikke right? Oh God, she *was* right. Beth had stupidly let Charlie back into her life — into her home — after he'd hurt her, made a fool of her.

'How long will he be there for?' Rikke was asking.

'I'm not sure. Maybe a week.'

'A week!' Rikke groaned theatrically. 'Do you think you can keep him out of your bed that long?'

'Yes!' Beth snapped. 'I do have some self-control, you know.'

'I know you do, but this guy is a master manipulator, by the sound of him. He'll be doing everything right to get back into your life. Being the perfect guest, flattering you, explaining away his past sins. Do not let your guard down, Beth.'

Beth was silent, wondering if Charlie could be the man Rikke was describing. It didn't fit with what she knew of him. But then, she was already weakening towards him since he'd given her an explanation for his abandonment. She wanted to forgive him, she realised — because it took some of the old hurt away. Hell, she'd once given Free the same advice about Finn that Rikke was giving her right now — and yet she couldn't identify the deception in her own situation.

She truly was a sucker for Charlie.

'Beth?'

'I'm here.'

Rikke sounded worried. 'I don't want him hurting you again.'

'Yes, I get it. I'll be careful. I won't let him get close.'

She made an effort to change the subject, asking Rikke about work and her upcoming travel plans.

'Oh, hey,' Rikke interrupted Beth as she was attempting to wrap up their conversation. 'I got contacted yesterday by a guy I met at a professional development day a few years ago. Apparently he's working in Mount Clair now. Harry Sterrick.'

'The radiographer? Yes, I had to go see him on Thursday. I thought I might have fractured my tailbone, but it's just bruised.' Beth recounted the history of her injury, glossing over the circumstances of her fall. The colposcopy scheduled for Monday scuttled darkly across her mind. *Don't talk about it. Don't even think about it.*

'Ouch' was Rikke's remark. 'Well, I think you made quite an impression on Harry. He was Facebook-stalking you and saw you and I are friends, so he messaged me to rave about how funny and gorgeous you are, and to ask me if you were single.'

Beth shook her head. 'Seriously? I don't date guys who still qualify for student concessions.'

Rikke gave her throaty laugh. 'He's thirty-one, you silly girl.'

'What? Rubbish.'

'He is, I swear on my *Downton Abbey* box set. I gave him my blessing, Beth. He's a lovely guy. Very genuine. And very cute.'

Beth wrinkled her nose. 'Cute is right. Baby-faced.'

'Okay, he has a youthful face, but he's a man where it counts, I have no doubt. You should give him a shot. Let him take you out. It would be a good way to get your mind off the master manipulator.'

Rikke wouldn't let Beth go until she'd promised to consider a date with Harry. When she'd said goodbye, Beth opened her office door to the hall but stayed where she was, writing up consultation notes from her visit to Madjinbarra and keeping her ear on the living area, wondering what Charlie was doing. At last she heard a rustle in the hall and glanced around to find him standing in the doorway to her office.

'I'm just going to take a quick shower, then I'll head for bed,' he said. 'See you tomorrow.'

'Goodnight, Charlie.'

Beth waited until he was safely in his room, then took herself to the bathroom for her turn in the shower. Now that he was in bed, she felt like she could breathe again, although the thought of him naked in this shower just minutes earlier didn't help her peace of mind. Her old memories of Charlie's smooth, tanned skin, his broad shoulders and those vivid eyes on hers intruded on her thoughts. His body was bigger, stronger these days, and she'd seen a hint of hair on his chest when he wore a shirt open at the collar, and there were tattoos as well. What would that big, strong body feel like against hers? She could almost imagine it was his hands running over her body as she soaped herself under the warm water —

Oh, for Chrissake, Beth. Just stop.

15

Charlie took Pearl to the park for a play the next day, and they were out for several hours. Beth finished her notes, emailing them to the remote health body that funded her monthly trips to Madjinbarra. Then she vacuumed and did some washing, digging the small collection of clothing out of Pearl's backpack to throw into the machine too. She straightened Pearl's room while she was at it, making the bed and packing her books back up in a stack beside the Barbie lounge.

Pearl had left her toys out in the living room, and Beth was about to pack them away when she realised it was an intricate little zoo. Pearl had created a red block enclosure for her beloved carnivorous zebra herd, a blue one for the big cats, and green and yellow for the giraffes, rhinos and hippos. A zebra and a hippo were having a genial conversation over one of the block fences. Beth couldn't bring herself to dismantle it.

She was outside pegging wet washing on the line when she heard Charlie and Pearl arrive home. She finished the job and went inside, where Charlie was setting out lunch on the kitchen table.

He'd bought fresh grainy bread, ham and salad to make up sandwiches.

'Hungry?' he asked.

Beth nodded. 'Looks good.'

'I been swinging,' Pearl informed Beth.

'Have you? At the park?'

Pearl nodded, her big dark eyes on Beth as she munched a piece of ham.

'Did you see any other kids there?'

A frown creased Pearl's little forehead. 'They not wanna play with me.'

Beth's heart dropped and her eyes flew to Charlie.

'They just didn't know you,' Charlie assured Pearl. 'Maybe next time.'

Poor little thing. There was plenty of racism in Mount Clair, Beth knew, and kids who didn't understand Pearl's disability might also be put off by that. For an instant, she got Charlie's point about why Pearl would be happier at Madjinbarra, where she was accepted as one of the crew. But what he'd just said was true as well. If the Mount Clair kids got to know Pearl, Beth had faith they'd accept her.

They ate lunch together, but Pearl was the most capable conversationalist among them. It didn't seem to be getting any easier, having Charlie in the house. Beth hoped it wouldn't be a whole week of this tension.

'Kanga had ice-cream,' Pearl announced unexpectedly.

'Oh, yeah, Kanga's in town,' Charlie said. 'Got here yesterday. We saw him at the shop this morning.'

'Oh, good. He was going to bring Billy Early in. I haven't heard from the hospital, so maybe he hasn't admitted himself yet.'

Charlie twisted his mouth, looking doubtful.

'Kanga didn't mention Billy. Are you sure he came in with him?'

'That was the plan.' Beth sighed. 'Damn. Billy really needs to be in hospital for his feet. If he's not here, I'll have to request ambulance transport.'

'I'll see if I can get hold of Harvey and find out,' said Charlie.

The afternoon passed slowly and quietly. With the house tidy — well, as tidy as it could be with a toddler staying in it — Beth found herself at a loose end. She found jobs. She tended to her pot plants, then paid a couple of bills online and exchanged messages with her sisters, almost looking forward to work in the morning so she could get out of this uncomfortable home environment. Pearl came to find her as the sun dropped and Beth had begun to contemplate cooking dinner.

'I thought I might make spaghetti,' Beth told her, knowing this was a universally acceptable meal for children, and one that she could hide vegetables in.

'I help,' Pearl announced, dragging a chair towards the kitchen bench.

At first, Beth was concerned Pearl might tumble off the chair, but she seemed pretty secure up there on her knees, shoulders barely clearing the top of the bench. Beth racked her brain for something Pearl could do to help that wouldn't end in grated knuckles or sliced fingers.

'Pearl, could you break the stems off the mushrooms, like this?' She demonstrated.

233

Pearl nodded vigorously, curls bobbing. The job was done in no time, and Beth had to find more things for her to do. She got her stirring a jug of tomato puree, red wine and herbs — a task Pearl seemed to find riveting, and which resulted in substantial splatter. Beth chopped onion and set the beef mince frying, handing Pearl the garlic to peel. Then she took her outside to cut basil and oregano from the garden. This was definitely Pearl's favourite part of the process, and she did a good job of tearing the leaves off the stems. Just when Beth had run out of jobs for Pearl, Charlie appeared in the kitchen with a handful of DVDs.

'Do you want to watch something, Pearl?'

Pearl did. She slid off the chair, hitting the floor with a splat that didn't seem to do her any harm, and bum-shuffled after him into the living room. Charlie set her up with a movie that, from what Beth could hear, starred Barbie as the main character.

'Barbie's an actress these days?' she asked Charlie when he returned.

'Apparently so. Not a good one. There's something a bit unnatural in her performance.' He sank onto a stool on the opposite side of the bench. 'Can I help with anything?'

'It's almost all done,' she said. 'Pearl was very useful.'

He looked at the splatter of pasta sauce on the benchtop and the floor, and a corner of his mouth tugged upwards. 'How about a drink, then?'

'An alcoholic drink?' she asked, pausing in her

task of grating parmesan cheese to regard him with surprise.

He shrugged. 'We're not at Madji any more.' He paused. 'And it might take the edge off the awkwardness.'

Thank God he'd acknowledged it. She nodded and he went down the hall, returning a moment later with a bottle of good-quality whisky.

'Got any Coke?'

'No, but I've got soda water.'

He reached for two tumblers on the shelf above her microwave oven and she went for the soda water. It wasn't cold — it had been sitting unopened in her pantry — so she collected ice from the freezer and dropped a handful of cubes into each glass. Charlie mixed the drinks and handed one to Beth. They clinked glasses and drank, watching each other's eyes as though waiting to see who would be the first to attack. Charlie turned to the sink and wrung out a sponge, wiping down the mess Pearl had made on the bench and the cabinet door, and took some paper towels to the floor before reclaiming the stool.

'I haven't seen Pearl having any seizures since she's been on those pills,' he said.

'Nor me. Great sign. Have you reported back to Mary?'

'Yeah.' Charlie swirled his glass so the ice clinked. 'I sent some messages and Aunty Mary replied, then Jill got hold of Aunty's phone and left me a voicemail. It was a pretty rough line and I couldn't make sense of much of it — you know what the signal's like out there. She's still pretty upset, though — that came through loud and clear.'

'Worried about Pearl?'

'Yep. And pissed off she wasn't allowed to come to town.'

'She asked me to speak to you,' Beth confessed. 'About coming to school in Mount Clair. I said I would, but only because I didn't know what else to say to her. She seems to think I can influence your decision.'

Charlie was silent for a few moments. 'She doesn't understand the bigger issues.'

'I think she does, actually. She knows exactly what the bigger issues are, but she still wants to go. She wants to go to university.'

'There's plenty of time for that,' he said in a voice that indicated he didn't want to discuss the issue.

Beth ignored his tone. She wasn't his niece — she could say what she wanted. 'Maybe so. But Jill wants it now. She wants to bring skills to Madji to manage Pearl's disability and contribute to the community's health care. She's desperate, Charlie.'

Charlie took another sip and didn't answer. Beth finished grating the cheese and stirred the pot of pasta sauce, thinking of Jill back in Madjinbarra. Then she thought of a different Madjinbarra — one with a pub nearby; one where people could readily sink their sadness in drink. How would Jill fare there? What sort of future would that be for the girl?

'The word is that the minister is making a decision about the mine soon,' she said.

Charlie nodded. He'd obviously heard the rumours too.

'How would you feel about shifting the whole community somewhere else?' she asked.

'What do you mean?'

'I mean, if all the kit homes got packed up and you literally relocated everyone to another spot, away from the Gargantua mine.'

Charlie looked surprised for a moment, then his brow creased as he considered the idea. 'The location is meaningful to us.'

'Yes, of course. But if the mine is approved, and a wet mess goes in, then everything you've worked for could crumble. Maybe if you shifted everyone somewhere else, you'd have more security.'

'Shift everyone?' His mouth grew tight. 'That's the main thing Harvey remembers of his younger days, you know. The whites shifting people around from camp to camp, like cattle.'

Beth was disgusted at herself for making the suggestion. He was absolutely right. She stirred the sauce in silent remorse.

At length, he spoke again. 'Look, if it came down to it, I'd consider it. But I'm not sure we could afford a move like that, even if we wanted to do it. We're talking big dollars to pack everyone up, all the houses, and buy new houses to replace the ones that aren't transportable. And where would we go? What if it broke up the community? If we're moving, some people might see it as an opportunity to go somewhere else, or just stay put in Madji to work on the mine.'

Beth chewed her lip. 'That's true. But if your

only other choice was staying while Gargantua moved in . . . ' She watched him.

'As for the cost, what if it was funded?'

'Funded by who?'

'Gargantua or the government.'

'That would make it more feasible, but I'd rather we stay where we are.'

'Yes, absolutely.' Beth sipped her drink, staring absently at the pile of grated cheese on her cutting board. He'd heard the idea with much more openness than she'd expected. Maybe it had potential, as a last-ditch solution.

'Where did this come from?' he asked.

She almost told him, but stopped herself at the last moment, recalling the issues he had with Lloyd Rendall. If he knew Lloyd had presented the idea, Charlie would probably dismiss it without another thought.

Beth shrugged. 'I heard it worked for another community, over east somewhere, I think.'

'I see.' Charlie looked like he was turning the idea over in his mind, but a moment later, his gaze came to rest on her face again. 'How many nieces and nephews have you got?' he asked.

'None yet.' She put down her drink and dug in her pot drawer for a saucepan suitable to boil water for pasta.

'But there's one on the way?'

Beth glanced at him. 'How did you know that?'

'I didn't know. It was a guess. You've got a kid's room set up at your house, so I figured you must have kids staying here sometimes. You don't have kids of your own — not that I know of, anyway.'

She laughed. 'No, I don't have children hidden in a closet somewhere. Willow's pregnant. She hasn't told the world yet, though.'

Beth didn't directly address the fact that she'd set up the room for Pearl and no-one else. That was her business.

'Willow's younger or older than you?' he asked.

'She's three years younger. She got married last year. She's running Patersons now.'

'You've got another sister, too, yeah?'

Beth nodded, relaxing a little. She could do small talk. She set the saucepan of water on the stove and added salt. 'Free. She's the youngest. She teaches art locally and runs an art supplies business. She lives in town with her boyfriend — a cop.'

'They've both settled down, your sisters.'

He left the unspoken question hanging in the air, but Beth refused to take the bait.

'Yes, they're both doing really well. I was worried about Free for a while. She couldn't seem to settle down to anything. But she found something she enjoys doing and seems pretty happy nowadays.'

Beth had her back to Charlie but sensed him watching her. She stirred the sauce again, although it didn't need it. At last she could delay it no longer, and she turned around. Charlie's eyes, the green of a glacier wall, were focused on her with an intensity that sent a jolt through Beth — something between fear and desire. Beth wrenched her gaze away and focused on fetching herself a stool from against the wall. She brought it around to her side of the bench, perching gingerly on the edge, then grabbed her glass and took a sip.

Don't ask. Don't ask.

He asked. 'You never got married?'

'Not everyone has to get married,' she said sharply.

'I didn't mean getting married, specifically. I meant finding one person. Settling down.' He paused. 'I wouldn't think it'd be for lack of offers.'

She became aware of the tension in her shoulders. 'I'm not sure this is something I want to talk to *you* about.'

Charlie looked away at last. 'Fair enough.'

Although she'd been the one to shut him down, she couldn't restrain herself from launching a counterattack. 'You're not married either.'

Dammit. That brought his extraordinary eyes straight back to hers. 'No.'

'Why not?'

Surely he would take the opportunity to tell her it was none of her business, just like she'd done a moment before.

'Never met anyone I wanted to settle down with,' he said. 'Not likely to happen, either.'

She attempted to keep her tone as casual as his. 'I guess it's a transient lifestyle you lead, touring and shows, stuff like that.'

He tipped his head in a sort of gesture of agreement. *Pathetic answer.* Beth pressed her lips together and slipped off her stool, gathering plates and cutlery.

'Why don't you get Pearl cleaned up for dinner? The pasta will be ready in fifteen minutes.'

Charlie frowned. He put down his glass and stood, but Beth kept her eyes on the plates, shuffling them around on the benchtop as though she had to get their position just right. At last, he turned and headed for the living room, where she heard him pause the DVD, to Pearl's ire, and cart her off for a bath.

God, this was such a huge mistake, inviting him to stay here. There was too much between them. He was too proud; she was too resentful. There was no way to back-pedal, either. Pearl needed stability and calm at the moment. Beth fought the emotion coursing through her and tried to keep her focus on Pearl. She could do this. She would ignore Charlie and be there for Pearl.

Pearl was annoyed when her uncle made her have a bath, but she was even more annoyed when he made her get out. Listening from the kitchen, Beth had to hand it to Jill. If this was what she managed every day, the girl must have the patience of a saint. She served the meal, bringing three plates to the table just as Pearl appeared, clad in a My Little Pony nightie. The sound of water screeching down the plughole followed Pearl into the kitchen.

'All squeaky clean?' Beth asked brightly.

'I hungry,' Pearl replied, clambering onto a chair.

'Good. Do you want cheese?' Beth put a mug of water onto the table for Pearl to drink.

The child didn't reply, diving into her dinner with her fingers. Beth was torn between being glad Pearl's fingers were clean after her bath and realising with dismay that she would need another bath after dinner. Charlie appeared and observed his niece.

'Well, that was a bloody waste of time,' he said.

He turned back down the hall. A moment later, the water stopped *shlucking* down the drain as Charlie conserved the remains of Pearl's bath for a repeat later.

Beth's manners wouldn't allow her to start without Charlie, even though Pearl was eating as though her life depended on it. She made a mental note to speak with an OT about the appropriate stage to get Pearl using cutlery. Charlie returned and refilled his glass from the whisky bottle. Before she could protest, he'd grabbed her glass and refilled it as well. No soda. No ice.

Screw you. She could drink moodily with the best of them. Beth took a swig.

They ate in silence, except for Pearl's occasional pauses in eating to make worldly three-year-old observations about spaghetti, Barbie or the lack of juice with her dinner. When they'd finished, Beth stood up, announcing that she would clean Pearl up. She carried Pearl to the bathroom, topped up the bath and plonked her in. Pearl was delighted. Beth attempted to clean spaghetti sauce off the pony nightie and

242

dry it with her hair dryer while Pearl splashed contentedly with her zebra and hippopotamus.

By eight p.m., Beth had come to understand that children of three years did not want to get into the bath, did not want to get out of the bath and did not want to go to bed — at least, not without an exhausting emotional battle. She read every single book she'd bought aloud to Pearl, and then lay down on the mattress to discuss the farm animals hanging from the mobile. The whisky had made Beth sleepy and she relaxed beside Pearl. The smell of clean child was more delicious and soothing than a bedtime hot chocolate, and she found herself drifting off at the same time.

She woke to quiet, Pearl sleeping soundly beside her, an arm hooked over Beth's neck. Beth rolled over slightly, wincing at the pain in her tailbone, and stared at the mobile spinning slowly above her head. After a minute, she disengaged Pearl's warm little arm from around her neck and eased herself up off the mattress. Charlie's bedroom door was closed. Beth headed down the hall to tidy the kitchen before bed.

The kitchen was clean. The table had been wiped clear of Pearl's spillages. Even the floor beneath Pearl's chair was spotless.

She opened the fridge and saw a container of leftover spaghetti on a shelf. The dishwasher was gurgling and clunking contentedly in the darkness. *Okay.* The only thing out of place was the bottle of whisky and the glass on the bench. *Why not?*

Beth poured herself a splash and threw in a

couple of ice cubes. She would bloody well wind down before bed. She would take control of her Sunday night, despite Charlie Campbell's best efforts to disconcert her. She paused to rub her forehead for a moment, closing her eyes. Then Beth pulled her shoulders straight. Yes, she'd made a mistake when she offered Charlie a place to stay, but she'd done it with the right motives, and once Pearl's seizures were under control, Beth could reclaim her life and her habitat. She might even try a date with Harry Sterrick. She sipped her whisky as she headed for the living room, rolling its spiciness over her tongue.

Beth rounded the corner and found Charlie sitting right in front of her on the sofa. She jerked to a stop and almost dropped her glass. 'What are you doing?' she demanded.

'Waiting for you.'

'Why?'

'Because you fell asleep with Pearl and our conversation wasn't finished. Not the one we had tonight, or the one we had on the road back from Gurrungah's camp, *or* the one we had before everyone woke up on Wednesday.'

Beth glared around the room, looking for something to blame for her discomfort. 'What's the time?'

'Just after ten.'

She frowned at him. 'Are you drunk?'

Charlie frowned back. 'No. I don't get drunk.'

She regretted her accusation for an instant. Then her resentment returned. 'I don't want to finish this conversation,' she said.

'I need to know what really happ — '

Beth could hardly believe what she was hearing. 'This is my house. Don't you dare question my honesty, not here.'

He was silent. Beth stepped forward and sank onto the sofa that sat at a right angle to his. She stared at the reflective surface of her coffee table.

'You wanted to know why I'm still single,' Charlie said.

Beth didn't speak or meet his eyes.

'It's because I've got trust issues,' he said.

Her anger boiled to the surface. She sucked back the whisky and slammed down her empty glass on the table, throat burning.

'Is that so?' she spat when she could speak. 'Maybe you should work on that. Sometimes trust issues find their basis in nothing but insecurity and paranoia.'

He didn't answer and she met his eyes, defiant as hell. She waited for him to slink away, but he didn't, so she piled on more fuel.

'It's funny. I've got trust issues too. I got abandoned when I was eighteen and stupidly in love.'

Charlie leaned forward, placing his glass slowly on the table. He stood, moving towards Beth until he was right in front of her, eyes not moving from her face. Beth stood up too. She wasn't about to be intimidated — not by *him*. He was close to her, so close she could feel the warmth of his body.

Beth didn't give an inch. 'You really have the *gall* to say you need to know the truth? To ask if you can *believe* me?' She shook her head, as much at herself as at him.

'I believe you.'

She narrowed her eyes. 'Oh, good.' The sarcasm was thick in her voice. 'I'm so relieved. Hopefully you're at peace now you know you didn't get screwed over. You did the screwing over. Goodnight. Sleep well.'

Charlie didn't budge. 'I'm sorry.'

'Not good enough. Nowhere near.'

'I won't sleep well.'

'Good, because you're an arsehole and you don't deserve to sleep well.'

His lips twisted, trying to suppress his amusement. 'Fair call.'

'Screw you,' she whispered.

And suddenly there was no humour in his face, only sorrow. He brought a hand up, laying it against her cheek, and stroked a thumb over the skin beneath her eye. Her body sprang to life at the very same moment that her fury rose another notch. She shoved his hand away.

'Don't mess with me. I'm not the naive girl I was back then.'

There was a tense moment while Beth's fists clenched and she silently challenged him to just try and touch her again. He wasn't afraid, but he comprehended just how angry she was and took a reluctant step back. She used the opportunity to make her escape, diving for the living room doorway.

'Beth.' His voice arrested her. 'Do you hate me?'

She didn't turn her head to look back.

'No, Charlie, I don't hate you. We're *nothing* to each other, just like you said.'

16

It was satisfying. Beth had said the things she'd wanted to say to Charlie for years. It hadn't erased the past, but it had taken the edge off her resentment. Maybe she could move forward now, knowing not all men were evil. Only some of them.

And the rest were stubborn morons.

In the morning, Beth decided she did not wish to face Charlie and departed early for the clinic. She switched on all the consulting room lights and sat down at her computer to check her appointments for the day. She'd avoided her email on Friday, and now there were over 140 unread messages in her inbox, including dozens of newsletters from various health foundations, peak bodies and the Chamber of Commerce. She filed them for later, prioritising anything that related specifically to her patients or the clinic.

Carolyn had arranged an appointment for Beth to have genetic counselling by telephone. At first, Beth had tried to skip this step but Carolyn had reminded her that she couldn't get the testing done without doing the counselling. When the call came in at nine, Beth faked being upbeat and calm about the whole testing issue, assuring the counsellor that she definitely wanted to know the result. The counsellor told her she could get the blood test done at the hospital's pathology clinic and her samples would be sent to the genetic laboratory, with results available in a few months. Beth opted for the results to be sent to Carolyn and claimed she would be glad to know the outcome so she could take proactive steps. Once the phone session was done, Beth took deep breaths and tried to believe her own lies.

She was due at the gynaecologist's rooms for her colposcopy at eleven-thirty. She saw several patients before that, then had to run to her car to make the hospital appointment. She'd known the specialist professionally for years but had never had the dubious honour of revealing her lady parts to him. She tried not to think about how cringe-worthy that was. *He's the best in Mount Clair, and he's seen thousands of these bits before.* Somehow it wasn't much of a comfort — but she couldn't delay this procedure until her next visit to Perth or Darwin.

Gavin Bainbridge was a quietly spoken man. He outlined how the colposcopy would work, then sat patiently through Beth's nervous jokes. He'd clearly heard them all before. When she'd exhausted her repertoire, she stood up.

'Right, let's get this over with.'

The procedure itself wasn't a big deal. It was much like any other gynaecological check. When it was over, she pulled her clothes back on and sat at his desk, waiting for Gavin to finish tapping notes, her heart racing.

'All looks okay to me,' he said at last.

'Sorry?'

Gavin looked up. 'No sign of any problems. I've taken a biopsy, but I certainly didn't see anything sinister, Dr Paterson. Hopefully the results will be fine — if so, I won't be recommending another screening before the usual time frame.' He offered her a small smile.

'Thank you,' she said rather stupidly.

She left the room wondering if Gavin Bainbridge really knew his stuff. Then she laughed at herself. Of course he did. The wave of relief was as powerful as it was short-lived. It wasn't just the biopsy; she still had the genetic testing to get through. Beth dug her blood test request out of her handbag and headed for pathology. Minutes later, it was done. It would be an awful wait until she found out if she had the gene. Part of Beth wished the result would get lost in the mail; at the same time, she foresaw herself hounding the lab for her results within a fortnight.

She cast the whole matter from her mind and swung by admissions to ask if Billy Early had been in touch. He hadn't. Beth sat in the Beast and sent messages to Mary and Harvey, hoping they would receive them sooner or later and use their sway with Billy to get the stubborn bastard into town to get those feet treated.

Beth got herself back to the clinic and dived back into appointments. It was past lunchtime before she picked up her phone and noticed a social media connection request from Harry Sterrick. Beth accepted, and within minutes he sent her a message.

Hi there! How's the injury? I hope the pain's settled down.

It's much better since I found out it wasn't

249

serious, Beth replied. *Funny how pain and worry go hand in hand.*

Harry replied immediately. *There's a research paper in that, I'm sure.*

She sent a smiley face and began a message to her father, but Harry wasn't finished.

Wondering if you're free this week? Maybe we could grab dinner together one night?

Beth considered it, Rikke shouting in her conscience. The thought of Charlie back at her house, looking after Pearl, wandered through her mind as well. Dating Harry was a good idea. It would get her focus off Charlie — it would help her close that damn door.

Sounds good, she answered. *Did you have a specific day in mind?*

Tonight? He added a smile to show her he meant it, but she could knock him back and he wouldn't mind.

Whereabouts and what time? Beth answered before she could change her mind.

They made arrangements to meet at the Sawmill at six, then Beth spent every spare moment between appointments second-guessing her decision. Was she in the right headspace to take this step? The last few days — weeks — had been emotionally tumultuous, to say the least. She messaged Rikke to tell her she was going on a date with Harry and Rikke sent back all manner of celebratory emojis. It cemented her resolve.

She also sent a message to Charlie.

Eat without me. I'll be late tonight.

He replied. *No problem.*

How's Pearl? Anything to report?
All clear.

That was something. Soon Pearl would get the okay from Dr Grahame and Charlie could take her home. Then he could get on with the job of saving his community and being a successful musician, and Beth could get on with her life.

★ ★ ★

'Have you been here before?' Harry asked as they followed Letitia to their table.

'Yes, a few times,' said Beth. 'It's been open about five years and it's definitely the best place to eat in town.'

'First time for me,' he said. 'Great spot, isn't it, overlooking the lake? Thanks,' he added to Letitia when she handed them menus.

Beth shot the girl a smile.

'Would you like to see the wine list, Doc? I mean, madam?'

'Thanks, Tish.'

Letitia handed them a wine list and left them to it.

'She's a patient?' Harry asked.

Now she got a proper look at him, Beth realised he wasn't as baby-faced as she'd first thought. Sure, he was soft-skinned, but he had a respectable amount of facial hair, shaved close. It was light in colour to match the blond hair on his head, so naturally it was less visible. His eyes were a soft, twinkling blue.

'Tish is from a remote community — the same one I go out to visit once a month.'

251

'Oh, yes, I think I heard that you do a regular FIFO job out at a community. That's a well-paid gig, I believe.'

Beth must have looked a little surprised because Harry back-pedalled. 'Not suggesting you're just doing it for the cash,' he said.

She laughed. 'That's okay. It *is* good money.'

'For one day's work. A hard day's work, though, I imagine.'

'I find one day's too short. I stay for three in the dry season.'

Harry tipped his head. 'So, you fly in and stay for three days before flying out again?'

'Well, I can't fly because the charter flight's only covered if I do a same-day turnaround. I opted to drive out there instead, if the roads are passable. I drive for a day, stay for three, then drive home. If I leave home on a Sunday, I only miss four days at my clinic.'

Harry was watching her in amazement. 'Hang on, you spend two full days on the road, work for three — but only get remunerated for one day's work?'

She dropped her gaze. 'I get a fuel rebate. One day's not enough to see everyone who needs medical attention.'

'That's huge, what you're doing,' he said. 'It can't be pleasant out there, but you're essentially volunteering your own time to stop up a hole in the health system.'

'Wine?' she said. 'Red or white?'

Harry smiled. 'Am I embarrassing you? Sorry. Your fault, for being so incredible.'

She rolled her eyes. 'Red or white?'

'White.' He was chuckling now.

Harry was good company — he was bright and attentive, and he laughed at her jokes. After a glass of wine, he looked even cuter. *Good call, Rikke,* she thought as the night went on. This was fun. Two adults. Clean slate. It was fun and . . . *functional.* Nice and slow, too. Harry didn't make any hasty moves. He was a gentleman. He walked her to her car at the end of the night and put a hand on her upper arm as he moved in for a brief, light kiss on the cheek. Beth smiled and agreed with Harry when he said they should do this again.

She drove home, easing the Beast past Charlie's battered 4WD, into her little carport. It was after ten and she expected Charlie would either be in bed or winding down in front of the television. She entered the house quietly, not wanting to disturb him if he was asleep.

Music was coming from the living room. Beth peeped around the corner to find Charlie sitting on the sofa, head bent over his guitar, fingers tripping up and down the strings as he softly sang a line, stopped, tried it again with a slightly different melody, then reached for a pencil on the coffee table to scribble on the page of a notebook. When he looked back down at his guitar strings, his long hair flopped over his face and hung in one eye. He shoved it back with an impatient hand.

Oh. My. *God.*

She would have pulled back out of view to compose herself but at that moment he caught sight of her and stopped, laying his guitar aside.

'Hi.'

Beth stepped forward. 'Hi. I didn't mean to disturb you. That was — it sounded good.'

His face brightened. 'Thanks.'

She couldn't think of anything to say and didn't want him to see how she was trembling with sudden, insane need so she crossed quickly to the kitchen, putting down her bag. A plate covered with foil sat on the clean bench. She paused to check what was under it and discovered a portion of steak, mashed potato and greens.

Wait — he'd cooked for her?

Charlie appeared behind her. 'I wasn't sure if you'd get a chance to eat tonight.' He examined her face. 'Were you called in to the hospital?'

Oh *shit*. He'd cooked her dinner and then sat on her sofa, composing music, waiting for her, sexy as hell — and now she had to admit she'd been out on a date with nice, functional, baby-faced Harry. She attempted to think of a way around telling Charlie the truth but there wasn't one. Her heart was thumping so hard she could feel her pulse in her throat and it seemed to be blocking her vocal cords, too.

'Um, no,' she managed. 'Thank you for cooking, but I had dinner with a colleague.'

'Ah. Right.' He didn't take his eyes off her face. 'You were on a date.'

She swallowed against her dry throat, leaned back on the bench and nodded. His green eyes didn't even flicker. She waited, breathing shallowly.

'Good time?' he asked.

Beth shrugged.

'Will you see him again?'

'I don't know.' It came as a whisper and she cleared her throat. 'Do you want a cup of tea?'

Charlie was already moving when she stepped towards the kettle to switch it on. He intercepted her, catching her face in his hands and crashing his lips onto hers, kissing her as if he didn't care if either of them ever breathed again. Beth was held in place by his hands and lips, helpless to do anything except be kissed by Charlie and long for more. He turned her whole body around, pushing her so she had her back against the pantry door and kissed her even harder. Charlie's solid chest crushed Beth's breasts, making heat roar through her, and he made a noise like a deep groan of hunger as his lips slid sideways down her neck. Her hands closed on his upper arms, fingers digging in, registering the hard muscle like a cherished memory.

Without removing his mouth from her even for an instant, Charlie slipped his hand beneath her top onto her bare stomach, moving upwards, fingers tracing their old, familiar journey along her skin.

Beth's phone pinged with a message inside her handbag on the bench, and Charlie stopped, releasing her. She dropped her hands but stayed where she was against the louvred pantry door, trying to recapture her breath, almost dizzy with desire. They stood inches apart, chests heaving.

'Beth,' Charlie breathed, his eyes intent on hers. 'I — '

She straightened her top and slipped out from

her position between him and the door.

'Jesus, Charlie.'

Charlie simply watched her, his face completely open, just as it had always been when he was younger. Was he regretful? Annoyed? Sorry? She studied him but couldn't work it out. His expression seemed to emanate, if anything, acceptance. Perhaps even patience.

Screw that.

'If you try anything like that again, you'll be out the door, Pearl or no Pearl.' Beth crossed to the bench, snatched up the dinner plate covered in foil and shoved it into the fridge with a clatter. She fished in her handbag, refusing to look at him, and found her phone.

I had a great time tonight. You're pretty special, you know that? Are you free on the weekend? I was thinking of doing one of those touristy sunset cruises on the river and I can't think of anyone I'd rather drag along with me. Harry's message finished with a smiley face.

Beth looked up and found Charlie's eyes locked on her phone screen, where the name 'Harry Sterrick' was clearly visible. That steadfast look remained, although something like hurt flickered across it. Defiant, Beth raised her eyebrows at him, turned her back and started tapping a reply to Harry. Charlie left her alone, heading down the hall to his bedroom.

Beth gave up on thoughts of tea and went to sit in the living room, but evidence of Charlie was everywhere and she couldn't get the feel of his kiss off her lips. Her eye fell on the scrawl of lyrics and musical notes in his notebook. She picked it up, the spidery, flowing handwriting painfully familiar.

Never did anything, anything but loved you from the start Too young and foolish, my pride, it tore your love apart Should've been forever, instead I got this shadow on my heart . . .

Beth shoved the notebook away and jumped up. Just some stupid, meaningless lyrics. Sleep. She needed sleep.

But she cried in bed, just as she had in Durack all those years ago, fighting to stay silent. She didn't want to cry — it made her furious — but the tears wouldn't stop. God, she *loathed* this Beth. She was out of control, swinging between emotions like a teenager, lashing out, dealing low blows — unable to just bloody *grow up and get over it.*

★　★　★

The next day Beth felt calmer, almost emptied out of the fury that had kept her stitched together for the past couple of days. She tested the pain of her bruised tailbone with a dawn run and it was bearable. She couldn't run as far as usual, but at least she was on the road to recovery. She returned to the still quiet of home and showered, planning to get out of there early again, before Charlie or Pearl got up. She hesitated on her way past Pearl's room, looking in to see the child sprawled across her covers, curls silky and pale in the morning light. Beth felt bad. Tonight, she would do a proper assessment to see if there were any signs of seizures, reactions to her medication or anything else out of the ordinary. And she would spend time playing with Pearl.

During a short break in her morning, Beth called Gavin Bainbridge for her biopsy results. He chased down the lab for her before calling back to tell her the biopsy was clear.

'Are you sure?' she asked, hardly able to believe her luck. 'Completely clear?'

'The result is completely normal,' he assured her, humour in his voice. 'You know the old joke that medics either ignore their health problems or build them up into the most serious condition they can imagine? You're living evidence, Dr Paterson. Beth, you do not have cervical cancer.'

'Sorry, I'm not normally such a pessimist,' she said, laughing with sheer relief. 'I've just had such a crazy bunch of things going on lately, I was starting to think everything that could go wrong, would.'

'Well, this is one thing you can strike off the *things going wrong* list.'

She thanked him and hung up, then made herself a cup of tea to calm her nerves. *Don't get too cocky.* She still had the genetic test hurdle to clear.

Harry had been messaging her so Beth squashed down thoughts of Charlie's horribly amazing kiss and arranged to go out with him again on Saturday evening. The river cruise was booked out with tourists so they decided on a pub meal instead. Then Beth worked through the rest of the morning. Just before noon, Free called her phone and left a voice message.

'Hi, Bethie! Do you want to grab lunch with me? I need to talk to you. Come over to Galileo's. Oh, you probably can't leave your clinic, can you? Do you even take lunchbreaks? Sometimes I think you're superhuman and you don't actually stop and eat like the rest of us. How about I bring you something to eat? You *are* human, you know. This could be, like, an intervention. Yeah! I'll bring you a panini. It's a panini-tervention. And I'll even bring you a coffee! No, I know, I'll bring you a kombucha. *So* healthy. Okay? I'll see you soon!'

Free arrived with panini and colourful kombucha drinks around twelve-thirty. Beth was able to squeeze in a fifteen-minute break for lunch with her sister. They sat in the tiny break room together and unpacked paper bags printed with the Galileo's telescope logo. Free's eyes were bright with suppressed excitement.

'Willow rang me this morning and told me the news. I've been shopping ever since.' She abandoned her panini for a moment to fish in her bag, then presented an array of tiny baby clothing, mostly pink. 'Check out this one.' She held up an impossibly small hot-pink T-shirt that said *Cowgirl in Training* in glitter applique.

Beth chuckled. 'Perfect. Except it could be a cow*boy*.'

'No, it's a Paterson girl.' Free had absolutely no doubt in her voice as she packed up the items and returned them to her bag. 'And sorry,

Bethie, but I'm planning to be the favourite aunty.'

Beth gave a nod. 'Challenge accepted.'

'Eat!' Free ordered.

Beth ate. 'Thanks for bringing lunch,' she said between mouthfuls.

'I'm totally taking care of you.' Free smiled with pride. 'I can't wait to tell Dad.'

Beth grinned. 'I'd starve if it wasn't for you.'

'You are looking a bit skinny.' Free's eyebrows pulled into a frown as she cast a gaze over Beth's arms and legs. 'Are you stressed out, or sick, or something?'

'Not stressed out,' Beth lied. 'Just worn out.'

'You really need a holiday. Big-time. Look at you. Your eyes are kinda puffy, too, like mine look when I stay up too late crying over a book.'

Beth dropped her gaze. 'I'm just tired.'

'Why don't you go home and rest this afternoon? Take a sickie.'

'It doesn't quite work like that. I've got about twelve patients to see this arvo.'

Free shrugged, lifting her panini to her mouth. 'Work, work, jogging, networking meetings, community visits, jogging, work. Something's gotta give, sooner or later.' She took a big bite, nodding sagely at Beth.

Beth ate in silence. A thought seemed to occur to Free while chewing, and as soon as she had swallowed her mouthful, she launched back into speech.

'You know what? You're just like Dad. Always working or worrying, and look where it got him. Heart attack before the age of sixty.'

260

'I always eat well,' Beth reminded her. 'And I exercise.'

'Yeah, but you work too hard and worry too much.' Free stopped and gazed at Beth. *Uh-oh.* Beth knew what was coming next. Sure enough, in moments Free's eyes were swimming with tears. 'You mustn't let yourself get run-down, Beth. I lost Mum and I nearly lost Dad. I couldn't stand to lose a sister.'

'Jesus, Free.' Beth's impatience crumbled at the sight of Free's tears, and her thoughts flew to the genetic testing. Did she even want those damn results? She reached across their sandwiches and hugged Free. 'I'm perfectly healthy and a hundred per cent well. Please don't worry about me.'

Free wiped her eyes. 'Sorry. I just don't like seeing you looking sorta flat like that. It spooks me.'

'I've had a lot to think about, what with the Madjinbarra battle with Gargantua, and a couple of issues with patients.'

'What's going on with the Gargantua thing?' Free resumed eating, her tears already a thing of the past.

'I don't know. We're in limbo while the Department of Mining makes a decision. There are some options floating around but no-one seems to want to make definite plans.' She heaved a sigh. 'Lloyd Rendall's offered a kind of solution but I don't even know if it's really on the table, because nothing's appeared in writing yet.'

Free swigged kombucha, eyeing Beth. 'He's

that old lawyer dude, right?'

Beth smiled. 'He's in his forties, so not that old. But yes, he's a lawyer.'

'Finn knows him from court. After you went home on Friday night, Kate was saying . . . ' Free trailed off, poking at some lettuce hanging out of her sandwich.

'Let me guess. That I'd been spotted out on a date with Lloyd?'

Free tucked a wayward curl behind her ear. 'You are going out with him, then?'

'God, no. I met him for a business dinner, that's all.'

Free looked immensely relieved. 'Oh, good, because Finn doesn't think much of him and I didn't like the thought of you being with someone who might not have . . . have *honour*.'

Beth couldn't help a cackle at her sister's choice of words. 'Don't worry, *honour* is right at the top of my wish list when it comes to a prospective life partner.'

Free didn't quite see the joke and nodded vigorously. 'Me too. I mean, without that, what are we? Just a bunch of bald monkeys crawling around the planet trying to get hold of more bananas than the monkey next door? Right?'

Free bit into her panini, her big green eyes on Beth's, full of trust.

'Right,' said Beth.

17

Beth was home in time to cook, but Charlie had already started preparing vegetables and had some chicken marinating in a bowl of sauce. She wondered when he'd learned to cook, in between touring and recording albums as a famous musician. He'd been out and bought the food, too, rather than using hers. His pride, she guessed. He didn't want to feel like he was sponging off her.

'Hi,' she said, hanging her bag over the back of a chair and pretending he hadn't kissed the hell out of her in this very room the night before. 'How's Pearl?'

'Good,' he said, also diligently pretending. 'We've got an appointment with the doctor for Thursday. Hopefully she'll get the all clear and then we can get out of your hair.'

Beth nodded, pleased with how well they were faking civility.

'I spoke to the hospital admissions staff again today,' she said. 'Billy Early still hasn't been in.'

Charlie sighed. 'Okay. I'll chase that up, too. When I take Pearl home, I'll kick his arse.'

'Good. His situation is much more serious than he's willing to accept.' Beth paused. 'Where is Pearl?'

'Playing in her room.'

She went down the hall and found Pearl

seated on her mattress-bed, gazing at a picture of a zebra in a book, a plastic version of the same animal clutched in her hand.

'You like zebras, don't you, Pearl?' Beth said.

Pearl looked up and nodded, showing Beth her plastic zebra. Beth slipped off her shoes and joined Pearl on the mattress, leaning her back against the wall. Her bruised tailbone coped admirably. Pearl gave her the book.

'Do you want me to read it to you?' Beth asked.

Pearl climbed onto her lap. Beth's tailbone complained a little this time, but dealt with it. Beth opened the book, titled *Zoe the Zebra*, to the first page.

'Zoe the zebra lives with her herd,' she read. 'Zoe the zebra looks at a bird.'

Pearl made a noise of agreement, pointing at the bird.

'Zoe the zebra visits the llamas. Zoe the zebra has stripey pyjamas.'

'Jamas,' echoed Pearl, the thumb sneaking its way up to her mouth.

Beth dipped her face down to kiss Pearl's soft curls. 'Zoe the zebra nibbles the grass. Zoe the zebra watches the lions go past.'

'Zoe the zebra should work on her meter.'

Beth started at the sound of his voice. She lifted her eyes to Charlie, where he leaned against the doorframe observing her and Pearl. He wore a look that rattled her to her core, it was so full of tenderness. She gazed back at him, the last remnants of her anger dropping away. *Shit*. If she couldn't hang on to that anger, how could she deal with this situation? How could she protect herself?

'She'd better watch out, or the lions will eat her,' he added.

Pearl popped her thumb out. 'Zebba,' she demanded.

Beth forced her eyes back to the book. 'Zoe the zebra takes a walk down the path. Zoe the zebra loves Ginny Giraffe.'

'Zoe the zebra is experimenting with a bit of inter-species love,' Charlie remarked. 'But who's judging?'

Beth fought to control a smile, fixing her eyes on the book. 'Zoe the zebra shoos flies, her tail wagging. Zoe the zebra zips, zigging and zagging.'

'Jesus, now she's resorted to alliteration.'

Beth couldn't help her laughter this time. 'So you did learn something in Year Eleven English?'

'Zebba!' Pearl shouted.

'Okay, sorry!' said Beth.

There were only two pages to go. 'Zoe the zebra cools off in the water. Zoe remembers what her mummy taught her.'

'And here comes the moral . . . ' Charlie put in.

'Zebba!' Pearl scowled at her uncle and he lifted his hands in surrender.

'Zoe sleeps soundly at the close of the day, and wakes up each morning, ready to play.'

'Kapow,' said Charlie. 'There it is. Get to sleep, kid.'

'No sleep,' Pearl said firmly. 'I hungry.'

'Dinner's coming.'

He headed back down the hall. Pearl clambered off Beth's lap and, with a monumental effort, stood up, wobbling. Beth gave a slight gasp of surprise, and Pearl shot her a look filled with triumph.

'I *walking*.' She staggered away after her uncle.

Beth stayed where she was sitting for a moment, with Gummy the elephant and Zoe the zebra. Dear God, she would be lonely when they left. She would miss Pearl's indomitable spirit, and she would miss Charlie, although she knew she should not. She would be obliged to pack up Pearl's bedroom, send the toys off to Madjinbarra with the two of them, load the sage sheets into the washing machine and pass the mobile and bunting to Willow. Make her spare room a spare room again. Bring the floor-standing vases back out. Get the white rug steam cleaned.

The thought left her bleak. Empty.

Beth got to her feet and went into her bedroom. She changed out of her work clothes and into a tank top and shorts, pulling her hair out of its customary knot at the base of her neck, then lay on her bed for a couple of minutes, staring at the ceiling. She thought about her date with nice, functional Harry, scheduled for Saturday evening. And that senseless, goddamned amazing kiss with Charlie the night before. Would Harry kiss her like that? She doubted it. And even if he did, she wouldn't feel anywhere near as much deep, real want as she had last night.

Shit.

Shit.

'Well, Pearl ate a lot more vegetables in your stir-fry than she did in mine.'

Charlie sank onto the sofa angled across from Beth's. 'Bribery and deception. And carrots. And overcooking the vegies just a bit.'

'I've got to hand it to you. You know your stuff when it comes to child rearing.'

'Maybe with toddlers. Teenagers are a mystery to me.'

Beth cocked her head. 'Have you heard from Jill?'

Charlie's face became remote. 'She left a message on my phone. She was crying. Angry. Demanding to know about Pearl — when she'll be back, what the doctor said. You should've heard the language she used.' He shook his head in disbelief.

'She's just worried, Charlie. She's taken on a parenting role with Pearl.'

He half-nodded. 'Yeah. I'll send her a message later to explain it more fully. I forget sometimes that Jill's old enough to understand things nowadays.'

There was a silence, during which Beth gazed at her toddler-finger-smudged coffee table, thinking about the girls.

'What are you going to do about her wanting to go to Mount Clair High School?' she asked.

'I'll talk to her. I'll help her understand why it would be better for her to wait.' He caught Beth's eye. 'I know I don't always get it right. I've fallen into the habit of just telling Jill what

267

I've decided, without explaining why. But you're right. She might respond better if I talk to her like an adult.'

Beth wasn't convinced Jill would accept his decision, but she nodded.

'I've been thinking,' she said. 'I know an occupational therapist who works with a lot of kids with disabilities. Would you be willing to take Pearl for a visit while you're in town? It might be a good way to get ideas to manage her cerebral palsy, to help her mobility and speech, her fine motor skills — that sort of thing. I think I could probably arrange an appointment at short notice, if you're willing to take Pearl along . . . '

Charlie's face was wary. 'There wouldn't be any reporting to authorities, would there?'

'What do you mean?'

'This OT won't report back to the government on Pearl's condition, recommending she gets moved out of Madjinbarra?'

Beth comprehended. 'I'll check, but I don't think so. I believe any reporting would simply be statistical, no names attached.'

'Then yes, I'll take her to an appointment.'

That had been unexpectedly easy. 'Great! I'll message Viv right now.'

Beth tapped out an email on her phone. Charlie seemed restless and fidgeted with his own phone for a few moments.

'I might take off and sit in my room,' he said at last. 'I'm halfway through writing a song and I think I've got a bit of it worked out — a bit I've been struggling with. Not being rude, I just need to get it down while it's in my head.'

She glanced at his leather guitar case, leaning against the living room wall. 'You don't have to hide in your room. It won't disturb me — unless you want privacy.'

'Cheers. It's easier out here. More space.'

He fetched the guitar and his paper and pencil, and began playing, humming and murmuring the song lines she'd read the night before, trying different snatches of music. Beth finished sending her occupational therapy contact a message and then pretended to do things on her phone while listening hungrily to Charlie's music. It felt like the song was sinking deeper into her every time he sang a line until she knew she'd never forget it, even if she never heard it again.

A memory pierced her consciousness: Charlie lying beside her on the grassy bank, hidden from the main road by a row of cycads. Heads touching, eyes on the clouds. He'd said that if he ever made anything of his music, he would kidnap her from her job or studies, or whatever she was doing, and take her on tour with him. They would go on the road together, he told her, driving from state to state in a Winnebago, and he would perform at all the coolest venues. They would find places to stop and explore along the way. They would lock themselves in the caravan to touch, play and kiss all night long. She'd laughed and asked when they were supposed to get any sleep, and Charlie had assured her that he'd give up sleep for the rest of his life if it meant he could spend all that time on her body.

Beth had told him quite firmly that she couldn't just drop everything and go on tour with him. But deep down, she'd suspected she would. All he had to do was ask.

Beth's fingers had fallen inactive over her phone and she found herself staring at the timed-out dark screen. She looked up to make sure Charlie hadn't noticed. He had. He was gazing at her, his expression puzzled, fingers still moving gently over the strings.

'Thinking?' he asked.

'I'm tired,' she said quickly.

He didn't buy it. 'Go to bed, then.'

'I will soon.'

Charlie didn't stop his soft playing, but he didn't take his eyes off her either. 'I don't want to be at war with you.'

She nodded, not trusting her voice.

Charlie looked down at his guitar for a moment. 'I know you're angry about what I did when we were at school — listening to gossip instead of trusting you or talking to you.'

'I don't think I'm angry any more,' Beth said. 'But no promises.'

Light sparked in his eyes. 'You might explode at any moment?'

'Anything is possible.'

He paused in his playing to push his hair back from his forehead, then resumed — but never once took his eyes from her face.

'You've been amazing with Pearl. Thanks.'

She half-smiled. 'You've got very cool nieces. I can't believe I've been working with them for two years now and I didn't pick up that they were related to you.'

His eyebrows rose. 'Really?'

'I had no idea. I mean, I'd heard them talk about an uncle but I never put two and two together.'

'You knew where I came from, though.'

She shook her head, embarrassed. 'I didn't. I knew you were Gwini but I didn't realise that, once a month, I've been visiting the place where you grew up. Staying with your aunt.'

'Huh.' He seemed to be thinking about that, his fingers dancing almost absently over the strings.

She wanted to be sure he believed her. 'I never saw you out there. But I guess you don't necessarily get out there that often, what with your work.'

It was Charlie's turn to look awkward. 'Actually, I knew you were our doctor. I made a point of finding out when you would be in town so I could make sure I wasn't. I didn't want us to have a difficult time if we saw each other out there.'

'Ah. You deliberately avoided me. I didn't realise you knew I was doing the remote health program.'

His mouth tugged up on one side. 'I heard about the new doctor from Jill first. *Doc* this, *Doc* that. But I got a bit of a shock when Aunty Mary mentioned the new doc's name.'

'Jill's so sweet. I think she's got a solid career in health ahead of her.'

'You realise you're a hero to her?'

Beth shot him a sceptical look. 'That's going a bit far.'

He snorted and did a fangirl voice. 'Uncle, the doc says I'm really good at managing Pearl's disability. Doc says Pearl needs physio. Uncle, the new doc, she's so pretty — you should see her. She should be on *Home and Away*.'

'Rubbish. Jill didn't say that.'

'She bloody did.' He was grinning now. 'She's your biggest admirer.'

'That's — *wow*.' Beth's heart ached for Jill, the girl who longed to follow her aspirations but was prevented from doing so by so much broken cultural history. She couldn't help but feel ashamed of her privilege, with her own personal history of a stable education and supportive parents.

Charlie put his guitar aside. 'In the interests of honesty, I need to admit something to you.'

'Jeez, something else?'

Charlie broke into laughter. 'Okay. I'll take that on the chin.' He grew serious again. 'This is going to sound self-obsessed, but when I heard you were doing the medical visits to Madji, I figured you were shoving the past in my face — what you did to me. What I *thought* you did to me. I thought you chose that particular community because you knew I would hear about you coming.'

Pain constricted something in her chest. 'Bloody hell, Charlie.'

'I know.' He rubbed his forehead. 'I'm starting to realise what a paranoid dickhead I've been.'

'What did I do to make you think so badly of me?' The question burst from her, as plaintive as a child's 'not fair'. 'You thought I slept around, made fun of you, and then came after you years later to drive the point home? What the hell did I ever do to make you think I would act that way?'

Her voice wobbled slightly and he moved so he was beside her on the sofa, his face full of remorse. Charlie looked for an instant like he would put his arms around her — but thought better of it.

'I don't know. You did nothing. I could apologise forever but it won't change anything. I don't know why I was suspicious. Pride, I guess.' He ducked his chin so he could see more clearly how valiant a fight Beth was putting up against her tears. 'I always felt like the world was going to get me, one way or another. Then, when it was kinder to me than I expected, I couldn't trust it.'

Beth was damned if he would see her cry. She held herself rigid. 'I understand.'

He moved back to his own sofa somewhat reluctantly. 'I don't know if you do.'

'I do. I understand the context — why your trust was easy to lose.'

'Doesn't make it feel any better though, right?' Charlie's voice was low. He took a breath. 'I want you to know I trust you now, and I want to prove it. It won't make up for what happened but maybe it will help make peace between us, and I want that — I really do.' His eyes were utterly earnest.

Beth shook her head. 'You don't have to prove anything to me. I'm not angry any more.'

'I want to. My nieces — my girls — they love you. They trust you. You earned that. Our elders, Aunty Mary and Harvey, they trust you too. So

I'm going to stop being a paranoid dickhead and show some faith in you too, if you're still willing to speak to me after the way I've acted.'

Beth smiled with an effort. 'That'd be good, Charlie. I appreciate it. It would be nice to be friends.'

His expression seemed to flicker but he put a hand out for her to shake, and she took it.

'Friends,' he said.

Beth shook.

18

On Thursday, Dr Grahame gave his blessing for Pearl to go home with her new medication regime. The occupational therapist, Viv, was able to see Pearl on Friday. Beth went to work feeling hopeful that the child would have some new strategies in place by the end of the day, and perhaps some recommendations for new equipment to help her motor development. She looked forward to hearing back from Charlie about the appointment. He was planning to drive Pearl home on Saturday morning and to bring Billy back to town with him sometime in the following few days.

When she got home from work on Friday afternoon, she discovered a blanket cubby in the living room. Beth ducked her head to peer into the cavern of fabric.

'Oh, hi,' said Charlie. 'You're early. I was going to get this all cleaned up before you got home.'

Beth stared at him. He and Pearl were beneath a fawn throw draped across two kitchen chairs. They sat on a pile of cushions, surrounded by toys and books.

She smirked. 'I really want to take a photo and tag your Instagram profile.'

Charlie frowned. 'I have an Instagram profile?'

She burst out laughing. 'Don't give me that rubbish. My sister and her friends reckon you're chatty and active on your social profiles.'

He looked puzzled, then abruptly enlightened. 'Oh, yeah. My manager said he was going to get a publicity person to manage my social presence. Must be that.'

'Well, I believe your fans are in quite a frenzy over your posts. I hope the man or woman who's doing it is being paid handsomely.'

'It's a she, I think,' he said, crawling out of the cubby. 'I get messages from someone called Shawna every now and then, asking me to send her a selfie or a photo of wherever it is I am. I won't do that selfie shit, but I send her photos of town signs, highways, stuff like that.'

Beth couldn't resist taking a look. She put her bag away and searched for Charlie's Instagram account on her phone. Then she sank onto a sofa and giggled at it until he couldn't repress his curiosity and came closer.

'What are you sniggering about?'

'Your Instagram.'

Charlie's eyebrows pulled down. 'What about it?'

She held it up to show him. He took her phone and scrolled slowly, his frown growing heavier and heavier.

'What the actual . . . '

Beth gave a little snort, she was laughing so hard. 'You're getting a lot of *likes* on those pics.'

'Half of these aren't even me!' he exclaimed, zooming in on one of them. 'Jesus. Who is this bloke with the guitar and the chest? I never had that photo taken. That's not even my chest. I mean, that's my tattoo, but it's not my chest. How the hell . . . ?'

'I think Shawna's been getting creative with Photoshop.' Beth craned her neck to see. 'Look, she's carefully excluded the face so your fans will think it's you.'

'Christ.' He kept scrolling and yelped when he found an artsy black-and-white shot of a guy with a muscled back, facing away from the camera, cowboy hat on. Only a guitar slung strategically across the back of him hid his bare arse. 'Okay, I'm emailing my manager. That one's gotta come down.'

Beth retrieved her phone, still giggling, and perused the photos more carefully. His account featured plenty of outback shots, venue photos and cityscapes, but Shawna hadn't gone light on the photos of Charlie, either. There were many of his face — smiling, brooding, candid, or close-ups of his amazing eyes. Some showed his hands playing the guitar. And, of course, a good serving of the fake-Charlie shots of muscled chests and backs.

'Maybe you should leave her to it,' she said. 'You're getting great engagement.'

'I can't have her posting shots of other blokes and pretending it's me!'

Beth shrugged. 'You should pose for some of those sexy shots yourself then.'

'Not a chance.'

'Well, you left her no choice.'

Charlie opened his mouth to argue but realised she was teasing him and shot her a faux-glare instead. 'I don't appreciate being objectified.'

'You should have thought about that before

you became a hot rock star,' she chuckled.

He glanced briefly her way, and in it she saw something between confusion and appreciation.

Ah, I just called him hot. Oops.

'How did the OT visit go?' she asked, pocketing her phone.

Charlie's face fell. He crossed to the kitchen table and picked up a sheaf of printed pages stapled in the top corner. He brought them over to Beth.

'Pearl needs a lot of stuff. A lot of therapy.'

Beth flipped through the pages Viv had printed for Charlie. There were recommendations for therapy schedules and lists of local specialists they could see, equipment to purchase, ways to help prepare her for school, adjustments to make to her home environment . . .

To Beth, the list looked appropriate and doable, but not if Pearl stayed out at Madjinbarra. She noted Charlie's expression: the frown and the tight jaw.

'Jill and Mary would be able to cope with a lot of these suggestions,' she said.

'Physio once a week? Regular speech therapy? And did you read the bit at the end where the OT recommended a hearing assessment? She thinks Pearl might be partially deaf.'

Beth flicked to the last page and read what Viv had written. *Cannot consistently identify where noises are coming from; possible sensorineural hearing loss to one ear.*

'Pearl's issues seem to be getting more and more complicated,' Charlie said with a sigh.

He gazed at his niece as she built a stack of

books, gabbling to her animals in her rug tent. Beth wasn't sure what to say.

'I know what you're thinking,' he added. 'She should come and live in town.'

'I wasn't thinking that, actually. Not this time.'

Charlie was silent for a few moments. *I'm* starting to think that,' he admitted at last. 'But how — how can I do that to her?'

'I get it,' she said, heart twinging.

'But?'

'No *but*. I get it, full stop. I wouldn't want her living with strangers, either. Pearl might cope okay, but it would hurt Jill to lose her sister. And she's so little. What if she forgets her own family?'

Charlie wore a look of immense relief.

Beth bit a nail. 'If I tell you something, do you promise not to come down on Jill like a ton of bricks?'

Charlie sat down near her. 'Okay.'

'I mean it. It's a betrayal of her confidence, and I don't want Jill turned against me. I'm telling you this because I know you want the best for them.'

'You have my word,' he said.

'Jill hinted that she wanted me, as her doctor, to recommend she and Pearl go into foster care.'

Charlie's expression changed to shock, then devastation.

Beth hastened to explain. 'Please understand, she feels helpless. She believes Pearl needs to be near health facilities, and she's desperate to go to school in town. She knows you won't let them leave, so she's trying to come up with a solution.'

Charlie swore, stood up and paced the little living room in agitation.

'On what grounds?' he snapped.

'Pardon?'

He glanced her way and adjusted his tone. 'On what grounds did she want you to recommend she go into foster care?' He sucked in a breath. 'This will kill Aunty Mary.'

Beth suddenly wished she hadn't said anything. 'No grounds. Charlie, it never got that far. Jill isn't plotting any allegations. She loves you and Mary. But she's fifteen, and she doesn't know what else to do to make you listen.'

He stopped that angry pacing and met her eye. 'Are you sure?'

'God, yes.' Beth was emphatic. 'Absolutely. Where's your trust, Charlie?'

She hadn't been referring to their history but Charlie looked like he'd been slapped. Beth froze.

Unexpectedly, he sank back down on the sofa alongside hers. 'You're right. But, bloody hell, *foster care?* I had to fight that dick-head Rendall to get her out of foster care once before. For Jill to jump straight to that — it's a kick in the guts. She didn't even ask if she could live with *me* here in town.'

'You're always on the move, Charlie. Of course she didn't think of that. She knows you can't give her a home here.'

He tugged his hair back from his forehead. 'Jesus. I'm really messing things up with these girls.'

'You're not!' Beth exclaimed. 'You're a wonderful uncle. They couldn't ask for better. But things have changed for both of them and . . . and maybe you need to work *with* Jill to find a solution, instead of against her.'

Charlie shook his head. 'You're a bloody masterclass in teenage-girl parenting,' he said, a half-smile twisting his mouth.

Beth laughed weakly. 'I don't know what I'm talking about, to be honest. Not a parent. Or even an aunt, yet.'

'But you've been a teenage girl. That makes you much more qualified than me.' He sighed and muttered. '*Jill.*'

His love for his nieces humbled Beth. 'Look, you've got a few days with Jill this weekend. Maybe you could talk to her and find out if she's got any ideas. Pearl needs hands-on care around the clock that Mary can't provide — but with Jill in a boarding school here, she won't be able to provide it either. So I guess the real problem is, who will care for Pearl if Jill comes to Mount Clair for school?'

'And can Pearl realistically stay in Madjinbarra, with her health so unstable?' he added, his eyes fixed on the coffee table.

'Perhaps if Pearl went into foster care here in Mount Clair, Jill could spend weekends with her,' Beth suggested. 'It's not ideal, but better than nothing.'

'Hmm.' Charlie looked wrecked.

She leaned forward and put a hand on his knee. 'Charlie. They're such amazing kids. Switched-on, love their family, want to do well.

Whatever happens, they'll be okay — I honestly believe that.'

Charlie nodded an acknowledgement of her words but then his gaze switched to his knee, where her hand rested. Beth withdrew it hastily.

He met her eyes. 'Let's eat out tonight,' he said. 'My shout. I want to say thanks for letting us stay with you this week.'

'Okay.'

'Pearl,' he called. 'Should we go out to get dinner?'

'I hungry,' she called back.

'I'll just get changed out of my work clothes.' Beth got to her feet. 'Where are we going?'

'Somewhere that is okay with extremely messy eaters.'

'Hmm. That only leaves Mountie Fried Chicken, I think.'

Charlie screwed up his nose. 'God, please no.'

Beth thought of an alternative. 'Oh, hang on, what about fish and chips? We can eat at the lake.'

'Sounds good.'

Beth went to change out of her work pants and blouse and into a pair of shorts and a tank top, relieved she didn't need to dress smartly for a restaurant. The three of them piled into Charlie's vehicle. Although the body was rough, it was relatively clean inside the dual cab. Pearl perched in her booster seat in the back, shouting about chips like a small dictator.

Charlie drove them to the foreshore car park on Lake Road and left Pearl with Beth while he went to sort out the food. Beth held Pearl's hand, encouraging her to walk on the grassy strip that bordered the red shore and the water beyond. It was still warm, but the sun had dropped enough that the air felt balmy, rather than oven-like. A breeze tickled through her hair. Beth found a spot and spread out a blanket, sprayed Pearl with insect repellent and sat down to wait for Charlie. Pearl did a little triathlon of crawling, bum-shuffling and staggering after seagulls, and Beth laughed at the way she yelled at them, as if outraged by their very existence.

Ten minutes later, she glanced around and spotted Charlie making his way across the grass towards them, carrying a paper-wrapped package. Her breath caught.

If his Instagram fans could see him now . . .

'Now, it's going to be hot,' he told Pearl as he sat down across from Beth. 'Let the chips cool down before you eat one. Here, I got you some sauce.' He shot Beth a rueful look. 'Sauce was probably a mistake, yeah?'

She managed a smile, still a little shaken by that vision of Charlie striding towards her in shorts and a snug-fitting T-shirt, hair pushed back off his face, frowning into the glare of sunset. His *holy-hell-gorgeous* body was obvious, even covered by clothes. He unwrapped their dinner and they tucked in.

'Not as healthy as you're used to,' Charlie commented.

'It's so good,' Beth said, smiling. 'Can I have some sauce too, Pearl?'

Pearl passed her a grease-covered sauce sachet. They ate, watching the sun sink beyond the lake. As soon as she'd finished, Pearl smeared cold chip across the blanket, setting off to banish the seagulls attempting to settle on the grass for a night's sleep. Beth dissolved into laughter, watching Pearl shout every time one dared land again. She opened her mouth to make a remark about it to Charlie, but when she turned and saw his face, the words died on her lips.

Charlie was looking at her with an expression that sent a jump-start through her chest. His eyes, green as sea glass in the fading light, were enthralled yet terribly sad — like an old ache had been triggered. Although she was sitting there in boring shorts and a tank top, fingers covered in salty chip grease, hair knotted by the sea breeze, it was as though Charlie saw something truly incredible.

'I lied,' he said. 'It wasn't just trust issues. That's not why I never settled down.'

Beth waited. She had somehow forgotten the simple process of breathing.

'It's because I never met anyone who even remotely measured up to you.'

Beth dragged her eyes away. Now she understood why she'd never found anyone either.

★　★　★

All the way home, Pearl sleepily discussing chips, seagulls and zebras in the back of the car, Beth fought with herself. She should have known this would happen. She should have predicted that there was a chance her feelings would be reignited. How could she have allowed it? Hell, she'd invited Charlie to stay in her home, invited him back into her life. She might as well have put a big sign on her door saying, *Come in and take advantage of me if you want, because I'm spineless where you're concerned.* And even if that look in his eyes was real, even if he really cared, Charlie was leaving tomorrow, and he would always be leaving. He lived a life on the road. There was no way they could make anything of this . . . this *thing.*

We already have, her heart whined. *We've already made peace, cleared up the past, come together and forgiven. He still cares about me, and I still hold a candle for him — a great, big, fiery, gun-powdery candle.*

Too much history, her brain answered patiently. *He will be touring, looking after his family. He won't be able to give me the commitment I want.*

Her heart — and other parts of her body — pictured Charlie walking across the grass in the setting sun and didn't give a damn whether commitment was forthcoming or not. Beth panicked silently as they pulled up in her front yard. She wanted him so much that she wasn't sure she had the fortitude to protect herself. This could hurt. And she'd promised herself a long time ago that no man would ever hurt her again — least of all this particular man.

Pearl had fallen asleep during the five-minute ride. Charlie released her seatbelt and untangled her arms from the harness, heaving her out onto his shoulder, and Pearl didn't even murmur.

Beth let them into the house and helped him get the child into bed, ensuring Gummy the elephant was tucked in beside Pearl. Then she went to the kitchen on trembling legs, poured herself a glass of wine and waited for Charlie.

'Do you want a drink?' she asked when he arrived, his eyes veiled.

He hesitated, then nodded. He reached for the whisky bottle he'd left on the bench a few nights before, and she got him a glass with some ice. They sipped their drinks, avoiding each other's eyes. Beth went into the living room and sat down on a sofa.

Charlie followed, sitting opposite. 'It was easier when we were kids, wasn't it? Gargantua and their workers' camp, that would've been the grown-ups' problem. A Gwini kid being relocated to another family — not our call or responsibility. We would have been affected by the outcomes, but we didn't have to make the decisions or fight them ourselves.'

'Maybe it's because we *are* willing to fight that it's harder,' she said. 'Some grown-ups just watch things happen. You and I get involved, whether we're likely to make a difference or not.'

He nodded. 'I suppose we're lucky. We've got the resources to get involved.'

'Yeah. But I hear you on how hard it is. Sometimes I wish I didn't have to get involved.' Beth put her head back against the sofa and stared at the ceiling. 'It starts to feel relentless.' She shot Charlie a half-smile. 'I need a bloody holiday.'

'Where would you go?' he asked. 'If you could

286

take off tomorrow?'

Beth thought about it, gazing unseeingly at her light fitting. 'Somewhere with a pool, a view, a pile of books and nobody I know.'

Charlie made a noise of agreement. 'Throw in some fishing and I'm there.'

She laughed. 'You fish, I'll cook.'

'You're on.'

She dropped her chin and caught his eye, her smile fading. Everything between them had always been like this. Pipe dreams or memories. Charlie read her face.

'Please, Beth,' he said, his voice low.

She waited, knowing it was hopeless, but needing more anyway. Charlie pushed his drink onto the coffee table and then he was beside her on the sofa, one hand coming up to lay a warm palm against her cheek, the other taking her wineglass and setting it on the table.

'I can't believe I threw us away. If I could meet my eighteen-year-old self, I'd punch him into next week.'

'There's no point regretting it any more,' she said.

'I'll regret it for the rest of my life.' He stroked his thumb across her cheek and took a breath. 'And I'll regret it more if I don't ask — am I really *nothing* to you?'

Without hesitation, Beth shook her head. Hope fired in his beautiful eyes.

'I'm not too late?'

'No.' She sighed the word so quietly she wasn't even sure she'd heard it herself.

Charlie would never be too late, damn him.

She was his forever. Even if they couldn't be together, he had her. Even now, her brain was still tutting away about commitment and distance, but her heart was completely, wildly, blindly *his*.

'Thank Christ,' he muttered, slipping his other hand up under her hair and pulling her close enough to kiss.

Everything that had been brewing between them for the past couple of weeks sat under that kiss, and within moments it wasn't just a kiss any more. It was a frantic, full-body event: hands, lips and tongues. Clothing was nothing more than a diabolical inconvenience and Charlie made short work of it, using both hands to grasp the hem of her tank top and whip it up over her head before he crushed his lips back onto hers, fumbling with the button of her shorts with one hand and the catch of her bra with the other. It was only when she found herself naked that he suddenly slowed down. Charlie's eyebrows knitted and he drew his gaze down over her whole body, studying every inch with avid appreciation.

'Bloody hell, Beth,' he breathed. 'You're even more gorgeous than I remember.'

In answer, she pulled his shirt off and kissed the tattoo of a bird of prey that stretched across his chest, her hands urging him to get rid of the rest of his clothes. Then there was nothing between them but need, and they made short work of that, too.

The initial desperation out of their system, they collapsed back against the sofa cushions and Charlie pulled her into his arms. He kissed and touched her relentlessly, poring over her body like he had to know every part of her. No — like he had to *reacquaint* himself with every part of her. After years of sporadic, adequate encounters with guys who didn't mean an awful lot to her, Beth was immensely relieved to find she hadn't lost the capacity for mind-blowing sex. Charlie knew how to shine a light into the very back of her heart, where all her secret desires lived. After all, he was the one who'd originally put them there.

She gasped his name over and over, and he murmured hers back to her. At last he stood and pulled her to her feet.

'Come on,' he said. 'Bed.'

'You're tired?' she said.

'Hell, no. But you might as well get comfortable because I'm nowhere near finished with you.'

As they went, Beth registered that they'd somehow knocked over her glass of red wine and it had run across the table, dripping like blood onto her white rug.

Oh, well. White floor rugs were stupid, anyway.

19

Beth barely had time to yank a sheet over herself when Pearl bum-shuffled into her bedroom in the morning, demanding to know where *Unca Jarlie* was. Charlie shifted against Beth's back as he woke up.

'Why you no in your bed, Unca?' Pearl wanted to know.

'Morning, Pearl,' he murmured, strategically ignoring the question. 'Have you been to the toilet?'

'Yeah. I hungry.'

He sighed and slid a hand from Beth's thigh, up over her hip beneath the sheet, pressing his lips to the back of her neck.

'Don't move,' he said firmly. 'I'll make you a coffee.'

With a little deft manoeuvring, Charlie snatched a throw rug off the floor and wrapped it around his waist like a towel.

'Come on, Pearl. I'll get you some Rice Bubbles.'

'Why you no in *your* bed?' she repeated, following him down the hall.

'Because I wanted a cuddle with Beth,' he said.

Pearl was offended. '*I* want cuddle.'

'C'mere, then,' he said, and a delighted squawk indicated he'd swung her up into the air.

Beth listened to them as Charlie made Pearl breakfast and boiled the kettle. Pearl clambered loudly up onto a kitchen chair and talked about why she wanted sugar on her Rice Bubbles until Charlie relented and agreed to drizzle a little honey on them. Then he implored her to try using her spoon, and eventually groaned that she would need a bath before they left.

A few minutes later, he brought Beth a mug of coffee and sat on the edge of the bed to explore her face and the outline of her sheet-clad body with those glass-green eyes.

'I should be back in town on Monday,' he said. 'The only thing that would mess with that is if I have trouble with Billy.'

Beth took a breath. 'Will you stay with me again, when you get back?' she asked. She'd tried to sound casual but it came out shy and awkward.

A smile curved his lips as he stood. 'Definitely. Now, I'd better go and sort Pearl out before she comes looking for us. She's swimming in Rice Bubbles. And it looks like a crime scene in the living room,' he added. 'I wiped up the red wine, but that rug . . . '

'It survived a week of Pearl but it couldn't survive *us*,' she said.

He shot her a grin. 'At this rate, your house might not even be standing by the end of next week.'

Beth found a T-shirt and slipped it on, sitting up in bed to drink her coffee. She felt almost giddy, there was so much joy buzzing around inside her. She tried to control it but it kept lifting her up, flying off with her heart until the ground had practically disappeared from sight.

He was coming back to stay with her.

Beth listened to Charlie bathing Pearl, then having a shower himself. She should get up and tidy the house. But she stayed where she was, sipping her coffee, listening to their activity. Revelling in her happiness. Eventually Charlie came back in, dressed for his long drive, and handed over her phone.

'It's pinged about a thousand times,' he said, a slightly odd expression on his face.

She checked the screen and saw messages from Free, Willow and Rikke. And nine from Harry, the final one still sitting visible on the screen.

Anyway, no problem if you're not interested. Just a thought. Either way, I'm looking forward to dinner tonight! x

She scrolled back up and read through the previous eight. Harry was telling her all about a film festival coming to Mount Clair in a couple of weeks and suggesting they go and see a couple of the movies together. Beth looked up at Charlie, waiting beside her bed with an expression somewhere between uncertainty and wry amusement.

'I guess I'll need to cancel my date with Harry for tonight,' she said. 'I'm glad you bothered to check the facts with me this time.'

Charlie scowled and was on her in an instant, burying stubbly kisses in her neck while she squirmed. When he discovered she still wore no knickers under the sheet, he made a delighted noise and it seemed he might settle in to stay a little longer but Beth slapped his hand away.

'Pearl could come in at any moment.'

'Yeah, okay.' His reluctance was plain. 'How's your bruised bum now?' he added.

'Feeling much better.'

'Good. I have to admit I completely forgot about it last night. I'm glad we didn't make it worse.'

Beth stretched languorously. 'There's a theory that it's impossible to feel pain at the same time as pleasure.'

He was smiling. 'So last night you were just testing a medical hypothesis?'

She shrugged. 'I'm committed to my work.'

Charlie chuckled and stood up. 'Well, we're packed and ready to go.'

'Did you get Pearl's Barbie sofa and books?'

He tipped his head. 'Aren't they for your sister's baby?'

'No, I got them for Pearl. She can take them home.'

'You sure?'

'Absolutely. And Charlie,' she said, grabbing his hand as he turned. 'Will you bring me my bathrobe so I can come and say goodbye?'

He did so and Beth found Pearl with Gummy tucked under her arm, thumb in mouth, watching *Play School*.

'Come on, Pearl,' Charlie said, arriving behind Beth with the Barbie sofa hanging from his hand. 'Time to go.'

She got off the sofa and, when Beth asked for a hug, put her arms out. Beth gave her a big cuddle, inhaling the child's smell — honey and soap.

'I'll see you next time I come to visit you at Aunty Mary's place,' Beth told Pearl.

'Jill,' Pearl replied.

'Yep, you're going home to see Jill. Give her a hug for me, too.'

Charlie loaded his niece and her gear into the back of his vehicle and came back to Beth, catching her around the waist.

'Be gentle when you break the bad news to Harry,' he said, giving his head a sorrowful shake. 'Poor guy's going to be devastated.'

She shoved him. 'Stop gloating.'

Charlie grinned and bent down to place a kiss on her lips. 'I'll see you soon.'

⋆   ⋆   ⋆

Beth put off contacting Harry while she did the laundry. Washing Pearl's bedding and taking down the decorations she'd put up in the spare room were sad tasks, but they didn't have that edge of loneliness Beth had expected. Inside she was clutching the beautiful knowledge that Charlie was coming back to stay with her. It might only be for a few days, but she would have him all to herself for that time.

Maybe she and Charlie *could* make it work. Sure, he had a lot of responsibilities, but he'd admitted he had never met anyone he cared about as much as Beth. Warmth flushed through her as she thought about it. Hell, she had her own responsibilities, too — her clinic and her work at Madjinbarra. But they could make time for each other, couldn't they?

Her mind accelerated into the future, calculating how they could arrange their lives so that they could spend more time together. She could cut back on hours — maybe consider adding a staff member or using the locum more. They could coordinate around Charlie's recording sessions and tours so that they could be together. If they communicated properly, it might work. Doubt crept in when she remembered that musicians generally toured for months on end. And who knew when he would flit off to do a collaboration or get invited to appear at some festival? She always needed a good month or two to arrange any time off work.

Worry about it later, she scolded herself.

She had a more pressing problem: Harry. She couldn't put it off any longer. She opened his most recent message and contemplated it. Maybe it would be smarter to claim some bogus emergency to bow out of tonight's date, and then fully withdraw from the fledgling relationship on a separate occasion. It seemed horribly cold to cut the whole thing off just hours from their date. Or maybe she should just go — meet him at the pub — and tell him face to face that it was over. No. That would be too public. At last she decided she was being cowardly and just had to bloody do it. She messaged him.

Hi Harry, are you busy? Have you got time for a coffee?

He replied a couple of minutes later. *Now?*

Yes, she responded. *I need to talk to you*

about a couple of things.

Okay. My place or yours?

Neutral ground, her logic warned her. *Do you know Galileo's?*

Yes. I can be there in twenty.

See you then.

She dressed modestly. If she was honest, she dressed as boringly as possible — some khaki cargo pants she normally wore to do the gardening, and a bland T-shirt. If she looked unsexy and plain, maybe Harry wouldn't feel too let down.

His face was fresh, young and hopeful when she spotted him in a booth at Galileo's. *Shit.*

'Hi, Harry.' Beth gave him a tight smile but he stood up and kissed her cheek. 'I'll shout you a coffee.'

'Only if you let me pay for dinner tonight.'

Beth gave him another smile but didn't answer. She crossed to the counter and ordered two flat whites — small size. *Let's keep this as quick as possible.*

'I didn't think I'd get to see you twice today,' Harry said when she returned, his blue eyes shining warmly into hers.

'Um, yes, well, I thought it would be better if I cleared this up before tonight.'

Slight caution entered his expression. 'What's up?'

She searched for a place to start. 'Our mutual acquaintance, Rikke — she's one of my oldest friends. She thinks a lot of you. In fact, she really wanted me to go out with you.'

He chuckled. 'Thanks, Rikke.'

Beth cringed inside. 'She's got great taste but she's not a hundred per cent in-the-know with what's going on in my life at the moment, and I have to admit I've made a mistake, Harry.' The cautious look returned and Beth ploughed on. 'I've got some complications happening that mean I'm not in a great space for dating right now.'

Harry looked concerned. 'Complications?'

The waitress arrived, holding their coffees. 'Two flat whites?'

'Thanks,' said Beth.

Harry waited while the waitress placed their coffees on the table and then returned his gaze to Beth's face. 'Anything I can help with?'

'No, it's personal.' She attempted a smile. 'I'm sorry.'

'Sometimes it can help to unburden yourself,' he suggested, stirring a sugar into his coffee.

Ugh. 'Harry, you're such a lovely guy and I would hate to see you hurt. I'm just . . . ' She went blank. How could she say she'd met someone else in the few days since her first date with Harry? She wasn't ready to tell anyone about Charlie yet, least of all Harry.

'Is it stress?' Harry asked. She was reaching for her coffee cup and he put his hand out, catching hers in his. 'I've noticed how stressed out you seem.'

'No, I'm fine. It's more that I have a lot going on.' She gently withdrew her hand and picked up her coffee.

'I'd like to help,' he said.

'It really is personal,' she said. The coffee was

too hot to drink. She was forced to put it down to let it cool. 'I appreciate your thoughtfulness, Harry — I honestly do. But I need to focus on my own stuff for a while. I'm not sure Rikke explained how full-on my work life is. Plus, I have family things happening, and involvement in community issues — I'm just not able to give enough of myself to be good company right now.'

To her dismay, Harry reclaimed her hand. 'I get it,' he said. 'You give a lot of yourself. You need to rejuvenate. But believe me, I want to help you do that.' He looked straight into her eyes. 'I've had a thought. I'm booked for a trip to Sydney next month. This is radical, but how about you come too?' Her face must have changed because Harry hastened to explain. 'Not like that. Just as friends. Separate rooms, but maybe some nice meals together, a bit of exploring . . . ' Harry's blue eyes were bright on hers. 'Galleries, restaurants. Maybe a show?'

This was almost traumatic. 'Harry, you are *such* a nice guy. Please forgive me, but I'm not someone you want.'

He laughed. 'I think I'll be the judge of that.'

'Seriously. I'm not.'

'Beth.' Harry squeezed her hand. 'I know what I want.'

'Harry, I just told you I'm not in the right space — '

'Yes, I know. I'm sorry.' He released her hand. 'I'm not pressuring you at all, I promise. I just want you to think about it. Don't give me an answer right now. Take the idea away with you

298

and think about it. We don't have to go to dinner tonight if you don't want. Take the time and space you need, but do me the favour of not turning down the Sydney idea right now.'

He looked so earnest and caring, and she was so damned relieved that he'd let her off the hook for their dinner date that Beth nodded. With an effort, she turned the conversation to work while they finished their coffees, and then claimed she had book work to get through for the clinic. As she drove home, she felt genuinely bad — not just that she hadn't been honest with Harry, but that she wasn't interested in the poor guy. Perhaps, in an alternative dimension, she might have been able to fall in love with Harry — in an alternative dimension where Charlie Campbell had never existed.

★ ★ ★

Beth was with Reg Craddick on Monday afternoon, discussing the likelihood that he had Lyme disease, when her phone buzzed with a message from Charlie. She saw it come through and would dearly have loved to snatch up her phone and read it, but she had too much respect for her patient, despite his chronic hypochondria.

'Just keep it clean, and if it does turn out to be a tick bite, we can always do blood tests. But honestly, Mr Craddick, I think it's just a mozzie bite.'

He departed, grumbling that if it turned out to be Lyme disease, it might be too late to do anything about it by then. Beth gave him a reassuring smile as he stumped away down the corridor. She seized her phone.

Back in town, with tag-alongs, Charlie had written.

She couldn't hold in a huge smile. *You know where the key is?*

He replied with a simple *Yep. Cheers.*

Beth wasn't sure how she would get through the rest of the afternoon seeing patients. The hospital tried her number three times during a consultation, and in between appointments, Dani popped her head around the door.

'Beth, could you call the hospital? They need to talk to you about an admission.'

She did so. This must be about Billy Early. Hopefully they were just seeking information. The reception desk put her through to Ed Hyem, an orthopaedic surgeon who did regular visits to Mount Clair. Her heart dropped another level.

'Hi, Beth. How's things?'

'Not bad. I didn't realise you were in town, Ed. What's going on?'

'It's probably a good thing I am in town. I've got your patient here — Billy Early, from a desert community.'

'Yes — what do you think?'

'I think he's going to need an amputation.'

Beth sucked in a breath. 'Oh no!'

'Gangrene's set in. I've got him on intravenous antibiotics and morphine for the pain but the infection's wreaking havoc with his blood sugar and the Doppler shows next to no perfusion in the lower leg. I really don't think the limb's viable. We'll send him to Darwin and monitor for improvement but I suspect it will be surgery. Below the knee at this stage — and then we'll keep an eye on things. Can you come and see him, Beth? He's agitated, says he wants to talk to you. We need a bit of help with notifying his next of kin, too. He says that's his father, but we can't get a response on the number we're trying.'

Dismay settling like a cold lump in her gut, Beth checked her appointments and those of Carolyn, the other GP currently in the clinic. 'When are you sending him to Darwin?'

'As soon as possible. It's very nasty.'

She promised Ed she would be there within the hour and went out to reception to ask Dani to shuffle her appointments. She treated the two patients who were waiting and dashed out to the Beast, dialling Charlie as she went.

'Beth?' he answered.

'Charlie, Billy's not in a good way. Can you meet me at the hospital?'

'I'm already here at the hospital. What's going on?'

Beth hesitated. 'You are? Are you with him?'

'No, I'm with Pearl.'

'Pearl!' she exclaimed. 'What? Why?'

'I didn't want to disturb you while you were at work,' he said, his tone apologetic. 'She's not quite right yet. She had a couple of seizures back at Aunty Mary's place.'

'Oh no,' said Beth. 'Bugger.'

'I brought Jill with me this time. We're here in

the ward with Pearl, settling her back in. What's going on with Billy?'

'The specialist thinks they need to remove his foot.'

There was a silence. 'What the *hell?*'

'It was bad, Charlie, even when I saw it a week or so ago. It's even worse now, and if they don't take it off, he could lose the entire leg.'

'Jesus.' He'd dropped his voice and Beth realised he must be trying to conceal his reaction from the girls. 'They can't try antibiotics, or something?'

'He's been on and off antibiotics, from what Maud and Christine told me. The ulcers are necrotic. There's nerve damage, no circulation. His whole lower limb is pretty much dead, and it will take the upper leg with it if they don't act now.' She paused. 'They need to do this, Charlie, or Billy might not survive.'

Charlie was quiet for so long, she wasn't totally sure he was still there. She checked her phone but the call was still connected. Was he going to argue? Try to tell her Billy would be better off keeping his rotting limb? At last, she heard a deep sigh.

'Right. I'll go see him,' said Charlie.

She drove to the hospital and sought out Ed Hyem.

'The RFDS can get Billy to Darwin in the morning,' the specialist told her. 'The foot is putrid and I'm not convinced the other one's going to last very long either, but I'll let Darwin make that call. I'm ninety-nine per cent sure he needs at least one amputation.'

'Did you tell Billy his other foot is in danger, as well?'

Ed nodded. 'He's adamant he'll be fine and keeps saying it doesn't even hurt any more — hardly a surprise now he's on strong pain meds. He was trying to prove it's still a functioning limb, wiggling his toes. I thought for a moment one of the toes might break off in front of me.' He paused. 'How did the clinic out where he comes from let it get so bad?'

'They did their best with him,' Beth said, defensiveness making her voice a little sharp. 'He's not what you'd call a cooperative patient. I told him over a week ago he needed to get himself to hospital but it wasn't until a friend went out to pick him up that we actually managed to get him here.'

Ed raised a hand. 'All right. I didn't mean to cause offence.'

Beth forced herself to back down. 'It's just, the clinic nurses out there are highly competent and work their arses off to look after the community. I wouldn't want any misinformation getting out about the clinic's capacity.'

'They'll have better access to facilities once the Gargantua mine is constructed, anyway.' Ed was glib. 'The Aboriginal Liaison Officer hasn't been able to see Billy yet. Could you try to calm him down a bit, Beth? He doesn't seem to trust me, for God knows what reasons of his own.'

Angry disbelief rose again but, thankfully, Ed turned and left Beth on her own in the bright corridor. She made her way to Billy's room. Charlie was already there, trying to reassure

Billy, whose face was grey with fear.

'Was it you?' Billy demanded when he caught sight of Beth. 'Did you tell 'em to cut me bloody foot off?'

Charlie jumped in. 'Don't be a silly bugger. You know her better than that.'

Billy slumped back on his bed, regarding his foul-smelling, bandaged foot with hatred, as if he would lop it off himself, given the right tools. Then his face crumpled and he heaved a sudden, dry sob. 'I don't wanna be a bloody cripple.'

Charlie grabbed Billy's shoulder and shook him gently. 'All right, mate. You won't be out of action long. We can get you a falsey. State of the art.'

Beth saw how badly Charlie wanted to take Billy's pain away, but Billy needed to feel this anger and sorrow; it was part of the process.

'I'm so sorry, Billy.' She stood at the side of his bed. 'It may be too late for your poor old foot. It looked very bad when I saw it a couple of weeks back. It must seem strange that you can still stand on it and move it, but that's just the tendons and joints in your leg. The foot itself is already gone — dead.'

Billy's face was still screwed up with awful grief, his eyes fixed on the pallid, cracked skin exposed between the dressings on his foot. She continued, keeping her voice low and calm. 'The fact that you can still walk is good, because it tells us the top part of your leg is still okay. If we remove the dead foot now, Billy, the rest of your leg has a good chance of being all right. Charlie's right, we can sort out a prosthetic — a good, strong artificial leg for you — as soon as the surgery's all healed up.'

Billy heaved another soundless sob, his lips pulled back in a grimace of sorrow.

Charlie squeezed the man's shoulder. 'Come on, mate. What would your dad say? He'd tell you not to be a dickhead, and to just get rid of the foot. It's bad for you. It's full of bad blood and rotten flesh. Let the docs take it off and the rest of you'll be well again.'

There was a long, long moment of silence while Billy brought his face under control and gulped some breaths.

'Take the bloody thing off, then.'

Beth brought them cups of tea and they all sat together for a while to discuss fishing and keep Billy's mind off darker things. A recent football game was replaying on the television so, after a short while, they left Billy in relative comfort, watching his favourite sport.

Beth and Charlie walked to the children's ward in silence.

'I should've gone and got him last week,' Charlie muttered at last.

'It was already too far gone,' said Beth. 'He told me he'd had those sores for a while but he was never around when I was visiting. Maybe that was deliberate. I could see how bad it was when he came into the Madji clinic last week, but he wouldn't agree to come to town with me.'

'You offered him a ride?'

'Yes, of course, but he said he'd rather catch a ride in with Kanga on the weekend. I didn't realise he'd wriggle out of it.'

Charlie groaned. 'Typical Billy. I'll keep trying Harvey's phone. He'll be gutted when he hears.'

They found Pearl playing with her little friend with the bandaged head. Jill was sitting in the chair beside the bed where the two played, flicking through a magazine. She jumped up and came forward to hug Beth when she saw her.

'Uncle Charlie said we could stay at your place,' she said, her eyes shining with excitement.

'Hey,' Charlie interjected awkwardly. 'I said I'd ask — '

'Of course you can,' Beth interrupted. 'I'd love to have you.'

'Uncle reckons Pearl's seizures stopped last week, but she had another one at home. I saw her.'

'Yes, I heard.' Beth crossed to the bed to kiss Pearl's silky hair. 'Hi, Pearl.'

'I playing with my *friend*.' Pearl was indignant at the interruption.

'Okay, fair enough.' Beth turned back to Charlie. 'Has Dr Grahame seen her yet?'

He shook his head. 'The nurse said he would be in sometime this afternoon.'

'I finished early. If you want to take Jill back to my place, I can stay with Pearl.'

Jill turned away to grab her gear but Charlie stepped closer to Beth.

'Would you take Jill home with you, instead? It's my responsibility to stay with Pearl, and anyway, I think I should be around for Billy tonight.' She nodded and he looked at her mouth for a long moment before apparently deciding it was not the time or place to kiss her.

She liked that he'd thought about it, though. 'Thank you,' he added.

Jill was perfectly happy to go home with Beth instead of her uncle. She loaded her bulging backpack into the rear of the Beast and climbed in beside Beth, already chattering away, a big smile on her face.

'Uncle Charlie says we're going to check out the girls' boarding house,' she reported.

Beth lifted her eyebrows. This was a significant change of heart. 'How exciting. Did he say you *might* do that? Or definitely?'

'Definitely. He wants me to tour the school and boarding house first, and then he said I could trial it for a term if I like the look of it.'

Although Jill had been to Mount Clair before, she was looking around at the place as though it was her first visit. Beth recognised the brightness in the girl's eyes. Jill was seeing Mount Clair as her new home.

'I know I'll like the boarding house and the school,' she added. 'But I said yes to it being a trial, to make Uncle happy.'

Beth laughed as they rolled down the main street. 'I think you might like it, too. I lived at Durack when I was seventeen. The same hostel nanny still runs the place — Hen. She's fantastic.'

Jill grinned at her. 'Thanks for talking Uncle Charlie into it.'

'I honestly didn't,' Beth replied. 'I just suggested he have a proper conversation with you about it.'

She wanted to ask if he'd said anything about

arrangements for Pearl but stopped herself. Perhaps Charlie was considering foster care for Pearl — and that could upset Jill and wreck her excitement.

'Uncle Charlie says you have a really nice house,' Jill said. 'With posh decor, like on *The Block.*'

Beth burst out laughing. 'It's not as posh as that. Don't get too excited.'

It was posh enough for Jill's tastes. She brought her bag inside and explored the interior, not even waiting for Beth to offer her a tour.

'Wow,' she said when she returned to find Beth in the kitchen. 'This is so nice. Everything matches. Where can I sleep?'

'You can take the guestroom. The spare room is Pearl's, and she should be out of hospital again in a few days.'

'I don't mind sharing with Pearl,' Jill said.

'You can if you'd rather,' Beth told her. 'But if you want your own room, take the guestroom.'

Jill's brow creased. 'The one with the blue doona and double bed?'

'Yes, that's it. On the left.'

Jill was grinning again. 'Awesome. It's huge! But what about Uncle Charlie? Does he have to go back and stay at the pub now I'm here to look after Pearl?'

A hot, embarrassed blush hit Beth hard. She'd unconsciously assumed Charlie would be in her own room, but they couldn't do that, of course — not with the girls here. She attempted a laugh that sounded a little strangled.

'No, of course not. I forgot about him. Maybe

you *should* bunk in with Pearl.'

'Or sleep on the couch.' Jill eyed the big sofas covetously.

Phew. Jill hadn't noticed Beth's momentary freak-out. 'Whatever you prefer. You and Pearl could even share my room, if you want, and I'll take the spare.'

'Nah, I'll sleep in Pearl's room.' She glanced around. 'Do you have internet here?'

'Yes. Want to have a play?'

Jill's smile couldn't have been any wider. Beth set her up on the computer and called Dani to rearrange some of her appointments for the next morning. She wanted to visit Billy again before he left for Darwin. Jill wandered in after an hour and asked if she could help with cooking dinner. Charlie arrived while they were chopping vegetables for a curry.

'Hey, Uncle,' Jill called as soon as he stepped inside. 'Is Pearl okay? Did you talk to her doctor?'

Charlie joined them in the kitchen. 'Yes, he's adjusting the dosage of her medication. He wants her to stay in the hospital for a few days while they get it right. If this doesn't work, he reckons it would be better to send her to Darwin to get it sorted.'

Jill's eyes lit up. 'So we might go to Darwin?'

Beth checked Charlie's face. He looked tired and stressed. 'If that's necessary, Charlie, Jill could stay with me,' she said. Jill frowned and opened her mouth to argue but Beth shot her a warning look. 'Your uncle needs to be able to focus on Pearl. It wouldn't be any fun for you,

309

anyway, because it wouldn't be a holiday. You'd be stuck at the hospital all day too.'

Jill thought the better of her protest and settled back into chopping onions. Charlie gave Beth a weary smile.

'Did you see Billy again?' she asked.

'Yeah. He wasn't in a good way, emotionally. The nurse gave him a sedative to help him sleep. I sat with him for a bit, but he fell asleep and didn't look like he'd be waking up anytime soon, so I came home.'

Beth wrestled down the wave of dizzy joy that rose in her when he called her place 'home'. She sliced the skin off a piece of ginger root and made herself think about poor Billy. 'I'm going to see him in the morning,' she told Charlie. 'I've swapped some appointments around.'

His expression softened. 'That'd be good. He's scared.'

Beth grimaced, reaching for the garlic. 'Who wouldn't be? Poor Billy. It's going to be hard work to get him to protect his other limb. And with a prosthetic — we need to make sure he keeps it clean and checks for rubbing sores, or he might end up in the same boat with his upper leg. Did you get hold of Harvey?'

'Yes. He's coming into town tonight and he'll fly with Billy.'

She fiddled with a clove of garlic, gazing at Charlie. 'Is Harvey okay?'

'A bit rattled, but yeah, he's okay.'

Their eyes locked, Beth saw all the pain of the exchange Charlie must have had with Harvey and ached to comfort him. Jill looked up at the clock, gasped and put her knife down with a clatter.

'Can I watch *Home and Away*?'

Beth nodded and Jill raced to the living room. With an air of relief, Charlie stepped nearer to Beth, pulling her into a tight hug.

'I hate bringing all this trouble into your home.'

'These are my concerns too. I wouldn't want you to exclude me.'

He pressed his lips to her forehead and stroked a hand down her arm. 'I've never wanted anyone's help — not for years. But there's something about you that makes everything feel easier.'

'Just let me know if I get pushy,' she said.

Charlie gave her a puzzled look. 'You're not pushy.'

'I've been known to . . . to organise people a little too energetically. My younger sister gave me a good telling off for it last year. I've been trying to control my urges since then.'

He squeezed her close. 'No need to control any urges around me.'

'How do you work this remote control?' Jill called from the living room. 'It's got, like, a thousand buttons.'

Charlie released Beth and went to assist, while Beth got on with cooking, warmth buzzing through her. *He'll leave*, came a whispered warning from somewhere at the back of her mind. She shoved the thought away. He wasn't showing any signs of wanting to leave. And anyway, he was here now. That was what mattered.

20

After Jill went to bed in Pearl's room, Charlie dumped his gear in the guestroom and went for a shower. But afterwards, instead of going to bed, he slipped into Beth's bedroom and shut the door — just as she'd hoped he would. He wore nothing but boxer shorts, which meant the great hawk tattoo across his chest flexed when he bent down to crawl into bed beside her.

'What?' he said, seeing her stare.

'You. You're just so — hot.'

Charlie snorted with mirth and leaned in to kiss her lips.

'You must be tired,' she said when he pulled back to see her more clearly.

'Yeah.' He dropped his head onto the pillow and Beth turned towards him so they could lie face to face. 'Long drive, then the stuff with Billy — not to mention Jill in my ear all day.'

'She said you're taking her to tour the school and Durack. Is that true?'

He nodded. 'I decided you were right. She seems to need this.'

'What about Pearl?'

Charlie dropped his gaze, taking her hand. He stroked her fingers absently. 'I don't know. I still don't know what to do about her. I need to think. There's a good foster family in town who might be willing to take her. The woman's Gwini, and they've got all sorts — a couple of teens, another Aboriginal boy about ten years old, and a little bloke with Down syndrome. But . . . '

'But?'

He met her eyes again. 'I swore I'd never let either of my nieces get taken away again. If I hand Pearl over now, will I ever get her back? She's so young. What if she settles in and doesn't *want* to come back?' He heaved a sigh. 'I don't know what to bloody do. I've even been thinking I should find a place in town and take care of her myself. I'd have to do it all myself though, because Aunty Mary's needed out in the community.'

Beth was startled. 'What about your career? If you're stuck here, you can't tour and perform, and then you won't have the money to support everyone like you have been. And you can't take her with you, either. Living on the road for months on end wouldn't be good for her health. Plus, she starts kindy next year. Anyway, how could you settle her in to all the therapies she needs if you're on the road, or in the city, recording?'

He was silent and she realised he'd been asking himself all the same things.

'Sorry,' she said. 'I didn't mean to slam the idea like that. Personally . . . ' Beth took a breath. 'Personally, I'd love to have you living in town permanently.'

An expression came over his face that she couldn't quite read, and Beth was suddenly aghast at herself for admitting this to him. She wrenched her gaze away and chewed her lip, trying to find a natural way to back-pedal. But Charlie reached up a hand and tipped her chin so she was forced to meet his eye.

'I still love you,' he said. 'Never stopped, even though I tried like hell.'

Emotion locked her throat tight for a moment, then Beth blinked her tear-blurred eyes and lunged forward to kiss him.

'Same. Exactly the same.'

Charlie pushed her back and swung himself over the top of her, pausing only to cast his intense eyes across her face. Then he was devouring her lips in a fierce kiss, and Beth surrendered to it, knowing they were done with talking for the night.

★　★　★

Charlie was back in his room when Beth awoke in the morning. She was glad. Jill didn't appear to be up yet but Beth didn't want the girl getting a shock. She would need to speak to Charlie about how to tell Jill they were *together* now.

She got ready early and went straight to the hospital to see Billy. While Beth sat with Billy, waiting for the RFDS team, she very nearly wept with a patient for the first time in years. He was terrified and angry. She put her arms around him and he grumbled, heaved and choked into her shoulder.

'Should've taken better care of it,' he berated himself. 'Was too scared and stupid to let you see it, Doc.'

314

'I understand. It's okay.'

He sobbed. 'I'm a dickhead,' he managed. 'Crying like a bloody baby.'

'Stop that,' she said, rubbing his back, willing her voice to stay steady. 'You're strong and bloody brave, Billy. I know you'll get through this and be all right.'

'How am I gonna coach the footy kids?'

'Just like you do now. It'll take a little while to get back to it, but you'll feel better, Billy — stronger and healthier inside. You'll still be able to run around with a prosthetic leg, once you're used to it. And what's to stop you being involved while you're recovering? Nothing. We'll sort you out with a megaphone and you can direct them from the sidelines.'

'Useless as tits on a bull,' he growled.

'That's enough. Who will do it if you don't? Those kids are depending on you to come back and coach them.'

He sniffed loudly in her ear and she sat back, fetching him some tissues. He blew his nose until it made a hollow honk.

'Young Jackon's come along,' he admitted at last. 'Couldn't even handball when he started, but last week he took a mark.'

'You're a bloody good coach, Billy.'

He nodded, accepting her compliment graciously. Beth continued this line of conversation in the hope that it would distract him.

'Pearl loves football,' she said. 'How can we help her play?'

'Get the little girl a footy and chuck it around with her,' he said immediately. 'And teach her to walk proper. Then she can have a real go on the field.'

Beth nodded. 'I'll get to work helping her learn to walk more.'

'Could she get crutches? Then she could knock a ball around with a crutch if her feet won't work proper.'

Beth considered. 'That's a good idea. I'll talk to someone about crutches.' Crutches weren't always a good thing when it came to learning to walk, but if they were kept for sports only, Pearl might be able to participate more. 'She'd be pretty good at kicking with a crutch, now I think about it.'

'There was a kid when I played, when Dad and me lived in Darwin. He was sick like Pearl.'

'He had cerebral palsy too?'

'Yeah, somethin' like that. He used one crutch. One of those elbow ones, with the bit you put your arm through, like a loop.'

Billy looked at her quizzically.

'A closed-cuff crutch,' she said.

'Sounds right. He wasn't a bad player. Could catch with his free arm, kick with his good foot. Just used his crutch to help him run around the field, you know?' Billy paused. 'I dunno. Maybe soccer would suit her better. Just kicking, no hands needed. Footy's a better game, of course, but maybe not for Pearl.'

'Good idea,' she said. 'So, you played in Darwin as a boy, Billy? I didn't know you lived there.'

'Yeah, the Dingoes. I was full-forward. I was there till I turned fourteen.'

Beth tipped her head. 'And then what happened?'

He shrugged. 'Moved away. Went to live at Madji for a while.'

She groaned. 'I bet they were bummed to lose you.'

Pride touched Billy's face. 'Best and fairest, two years straight.'

Beth raised her eyebrows. 'Holy cow.'

Billy nodded. 'Coach reckoned I could've gone all the way.' He heaved a sigh, regretting opportunities lost. Although his eyes were trained on his necrotic foot, Billy didn't appear to be thinking about it. He was remembering his golden days in Darwin.

Harvey had reached town overnight and he arrived with Charlie while Beth was there. She heard their voices greeting the nurses, so Beth told Billy she'd be back in a moment and went out into the corridor to greet them. Harvey looked older and somehow smaller than usual. He nodded when he saw her and Beth put her hand out, knowing he wasn't a hugger. He shook it and they paused outside Billy's room to speak.

'It's a bad business, this,' Harvey said with a shake of his head.

Beth nodded heavily. She thought of Billy winning 'best and fairest' of the Dingoes as a hopeful fourteen-year-old, his father cheering from the sidelines. Her heart lurched.

'That surgeon bloke reckons Billy might lose the other one, too,' Harvey added in a low voice. 'That can't be right, can it?'

'I don't know, Harvey,' she said. 'Billy will

need to take very good care of the left foot if he wants to save it.'

'We'll help him take care of it,' Charlie put in.

'I'd give me own bloody leg to him if I could.' Harvey's face was a topographical map of lines, furrows and sadness. 'I should've stopped him sooner, with the grog and the smoking and shit when he was younger. I only stepped in because he was getting into trouble. He went wandering as a young man, got into fights and trouble with women when he was young. A few years back, I brought him home to Madji again, got him cleaned up and he's been a good bloke ever since. Loves those footy kids. Lives for the coaching — for the game. I didn't think it'd all end up here, with the bloody diabetes taking his leg.'

Beth tried to steady her voice so she could answer. 'Harvey, you couldn't have done anything more than you did. You work damn hard with guys heading down that track, and there's only so much one person can do. We'll do everything we can to help Billy resume as normal a life as possible — the medical staff, me.' She watched him anxiously, wishing she knew how to comfort him.

'And I'll sort out a really good artificial leg,' said Charlie.

'Some things money can't fix,' Harvey said, making for the door to Billy's room.

Just minutes later, the medical officers came in to pack Billy up for the flight. Beth and Charlie walked with them to the ambulance bay and watched as Billy and his father were driven away in the transfer vehicle.

Charlie accompanied Beth back to the car park and she tried not to think about the shock and pain Billy would experience when he awoke after the operation.

'Where's Jill?' she asked.

'In with Pearl, keeping her company.' Charlie looked distracted and pulled his hair back off his forehead in that familiar gesture of worry. 'I need to find a vending machine.'

'There's one in the foyer,' she said. 'You need breakfast?'

He half-smiled. 'Pearl's hungry, even though she only ate an hour ago. And Jill's requested Twisties.' His smile dropped away. 'And I'm hiding.'

Beth frowned. 'From?'

'Jill's reading to Pearl,' he said. 'Zoe the goddamned zebra.'

She chuckled softly. 'Fair enough.'

Charlie kept his eyes on the bitumen. 'I keep wondering why the hell this had to happen to Billy.'

Beth reached out, her eyes filling yet again. She wasn't a crier, as a rule, but seeing all this pain — first from Billy, then Harvey, and now from Charlie — wrung her heart. She placed a hand on his lower arm and waited.

'I saw Billy's face when they shut the ambulance door. He looked confused, terrified. Jesus, in a day or so he's going to be missing a limb.' Charlie looked up and caught Beth's eye. 'It's relentless. The problems.'

With a monumental effort, Beth held it

together. She put her arms around Charlie's waist and held him close, sensing how he felt — like a man in the eye of a hurricane, trying to hold onto everyone he cared about.

'You're not alone,' she said.

Charlie tightened his arms around her and they stood that way for a long time. If only she could have him here forever, to hold or hold onto; to comfort or take comfort from. Charlie was everything that had been missing from her life, and he seemed to feel the same about her.

'You've got to get to work,' he said, pulling away.

Beth agreed. She kissed him briefly and he set off for the hospital foyer while she climbed into the Beast. She was already running a little late for her first appointment, and as Beth arrived at the clinic, her phone rang. She parked hurriedly and checked it — it was Pam Twomey from the chamber. That could wait. Beth let it go to voice-mail and dashed inside, apologising breathlessly to the grumpy construction worker she'd kept waiting for his sick-leave certificate. She texted Charlie in the short break she got around midday, while she ate a banana and a handful of almonds for her lunch.

Any word on Billy? she wrote.

They made the call. He's going in for surgery tonight, he replied.

She emailed the hospital in Darwin to make herself known as Billy Early's GP and to request a status report after the surgery concluded. Then Beth dived into her afternoon consultations.

320

$\star$ $\star$ $\star$

Jill and Charlie were cooking and arguing when Beth got home. For a moment, Beth grew worried, but it quickly became apparent that this was good-natured family bickering. Jill was ridiculing Charlie's method of peeling vegetables, and Charlie was pretending to scold her for being disrespectful. Beth grinned to herself. He thought he wasn't great with teenagers but he didn't seem too bad to her.

Charlie spoke to Harvey on the phone for a while after dinner and was able to report that there had been no complications with Billy's surgery and he'd awoken in reasonable spirits. Jill watched her beloved *Home and Away*, then they all sat in the living room together. Beth listened as Charlie worked on his song, and Jill messed around with her uncle's phone, watching videos and playing games. Finally, the girl stood.

'I'm going to bed. Can I sleep in the big bed in the guestroom tonight?'

Charlie frowned. 'You've got a perfectly good bed in Pearl's room.'

'Yeah, but it's not like anyone else is using the guestroom, are they, Uncle? So I might as well have it.' She smirked while Beth froze in horror and Charlie's colour deepened. Jill was barely holding in her laughter. 'So, can I?'

Charlie grabbed a cushion and threw it at Jill. 'Get out of here, you cheeky little bugger.' He was laughing too by now, although Beth cringed with mortification.

Jill tossed the cushion back and departed. 'I'm

321

taking the guestroom,' she called from the hall.

'Well, I guess that solves the problem of talking to her about *us*,' Charlie said, shooting Beth a rueful smile.

'Oh my God. I thought we were being so careful and quiet.'

'She doesn't miss a trick.'

Admittedly, it was good to be able to wake up beside Charlie the next morning — *good* in the same way that finding out she'd made it into the medicine course at eighteen years old had been good. Good in the way that winning awards or curing diseases felt good. Everything was somehow more enjoyable, from taking her morning run, to opening up the clinic and making herself a coffee, to telling Reg Craddick that his head cold and prickly heat rash were unlikely to be a meningococcal infection. The only thing that marred Beth's day was an email from the team in Darwin to say that Billy's temperature was running high. They were on watch for septicaemia and giving him intravenous antibiotics. She contemplated forwarding the message to Charlie, then decided there was no need to worry him at this stage. If they had put Billy straight on the IV, that should sort out the start of a blood infection.

Beth stopped in at the Mount Clair hospital to visit Pearl on the way home, taking her some of the pharmaceutical company merchandise she stashed for her younger patients: a blue stress ball with an erectile dysfunction medication logo, and a plush worm from an intestinal worm treatment company. Pearl accepted her gifts graciously and introduced the fluffy roundworm to Gummy the elephant. Mary was there as well, and she greeted Beth with a hug.

'I'm off out of here shortly,' she said. 'Charlie and Jill were in here for a few hours today, and Pearl's happy enough with her little mate.' Mary indicated the boy with the bandaged head, who was watching ABC Kids on the bed opposite.

'Where are you staying?' Beth asked.

'With an old friend — Colleen,' Mary said. 'She doesn't live far from here. I can walk in from her place to see Pearl.'

'That's convenient. And have you got dinner sorted out for tonight? You could come back to my house and eat with Charlie, Jill and me . . . '

Mary considered the offer. 'No, I think Colleen's expecting me home for some tucker tonight. I'll catch up with youse later in the week.'

Beth stayed a little longer to read Pearl a couple of books, then she and Mary left the hospital together. She dropped Mary at her friend's place and went home.

'I was just about to start dinner,' Charlie told her when she came inside.

That crazy happiness rose up inside her again, inflating her heart like a balloon. 'I'll cook tonight,' she said.

'But you've worked all day.'

'I like cooking,' she reminded him.

'We went to the school and Durack today,' he told her as Jill appeared.

'Oh, yeah? What did you think, Jill?'

Jill's face was glowing. 'It was so cool. It's

huge, the school. Double storey and everything. They've got a whole block full of science labs, Doc. It's amazing.'

Beth nodded. 'The labs! My favourite part of the school too. I used to borrow prepared microscope slides from my biology teacher and bring them home to study using my own microscope. Liver flukes, paramecium.'

Jill clearly had no idea what either was, but she was impressed. 'You had your own microscope? That's awesome.'

Charlie quirked an eyebrow at Beth. 'You two are weird.'

'You were pretty good at biology, as I recall,' Beth told him.

'I had an extremely motivating teacher,' he shot back.

'What about Durack?' Beth asked Jill, carefully ignoring Charlie. 'What did you think of the old place?'

'It looked pretty nice.' Jill seemed less certain this time. 'I'd get used to it, I reckon.'

Poor kid was so used to a family home, Beth thought. It would be strange for her to live in a dormitory environment with a bunch of other girls. But she would enjoy it once she'd settled in.

'It's fun,' she assured Jill. 'Lots of craziness and laughing, and you start to feel like it's a second home. I'm still friends now with some of the girls I boarded with.'

After Beth's chilli beef and rice dinner, when Jill was contentedly watching *Home and Away*, Charlie sat with Beth at the kitchen table.

'Busy day for you, then,' she remarked. 'Spending time with Pearl at the hospital, and then school and boarding house visits with Jill.'

'I made some phone calls, too.' A shadow crossed Charlie's face, and Beth gave him a quizzical look. 'Nigel Winston's office,' he said.

'You spoke to him?'

He shook his head. 'I tried to speak to him. Apparently, he's 'not available' at the moment. So I asked to speak to the mines-planning people instead. What a bloody joke.' Annoyance flashed in Charlie's eyes. 'I couldn't get past some guy on a very low rung. I asked to speak to his superiors and got nowhere. Recommendations are forthcoming; all the facts and consultations are being taken into account, blah, blah. Then he proceeded to tell me in excruciating detail why my first album was still better than anything I've done since.'

Beth sighed. 'Great. Really useful.'

'Next I tried Gargantua. Asked to speak to the big boss. He's overseas. Asked to speak to the next guy up. He's in meetings, but if I go online and fill out the contact form, they'll make sure it gets to the right person.' He gave Beth a cynical look. 'Trouble is, these places are walls. Faceless walls, where no one person makes a decision. Gargantua's like a massive machine, ripping across north-west Australia, dredging every red cent out of the ground they can find. There's no-one to stop it. No-one to say, 'Hold on a minute, this could hurt people.''

She saw the helplessness in his face and wished she could do something to take it away.

'Could you try again? Ask to speak to the community engagement department, maybe?'

'Yeah, I will try again, but I think I'd better head down to Perth as soon as Pearl's better and park my bum in their office foyer until someone agrees to speak to me.'

She nodded. 'Have you thought any more about the idea of relocation?'

'We shouldn't have to bloody move,' he growled. 'We were there first.'

'I know. But if Gargantua wins, you need a plan B.'

Charlie was still frowning deeply.

'I know none of this is fair,' Beth said. 'I hate it too. And we won't give up, but if it doesn't work, then we really need a back-up solution.'

He still looked like he wanted to punch the corporate world in its collective face, but with an effort Charlie nodded. 'I have thought about the relocation idea. I even mentioned it to Aunty Mary today. She wasn't over the moon — but she wasn't dead against it, either. God knows where we could go.'

Beth thought about the map Lloyd had shown her. Why hadn't he damn well sent anything to her yet? She glanced at Charlie. Would he be willing to listen to anything Lloyd had said? If she could find the right words to put it to him, he might.

'I wonder,' she started, hesitating, 'if we made an appointment with Lloyd Rendall — '

'Rendall!' Charlie's face darkened. 'I'm not talking to that piece of shit.'

'He's involved,' she said. 'Gargantua's using

him as their local guy on the ground, I think. If we spoke to him — '

'Beth,' Charlie broke in. 'Do you know what he tried to do to my family? My sister, Justine — my half-sister.' Charlie paused and checked that Jill was still busy with her television program. 'She's a truckload of trouble. Men, drugs, grog. She had Jill at fifteen and went to live in Queensland in this god-awful relationship with some abusive dickhead. He broke her ribs once, and I told her to get her arse back to Madjinbarra. She came, but she was still a bloody disaster on legs. She was too rough with Jill. She was always angry, and she'd fly off the handle at the poor little kid.

'I was trying to make a bit of money in the music scene, so when I realised what was going on I asked Aunty Mary to take them in hand. Aunty tried but Justine wasn't exactly cooperative. She kept on doing what she was doing, then she started taking off and leaving Jill for months on end. Child Services placed Jill with this bloke who came out with his wife to do missionary work at Madji. Justine hadn't been around for ages. She was back in Queensland with that violent dickhead, doing drugs and getting arrested for assault, break and enter, you name it. Before you know it, this missionary fella puts in an application to *keep* Jill. Aunty Mary called me in to help her fight it and we ended up in court. Rendall was the case officer and, of course, he took the foster parents' side.'

Submerged anger was surfacing on Charlie's face, his words coming fast. 'That prick said I was just like my sister. I still remember his exact words — I was leading a *hedonistic lifestyle* in cities around the nation, in an environment that would place Jill in *grave danger of sexual assault* and exposure to drugs and alcohol.' Charlie paused and took a breath to calm himself. Beth checked that Jill was still watching television.

'I had to get lawyers involved. I had to produce evidence — affidavits and police records — just to prove I was fit to be Jill's guardian, and for Aunty Mary too. Only then did Child Services agree to return Jill to her own family. After it all ended, Rendall went up to my lawyer. I saw him. He shook his hand and said, 'Good match.'' Charlie's green eyes burned into Beth's. '*Good match*. It was just a game to him. If I'd had *any* chance of getting away with it, I would have pummelled him right then.'

Beth found her own fists were clenched. 'I would have pummelled him too. I've always thought he was an idiot, but I didn't think he'd sink that low. Arsehole.'

Charlie managed a half-smile. 'Yeah. So that's why I won't be paying a visit to Lloyd Rendall.'

Crap. Beth completely understood — but this made things even more difficult. She thought furiously. How could she get Charlie to seriously consider relocation if he knew it came via Rendall? It would be far better if it came from Gargantua. She resolved to contact Lloyd again and request that he arrange a solid offer from the mining corporation and keep his own name out of it.

'What about the media?' she asked. 'Mary said

you've got contacts. I reckon the Kimberley radio would love to talk to you. An interview and talkback, maybe. It's a hot topic — you might even get wider coverage than the Kimberley. It could put some pressure on the minister if people back you up — and you'll get a lot of support from your fans, won't you?'

Charlie nodded. 'Yeah, I'll set something up, if I can. I make some calls in the morning.' He watched Beth, giving a slight shake of his head. 'Thank you. I don't know where I'd be without you right now.'

21

Pam Twomey from the Chamber of Commerce called again during Beth's Wednesday morning appointments but didn't leave a message. Beth wondered if she should try to call on the chamber's support in the Madjinbarra affair. But the chamber members were all so focused on money and business and progress — she wasn't at all sure they would be on her side.

On her lunchbreak, Beth phoned Lloyd. He didn't pick up, so she emailed him instead to ask for Gargantua's relocation offer in concrete terms. Between patients, she checked a text from Charlie: *Speaking on the radio tomorrow afternoon. Drivetime talkback with Buster Carroll. Should get some attention.*

That was excellent news. Buster Carroll's show was the biggest regional drivetime program on the air.

She hadn't heard from the orthopaedic specialist in Darwin, so Beth guessed things were progressing well. Hopefully, Billy could be transferred back to Mount Clair for the rehabilitation process. Beth tried Mary's phone to check on Pearl, but she didn't answer. Then she became busy with patients until late in the day. It wasn't until nearly six that she made her way home, pausing on the front porch to water her pot plants, thinking about stepping inside to see Charlie's face waiting for her, in her house.

In her life. She couldn't repress the smile that arrived on her face.

Something seemed peculiar when she stepped inside. There was no smell of food cooking, no bickering or banter. The house was quiet, dim and still. Jill appeared, and relief washed over her face when she saw Beth. She hurried forward and lunged in for a hug, taking Beth by surprise.

'Jill! What's wrong?'

'Aunty Mary just left.' Jill's voice was muffled. 'My Uncle Bil — . . . my uncle, he's dead.'

Billy! Shock went through Beth like a blast of icy wind. There had to have been a mistake. But Charlie came around the doorway into the living room and Beth saw his face — and knew there was no mistake. She hugged Jill in silence, and after a few moments guided the girl towards the kitchen. Jill sank into a chair, still clinging to Beth's hand, and Beth turned to Charlie. She stepped into his arms, and held him tightly with her free arm.

'What happened?' she asked, her voice shaking.

'Aunty Mary doesn't know much,' he answered. 'Infection, they said. His heart just stopped.'

Beth understood in an instant. Post-surgery septicaemia that had raged out of control. Why hadn't they called her? God, she should have said something to Charlie yesterday. He released her and she sank into a chair beside Jill, who still hadn't relinquished Beth's hand. Beth looked from Charlie to Jill and their faces matched — pure, uncried hurt.

'Why did he die?' Jill asked.

'It's what Charlie said. An infection. His organs were already under strain from his diabetes. He never took his medication, so his body was weak. The infection would have gone straight to his vital organs. His heart must have failed under the strain.'

She rubbed a hand over her mouth, trying to think of something to say that wouldn't sound trite or pointless. *Goddamn it.* She was usually so good at knowing what to say. Beth looked at Charlie helplessly. 'I'm sorry. I should have told you they said he was running a fever, but I thought it would be okay.'

Charlie's face changed slightly. 'When?'

'Yesterday.'

He stared at the table. 'Wouldn't have made any difference, I guess,' he said, but she still felt terrible that she hadn't said something when she first heard.

'I should have got the ambulance out to Madjinbarra for him.' The words spilled out of Beth's mouth.

Charlie shook his head, meeting her eyes again. '*I* should've done something. I should've done a hundred bloody things. We all should have.'

Jill watched them anxiously.

'He never came to the clinic,' Beth said. 'I should have asked after him.'

'Yeah, he deliberately steered clear of the clinic,' Charlie told her. 'Maud shouted at him about it every time she saw him.'

'She did,' Jill confirmed in a hollow tone. 'She

was always shouting, 'Y'need to come and pick up your tablets, ya silly c — ' ' Jill stopped herself at the c-bomb.

'I should have realised he was avoiding treatment,' Beth said, the ache of grief taking hold. 'God, it's so *pointless*.'

Charlie didn't argue. Jill dropped her chin into her hand and poked at the table. Minutes stretched on while they sat in miserable silence.

'I should have gone straight back for him as soon as you told me his foot was serious,' Charlie said. He heaved a sigh that carried all his deep-running weight of responsibility and sorrow. 'I never thought something as stupid as sores on his feet could kill him.'

Unexpectedly, Jill gave a short laugh. 'It's not a competition for who sucked more at looking after Uncle, you know,' she said. 'Neither of youse win, anyway. Uncle wins. He sucked most at looking after himself.'

Beth forced a smile and Charlie pretended to clip Jill's ear. The girl was right, in a way, but there were so many more layers to this death than she realised.

'I'll need to go and help Harvey,' Charlie said. 'I'll go to Darwin with Aunty Mary tomorrow.'

Beth nodded. 'What about Jill? Will you take her or will she stay here with me?'

Charlie looked at Jill. 'Do you want to come, or would you rather stay in Mount Clair?'

'I'll wait here and look after Pearl,' Jill said immediately, and Beth was impressed with Jill's self-restraint. She knew how much Jill wanted to see a city.

Charlie nodded. 'I'll come back for you and Pearl to take you home for the funeral.'

The night dragged on, heavy with the remnants of shock that sank into deep sadness. Jill didn't want to watch *Home and Away*. No-one was hungry until later, and then it was a toasted sandwich dinner, with mugs of tea. They sat together at the table and talked about Billy — the good and the bad. Billy had been like an older brother to Charlie, who had plenty of stories about crazy things the guy had done — generally while fishing. Jill had her own share of stories and eventually Beth ventured one.

'Maud told me this,' she said. 'I wasn't actually there, of course.'

'You don't have to be there to be able to tell a story, Doc.' Jill was quite firm.

Encouraged, Beth went on. 'Apparently, this was when he was a teenager.'

She trailed off for a moment. Her thoughts had flashed to the glory-days football tale Billy had told her just two days before and she experienced a stab of renewed pain. But Jill and Charlie were waiting, so Beth endeavoured to focus on the story. She would have to take care not to upset anyone in the community by saying Billy's name aloud now he was gone — and that would go on for years. It was the rule.

'So your good uncle and a bunch of other kids went down to the waterhole to catch some barramundi. They were on the lookout for freshwater crocs, which had recently developed a habit of taking the barra right off the hooks. Your uncle and his mates had a few fish in the bag and were just starting to relax when he caught sight of a good-sized freshie heading in towards them. Sure enough, it tried to snatch the fish that one of the kids was reeling in. They chucked a load of rocks at it, but when it wouldn't back off, he jumped into the water himself and lunged at it, grabbing the croc and wrestling the fish free. All the kids were cheering for him, and he won the fight — came splashing out of the water holding the half-mangled barra. Your uncle was feeling pretty triumphant until he discovered that two crocs had found their stash of fish on the shore and were having a feast right under their noses.'

Jill burst into laughter and Charlie was grinning. 'True story,' he said. 'I was only about five or six, but I was there.'

'You should have told it!' she exclaimed.

'Nah. You're not a bad storyteller, Doc,' said Jill. This was high praise and Beth was honoured. 'Why do so many people have to die?' Jill added, surprising them both.

Beth opened her mouth to explain about chronic disease and lifestyle-based illness but then closed it, unsure if that was what Jill meant.

'It's the sadness,' Charlie said. 'It wears people down in the end.'

Jill nodded. She turned her eyes to Beth. 'I'm going to get my degree and do something to help.'

★   ★   ★

When Jill was long asleep, Beth and Charlie turned out the lights and lay curled close

335

together in bed. She struggled to get to sleep, thoughts wandering between the loss of Billy, worries about Madjinbarra and memories of her own mother's death. She kept coming back to the need for Charlie to meet with Gargantua and negotiate a solution. How could he make it happen if he had to attend to Billy's funeral and be there for the bereavement period? She'd seen sorry business before. It often took several weeks, especially with a loved member of the community like Billy, and couldn't be hurried or neglected.

She eventually fell asleep but woke again in the darkness, her phone showing her it was almost two a.m. For several minutes, she thought about her blood sample sitting in a laboratory in Perth, waiting to be subjected to genetic testing. It was just blood, sitting there in a vial, but in Beth's imagination it turned black with terrifying hidden disease.

Charlie's breathing sounded laboured and broken beside her. She listened for a few moments, wondering if he was dreaming. Quite suddenly, Beth realised he was weeping. She lay still, her heart squeezing as she heard his hidden grief pour out. She didn't move for a long time, tears blurring the rectangle of light around her bedroom door from the hall lamp. She wanted to give him the dignity of weeping in secret — clearly, that was what he wanted. But eventually she could stand no more and had to comfort him. She rolled over and slipped an arm over Charlie, pressing herself against his back. Her hand came to rest on his chest and she held him tight, feeling the rhythm of his heart through her fingers.

To her relief, he didn't push her away. His broken, grief-stricken breathing continued and he slid his own hand up to cover hers as though he didn't want her to remove it. She rested her cheek against his back and they stayed that way until eventually Charlie's grief gave way to exhaustion and his breathing evened out.

They slept.

22

Charlie's flight to Darwin was scheduled to leave just after midday.

He would leave Jill at the hospital to sit with Pearl for the day. Beth said goodbye to them both in the morning and, as soon as her final patient departed that afternoon, she left work to see the girls. When she started up the Beast, Buster Carroll's gravelly tones were on the radio and she remembered Charlie's drivetime radio appearance with a jolt of worry. Charlie would have cancelled the interview before he left. He must have.

'Well-l-l, it's four-fifty-three on a Thursday afternoon,' Buster said. 'You've been listening to James Reyne and James Blundell's nineties hit, 'Way Out West'. If you've just joined us, we're talking today about a new mineral ore operation coming to the Kimberley. This will be a Gargantua mine, and it's set to create a lot of new jobs out here. The application's sitting with the government's mining department at the moment, and word is they'll be making a decision on the matter any tick of the clock.

'The problem is, the mine happens to be going in right next to a remote community that's home to a couple of hundred people, the majority of them being the Gwini people, who have lived in the area for as long as fifty or even sixty thousand years. The town, named Madjinbarra,

338

was set up about forty years ago, originally by missionaries, although they're an independent community these days. The community is a dry one, which means no alcohol. They don't sell it, you're not allowed to take any in, and it's been that way for at least fifteen years. The elders say this has made them a stronger community, and they certainly seem to be doing better than the average statistics illustrate. Less family violence, less crime, better rates of staying in school, and better overall health. Now, if Gargantua builds a mine and an accommodation camp right next to Madjinbarra, they'll be wanting a wet mess — a bar. So essentially, Gargantua will be bringing jobs and infrastructure, but it will also be bringing booze — and that's a problem . . . at least, that's what their spokesman says — a bloke I'll be speaking to very shortly.'

Beth's spirits rose. It sounded like he had Charlie on the line, waiting to speak. *Phew.* She hadn't even been sure Charlie would have landed yet.

'Now get a load of this.' Buster's tone changed to one of intrigue. 'The humble desert community of Madjinbarra has produced a celebrity. You may know him from such massive hits as 'Keep it Coming' and 'Strange Days'. He's a nation-wide star who performs at major concert venues and festivals, and has a vast online following. The girls in the team here at *Afternoons with Buster* assure me he's a bit of a heart-throb. This bloke was born into the Wirra family — a family that's been living in the Madjinbarra community for forty years or so.

He's also the son of one of my favourite country and western artists, Dusty Campbell. You've gotta know who I'm talking about now . . . ' Buster paused for effect. 'And if you don't, let me jog your memory with this track.'

A song came on. Beth parked at the hospital and listened impatiently. She softened as she felt Charlie's beautiful voice wind its way through her, the sound of his guitar unmistakable even with the rest of the band playing.

Buster returned. 'That was, as I'm sure you know, Charlie Campbell with 'Unbroken'. Charlie should be speaking with us very shortly, but in the meantime, we've got a couple of callers. Kevin from Derby, hello.'

Beth tried to be patient with the opinions of the callers. Most of them seemed to be in favour of the mine and dismissive of the problem of the wet mess. Her indignation rose as she listened to their comments that 'no-one would be forcing the local Aboriginal population to go to the pub', and 'it's all about self-control, Buster'.

Beth texted Charlie. *Good luck for your interview. Are you on soon?*

Another track was played. This time, it was Dusty Campbell's 'Long Road Home'. More callers. More chitchat. Buster mentioned Charlie again but sounded less certain that he would be speaking. Beth's tension mounted. She tried calling Charlie but it went to voicemail. She tried Mary — same deal. The callers continued.

'Well, Buster, I'm a resident of Mount Clair, and I've got to say, the locals are pretty excited about Gargantua opening a new mine.'

Beth knew that voice. *Bloody Lloyd Rendall.*

'Is that right, Lloyd? The area's main source of employment at the moment is — what, agriculture? And the Herne diversion dam, I suppose, if and when that ever gets back on track.'

Beth scrambled to look up the radio station's phone number. She dialled but got the busy tone.

'That's right, Buster, but with work on the dam at a standstill, the locals need the jobs that a new mine in the region would offer.'

Beth dialled the station again. Still busy.

'I see,' said Buster. 'So, the people of Mount Clair are expecting to find jobs at the mine?'

'Absolutely. It'll be just the boost the town needs, economically and in terms of employment.'

'And what about the people of Madjinbarra?' Buster asked. 'What do you say to their concerns over a wet mess?'

'Well, I can't speak for *them*, obviously, but they've managed to stay alcohol-free all through their regular visits to places like Mount Clair, Broome and Darwin, and there's absolutely no reason why they won't maintain their community principles with a wet mess nearby. It won't be a pub in the middle of their town, after all — it will be in the mining camp itself, intended mainly for the use of the workers.'

'But surely they'll be wanting to get jobs at the Gargantua mine, too,' Buster said. 'And the bar will be open to visitors and the general public, am I right?'

'Well, that's partly correct,' Lloyd admitted. 'It'll be open to anyone, I suppose, but it's really meant for the workers.'

Beth wanted to scream at the radio. 'You utter wanker, Rendall,' she growled, trying the station number again. Still engaged.

'Unfortunately, it's looking like we won't be speaking to Charlie Campbell after all.' Buster let his regret be known through his expressive voice. 'We need to wrap up this discussion now, what with the footy about to start, and we haven't been able to pin him down.' He gave a chuckle. 'I suppose he is a rock star, after all. Perhaps he got caught up with something else this afternoon and missed our appointment.'

'Could be running on Gwini time,' Lloyd managed to get in just before they cut him off.

Beth swore loudly and hit the button to switch off the radio.

⋆ ⋆ ⋆

Each day that week, Jill spent time with Pearl at the hospital, then Beth collected her after work and took her home. Jill seemed to enjoy her days with the hospital staff, and her stories over dinner suggested they were almost treating her as a work experience student. Dr Grahame was very happy with Pearl's progress on the new medication and started to talk about discharging her from hospital.

Charlie sent a number of texts to Beth each day. He had remembered the radio interview on his flight to Darwin — but a delay in the flight

342

meant that by the time he'd landed, it was too late. Either way, being there for Harvey and helping make arrangements for Billy's Madjin-barra funeral had to take priority. Beth didn't tell him what she'd heard on Buster Carroll's program. Charlie would be gutted if he knew how badly it had gone.

Jill was brave after the initial shock of Billy's death. She and Beth even managed to find some moments of enjoyment on the weekend, visiting Pearl, then shopping for shoes and clothes at Mount Clair's tiny department store. Beth helped Jill pick out a pair of good-quality joggers and a few T-shirts. She bought Jill a new skirt and top for the funeral, and they selected clothing for Pearl as well. Jill mumbled something while they were standing in the women's clothing section, and Beth had to ask her twice to repeat herself before she caught it properly.

'I wish I had a bra.'

'Oh, you don't have one?' Beth had to conceal her surprise.

'Nah. I gotta wear these stupid crop tops, hand-me-downs from Tish. All stretched.' Jill didn't meet Beth's eyes.

'Let's get you a couple, then.'

Beth took her into the underwear section, where she quietly explained how to fit a bra, picked a couple of likely sizes off the rack and sent Jill into the change room. 'Just whistle if you need help,' she said.

Jill was out ten minutes later. 'This one fits,' she said, showing Beth.

'Great! We'll get you four of that type, in different colours. That sound okay?'

Jill wore a big smile on her face. 'Thanks, Doc.'

Beth was glad they'd sorted that out before Jill started at the local high school. There were some things a teenage girl would not want to ask her uncle, no matter how close they were.

After a few days, Charlie messaged Beth to say he and Harvey were back in Mount Clair. He didn't have a lot of time to see her because he had to drive Mary, Harvey and his nieces back to Madjinbarra. They would be receiving extended family from far and wide in the lead-up to Billy's funeral, and Charlie needed to spend time with Billy's footy kids.

Charlie phoned from the clinic car park before the long drive. Beth dashed outside to see him in between patients. He was alone, thankfully, and she found herself clinging to him like she hadn't seen him in months. She didn't care who saw her making a spectacle, either. It was gratifying to realise Charlie was holding her just as tightly.

'How's it all been going?' she asked. 'Can I do anything to help?'

'No, we're getting organised. We need to get home today so Harvey can be there to greet everyone. His sister's due in Madji today but her boys and a few others can't get there until next week. They're waiting for payday to get flights.' He pulled back a little to catch her eye. 'Thanks for sorting out the girls' funeral clothes. That saved me a scramble today.'

'It's nothing. As soon as you have a funeral

344

date, let me know so I can get a flight out to Madji.' She hesitated, then blurted out her next question. 'I know you need to help out and organise the funeral, but do you think you'll be able to get to Perth to see Gargantua any time soon?'

Charlie's voice was hollow. 'I can't rush this.'

Beth grimaced. 'I know. I get it. It's just, I heard that a decision might come through from the department any day now.'

His jaw tightened. 'Christ, I don't know what else to do, Beth. I can't just take off and go to Perth while everyone's arriving and getting ready for the funeral. They're family. Kin. They'd have to delay the funeral even longer to wait for me to get back, and everyone's already taking leave from their jobs and making travel arrangements. I just — I can't. It doesn't work that way.'

Beth was nodding. She'd witnessed sorry business many times before and comprehended its importance. 'Is there some way I can help? I could try to set something up for you, maybe? A phone call or an appointment for when the funeral is over?'

'No, I'll sort it out. As soon as I'm finished at Madji, I'll bring the girls back to Mount Clair and fly straight down to the city to meet with Gargantua.'

'The girls can stay with me while you're in Perth,' she said.

He pulled her close again. 'I can't believe I ever doubted you,' he said into her ear, his voice soft. 'I'm sorry.'

Her love gushed up inside her, so deep and

wild it took her breath away for a few moments. How had she kept this concealed, buried for all those years? She held on tight and murmured against his shoulder, 'I'll be thinking of you, Charlie. Don't hesitate to call if there's anything at all I can do.'

★ ★ ★

They exchanged intermittent messages during Charlie's absence, but with Madjinbarra's mobile signal so poor and his grim duty tying him up, Beth didn't expect much communication. It was two weeks before he was able to send her an official funeral date and Beth scrambled to rearrange all her appointments and book herself onto the early-morning flight for the nominated day. The small plane was filled with Billy's family and friends. A couple of blokes in Gargantua shirts were on the flight too. *Their timing sure sucks.* Maybe they were attempting to curry favour with the Madjinbarra elders by attending the funeral. It would have been more respectful of them to leave the extra plane seats for real mourners, Beth thought, ignoring them.

Charlie walked out to meet the plane when it settled on the airstrip. She gripped his hand, seeing the strain and sorrow in his eyes. Charlie spotted the Gargantua guys and, after a moment's staring, rammed his sunglasses onto his face. Although he kept his expression neutral, Beth could read his disgust.

She squeezed into Charlie's vehicle with several members of the Early family. Harvey's place was a stream of visitors before the funeral. Beth approached the elder to offer her sympathy, a little fearful at first. Was he harbouring anger towards her? But he simply thanked her for trying to save his son at the end. Harvey's voice shook and Beth was wiping away tears as they talked about Billy's reluctance to accept medical treatment and his last few days.

In the early afternoon, the funeral director's vehicle arrived with Billy's coffin and they all set off in a convoy to the old cemetery. It was hot and dry out there, with little shade over the dusty ground. People crowded beneath a couple of spindly trees between the head-stones. The young men of the community bore Billy's timber coffin to the freshly dug grave, sweat seeping through their new buttoned shirts, red dirt powdering the cuffs of their black trousers. Everyone ignored the two men from Gargantua.

The elderly priest from Madjinbarra's church gave the funeral sermon, during which Pearl waved at Beth several times from her big sister's arms. Both girls wore their new skirts. Beth tried to acknowledge Pearl without being insensitive to the other mourners, and Jill shushed her little sister every time she squawked. Pearl cried a few times, especially when Jill did, but didn't seem to understand much of what was going on.

At the end of the service, everyone took turns to come forward and drop a handful of red earth onto the coffin. The sight of the teary footy kids, as well as the sobs and wails of the family, cut into Beth's heart. She dropped her own handful in, apologising silently to Billy for not nagging him harder, and stood back with her eyes down as the young men took up shovels to fill in the grave. The task took almost an hour, punctuated by the grief-stricken cries of the congregation. At length, the final scoop of dirt fell and the last flower was placed. People turned for the cars, exhausted from their tears and sweating in the dry heat. The Gargantua executives hadn't said a word throughout the service but they both shook Harvey's hand before climbing into their hired white ute. Beth could have sworn she saw one of them retrieving bottles of beer from a cooler bag.

She sat with Jill and Mary for most of the afternoon, listening as they caught up with old friends, talking to people who approached her, and even sneaking in a little medical assessment for Debra's baby, who was running a fever. People wept for Billy, calling him 'that good coach' and reminding one another of his prowess on the footy field or at the fishing hole. However, her flight was to leave at five, and when the sun started to sink in the sky, Charlie drove her to the airfield.

'I'll stay until you board,' he said when she kissed him goodbye.

She half-smiled. 'No, you need to get back to Harvey's place. I saw people setting up camp. You'll need to fire up the barbecue shortly because Pearl will be wanting a *shoshage*.'

He gave a soft chuckle. 'Pearl's been fine on her new medication, by the way. No seizures. I think the epilepsy's under control — for now, anyway.'

'What are you going to do?' she asked. 'Leave

348

her here with Mary or bring her back to Mount Clair?'

'Mary says she might know a good place for Pearl to live in Mount Clair during school terms.' Charlie rubbed his chin, clean-shaven for the funeral. 'She wants us all to go and meet the family together to see what we think.' He shook his head briefly. 'I don't know, though. I'm not sold on the idea. But I can stay in Mount Clair for a while longer before I'm needed for work, so I've got a few weeks when I can look after Pearl myself. And make a decision.'

'When do you think you can get away from Madji?'

'Harvey understands I've got to meet with Gargantua as soon as possible,' Charlie said. 'If I don't leave tomorrow, it will be the day after.'

'Good. And the girls will stay with me while you're away, yes?'

His smile returned. 'Yes, Beth. You can have the girls while I'm away. I don't think Mary will mind having a break.'

Beth and the handful of other passengers were called for boarding, and Charlie touched her cheek briefly. For a moment, Beth thought she might cry again, simply at the idea of leaving him. *Jesus, it's only a couple of days,* she rebuked herself.

But Charlie's regret was plain in his face, too. 'I'll see you soon,' he said.

23

Back in Mount Clair, Beth churned through her backlog of postponed appointments. It was late on the day after her return when Lloyd Rendall phoned her. She groaned when she saw the caller ID. If she never had to talk to Lloyd again it would be too soon, but she took the call out of a sense of responsibility to the Madjinbarra community.

'I was wondering if you've got anything on tonight, Beth?' he said in his usual confident tone. 'I thought we could have a catch-up.'

'What for?' she asked, her voice stony.

If he noticed her coolness, Lloyd didn't show it. 'Dinner, mostly.' When she didn't reply immediately, he added, 'And perhaps another chat about the mine at Madjinbarra.'

'I'm still waiting for information from you on the relocation deal, Lloyd.' Beth barely tried to keep the annoyance out of her voice. 'I've emailed you repeatedly and received nothing. What's going on? Was there ever really a deal, or were you just buying time for Gargantua?'

Lloyd was silent for a moment. 'Wow. Okay. Yes, there was a deal, as a matter of fact, but with things moving so fast with the application, there hasn't been much time for anyone to focus on the relocation idea. Gargantua has been too busy crossing t's and dotting i's for the mining department to worry about much else.'

Things were moving fast in the mining

department? Panic seized Beth. If Gargantua was honestly in final negotiations with the government, why would they bother to discuss any kind of solution with Charlie at all? God, she needed Charlie to get back — pronto.

'Have you got anything *new* to say about how Gargantua will support Madjinbarra if they get mine approval?' Beth controlled her voice carefully.

'Ah . . . '

Too slow, Lloyd. He'd revealed his hand: he had nothing new.

'I'm busy tonight,' she said before he could make something up. 'Please urge your contacts at Gargantua to do the right thing. Charlie Campbell will be setting up a meeting with them as soon as he's finished with the sorry business for Madjinbarra's football coach.'

Beth didn't even wait for him to say goodbye. She hung up, thoroughly disgusted with Lloyd's smoke-screening, and muttered a few words she felt accurately described the guy.

She composed a text to Charlie: *Govt decision may be imminent. Not sure how things are going out there but I hope you're able to get away soon.*

Beth hit send, hoping the phone signal would understand its importance and carry it swiftly and reliably his way.

★ ★ ★

A day later, a message arrived from Charlie to say he was back in town with Mary and the girls.

Beth could not have been more relieved — for her own sake as well as Madjinbarra's. Charlie was scheduled to fly to Perth the next day but would spend the night with Beth — he would be at her house when she finished work, he wrote. Beth's heart became all thumpy and the morning seemed longer than any morning she'd ever worked.

Pam Twomey had been phoning persistently over the past few days but Beth had avoided calling her back, unable to deal with chamber matters while the rest of her life was so complicated. But when an unexpected break arrived in the form of a cancelled appointment, Beth figured she could kill a little more time in the torturous wait to see Charlie by phoning Pam.

'Hi Pam, it's Beth. Sorry I missed your calls.'

'Oh, hello, sweets. Goodness, you're a hard girl to get hold of. I've emailed you about six times in the last week. Didn't you get them?'

Beth thought of all those unopened Chamber of Commerce emails with a guilty pang. 'I'm so sorry, Pam. I've been insanely busy.'

'That's all right, lovely. I just wanted to check if you needed anything for tonight.'

Beth was silent.

'You there, Beth?'

Oh, holy shit. The networking meeting. It was her turn to host.

For a second Beth thought Pam must have the dates wrong. There was no way she would screw up something like this. But no — some hasty calculations told her it was the third Tuesday of the month and it was she who'd messed up, not Pam.

'Yes, I'm here,' Beth said through a dry mouth.

'Is everything all right?'

'Yes. How many are coming?' Beth's heart was racing, her nausea growing.

'We've had a great response this month. You're popular, lovely!' Pam chuckled. 'Forty-three confirmed.'

Nausea transformed into full-scale panic. 'That's great.' Somehow, she sounded calm. 'I've catered for fifty, just in case.'

'Good on you, sweets. Now, do you want me to sort out a door prize? Or have you got something? Snowman Air last month, they offered a free aircon service, but you can't really offer anything like that, can you? A free urine test, maybe?' Pam trilled a laugh.

'No, it's fine. It's all in hand,' Beth heard herself say. *What the hell is wrong with me?* 'I've come up with the perfect door prize.' *Jesus, Beth!*

'Oh, what is it?'

'It's a surprise.'

'You're such a gem,' Pam told her. 'I'll be there a few minutes early to set up my welcome table, all right?'

'Great.' Beth felt numb. 'See you then.'

She ended the call and stared at her desk while she tried to work out where to start. Dani popped her head around the door, eyes unusually bright.

'Um, Beth — I mean, Dr Paterson — you have visitors.'

Was Dani panting? Beside the young receptionist, Charlie appeared. That explained the panting. Mouth slightly ajar, Dani watched him manoeuvre past her to enter Beth's office, a plastic bag hanging from his hand. Then Dani made way for someone else following behind: Free.

Free's face was full of scandalised glee as she stepped in after Charlie and plumped herself down in a chair. Dani reluctantly withdrew.

'Well!' Free's bright eyes interrogated Beth's face. 'Look who I found in the waiting room. *Charlie Campbell*,' she added, as if Beth might not be sure.

'Yes, I know who he is.'

Charlie put his plastic bag on Beth's desk, a hint of amusement in his face.

'I've already introduced myself,' Free said. 'And I brought you lunch as a surprise, Bethie.'

'Me too,' said Charlie.

'Lucky me,' Beth said weakly. 'I get to choose.'

Free was clearly busting to demand the truth of Beth, but she glanced at Charlie and exercised all her self-restraint.

'I brought panini,' she said.

'I brought Vietnamese spring rolls,' Charlie said.

Beth gave Free an apologetic look. 'Sorry, Free. I love Vietnamese spring rolls.'

'But I love panini,' Charlie told Free, whose face lit up.

'Cool! We can have a sharing platter.'

A platter made the thought of the networking night pop back into Beth's head and she held in a groan. Charlie unpacked his container of spring rolls and Free unwrapped her panini, chattering about how she could cut them up, before departing Beth's office in search of a knife.

'Sorry,' Charlie said, leaning in to kiss Beth's lips quickly. 'I shouldn't have done this. I didn't realise you had a lunch date with your sister.'

'I didn't. She surprised me. You both did.'

A smile stole over his lips. 'She had to find out sooner or later.'

What did that mean? Did he mean he intended to stay — with her? In her life?

Free reappeared. 'I could only find a butter knife,' she said, waving it. 'But I reckon I can use it to hack at the panini and eventually they'll end up in pieces, neat or otherwise. Do you like chicken?' she checked with Charlie, studying him shamelessly. *Classic Free*, thought Beth, unable to repress a smile. 'Chicken, avocado and sprout, or salami and Italian roasted veg?'

'I'll have whatever you don't want,' he said.

'I like both but I got the chicken for Beth, so she doesn't breathe salami breath all over her patients.' Free bisected the panini inexpertly. 'How about we go halvies? Can I taste one of your spring rolls, Beth?'

'Of course.' She checked Charlie's face. 'How's Harvey?'

'Pretty broken. But he'll be okay.'

Free was eyeing them curiously but she didn't ask. Beth took a napkin and reached for some food, thoughts zipping between Harvey, the forgotten networking function and now this bizarre luncheon. What had Charlie said to Free about them?

'You all right?' Charlie asked Beth as she toyed with her spring roll.

Beth hesitated, then — almost against her will — poured out the story of her lapse in memory, and the function she was unexpectedly hosting in about six hours.

'Oh my God!' Free breathed. 'What are you going to do?'

Beth shook her head helplessly. 'I don't know. I can't cancel. Forty-three people are coming. I'll look ridiculous if I cancel now. I need to find a caterer.' To her embarrassment, tears came to her eyes.

Charlie leaned forward. 'We can find a caterer, no problem. Have you tried anyone yet?'

'No. I can't think.' A headache started with blinding suddenness and Beth rubbed her forehead.

Charlie took her hand in one of his. 'Leave it to me.'

Free's face lit up with stunned delight.

'What?' Beth managed.

'I'll sort it out. Catering, drinks for forty-three? No problem.' He looked completely confident.

'No, this is my screw-up — '

'What are your appointments like for the rest of the day?' he interrupted.

Beth hesitated, then checked her schedule on the screen. 'Back-to-back,' she confessed. 'Until five.'

'Okay — at five, you get the place sorted out

for guests. I'll have the food and drinks here by five-thirty.'

'I'll help,' Free said eagerly. 'Do you need decorations?'

'No,' said Beth. 'Oh — but I do need a door prize. It's supposed to be related to my business, somehow.'

'Ooh, I can get that!' Free bounced slightly and took a big bite of salami panini.

'I'll stay and help at the event, too,' Charlie said. 'I'll serve drinks.'

Beth laughed, sounding slightly hysterical. 'Charlie, I can't have a famous musician serving drinks at my networking event. That's insane.'

'Would you rather I play a few songs, then?' Charlie was grinning and Free just about spat out her mouthful in excitement.

'I'm serious,' Beth said. 'Anyway, you have to look after Jill and Pearl.'

'Jill can come along and hand around trays of food,' he said. 'And Pearl can stay with Aunty Mary at Colleen's place.'

'Wow.' Free was watching Charlie with admiration. 'He's really organised. Even more than you, Beth.' She seemed quite pleased that Beth's skills had been surpassed. 'Oh, and I'll come and help with serving too.'

Beth could have wept with gratitude. 'Thank you. Both of you.'

'Any time.' Free swigged kombucha. 'I'll sort the prize thingo. Charlie, you just let me know what I can do to help with the food and stuff, okay?'

She dug in her bag and located a business card

printed with *The Art Fairy* and her phone number. Charlie took it from her. Dani popped her head around the door again to report that Beth's next appointment had arrived, although Beth couldn't be sure if it was because the patient was waiting, or because Dani wanted another look at Charlie. Free and Charlie left her to work, Free nattering to him all the way down the hall as if he were an old friend.

Beth wondered all afternoon if she should actually leave the two of them to organise her event. This was Beth's event — Mount Clair Medical's reputation — and she'd entrusted its management to a roving rock star and an art fairy. What if they couldn't get things sorted out? What if there was nowhere in town that could supply food? Oh, crap — she should have told them to pick up disposable cups and plates. Maybe she could rush out and get some after work — or ask Dani to do it. She messaged the other staff frantically. Her practice manager was still on holiday, and Carolyn had her beloved tennis on Tuesday nights, so she politely declined in the name of 'me-time'. Paul could make it. Beth didn't hear back from one nurse, and Brianna, who was on duty, was a single mum so she probably wouldn't be able to come. Bloody hell, why hadn't she remembered this networking thing before today?

And, oh God — what would Free bring back as a door prize?

As soon as her last patient departed — well after five — Beth raced out into reception and begged Dani and Brianna to stay and help her tidy up. Dani was happy to oblige, but Brianna had to go home to her kids. Paul helped for a few minutes, then said he needed to feed his dog but would be back for the event by six. Together Beth and Dani vacuumed, moved furniture and opened up the sliding doors into the courtyard.

'Hmm, there's a lot of dust and leaves out here,' Dani remarked. 'I'll sweep up.'

She headed for the cleaning cupboard. So much for sending Dani out to get disposable crockery. Then Charlie arrived, carrying a large tray covered with foil in one hand and a bag of ice in the other. Jill trotted behind him with another tray and a big smile.

'Food tables?' Charlie asked.

Beth pointed wordlessly. He and Jill deposited the trays and Charlie stepped outside to lean the ice against the courtyard wall, Jill following.

'I reckon the esky should go over there, Uncle, next to the little palm tree. Then you can pour the drinks at that table.'

Beth checked under the foil of the tray and discovered tiny shortcrust quiches. She picked one up and inspected it. It was hot and smelled good — like bocconcini and sun-dried tomato.

'Does it pass the Pastoral Princess sniff test?' Charlie's voice came behind her, full of amusement.

'What's *that?*' Free asked with interest, arriving with another tray and a plastic bag. 'Is that the brand of pastry — Pastoral Princess?'

Charlie cracked up. 'Not quite. Did you show Beth what you got for a door prize?' he added as he headed out the front door again.

'He got loads of food,' Free said in a low voice. 'We used your oven and mine to heat it all up. Chicken skewers, pastries, samosas, and there's heaps of dips and stuff, too. And he got cartons of bubbly and beer. It's all packed in the back of his car.'

'What about cups and plates? Napkins?'

'Yeah, it's all there.'

A wave of relief hit Beth hard. He'd come through. She was about to host her first chamber event and it wasn't a balls-up — because Charlie had rescued it.

'What's going on with you and Charlie Campbell?' Free whispered.

'I'll tell you later,' Beth said. She made for the door so she could help with unloading his car, but Free grabbed her arm.

'Look,' she demanded. 'I got you a *killer* door prize.'

Free's soft eyes, just the same soft green as their father's, shone with hope when she opened the store bag to show Beth. It was a child's play medical kit with a red plastic stethoscope, a yellow syringe and even a bright green blood pressure cuff.

Beth snorted with mirth. 'It's perfect — and the most unique door prize the chamber's ever seen, I suspect.' Free gave a little cheer of triumph.

They set up a drinks area, loaded the food table and lit up the clinic so it looked bright and welcoming. Free wrapped the door prize using Beth's roll of examination table paper and bandages for ribbon, then she blew up some colourful latex gloves and arranged them in bunches around the reception area and court-yard so it looked like friendly hands were waving a greeting to their guests. She offered to man the drinks table, and Jill got her trays in order to start serving just as Pam arrived with her little card table and tin of raffle tickets.

'The place looks wonderful!' she exclaimed. 'Oh, look at all that food! Who did your catering, sweets?'

'Pastoral Princess Catering,' Charlie said, grinning at Beth.

'I don't think we've met . . . ' Pam eyed Charlie, a flash of recognition in her eyes.

'This is Charlie Campbell,' Beth said.

Pam shook his hand. 'And Charlie's your . . . ?'

She waited, but Beth had gone blank. Free's eyebrows knitted in puzzlement while Jill craned her neck curiously.

'My friend,' Beth said at last, practically choking on the words.

'Boyfriend,' Charlie corrected, and Free's jaw dropped.

'Lovely!' Pam exclaimed. 'I thought you were seeing . . . ' She stopped herself. 'Just small-town gossip,' she finished with a chuckle. 'Anyway, he'll be here tonight too.'

Beth didn't get the chance to find out what Pam had meant because people started arriving — a good twenty minutes before the official starting time of six-thirty. Charlie attracted quite a crowd of fans among the chamber members, which prevented him from serving, but Jill and Free seemed to have it all under control. He mingled with the business owners like he was an old hand at this kind of thing, Beth saw with some shock. Then she was annoyed at herself for being shocked. Of course he was good at small talk and meeting new people. He was a famous musician, for Chrissake — he hadn't been living under a rock since he'd left Mount Clair seventeen years ago.

Beth got caught up chatting with a local physiotherapist and noticed, with dismay, that Harry Sterrick had arrived with his pathology associate. Pam was sticking name labels onto their chests and pointing out the food and drinks. Harry smiled when he caught Beth's eye and she gave an uncomfortable wave. He made his way towards her and leaned in to kiss her cheek.

'Hello, Beth. You look lovely tonight. Your surgery is great!' He indicated his companion. 'Do you know Ginny?'

'Yes, of course.'

Beth gave Ginny a kiss, too, so it wouldn't look odd that Harry had kissed her. She checked on Charlie but he was busy talking to the advertising manager of the local newspaper. She was able to effect a reasonably natural escape from Harry when Pam came and fetched her to meet a couple of new members. Beth made light conversation with the newcomers, asking them all about their businesses — a pool supplies shop and a sign-writing service.

'How did you get Charlie Campbell here?' the sign-writing man said, dropping his voice. 'Is he a friend of yours?'

'Yes, we go way back,' she said, trying not to show how ridiculously happy the very thought of Charlie made her feel.

'And he helped me organise things tonight.'

'So he's not a chamber member? I didn't think he needed to promote his business, somehow.' The man chuckled. 'I recognise that bloke he's talking to, as well. He works at the hospital. He X-rayed my daughter's arm last week when we thought it might be broken.'

Beth went cold and swung around to look. *Crap!* Sure enough, Charlie and Harry were deep in conversation. She turned back to her companions, but it was useless: Beth couldn't focus on a thing they said any more. And even worse, Lloyd Rendall had just walked in. His face brightened when he spotted Beth so she excused herself, pretending not to have noticed him, and made for the food table. Now much closer to Charlie and Harry, Beth could almost catch some of the things Harry was saying to him.

'*Something something* work, but when I *something something something* community. Obviously, *something something* too hard, but *something something* Rikke, who's *something* supportive of the idea. So now it's a matter of *something something* down, and then *something* to Sydney.' Harry gave a modest chuckle.

Christ, *no*. He wasn't telling Charlie their romantic history, was he? Oh, dear God, she should have told Harry it was one hundred per cent over, instead of chickening out and agreeing to consider going to Sydney with him. What the hell would Charlie think? She raised her head and looked over to see if Charlie looked upset. His green eyes were locked on her, eyebrows pulled down in a frown. Beth's stomach twisted.

'Come on, sweets, time for your speech.' Pam's voice broke the horrible moment.

She gripped Beth's arm, leading her to the side of the room. There, Pam waved her arms, shouting for a bit of quiet.

'Now's the time of the night when our host gets to introduce themselves and tell us all about their business and what they can do for us. We always encourage our members to support each other's businesses, as you know, and I hope lots of you will give Beth's clinic a go, or at least recommend it to your friends and customers. And after Beth's talk, we'll draw our door prize, which I'm sure will be very exciting tonight. I even took a ticket for myself, since Beth flat-out refused to tell me what it was. So without further ado, I'd like to introduce Dr Beth Paterson, the owner and one of the GPs at Mount Clair Medical.'

Everybody applauded. Beth, who had not prepared a speech, stood there for a blank moment, attempting to compose herself. She couldn't meet Charlie's eyes. Not now. If she saw him looking hurt or at all troubled, she might lose it.

'Thank you, Pam.'

Free was visible out in the courtyard, right at the edge of the crowd. She gave Beth an encouraging double thumbs up and Beth straightened her shoulders. She could do this.

She would damn well wing it.

She raised her voice so those at the back could hear. 'Well, I want to thank everyone for coming out to the clinic tonight, and I should make special mention of my staff and friends who helped make this happen. A little about me, to start. I've lived in Mount Clair my whole life. I was brought up on Paterson Downs cattle station, south-east of here, and went to the local school. In fact, the only significant amount of time I've spent away from the town was to go to university and get my medical degree. I never wanted to leave for long because the Kimberley runs in my veins and I love it.

'I knew for most of my childhood that I wanted to be a GP, and I couldn't imagine working anywhere else. I decided to open my own practice pretty quickly after I finished my degree. The town was under-resourced for medical care, so I figured it could sustain a second clinic. At first, it was just me and a nurse, but after a year or so things were busy enough to warrant bringing on another doctor. Then another clinic opened in Mount Clair, which eased the pressure. We trundled along quite comfortably here with just the two doctors for a year or so, but when Dr McInerney from the East Kimberley Family Practice retired, a lot of his patients seemed to head our way. That made things ramp up again, so I brought on a locum, Paul Lavigne, who's over there in the corner, to help with the overflow.

'Our beautiful town's not for everyone, though, and I lost my original colleague of seven years when she returned to the city. But one door closes and another opens. Paul threw in the towel on his locum lifestyle and joined us in a full-time capacity, plus Dr Carolyn Shen joined us soon after. So nowadays, we're a happy medical family here with practice manager Ben, our two nurses, Brianna and Kath, and our fantastic receptionist, Dani, who's been helping with serving food and drinks tonight. We have a very full schedule but I'm extremely lucky in that I've got a dedicated team, so we travel along together very nicely.'

'Tell them about your award, Beth,' Pam called.

'Oh, yes.' Beth felt awkward about mentioning it, but she could hardly refuse after Pam's demand. 'Two years ago, we were honoured to win a Chamber of Commerce award for Best Professional Practice.' She pointed towards the trophy and certificate that sat on a shelf behind Dani's desk.

'The judges were very impressed by Beth's community work,' Pam put in loudly. 'She goes out to a remote community every single month and looks after the poor Aboriginal people out there.'

Beth was momentarily speechless. This was just like in Principal Ogilvie's office all those years ago.

'It's a paid position,' she hastened to clarify. 'I'm extremely lucky to have got it.'

It was an odd note on which to finish her speech so Beth smiled brightly around the crowd. 'Thanks again for coming along to check out the clinic. We hope you enjoy the night.'

'Oh, you're not getting out of here that easily, Beth!' Pam trilled. 'First, you need to draw the door prize!'

Beth did so. It was won by Gino from Safe-Tee-Quip, who was delighted, claiming the colourful doctor's kit was the perfect toy for his grandchildren. At last Beth was released from the public eye and permitted herself a fearful glance at Charlie. He was standing alone in a dim corner, his gaze fixed on her. As soon as their eyes met, he started across the room towards her.

'Good speech, Beth,' came Lloyd's voice.

God, not now. She mustered some fortitude. 'Thanks, Lloyd.'

'Drink?' He pushed a plastic cup of sparkling wine into her hand. 'Toast with me.'

'What are we toasting?'

Charlie arrived at her side and she looked up at him gratefully, glad he hadn't changed his mind about approaching when he saw Lloyd.

'Oh, you haven't heard?' Lloyd even sounded slimy.

Beth brought her eyes back to his face and frowned. 'Heard what?'

'The department has approved the Gargantua mine.' Lloyd nodded at Charlie. 'This should bring a lot of work and money the way of your community.'

Beth froze.

'Bullshit,' said Charlie.

'Not at all. I got official notification from Gargantua this afternoon.'

367

'We'll appeal.' Charlie's voice stayed cold and steady.

Lloyd tipped his head. 'I don't think you'll get very far. It's a done deal and the minister seems pretty happy about it.'

'Show some damned decorum, Lloyd,' Beth snapped.

'What? I'm not gloating,' he said, although he plainly was. 'I'm simply at a loss as to why you never considered the relocation deal, Charlie.'

'What relocation deal?' asked Charlie.

Lloyd glanced at Beth. 'The relocation offer I told Beth about on the dinner date we shared a couple of weeks ago. I asked her to speak to you about it. Did it slip your mind, Beth?'

She glared. 'I asked you for more information and you never sent anything to me. How is that an offer?'

Lloyd made a tiny movement of his shoulders that was almost, but not quite, a shrug.

'Why don't you try presenting *me* with an offer?' Charlie's voice was dark and growing darker every moment.

Lloyd sipped his drink, apparently unfazed by Charlie's manner. 'I'll have a chat to my friends at Gargantua and see if they're still interested. It might not be on their agenda any more.'

Beth was growing more and more alarmed. Outwardly, Charlie seemed relatively calm, but she knew him and saw the anger winding up inside him. She cast around wildly for a diversion but could think of nothing.

'Tell your friends at Gargantua they'll have protests, legal appeals and a whole lot of trouble on their hands if they don't come up with something worth our consideration in the next few days,' Charlie told Lloyd.

Jill arrived, offering a tray of food. 'I'll see what I can do for you, mate,' Lloyd said, taking a chicken skewer from Jill's tray. 'Thanks, sweetheart.'

'Don't you call her that,' Beth said, forgetting to be fearful in her disgust.

'No harm meant. Nice do you've put on tonight, Beth.' Lloyd winked — actually winked — at her. 'I'll give you a call sometime.'

In an instant, Charlie had stepped closer to Lloyd — so close their chests were almost touching. Beth repressed a cry. Charlie was breathing shallowly, staring at Lloyd's face until the man's eyes dropped and he raised his hands.

'No need for that, mate.'

Charlie didn't move and Lloyd looked around like he was searching for help. The other partygoers chatted and drank without noticing a thing. After a moment, Lloyd backed away a couple of steps before slinking off without another word.

Jill's eyes were wide as she stared after Lloyd. 'What was that about?' She turned back to Charlie and Beth. 'What's wrong, Uncle?'

Charlie turned sharply and strode away, leaving Beth gazing helplessly after him. She looked back at Jill's worried face but couldn't form a word.

24

The rest of the evening was a misery. Charlie didn't leave. He stood in a corner and conversed civilly when approached, but mostly appeared to be focused on his phone as the social gathering continued around him. Beth acted the cheerful host but longed for everyone to go so she could explain things to Charlie. Free was so damn good at her job, Beth reflected sourly, observing her sister serving drinks and chatting vivaciously to the guests. Beth was almost tempted to ask her to stop serving so everyone would bugger off.

At last they started to trickle out until it was only Pam, packing up her card table, and Free, clearing trays and rubbish with Jill while Charlie loaded empty trays into his vehicle.

'Lovely night,' Pam commented. 'Are you happy with how it went, sweets?'

'Yes,' Beth answered mechanically. 'It was great.'

'I might join the Chamber of Commerce,' Free chimed in. 'I met so many cool people tonight. The home care lady wants me to run art sessions with her old folks.'

Pam had lots of information and forms to give Free, so Beth worked as fast and hard as possible to return the clinic to its usual tidy state. Charlie helped her move furniture back into place, and just as they replaced the last table, she caught his eye across the white laminate and saw all the angry confusion he'd been hiding. He turned away and Beth fought to control her emotion.

The clean-up seemed to take forever, but eventually Pam left, so Beth kissed Free and thanked her, then set the alarm in the darkened clinic. Charlie and Jill got into his car. Beth climbed into the Beast and turned for home.

Once they were inside, she and Charlie were obliged to wait for Jill to get herself sorted out for bed. At last they were alone, standing in the kitchen, watching each other across the kitchen bench.

Beth went first. 'Please don't judge me on what you may have heard about me tonight. Don't do *that* again.'

That threw him. Charlie dragged a hand through his hair, a crease fixed between his eyebrows. Then he stopped and looked deep into Beth's eyes. 'Did Lloyd Rendall tell you about an offer to relocate Madjinbarra?'

Beth tried to find a way she could say no. There wasn't one. 'Yes.'

Charlie's colour seemed to drain. He slumped into a kitchen chair. 'You didn't tell me. *Why?*'

She pushed back against the sick feeling rising in her stomach. 'This was weeks and weeks ago — not long after the first stakeholder meeting. Lloyd said he had something he wanted to discuss — a possible solution — and insisted on a dinner meeting. He told me about the relocation idea and asked me to speak to you about it. Showed me a spot on a map. I told him you and I weren't friends, and suggested that

Gargantua go to you direct, but he thought I should raise it with Mary and Harvey. I asked him to send me something in writing. I was going to pass it on to you, or maybe print it out and talk to Mary about it, but he never sent anything. I even reminded him a few times, but he still didn't send me anything.'

She waited, heart thudding.

'Is this why you suggested relocating the community?'

She nodded, and Charlie swore. Loudly.

'Why didn't you tell me the idea came from *Rendall*?'

'Because I thought you'd just ignore the idea if you knew where it came from, and I believed it deserved honest consideration.' Beth's voice had risen too. 'You don't have any patience for Lloyd, and I was worried you'd dismiss the opportunity without a second thought.'

His eyebrows shot up. 'Maybe you should have shown me some trust! I wouldn't throw Madjinbarra to the wolves over my personal issues with that wanker.'

She took a breath. 'Okay. Yes, Charlie, you're right — I should have told you straight up. I didn't because I wasn't sure what to do. I hoped to introduce the idea to you first, gauge your response, and then show you their offer.'

Her apology didn't appear to register. Charlie was fuming. 'You crossed a line, Beth. This is *my* community. You don't withhold information from me about *anything* to do with Madjinbarra.'

'Charlie, this is an overreaction. All I did was fail to mention where the idea came from. No offer ever arrived. There was nothing to pass on or withhold.'

'An overreaction?' he hissed. 'I find out you went on a cosy dinner date with Lloyd Rendall, discussed the future of my family's home, and hid it all from me — and now I'm *overreacting?*'

Beth jumped in. 'Hang on, is this because you think I would exclude you from something to do with the community? Or is it because I went on a 'date' with Lloyd Rendall?'

His eyes glittered with anger. 'Both thoughts make me sick.'

'Forget about the date thing, that's — '

Charlie choked. '*Forget* about it? Jesus fucking Christ, Beth!'

'Don't talk to her like that.' It was Jill, standing in the dim hallway in her pyjamas, her eyes dark and fierce.

'Go back to bed,' he said shortly.

'No. You can't talk to the doc like that, Uncle. You can't boss her around. She's a grown lady, and if you reckon you're her boyfriend, you better treat her proper.'

'This is nothing to do with you, Jill,' he growled. 'Get back to bed.'

Jill didn't move. 'Why don't you trust Beth? She wouldn't do anything to hurt the community.'

Charlie looked so mad now he appeared to lose the power of speech for a moment. Then he stood. 'Jill, get your things. We're leaving.'

Pain shook Beth like a punch to the gut but Jill was standing next to her in an instant, clutching her arm.

'No.'

'Get your things,' he repeated evenly.

Jill erupted in sobs. 'No! I'm not leaving. I'm staying here with Beth. I'm sick of you running my life. Beth wants me to live in town, go to school — she *gets* what I want to do. All you care about is what you want! I don't want to go with you or go back to Madjinbarra. I want to live with Beth and go to Mount Clair High School! Beth can take much better care of me than *you*.'

Charlie's expression swung between fury and devastation, then he spun on his heel and strode down the hall. Beth held on to Jill, shaking as the girl wept against her. She heard the shuffling of things being shoved into Charlie's bag, then the zip being done up. Charlie emerged, pausing for a moment in the kitchen doorway to give Jill a long look.

'I'm not coming,' the girl said, clutching Beth harder. Instinctively, Beth tightened her arm around her.

Charlie wouldn't even meet her eye. He was gone an instant later, the front door banging behind him.

★   ★   ★

Beth made Jill a hot chocolate, and they sat down on the sofa together to watch trashy television and attempt to calm down. A few times tears were so close that Beth thought she might crack in front of Jill. *Dried flower arrangement, coffee table, slight red wine stain on the carpet where the wine went through the rug, Pearl's Barbie sofa.* God, that didn't work. How could she distract herself when everything in the room reminded her of Charlie and the girls? *Jill.* She had to focus on Jill.

'Your uncle needs time to cool down,' she said, squeezing the girl's shoulders.

'I've never seen him mad like that before.' Jill blinked and wiped her eyes, pulling her feet up to tuck them beneath her. 'Why was he so pissed off at you? I heard everything. You didn't do anything wrong.'

'There's talk of relocating your community as a way of avoiding the problems Gargantua might bring. I should have told Charlie upfront that Lloyd Rendall was the one who suggested the relocation.' Beth let out a shaky breath. 'I was just worried he'd freak out.'

'And you were right. He did.' Jill brought her big dark eyes to Beth's. 'It's not like Uncle Charlie.'

'There's some history,' Beth said, hesitating. Did Jill know the story about her foster parents? 'With him and Lloyd — and with him and me. It's a bit complicated.'

'Is he jealous? 'Cause you went out with some other bloke?'

'I don't know. Maybe that's part of it.'

'You weren't playing around but, were you?' Plainly, Jill had utmost confidence in Beth's fidelity. 'It was just a business thing.'

'Well, I wasn't even *with* Charlie when I went out with Lloyd. But yes, it was a business thing. I can't stand Lloyd, to be honest. I . . . I probably should have mentioned the relocation offer earlier, that's all.'

'You shouldn't apologise, Doc,' Jill declared. 'Uncle Charlie stuffed up, not you. You said straight up that you were sorry for not telling him, and he was still mad at you. It's gotta be jealousy. He should be the one to say sorry.'

'I don't think that's very likely,' Beth said. 'I doubt Charlie thinks he's done anything wrong.'

'He needs to say sorry,' Jill insisted. 'And if he doesn't, you should tell him to piss off.'

'He's your uncle, Jill,' Beth chided. 'Where's your loyalty?'

'I'm loyal, but he's gotta deserve it.'

Beth was secretly impressed. There was plenty of Mary's strength in Jill. Maybe the girl was right: after all, Beth had always acted with the right intentions. She'd admitted she'd got it wrong by not being open about where the relocation idea had come from, and Charlie was still furious. And he'd left. Instead of staying to work it through, he'd left — again. *Just like you always knew he would*, her brain whispered.

She tried to shut out her memories of the past few days — that magical reunion with Charlie, and their rapid descent into misunderstanding and conflict. Her thoughts drifted back to how it had all started and ended seventeen years before. They would never have made it. Charlie was too defensive and impetuous, Beth too anxious to protect their love — to the point where she tried to control everything about it, right down to who knew about them. They were a disaster waiting to happen, and sure enough, it had happened.

And now it had happened again. Seventeen

years and they'd got nowhere.

Tears threatened once more. *Mug on the table, coppery floor vase, stupid television program, a pair of seaglass-green eyes . . .*

'Are you crying, Doc?' Jill wriggled out and stretched her own slender arms around Beth. 'C'mere. It's okay. You want a tissue?'

★   ★   ★

'*Why do you want to be a doctor?*' *Charlie asked.*

'*Because I'm good at science, and I want to cure people.*'

'*Of what?*'

'*Diseases that might kill them.*'

Charlie was resting his chin on an arm slung over his knee, looking out over the town. They had found a shaded bench at the top of red, knobbly Mount Clair — which wasn't actually tall enough to qualify as a mountain.

'*Like your mum's cancer?*'

Beth scuffed the gravel under their bench with one shoe. '*Yes.*'

He was quiet for a few moments. '*Sometimes you might not be able to cure them.*'

'*I know.*'

'*They'll die, sometimes, no matter what you do.*'

'*Don't you think I know that?*'

He nodded. '*And what about other things? What else do you want to do?*'

Beth frowned. '*What do you mean? If I keep my grades on track, I'll get into medicine.*'

He laughed. 'I know you will. But what else do you want to do — you know, in life? Like travel, get married, have kids? Own a Maserati? Climb a mountain?'

'Travel — yeah, I want to see a few places around the world. Not interested in owning a Maserati. I'm not even sure what they look like, to be honest. I wouldn't mind a big four-wheeler to get out into the gorges. As for climbing a mountain, this one will do me.'

He turned to meet her eye. 'And getting married? Having kids? Are they in the grand plan?'

'I want kids one day. Definitely.'

'What should we call them?'

She laughed. 'You're planning to be the father?'

He gave her a mock glare. 'Who else?'

She contemplated him. 'You'd be a good dad, actually.'

'You bet I will. I'm prime husband material.'

'What are you suggesting, Charlie?'

He shrugged. 'Just putting it out there.'

'We're eighteen.'

'I don't mean tomorrow. But one day.'

Beth felt shy suddenly and couldn't think of anything to say. Charlie dropped his chin back onto his arm and regarded the red, boab-dotted landscape, skewered with telecommunications and radio towers, with the odd bump of a rosy rock formation.

'You've got to become a famous singer first,' she said.

'And a lawyer. Or an engineer. Or a businessman.'

'But definitely a famous singer, because I've heard you sing and play, and the world will be a sadder place if Charlie Campbell doesn't become a singer.'

Charlie seized her and buried his face in her neck, kissing her. 'And you can marry me and be a famous singer's wife,' he said against her hair.

She squirmed, laughing. 'And a doctor.'

He let her go, eyes glinting. 'Yeah, okay. You can be a doctor, too.'

'But won't you need other girlfriends — you know, for your songwriting?' she teased. 'As far as I know, all famous singers have broken a girl's heart, or had their heart broken. Maybe even had a girlfriend die.'

'You'd better not die, or break my heart.'

'I guess you'll be breaking mine, then.'

'Never.'

'Charlie, how are you going to write good love songs, then? Who on earth are you going to write about?'

'Every love song I ever write will be about you.'

★   ★   ★

The dream murdered sleep and Beth lay awake from four a.m. By seven, she was wishing she could simply go back to bed while across the table Jill spread jam on her toast.

Jill fixed her eyes on Beth. 'I've got an idea. What do ya reckon about this?'

Beth waited, popping a slice of apple into her mouth.

Jill spoke in a rush. 'You foster me and Pearl.'

Beth stared. She swallowed the apple with difficulty.

'Uh . . . '

'I mean, if you want to. Then I could live here at your place instead of Durack, look after Pearl and go to school, and she could get all the stuff she needs from therapists here in Mount Clair.'

'I couldn't . . . '

Beth trailed off. To her astonishment, Jill's idea had shot into her soul, instantly sprouted and was now growing rapidly, spreading through every part of her, bringing light and warmth she hadn't even known she was missing. Beth imagined Pearl playing in her backyard, bashing at a soccer ball with a crutch, Jill doing her homework at the kitchen table. She saw herself creating meals for other mouths — delicious, healthy meals that would make the labour of cooking worthwhile. She saw a pretty lilac bedroom decorated with the silhouette of a zebra in stripey wallpaper, shelves of books and a little white bed. Barbie nighties, soccer uniforms and teenage bras hanging on the washing line.

It was all there before her in breathtaking, wonderful detail. Something worth coming home to every night. Something that would even start to soothe the dreadful gaping loss of Charlie and the cold fear that her genes would give her cancer. Beth's heart galloped away towards the horizon with these warm thoughts and refused to let go.

What is going on here?

Jill still had an expectant look on her face, her toast forgotten.

'Um, I work full-time' was all Beth could think of to say.

'Yeah, I know. But there's day care, and Pearl will be at kindy next year, and I'll be able to mind her after school. I'm helpful. I do lots of stuff at home. Cooking, washing. And I think foster carers get a bit of money from the government to help with costs, yeah? So that might cover our food and clothes. We don't need much.' She remembered her toast and took a bite, crunching, her brown eyes on Beth.

'I'd need the consent of your family,' Beth recalled, the beautiful thought shattering.

Jill's face clouded. 'I reckon Aunty Mary would say yes.'

'But Charlie's your legal guardian, too.'

Jill stared absently at the table. 'Yeah,' she said at last, and had nothing more to add.

They ate in silence for a few moments.

'Are you going to be all right here for the day?' Beth asked. 'You could come with me to the clinic if you want.'

'Can I go on the internet, if I stay here?' Jill asked.

'What do you want to do on the internet?'

'Look up courses. Universities. Listen to music. Play games. Watch cat videos.'

Beth smiled. 'Look at you. You've had decent internet for one week and you're already a pro.'

She left Jill sitting contentedly at the desktop computer and went to work. Beth was thankful for her busy schedule. Any time she had a moment to think about Charlie, she sank into misery. She tried to imagine a time when she might feel healed and ready for a relationship again. A functional relationship.

It was tough. She'd never got over Charlie the first time round, and his return to her life had done nothing but open up her heart all over again, leaving it exposed and tender just like it had been when she was a teenager. *Damn him.* Damn him for owning her heart when he didn't bloody deserve it.

And damn me, for deluding myself that I'd stopped trying to control people and life. Beth had thought she'd quit doing that after Free confronted her last year, but she hadn't at all; she was just better at hiding it.

She got through the day and went home, half expecting to find it empty. Maybe Charlie had come to collect Jill? But when she went inside, Jill was still there, smiling, her hands in a bowl of mince and diced onion.

'I'm making us meatloaf.'

'Wow, thank you.' Beth put her bag down. 'Has your uncle been around today?'

Jill shook her head.

'Should we go and see Aunty Mary and Pearl once we've eaten?'

'Yep. I'll get this in the oven and peel some potatoes.' Jill grabbed a big double handful of meat and slapped it into a loaf tin.

'Let's do some greens, too,' Beth said.

'Okay.' Jill's voice expressed a distinct lack of enthusiasm.

'With gravy, of course.'

Jill brightened.

They cooked and ate together, then climbed into the Beast and drove to where Mary was staying with her old friend Colleen. They found Mary sitting at the table with Pearl, trying to convince her to eat her dinner. Pearl was continually clambering off her chair, complaining loudly that she wanted to play with her 'am'mals'.

'Oi, Pearl.' Jill scooped her up and placed her firmly on the chair. 'You've got to have your dinner or no animals.'

Scowling, Pearl snatched up a piece of carrot. 'Am'mals,' she demanded through the mouthful.

'Not yet,' said Jill. 'You've got to have a piece of chicken, a piece of broccoli, and ten bits of corn. Then you get your animals.'

Pearl attempted to cram as much of the list as possible into her mouth. Mary smiled at Beth.

'She knows how to handle Pearl, does Jill.'

'Sure does,' Beth agreed. 'Do you want us to take Pearl back to my place tonight? Give you a break?'

'Charlie said to keep her here. He reckons he'll come and get her in the next couple days. Said Jill should wait here for him too.'

Jill shot a quick look at Beth and Mary saw it.

'What's going on?' she said sharply.

Jill hesitated for a moment, but she knew better than to disobey Mary. 'I want to live with Beth. Uncle's pissed off with me. With both of us.'

Mary regarded them both with surprise. 'You want to live with the doc?' She frowned at Beth.

'What *d'you* reckon about that?'

Beth tried to word her response carefully. 'There are a few issues to consider.' She nodded towards Pearl to express her meaning. 'But I'm open to the idea.'

Mary considered it in silence. 'Hmm,' she said at last — and nothing more.

'But Uncle Charlie's really mad at her,' Jill put in.

'Why?'

Jill and Beth exchanged another look.

'How about I fix us a cuppa?' Beth said, and made her escape to the kitchen.

She dithered over the tea-making, putting off going back out, while Jill's voice softly explained something to Mary. Beth couldn't face talking about last night's debacle. She wasn't sure she could do so without breaking down in tears — and she mustn't do that in front of Pearl.

At last Beth steeled herself and carried the teacups back into the other room. The look on Mary's face showed Beth that Jill had told her all. Beth gave Mary a cup of tea and sat down with her own cup to watch Pearl playing with her animals. She tried to switch on her doctor brain, examining Pearl's eye movements and muscle spasms, but even the sight of the little plastic zebra in the girl's hand brought a wave of anguish. How could she have been so stupid, to let Charlie back in when she knew all along he would abandon her as soon as things got tough? She wasn't even mad at him this time — nowhere near as mad as she was at herself.

When it was time to go, Mary walked them to

the door. 'I don't see the harm in Jill staying with you another couple of nights,' the woman said as they stepped outside. 'I'll have a chat to Charlie about the fostering thing, see what he reckons.'

Beth thought to herself that they had Buckley's chance of getting Charlie to agree to Jill living with her after last night. She hugged Mary and they drove home.

25

The next day, Jill wanted to stay home and use the internet again. She promised to do some washing as well. Beth told her it wasn't necessary, but Jill was adamant.

'You need anything else done, Doc?' she asked. 'You want me to clean anything?'

'No, it's all under control.'

'What about the garden?'

Beth hesitated. 'Actually, if you could water the pot plants on the porch, that'd be great. I haven't had a chance in the past couple of days.'

'Yeah, no worries.' Jill gave her a bright smile.

Beth was touched by how much Jill wanted to stay — the lengths she was going to just to prove she would be a help and not a hindrance. That fantasy of a warm, busy house full of children, or even one child, kept intruding, making her heart yearn for something that seemed impossible. But Charlie would never go for it. He was so protective of the girls, and so committed to bringing them up the way he'd planned.

Beth turned from this line of thought and left for work. She was getting good at avoiding thinking about Charlie. She had plenty of years of practice to draw on. Towards the end of her work day, Beth was called in to the hospital to assist for a short stint. Their regular Emergency doctor had gone home with a case of gastro and they needed someone to cover his shift until the next doctor came in at six.

Thankfully, it was quiet in Emergency — so quiet, Beth was able to check her emails and social media. She discovered that Harry had sent her a message a couple of hours earlier.

Hey, you. It was good to see you at the function Tuesday night. How are you? You got time for a coffee?

Hell, she really had to sort things out with Harry. But not right now.

Beth replied. *Thanks, but I have a house guest at the moment, and work's crazy. I'm filling in again in Emergency as we speak! Can I raincheck until next week?*

Five minutes later, Harry walked into the room.

'Snap,' he said. 'I'm working late as well.'

'Sounds like coffee might be on the cards after all,' Beth said with a nervous smile. 'I hope instant's okay.'

She made them both coffees, checked if the nurses needed anything, and then led him towards the break-out area.

'Who's your house guest?' Harry asked when they were seated around a big table in the brightly lit room, surrounded by pinned-up rosters and ironically demotivational posters.

'Daughter of a friend,' she said, and pushed past the topic. 'What are you doing working late tonight, Harry?'

'Just catching up on paperwork.' He watched her for a moment, his soft blue eyes contemplative. 'Everything okay?'

She shrugged. 'It's been a challenging week,

but I'm okay.' Charlie threatened to enter her consciousness. *Wall urn, coffee tin, unclaimed lunchbox collection* . . .

'I was wondering, have you had a chance to think about my idea?' Harry asked, his voice gentle. 'A Sydney getaway, I mean.'

Beth put her hands around the warm mug and tried to word it kindly. 'I have. I'm sorry, Harry, but I can't go. I . . . I can't take the time off work.'

'Boss won't approve your holidays?' His eyes twinkled but there was disappointment in his tone.

She laughed weakly. 'Uh, yeah. Something like that.'

He was silent for a moment and she sipped her coffee, willing him to take pity on her and move on.

'Can I ask the real reason?' he said.

Crap. 'It's what I told you before. I'm not in a good space. For a relationship. For . . . anything.'

'Really?'

'Really.' It was true this time.

'It's not because there's someone else?'

She was caught completely off guard. 'H-how did you . . . ' Beth clamped her mouth shut.

His mouth turned down at the corners but Harry said nothing. She took a breath.

'All right. There's someone. We're not in a relationship, but there's stuff going on and I can't drag you into that, Harry. You're too nice.'

He fidgeted with his coffee mug. 'Thank you for being honest.'

'I'm sorry — so sorry. I never meant to lead you on.'

Harry nodded and shifted, looking at the table. 'So you're not actually *with* Charlie Campbell?'

'No.'

'Everyone thinks you are.'

Beth sat up straight. 'Who's *everyone*?'

'Everyone here, in the hospital. All the staff. I think it's all around town.'

'I doubt that,' Beth said, but then she remembered the two Emergency nurses talking softly together earlier. They'd stopped when she entered the room. She'd assumed they were discussing something private — not her love life.

Harry tipped his head. 'I've heard it mentioned several times in the last two days.'

Pam, Beth realised, her insides flipping. The woman must have rushed around town spreading the good news after the function on Tuesday. If only Pam knew the 'boyfriend' thing had only lasted about two hours after Charlie said it. This was so humiliating! To be known around town as Charlie Campbell's girlfriend, and shortly to be known as his jilted conquest . . .

'Great,' she muttered.

'Sounds like things are complicated,' Harry remarked.

Beth took a glum sip of her coffee. Harry took the hint and, to her relief, started to talk about staff changes at the imaging clinic.

★ ★ ★

Beth left work and headed out to the hospital car park shortly after six. She hadn't even started her car when her phone rang. Rikke's name flashed up on the screen.

'Hi, Rikke.' Beth attempted to sound bright. 'How are things?'

'What did you do?' Rikke wailed. 'I'll tell you what you did! You dumped Harry! *Why?*'

Huh. Harry had wasted no time reporting back. 'Because it would be unfair on him to do anything else. I'm not into him, and my emotional life's in a big fat mess.'

'Why? Because of Charlie Campbell?'

Beth gave up trying to hide it. 'Yes. I'm still in love with him.' She took a breath and explained how she and Charlie had reconnected, keeping herself calm with a mammoth effort. Then she awaited Rikke's onslaught of recriminations.

At the end, Rikke was silent for a few moments. 'Oh, Beth,' she sighed at last. 'Why did you have to invite him to stay with you?'

'It's been going on much longer than that. I never really got over him, and I'm pretty sure I never will.'

'So, it's a thing now, is it? You two?'

'No. It all went wrong again.' It took all of Beth's strength not to crumble as she said this. 'I wasn't honest with Charlie, and he also thinks I went on a date with Lloyd Rendall, who he despises.'

'Hmm,' said Rikke. 'He doesn't know how to trust you?'

'It's not just that.' Beth rubbed her forehead and closed her eyes. 'I don't trust anyone either.

I didn't trust Charlie to do what was right for his community. I tried to control the information he got so he'd make a certain decision, and it completely backfired. I don't think Charlie and I know how to be together. Neither of us is any good at it.'

'I'm sorry, babe.' Rikke's voice had softened. 'I can imagine how much this hurts.'

'Thanks.' Beth could hear the tightness in her own voice. 'I didn't even tell him . . . ' She stopped.

'What?'

Beth forced herself to make the confession, although it felt like her life was being wrenched from her grip, spiralling into the distance. 'I didn't even tell him that I had a cancer scare.'

Rikke drew a sharp breath. 'What?'

'I had a dodgy cervical screen. It's okay,' she added quickly when Rikke's silence grew heavy. 'We did another check and it was fine. But I'm getting genetic testing because of Mum's breast cancer. I'm . . . I'm scared to death, Rikke.'

Rikke released her breath in a whoosh. 'Holy crap. You poor thing. Why didn't you tell me?'

'Because I have this crazy way of trying to control things by hiding them.'

Rikke was silent again. 'Are you okay?' she asked at last.

Beth took a couple of steadying breaths. 'I will be.'

'Can I do anything? Do you want me to ask my specialist contacts any questions?'

'No,' said Beth. 'I just need to wait for my

results and stop trying to control everyone and everything.'

Rikke sighed. 'Beth, let's book a holiday somewhere together. I need a break too.'

Beth forced a laugh. 'I can't get away right now — but I believe Harry's looking for someone to go to Sydney with . . . '

'Uh-huh, as his second choice? Not for me, thanks.'

'He speaks very highly of you,' Beth said. 'I think if he lived in Perth, you might find yourself his first choice.'

Rikke scoffed, then paused. 'What did he say about me?'

Beth dissolved into laughter — genuine this time. 'Rikke! Why didn't you tell me you liked him? You crazy woman! God, imagine if I'd ended up marrying the guy. You and Harry would be a torrid extramarital affair waiting to happen!'

'Stop that,' Rikke growled, although she was plainly repressing her own laughter. 'I would never do that to you.'

'Look, how about you give it a couple of days, and then let Harry know you're thinking of a Sydney trip yourself and would he like someone to hang out with? You just never know what might come of it.'

'Would you stop?!'

Rikke was coming over all outraged but Beth wouldn't be at all surprised if what she had suggested went ahead. She gave Rikke her love and drove home, half-smiling about the call and half-aching with the pain of loss. *Jesus*. Now she had yet more lonely years ahead of her, trying to get over Charlie all over again. She cast the thought away and wondered if Jill had started dinner. Imagine if she had more time with the girl — she could teach Jill how to make beautiful, healthy meals: ricotta vegetable bakes and Thai curries. And muffins — really good muffins — the batter just barely mixed so they rose beautifully and stayed moist and fluffy.

Beth turned into her street and her house was dark.

She parked, staring at the dim windows as she got out of the Beast. Beth climbed the porch steps apprehensively. The front door was locked, so she used the key to let herself in and switched on the lights. The house was clearly empty. Beth went to the kitchen and discovered a note from Jill: *Uncle Charlie's come to pick me up. I watered your pot plants. Sorry, Doc. Love, Jill xxx*

Beth sagged into a chair. Well, that was it, then. She was alone now — completely alone. And this was probably how it would be forever, because the one and only man she'd ever loved now hated her, and the children she longed to look after were gone.

Beth made herself get up out of the chair, but there was nothing for her to do. No point in cooking dinner when she had single-portion meals in the freezer. No clothes to wash or toys to tidy. She wandered down to the guestroom and flicked on the light. With the bed neatly made, the room looked like no-one had ever even stayed there. Beth continued down to the spare room and turned on the light to look over the bedroom she'd assembled for Pearl a couple of weeks ago. The bed was made and the animal mobile and bunting were up, ready for the little girl who wouldn't be coming back. Charlie's green eyes, full of angry hurt, came into her head and Beth bit her lip to keep herself together.

Her eye fell on the closed wardrobe door and she crossed to open it, pulling out the stack of storage boxes she kept in there. She found what she was looking for in the first box she opened. A good-quality document wallet containing her most treasured papers: cards from her twenty-first birthday, her original university acceptance letter, and a heartfelt thankyou note from a patient.

And her mother's letter.

Beth slipped the letter out of the wallet and sank onto Pearl's mattress bed. She manoeuvred the paper from its old, dry envelope and lay back on Pearl's pillow, holding the page above her face to read it once again. It was dated seventeen years earlier — almost to the day — written just weeks before her mother died. Robin Paterson's familiar curly handwriting ran in black ink across stationery that featured the moon and stars over purple-blue swirls of sky. Beth had read it so many times over the years she could almost recite it word for word.

To my Beth,
I know everyone is hopeful that I still
might beat this cancer but I've had my
doubts. I've seen your dad's and the doc-
tors' faces when they talk about it and I

know what it means. I asked Cathy Forrest to be completely honest with me yesterday and she got tears in her eyes and said she didn't think I would be alive for very much longer.

It's good to have some certainty. Now I can make a plan. I know you'll be able to relate to that, Bethany, because you understand all about the need for planning and certainty.

For the past few years, I've watched you prepare for your career as a doctor and have been left in awe of your dedication to your calling. Your hours at the kitchen table, revising and doing homework, ignoring the shenanigans of your sisters and the bellows of the cows. Your colour-coded study plans. Your methodical approach to your goals — it's simply breathtaking! I remember how you decided to study for an hour every day of the summer holidays, and even on Christmas Day you put aside your new novels, CDs and games, and disappeared away from the noise and celebration to study. Free was so indignant — she wanted to go and drag you out, to insist you take a day off, but I knew you needed to do it for your own reasons, so I wouldn't let her disturb you.

I love you so very much, my clever girl, my first baby. You have such capacity to care for people. I've never seen anything like it. I wish I were as selfless! You will be a wonderful doctor, and if you change your mind about that, I urge you to follow your instincts into a role where you can help people because that is most certainly what you were made to do.

Thank you, Beth, for making my life perfect and complete. I'm so sorry my body has decided to leave this world early. I know it will cause you and the girls great pain, and I would give anything to prevent that. But I also know you'll find joy in things again — in people, and love, and life. And know that I'll always be with you, somewhere in the stars, flying with dragons.

I want to leave you these two lists. The first is a list of things I have learned from you. Obviously there are more, but here are the three that jump into my mind right now.

1. A child's arrival into the world brings immense love — a level of love I never even imagined could exist.
2. My capillaries, if laid end to end, would circle the earth four times.
3. When someone, even your youngest sister, is being more annoying than anything else on earth, you can still find a reserve of patience.

The second is a list of things I have learned for myself and that I hope you will find useful.

1. People will say and do things you do

not expect or that make no sense, and there is nothing you can do about that. Trust others to make their own decisions. Right or wrong, they must be permitted to own their destinies.

2. Just barely mix your muffin batter, with a very light hand, or they will turn out small and tough.

3. If you can't think of anything to say to help someone who is suffering, you can at least make them a casserole or fold their washing.

Now, this part is important. I do not want you to think you must look after your sisters for me. That's not your job, Bethany, although I know you do it quite naturally. My heart is at its warmest when you listen patiently to Willow as she raves about her latest pet ecological project, or when you see Free looking wistful and ask her if she needs a hug. But looking after them is not your duty or your burden. Your father is perfectly capable of that, and I trust him completely. I will tell him tonight that I know the truth about my cancer and ask for his help to prepare. He can hold on to this letter for you until after I'm gone so that you can keep it and hear my voice again whenever you need to.

Beth, I only ask one thing of you, and that is to think more of yourself. Please remember that it's not your responsibility to try to fix things or learn other people's *lessons for them. All you can control is what you do, not what anyone else does. Focus on the things you can do — just give others support, kindness and love.*

And remember that you deserve those things too.

Love Mum

Beth wiped her eyes and held the page to her chest, trembling from the crying. The letter had never made so much sense.

26

At the end of work the next day, Beth sent a message to Mary to ask after the girls. Mary rang while Beth was driving home, and she pulled over to take the call.

'Pearl and Jill are still with me at Colleen's place,' Mary said. 'They're both fine. Have you heard the news?'

'What news?'

'Charlie met with some Gargantua blokes yesterday. He's made a deal to move the whole community away from the mine. The papers are being written up right now.'

Beth sat in stunned silence. 'You're moving?' she managed at last.

'Yep. Gargantua will pay for the move, pack up the dongas and give us new homes for anyone who has a house that can't be moved. They're going to build us a school, a community centre and a pool.'

Beth's head swam. 'What . . . how . . . ?'

'Charlie's idea. He talked me and Harvey into it when we were all at Madji last week. We're not over the moon about moving, but it sounds like it's going to be pretty good for everyone in the end.'

'What about Gurrungah?' Beth asked.

'Yeah, she won't move,' Mary admitted with a sigh. 'But some of the younger ones have already said they want to stay in Madji to work at the mine, anyway. They say they'll keep an eye on her.'

Beth gazed unseeingly at the dashboard. Charlie had taken the deal. He'd overcome his personal abhorrence of Lloyd Rendall and negotiated with that . . . that *asshat* to protect his community. He'd done what Beth wasn't sure he could do.

She was hit with a powerful wallop of regret. *Why didn't I trust him?* She should have told him straight away about Lloyd's deal. Of course Charlie wouldn't let his personal prejudices get in the way of protecting his loved ones. Of course he would put what was important first. And yet Beth had held back, wanting to manipulate things so that Charlie would make the 'right' choice.

If I had just told him up-front, we might still be together right now.

'I'm happy for you, Mary,' she said, keeping her voice steady. 'That seems like a good solution, under the circumstances. I have to get home now, but perhaps we can catch up and have a chat about Jill and Pearl in the next day or so. I'd really like to be involved in their lives, even if it's just having Jill for some weekends while she's living at Durack.'

'Yeah, let's catch up, love. I'll give you a call tomorrow.'

Beth sat there for a few more minutes, pulling her hair out of its ponytail and rubbing her neck to relieve some tension. She didn't want to go home and be alone. Maybe she could go to Free's? But Beth wasn't exactly good company right now, and anyway, Free and Finn had their own happy, love-filled lives to live. Beth got back on the road and headed home. She would go for a run. She would pick up the pieces and bloody well carry on.

When she turned into her street, Beth wasn't prepared for the sight of Charlie's vehicle parked out the front of her house. *Oh God, what now?* Had he come to have it out with her again? There was no sign of him but a light was on — he must have let himself in, she realised with some shock. Not really an acceptable thing for him to do under the circumstances. Beth's stomach clenched.

Willing herself to appear composed, she slipped out of the Beast and climbed the porch steps. Her watering can was sitting neatly by her pot plant collection. She dithered, buying time as she checked the soil and found it was still damp from Jill's efforts the day before. Tears came to Beth's eyes and she brushed them angrily away. Why did she have to lose anyone she loved? It was like she was cursed.

She breathed deeply for a few moments and waited for her eyes to dry, then pushed through the front door. She could smell dinner cooking — something with Italian herbs. *What the hell?* He was using her place to *cook?* She went cautiously towards the kitchen and gave a violent start when Charlie appeared in the doorway, a wooden spoon in his hand. Her mouth fell open and she almost dropped her bag, then placed it on the sofa to cover her reaction.

'Hello, Charlie,' she said. 'What — '

He tossed the wooden spoon, which clattered onto the bench, and in three strides Charlie was right in front of Beth, an anxious frown over his green eyes. He tugged her close, his lips seeking hers, hand tangling in her hair. More than anything else, Beth was flooded with confusion.

Charlie broke from the kiss and searched her eyes. 'Please. I can't lose you again.'

Confusion transformed into senseless joy. Beth's brain attempted to argue but she stomped on her doubts and sought his lips again. Charlie pulled her closer, holding on tight. Questions were flying around her head, but Beth didn't know where to begin. He saved her the struggle, breaking into speech as soon as their kiss ended.

'I shouldn't have left the other night. I was angry and bloody scared about what was happening to Madjinbarra. But the more I thought about it, the more I realised you weren't messing with me.'

Beth interrupted. 'No, I should have told you about Lloyd's deal as soon as he mentioned it.'

'I didn't make it easy for you to explain,' Charlie said, shaking his head.

Beth fell silent. Could this really be happening — were they actually apologising, forgiving, understanding each other?

'Shit!' he exclaimed, pulling away. 'The chicken!'

She followed him in a daze as he dashed for the kitchen and retrieved the wooden spoon to stir a pot.

'Turn it off,' she said. 'I need to talk to you.'

He switched off the burner and turned to face her.

'You do know I love you, and Madjinbarra, and Jill and Pearl, right?' Beth said. 'You know I would never do anything to harm any of you?'

'I know. I knew that all along, but I saw red when Rendall stuck his sleazy face in yours the other night. The things he said about the mine being approved, what he said to Jill, and the thought of you *seeing* him — '

'I never went out with Lloyd,' she said quickly. 'Not like *that*.'

'Yeah, I know. And even if you did, it's not my place to say a bloody word about it because I gave you up all those years ago. And it was all down to my own stupidity.'

'No, if I *had* dated Lloyd Rendall, you totally should have judged me.'

He laughed. 'I should have trusted that you had better taste than him.'

Beth clutched her arms across her stomach, trying to find a place to start explaining. 'That night was a mess, Charlie. The stuff with Lloyd . . . but also, I panicked when I saw Harry talking to you. I didn't know what he was saying. I told him last week that I didn't want a relationship, but he asked me to think about this trip . . . '

'Yeah, I think the poor guy still hopes you'll go to Sydney with him.' Charlie's lips twitched in amusement.

'Not any more,' she said. 'I've made things extremely clear now.'

Charlie regarded her. 'Harry told me something I didn't know about you.' Beth waited, her dread returning. 'That you do unpaid work out at Madjinbarra.'

'No,' she said, exasperated. 'It's *paid*, for God's sake. I've never pretended to anyone that it was anything but paid work.'

'You're paid for FIFO, one day a month. But you spend two days driving and then work for three,' he said. 'Because you care.'

Beth could think of nothing to say. Charlie saw her embarrassment and moved on. 'Anyway, it's all sorted out. We're moving.'

'Mary told me you accepted Lloyd's relocation deal,' Beth said.

He shook his head. 'No, not *his* deal. I brought it up with Harvey and Aunty Mary last week, and they identified a good spot for a new home. Harvey used to take his son and the rest of us boys camping there as kids. It's under native title, nice and close to the coast, with a good access road. Three and a half hours from Mount Clair. Better phone signal, internet coverage. We've already got agreement-in-principle from the land corporation. They'll sign a hundred-year lease for us. I took it straight to Gargantua and warned them not to involve Rendall.'

Beth stared. 'And they're paying for everything?'

Charlie half-smiled. 'I'm a persuasive negotiator when I need to be.'

'Holy crap, Charlie.'

'There are still hurdles. We'll have to go over the contract with a fine-tooth comb. I want time frames, contingencies, every little thing itemised. It's a loss to us — we're losing our home of forty years, so we have to be sure we're going somewhere even better.'

She nodded. 'And everyone at Madjinbarra's on board?'

'They will be, I think. Harvey took a bit of convincing, but Aunty Mary talked him round. And then today she tore strips off me for disrespecting you. She got the full story from Jill. Aunty Mary said I should have trusted you and informed me that I was a stubborn idiot.' Charlie paused, catching Beth's eye. 'I told her I'd already worked that out.'

Beth, who believed there was nothing to forgive, just reached for him. They held on to each other wordlessly and there was something unspoken between them; something that promised to do better. To trust and get it right.

'Aunty also told me that if I really knew what was good for my nieces, I'd let them stay with you.' Charlie pulled away to examine Beth's face. 'Is it true? You want the girls to live with you?'

She nodded cautiously.

'Why?'

'Because I love them. And I didn't realise how lonely I was until I had someone living here with me. I could maybe cut back on hours at the clinic and find some family day care for Pearl while Jill's at school and I'm at work . . . '

'I'm not sure about day care,' Charlie said. 'But maybe if there was another adult around to look after her while you're at work . . . ' He waited, watching her.

Her breath snagged. '*You?*'

'Well, I'm not talking about Lloyd Rendall, am I?'

Beth couldn't speak for a moment. 'You want to live *here* and look after Pearl?'

Charlie kept his eyes on her face. 'I want to be with you. And of course I will look after Pearl. And we can sort out something else for when I'm recording or touring.'

Beth cleared her throat but she still didn't seem to have a voice, so she cleared it once more. 'I'd like that. Very much.'

'I'll do as much as I can around here, and I'll cover all the expenses.'

'I don't think your pride would ever permit you to freeload, Charlie. We'll split the bills and the workload.'

'You're on.'

She looked up at him, a little frightened to breathe, trying to think of ways to be sure this wasn't a dream.

'Please just do one thing for me?' he said.

Anything, she thought. 'What's that?' she said.

'I know I fly off the handle sometimes, but I'm better than I was. I promise I won't just storm off again if I hear something I don't like. But Beth, you've got to tell me stuff. Don't hide things from me. I might not always react how you want me to, but I'll try to make the right choices.'

She'd already resolved to do exactly that — even before he'd asked — but she nodded to show him she agreed. Then Beth chewed her lip for a few moments before blurting, 'There is something else I should have told you. I . . . I might have the breast cancer gene.'

Charlie actually staggered — one foot went back so he could get his balance. He stared at Beth in horror. '*What?*'

'There's a history of cancer in my family. My colleague convinced me to get the test. I'm still waiting for the results. If it's positive, I'll be at an extremely high risk of developing breast cancer.' Now that she'd told him, the words spilled out in a crazed torrent. She couldn't have stopped them if she'd tried. 'I had an odd result on a cervical screening recently. It turned out to be okay but it made me realise I've been living under this cloud of fear and I needed to do something about it. Find some certainty.' Beth discovered she was crying, tears coursing down her cheeks.

Charlie dragged his hand through his hair, his eyes speaking his devastation. He caught her hand in his. 'Jesus, Beth. When did all this happen?'

'Just after we got back from Madjinbarra.'

He pulled her close and hugged her for a long time, letting Beth sob against his chest. When she grew calm, he pulled back just far enough so that she could see his face. Charlie still looked shell-shocked but there was a steadfastness there, too.

'I wish I'd known,' he said. 'You needed me.'

'It was another thing I didn't know how to say,' she admitted, wiping her eyes.

Charlie moved her hair away from her neck and ran his fingers down to a point just underneath her ear. He bent his head and placed his lips on the spot, kissing it softly.

'I'm here for you. Always. No matter what.'

Her eyes filled again. 'But Charlie, I might need to get a full mastectomy.'

'Then you get one.'

'I might get cancer.'

'Then you get treatment, and I look after you.'

'Charlie. I might *die*.'

'No. You do whatever it takes to stay here because I can't be lonely and mourning you for the rest of my life. I've done that for long enough. You are *not* allowed to die, Beth.' His vivid eyes bored into hers. 'Promise me you won't.'

Beth found herself promising Charlie she would not die. It was insane, stupid and completely irrational, but Charlie had always been able to make her do irrational things.

He nodded, satisfied. 'I'm going to make you so bloody happy. Every single day, you'll know I never did anything but love you from the moment we met.'

One Year Later

The ninety-minute drive to Paterson Downs was just the beginning, Charlie assured Beth. 'You might as well get comfortable,' he said. 'It's a bit of a journey.'

'Pearl's going to get bored,' Jill warned. 'You'd better have some good ideas to entertain her.'

'She's fond of I-spy,' Beth reminded Charlie with a smile.

'Oh God, yeah.' He rubbed his forehead. 'Maybe we can sing a few songs.'

'I know your uncle's favourite song,' Beth said over her shoulder to Jill and Pearl, turning the radio low.

'What is it?' asked Jill.

'Join in if you know it.' Beth launched into 'Do Your Ears Hang Low?' and Jill cracked up laughing as Charlie groaned. Pearl joined in with gusto, especially the 'wobble to-and-fro' sections. Clearly, she'd learned this one at kindy.

'Thanks for that,' he muttered when the song finally ended, several rounds later.

'Perhaps you'll tell me where our holiday is located next time, and not torture me with suspense,' Beth retorted.

He grinned with wicked pleasure, eyes on the road ahead. Beth studied his profile for a moment, revelling in her happiness. It was astonishing. Just ten months ago, she'd been living in fear of her life. Then the results from the

409

genetics laboratory had arrived and Carolyn had invited her into her office, handing her the letter with a glass of expensive champagne. Beth had cried so hard she hadn't even been able to take a sip. In an odd way, the negative result felt like a gift from her mother — like her mum was there, influencing this outcome, circling through the stars on a dragon, blessing Beth with this joyous release. Beth couldn't think about the look on Charlie's face when she'd told him, not without a surge of emotion that restarted those grateful tears.

'Uncle Charlie, your song's on the radio!' Jill cried.

Beth cranked up the volume. Charlie's latest single, 'Always You', was getting a lot of airplay. It looked like becoming his biggest hit yet. They all sang along, even Pearl, and Charlie pretended to think they sounded good. Pearl was just starting to talk about being hungry when they turned in at the stone-and-wood sign of Paterson Downs.

'Lunchbreak,' Beth told Pearl as Charlie parked outside the homestead.

Jill unbuckled Pearl from her booster seat in the back of the Winnebago and carried the wriggling child to the verandah, placing her on the decking. Pearl stood and staggered towards the door.

'Grandad!' she called.

Beth smiled. They'd introduced Barry to Pearl by name many months ago, but she'd picked up the 'Grandad' when Scarlet was born. Patersons was almost Pearl's favourite place in the world, topped only by the new community where Aunty Mary and Uncle Harvey lived with all her oldest friends.

Tom appeared at the door, baby Scarlet in his arms. 'Hello, Pearl!'

'Baby!' Pearl shouted. 'I wanna hold.'

'Yep, you can hold the baby,' he said, opening the door for Pearl, who thumped inside.

'Come here, beautiful bub.' Beth took little dark-haired Scarlet from Tom and kissed her velvety cheek.

Pearl had found Barry and was chatting energetically to him, mostly about horses. No doubt there would be a pony ride on old Tuffie before their lunch stop was over. Charlie and Tom shook hands, and Jill went to see if she could help Free in the kitchen — and probably to discuss the project they were working on in Free's weekly youth art circle.

'Where's Willow?' Beth asked.

'Out with the cows,' said Tom. 'She should be in soon. Mum and Dad will be here shortly, too.'

'I'm glad they could make it,' said Beth.

'Do you know where Charlie's taking you yet?' Tom asked.

Beth rolled her eyes. 'I've been told there will be a pool, ocean views and fishing.'

Tom looked highly entertained. 'That narrows it down to most of the Australian coastline, then.'

Beth crossed to her father and gave him a kiss. Finn, working on a jigsaw puzzle with Barry, stood up to greet her with a hug. Then the back door banged and Willow arrived, looking hot and dusty.

'Hi, all,' she said. 'I'll just duck in for a quick shower.' Scarlet squawked at the sound of her mother's voice.

'She's hungry,' Tom called.

'Milk bar will open in five minutes, Scarlet,' Willow called back.

'We'll distract her while she waits,' said Beth, perching on a sofa. She traced the baby's soft cheek and chin with one finger and Scarlet yawned.

'I hold?' Pearl said hopefully, clambering up beside Beth.

Charlie knew the drill. He arranged cushions on either side of Pearl and positioned himself on the sofa's arm, ready to catch Scarlet if she looked likely to spill out of Pearl's arms. But Pearl was an old hand at this now. She put her arms out and Beth leaned across, placing the baby gently across Pearl's lap.

'Baby.' Pearl's tone was reverential as she gazed down at Scarlet's face.

'Ohhh, that is so gorgeous.' Free had appeared now and whipped out her phone to take a photo of Pearl with Scarlet. 'Beth, will you come and do your special Caesar dressing? I brought avocados in the desperate hope that you'd make it.'

'Can do.'

Free headed back towards the kitchen and Beth checked with Charlie. 'Will you watch her?' She indicated Pearl, still holding the baby.

'Of course.'

Beth stood but Charlie caught her hand as she went to follow Free.

'Hey.' He pulled her down closer so she could hear him whisper. 'I've been waiting almost a year now. When are we going to have a go at making one of those?' He nodded towards Scarlet.

Beth caught her breath. 'You want that?'

'Absolutely.'

'Soon?'

Charlie tipped his head. 'We've got a three-week holiday at a mystery destination ahead of us. Seems as good a time to start as any.'

Beth wrestled down the exquisite happiness that was threatening to make her look like a grinning fool in front of everyone. She planted a quick kiss on Charlie's lips. 'You're on.'

Acknowledgements

In offering this book to the world, I would like to first respectfully acknowledge the traditional custodians of this country. I acknowledge the nations of the east Kimberley — the Miriuwung, Gajerrong and Gwini people who feature in this book — as well as the Wadjuk people, who are the rightful owners of the land on which I live in Perth. I offer my respects to the elders, past, present and emerging, and express my sorrow for the wrongs done to all Aboriginal nations, my admiration for the wisdom and resilience of Aboriginal culture, and my hopes for a more positive future.

The remote community of Madjinbarra is wholly fictional, and I hope I can be forgiven for creating a town name that is in the style of other Aboriginal place names in Western Australia. I did so because I did not want to suggest I was representing an actual place in WA. I also wanted to show that the fictional community had reclaimed ownership of a place that had been a white-run mission, similar to the renaming of Drysdale River Mission to Kalumburu in 1950. The word Madjinbarra is not, as far as I can discover, in active use in any Aboriginal language. If I have inadvertently hurt any individual or community with my use of the name, I humbly offer my apologies.

I would like to show my gratitude to my

family, who accept, tolerate and even enable my regular descents into my brain's writing zone. You've been patient during my countless writing and editing hours when, even if I'm not at the keyboard, I'm thinking about it. Thanks for understanding my absent presence.

A huge thanks to the people who gave me the opportunity to make a multi-purpose trip into the East Kimberley last year, in which I combined being a charity ambassador, volunteering at a writers festival and doing research for *Love Song*. Thank you to Peter Large and Julie Ditrich of Books in Homes Australia, who facilitated the trip so I could speak to school principals about the fantastic Books in Homes program, which brings books into the homes of children who may not otherwise have many (or any) books of their own. Thank you for working so hard to empower disadvantaged kids through literacy. Thank you to Jo Roach and Emma Day and their team, who do a stellar job of putting on the Kimberley Writers Festival each year, and who allowed me to volunteer at the event, even lending me a vehicle and arranging somewhere for me to sleep for the week. Thanks especially to Jo, who said yes when I asked if I could tag along to her Children's Book Week visits to schools in Kununurra, Wyndham, Doon Doon, Warmun and Kalumburu, and who let me drive her Nissan Patrol through a creek, inciting a number of excited squeals. Thank you to the principals and staff at those schools who were open to my questions and curiosity — and for the amazing work they do with the wonderful children in their care.

A vast, eternal thanks to Steve Kinnane, Miriuwung man and author, and Kathryn Trees, academic and my former PhD supervisor, both of Murdoch University. Steve and Kathryn agreed to read the manuscript of this book and then provided feedback and guidance on details of Aboriginal life and culture in the East Kimberley, as well as on the story more generally. As well as your help, you gave me the confidence to go forward with the book's plot and characters.

Thank you so much to Dr Sue Jackson and Georgia Bolden for your medical and pharmaceutical advice on these elements of the book. Sue also assisted with the medical elements in *Dear Banjo*. Without you both, there may have been some awkward mistakes (and if there are still mistakes, please don't blame Sue or Georgia because they never got to read it before it was printed).

A number of my friends, both writers and others, also gave me advice and encouragement that helped during the writing and editing of this book. Tess Woods' advice on the stolen kiss scene was brilliant! Thanks also to the writers who answered emails or questions during author talks about writing across cultures, the 'own voices' debate and other curly issues.

Many thanks my agent, Alex Adsett, and to the team at Penguin Random House: Ali Watts, Amanda Martin, Louisa Maggio, Penelope Goodes and the sales, publicity and marketing teams, all of whom worked so hard to bring this book into the world.

And lastly, a gigantic thanks to those who have supported the Daughters of the Outback series by reading, reviewing, telling people about or buying my books. Your enthusiasm for 'the next book' is no small source of inspiration.